I LOVE CAPRI

Belinda Jones's first paid job was on cult kiddy comic *Postman Pat*. Since then she has written for a multitude of magazines and newspapers including *Sunday*, *Daily Express*, *Empire*, *FHM*, *heat*, *New Woman* and *more!* magazine where she was a staff writer for four years. Belinda's widely acclaimed first novel, *Divas Las Vegas*, was voted No. 2 in the *New Woman* Bloody Good Reads Awards in 2001 and *On the Road to Mr Right* – a non-fiction travelogue love quest was a *Sunday Times* top ten best-seller.

Praise for *

'You won't want to pu
C

Praise for *On the Road to Mr Right*

'This is definitely worth cramming in your suitcase'
Cosmopolitan

Praise for *The California Club*

'A riotous page-turner, full of witty observations about life and love'
She

Praise for *I Love Capri*

'With more twists than a bowl of fusilli and more laughs than a night out with the girls, *I Love Capri* is as essential as your SPF 15'
New Woman

Praise for *Divas Las Vegas*

'Great characters . . . hilariously written . . . buy it!'
New Woman

Also by Belinda Jones

Fiction
Divas Las Vegas
The California Club
The Paradise Room
Café Tropicana
The Love Academy
Out of the Blue

Non-Fiction
On the Road to Mr Right

To embark on more fabulous journeys with Belinda Jones, visit her website: www.belindajones.com

I Love Capri

BELINDA JONES

arrow books

Published by Arrow Books in 2002

18 20 19 17

Copyright © Belinda Jones 2002

First published in the United Kingdom in 2002

Arrow Books
The Random House Group Limited
20 Vauxhall Bridge Road, London, SW1V 2SA

www.randomhouse.co.uk

Addresses for companies within The Random House Group
Limited can be found at: www.randomhouse.co.uk/offices.htm

The Random House Group Limited Reg. No. 954009

A CIP catalogue record for this book
is available from the British Library

ISBN 9780099414933

The Random House Group Limited supports The Forest Stewardship
Council (FSC®), the leading international forest certification organisation.
Our books carrying the FSC label are printed on FSC® certified paper.
FSC is the only forest certification scheme endorsed by the leading
environmental organisations, including Greenpeace. Our
paper procurement policy can be found at
www.randomhouse.co.uk/environment

Printed and bound in Great Britain by Clays Ltd, St Ives PLC

For my mother – Pamela Gwyther

(and everyone who's ever had a love affair with Italy)

Acknowledgements

Grazie Mille to: my exquisite, inspirational mother who should have been a 50s movie star; my flat-mate James 'ciao-ciao' Breeds for watching TV with head-phones on and supplying endless gourmet Italian dinners; Cabbage for being guardian of the suitcases; Emily 'Bella' O'Neill for that West Side Story moment on Via Emanuele – too absurd to even feature in the book!; Antonino Cacace of Massa Lubrense, the wondrous staff at the Hotel Luna, especially Andrea, Antonino, Luigi and Vincenzo. Plus, all at the Fara-glioni Restaurant, especially Mr Paradise.

Unlimited gelato to: Yasmin Sethna at Voyager PR, Gianni at Magic of Italy for expert translations; Fiona, Karen and Stephen at Orient Express; Camille at the Gabbia D'Oro; Christine and Helen at Wedding & Home, Carla Finer at L'Oreal for supreme hospitality/embracing my clumsiness and Sarah Harvey at Star-wood for the pistachio story and boundless joie de vivre.

Special mention to my lovely step-cousin Steven Lane who saved my parma ham with his incredible insight and calming influence the day before my deadline!

Frothy cappuccinos all round for: Bellagio-loving Gill and Derek, Bellini-clinking Graham and Andrew, Amarone-swigging Sandy Battaglia, Cardiff-capering Tahira Yaqoob, wise Welshmen Trefor & Gareth Jones, wanderlustre Charles Thom and sweetie-darling Sarah Green – here's hoping you and Stella get to Maiori one day soon!

Limoncello cheers to: Kate Elton, the most fabulous editor a girl could hope for – enthusiastic, encouraging, instinctive and wise; plus fellow Random House diamonds: Jo Craig, Ron Beard, Grainne Ashton, Sarah Harrison and Alison Groom.

Also Lizzy Kremer at Ed Victor Ltd for getting me into this novel-writing lark in the first place, and for suggesting I re-christen Luca!

And finally, my heroine, Claudia Cardinale for bringing Rosa to life for me.

1

Is £5,000 enough to change your life?

It doesn't sound much compared to the loot offered on 21st century game shows but the reason I ask is that I woke up this morning £5,000 richer. I didn't even do anything to deserve it – an old man in a foreign country dies and I get a lump sum transferred into my account. (Now that's what I call pennies from heaven.) No mourning required – I've never even met him – just *spending*.

So now I'm standing here holding the cash in my hands. We're talking one hundred bank-spanking new £50 notes. I feel compelled to fan them out like I'm in an ad for the *Sun* bingo and do a gleeful little dance.

It was my mother's idea to change up the money into high-calibre currency – she said I would have more respect for its worth that way. It sounded elitist at the time – only top-end notes command respect – but she had a point: you can bet your bottom buck that a £50 note will never experience the humiliating origami-scrumpling that fivers get subjected to as you ram your change into your purse at a busy M&S checkout.

I pity the poor, hard-working relations with their tattered edges, biro squiggles and smudges of chip grease. No amount of money laundering will get them clean.

Mum (who is always trying to change the way I look at things) went on to suggest that I spend some quality time with the money and feel a sense of duty to do something special with it. I have to indulge her. The old man was her father.

I take one of the pristine notes and hold it up in front of my lava lamp. The holographic foil looks like a transfer that's just been smoothed into place. I can tell these babies expect to go shopping at Voyage or recline on a silver platter alongside a bill for a bottle of Cristal champagne but I've got rather different plans. The second the £ signs ker-chinged on to my eyeballs I knew what I'd spend it on – Cleo and I had fantasized about it long enough. And yet we've avoided saying it out loud for a good two hours . . .

'Look! I'm a lapdancer!' titters Cleo, tucking a wodge of cash into her bra and thrusting her wannabe-cleavage in my face.

As that most freakish of creatures – dream flatmate – Cleo has more than earned a cut of my inheritance. Two years ago I was a mass of sodden tissues following a mangling break-up and she was the only person who understood that I needed to hide. Everyone else expected me to bounce back and be all Destiny's Child *Survivor* about it. (I'm still waiting for my surge of 'I'm Stronger!/Wiser!/Sassier!' empowerment.) We hardly knew each other at the time but she even upped sticks from Sheffield to coax me through the agonizing miseries and we've been best friends ever since.

I think part of the reason we clicked is that Cleo was a twin in the womb but only she survived the birth and she's always felt half of her was missing. Until me. Somehow I seem to fill in the blanks. In fact, she's such a good person I sometimes feel like her evil twin. Not that I do anything bad *per se*. It's just that compared to her sunny self, I'm a bit of a grump. She doesn't seem to mind. Cleo asks very little of life and in return life gives her just that. I'd like to think that one day I can do as much for her as she's done for me. All the same, I don't want her impaling these precious £50s on an underwire.

'Stop! You'll scrumple them!' I say, retrieving the dosh and smoothing it back to perfection.

'Since when did you give two hoots about money?' Cleo flumps on to our giant pink sofa. (Neither of us is particularly girlie but it seemed the least grown-up colour option and my mother thought it was vile so that pretty much sealed the deal.)

'Since I actually got some! Show a little respect,' I reply.

'Sorry!' Cleo humphs, then fakes an *a-a-a-TISHOO!* sneeze into one of the notes.

I give a testy sigh and get back to the tricky business of trying to decide what to spend the money on.

'We could blow it on a luxury cruise around the Caribbean. I think that's actually compulsory when you come into a few thou,' I frown.

'Only you don't like the humidity,' Cleo reminds me.

'And you're allergic to coconuts,' I counter.

'And we'd miss too much good TV.'

'If we hadn't bought our Sony home cinema system last year we could have paid for that,' I sigh, taking a moment to behold our rear-projection/surround-sound extravaganza. Our shrine. It wiped out all our savings but if you tot up the hours of pleasure it has brought us, it works out as an absolute bargain.

'We could re-decorate . . .' I say, looking around our dinky but deliciously toasty flat. One thing we can't seem to get enough of is cushions, especially those shaggy-sheep and faux-fur ones. Our most recent indulgence was a pair of duvets specifically for cosying up the sofa on video nights. We could do with a trunk to store them in. And maybe some bigger trays to accommodate Cleo's ever more adventurous dinners. (She's into multiple taste sensations at the moment – each served in its own little dish, like tapas. I think she got the idea from *Ready, Steady, Cook* – trying to create as many variations as possible from a set number of ingredients.)

'I'd quite like some new coasters,' I say, looking at the coffee table Cleo's brother Marlon made out of a door he found in a skip.

'That still leaves £4,988. You need to think bigger,' Cleo advises.

'Champagne!' I whoop.

'Just how drunk do you want to get?' Cleo hoots.

'No! I bought some to celebrate,' I say, scampering

to the kitchen. It's corner shop fizz that tastes like sherry zapped through one of those old Soda Stream machines but it'll do. (The off-licence is just that little bit too far at the moment.)

As I reach for the corkscrew, I catch sight of my sloppy-joe reflection in the window.

'New wardrobe?' I suggest.

'I'm happy with our clothes rail,' Cleo boom-booms.

'Very funny. If we used my mum's staff discount at Woodward's we could get a whole new rack of stuff.'

'I think you already own every style of pyjama known to mankind.'

'Meaning?'

'Kim, you never leave the house – I can't remember the last time I saw you dressed.'

'You only go as far as PhotoFinish,' I pout.

When Cleo decided she wanted to move to Cardiff and set up the Cleo Buchanan Home for the Emotionally Challenged she requested a transfer from the Sheffield branch of the done-in-a-flash photo lab she's worked at since she left college, but they didn't have an equivalent managerial position available. Even though she had to go down a level, she took the job. Such is her loyalty to me. However, it would seem that selected highlights from the Kaliko summer collection are not the way to repay her kindness.

'The last thing I need is a makeover from your mother. Everyone she dresses looks like they're either going to a wedding or about to read the news. I am New Look. Always have been, always will be.'

'Fair enough. But I might go travelling again. I'd

need at least four new business suits if I took that job in Paris.'

It sounds flasher than it is. It's also already gone. I dithered too long and they gave the contract to someone else, as Cleo rams home: 'You've been offered three amazing jobs overseas in the past six months and you've turned every one of them down so you can carry on translating computer games into German in a basement flat in Cardiff.'

She's got a point. In the beginning the idea of a jet-set lifestyle was the reason I studied so many languages, and they came so easily to me. It was such a kick being good at something and I felt a real citizen of the world. But then I became too game, too open, too trusting. After my last spectacularly disastrous trip to Sweden (whatever gives you the idea that there was a man involved?!) I swore 'never again'. I'd had my fun. That was two years ago, and now I like staying in. I've even stopped missing the adventures. Okay, so what I do now isn't glamorous but at least I don't have to stare at the hairy ears of international delegates or smell the noxious aftershave of fashion designers or wish it was my hand a Latin pop star was touching and not the flirty female interviewer from *Glamour* magazine. Really, it takes gooseberrydom to new levels: you're serving a vital purpose – helping these people to communicate with each other – and yet they don't even acknowledge your presence.

You get used to it, of course, being ignored. Lucky for me, I got in a fair bit of practice over the years with countless dinners to introduce me to my mother's latest beau. Each time I'd become redundant after the first flush of introductions. I couldn't bear the awkwardness of them trying to include me in their pet-name conversations so I became adept at blanding out – you'd barely notice I was there. I'd sit imagining I was being paid not to react and deduct money every time I made a sarcastic remark or felt the need to defend my father, who left when I was nine. (Because of *her*, I have to point out. She drove him to it.) Anyway, now when I'm on a translating job I show no expression at all, even when the person I'm speaking for is telling a joke or getting all steamed up. As my trainer told me, you're not re-enacting what they are saying, just repeating it, like a human tickertape.

My one unfulfilled ambition is to be one of the interpreters that speak for Miss World contestants. I've always thought they could help the girls out a bit with their answers. You know, the host asks, 'So, what two things do you think would make the world a happier place?' and in her native tongue she replies, 'An end to war and hunger.' But the interpreter could say, 'Laughing gas and calorie-free chocolate' and she would win the crown! Or better yet, 'When I look this good, does it really matter what I think?'

Maybe one day I'll get to do that. In the meantime the computer game contract suits me fine. Besides, the pay is better as I remind Cleo. 'Think of all the real holidays we can take with the extra money I'm earning!'

'Kim, you haven't been abroad in two years. The cat gets more use out of the suitcase than you.'

7

'I'll have you know I speak six languages.'

'Of which Spanish is your second most fluent and you've never even been to Spain.'

'I might go.'

'In which case I take it all back,' she mock-strops. 'There: FLAMENCO DRESS is top of the list!'

I peer at our heavily-doodled page of *Ways to Spend £5,000*.

'Happy?' Cleo snaps.

'I hate shopping,' I moan.

'Me too.'

We become briefly transfixed by our feet – 'I'm actually sprouting hairs on my big toe!' 'Me too!' – then I flip to the underwear section of our Freemans catalogue, scribble a quick calculation in the corner and say, 'How about 312 pairs of hold-your-blubbery-bits-in knickers?'

Cleo knows what's coming next and turns to me expectantly.

My heart starts to hammer and my mouth goes dry. I can't believe that after months of wishful thinking and speculation (beginning way before the money landed in our laps) I now have the power to make our greatest desire a reality.

'Or . . .' I begin, palpitating wildly.

Cleo takes a breath and exhales the word 'Or . . .', daring me to go on.

I reach for her hand and together we scream: *'LIPOSUCTION!!!'*

When you've got thousands of pounds at your

disposal, potentially disfiguring surgery is really the only option.

Toasting our decision, Cleo and I prepare to indulge in our favourite pastime: playing Who's Got the Grossest Bulgy Bit?

'You know how people say cellulite is like cottage cheese?'

'Yes,' I say.

'I think mine is the variety that comes with pineapple chunks!'

'That's nothing,' I giggle, sitting forward. 'Check out my Buddha-belly. You don't get a figure like this from eating raw seaweed!'

'I'm sure there's got to be some tribe in the world who'd consider us goddesses,' Cleo reflects.

'There is,' I assert. 'They're called cannibals. We'd be the equivalent of a KFC bucket for six to them.'

We fall about laughing. Okay, we're only a size 14 but for some reason we find it amusing to torture ourselves about our bodies. And what better way to celebrate the prospect of becoming fat-free femmes fatales than with a dummy run of our first plastic surgery consultation . . .

Taking turns with the red felt-tip pen, we mark the 'gotta go' areas. Despite the fact that the pen runs out of ink before we're done we still manage to look like human jigsaws. Before we move on to attempting home facelifts with Sellotape we stand side by side in front of the full-length mirror and decide that if we pooled our resources we could probably come up with a half-decent-looking woman: Cleo's long legs (her cellulite is imaginary), sleek shoulders and auburn hair, my 36C boobs, cat's eyes and disproportionately dainty wrists. Then we consider the monster our reject parts would form and are suddenly so grateful for what we've got that we nearly talk ourselves out of surgery altogether.

But no. That would be silly – it's our dream.

We've already chosen the clinic. Months before the windfall we whiled away a gap in our TV schedule by flicking through our leaning tower of women's mags and scrutinizing the back page ads offering plastic surgery: you know the ones where they show a dimpled, saggy crone next to some busty pert-buttocked nymph and claim it's a genuine before and after shot?

'Yeah, before and after the body double entered the room,' Cleo scoffed, though deep down I knew she was desperate to believe that such miraculous transformations were just a slice and suck away.

We settled on the 'New You Clinic', loving their TAKE A TRIP TO NYC! slogan.

'Just think – a week from now a surgeon could be looking down at our anaesthetized bodies thinking, "Look at the Empire State of that!"' Cleo chuckles, dancing around the room.

'We have to make a pact not to tell anyone,' I insist, gravely.

'What about your mum?'

'No way!' I protest.

I want this change to be mine. My mother has been trying to find a way to reclaim her influence over the way I look since I was old enough to rebel against her twirlie-girlie styling. If there was a culture that believed in arranged wardrobes rather than arranged marriages for their children she'd sign up straight away. Even my make-up – or lack of it – bothers her: 'You're looking a bit pale, darling,' she'd complain. 'Why don't you try this?' And then, out of nowhere, some sickly bright confection would appear – just call her Edwina Lipstickhands. But the bane of her life is my hair. I've lost count of the number of pictures she's sent me of Minnie Driver and Nicole Kidman with their naturally springy curls ironed straight. I did secretly try and straighten mine once but it just ended up looking like a perm that had given up the will to live. So I cut it all off. Then she said I looked like a boy. I just can't win with her. She's always had the better hand in the looks department. And she never tires of playing it.

'You know she'll notice. It's her job to assess people's physiques, you won't be able to hide it from her.'

'If she says anything I'll just tell her I've cut wheat out of my diet, she's always saying that's what gives me a bloated stomach.'

'So you won't be wanting your last slice of pizza, then?'

'You can have half,' I grant.

'It's funny how your mum is so into image but dead against surgery,' Cleo muses, sending a little pepperoni Frisbee in my direction as she yanks the dough base apart. 'I mean, she talks her customers out of boob jobs

11

and tummy tucks and then cons them into spending a couple of grand on a new wardrobe when if they'd gone ahead and had surgery they would look great in T-shirts and jeans for the rest of their life! Look at all the people we've seen on TV and in magazines saying how a quick nip and tuck has improved their lives.'

'Oooooh, do you remember that really awful scarring picture?' I say, face shrivelling with revulsion.

'All right she was unlucky,' Cleo concedes.

'Not that it really matters if we end up looking like we've been ravaged by sharks – it's not like anyone's going to actually see us naked, is it? It's just for the overall effect.'

I'm really not convinced that I'm ready to bare even a new-improved physique in public.

'Speak for yourself! If we go through with this we're having the heating up full blast every night so I can watch TV in my bikini!' Cleo chortles, draining her wine glass. 'Oh, Kim! We're really going to do it, aren't we? Just think of all the gorgeous men we're going to attract.'

'Heaven forbid!'

Cleo looks miffed. 'Not all of them are like—'

'Don't say his name!' I cut her off.

'You really don't want a boyfriend, do you?' she blinks in bafflement.

Cleo says she wants to meet someone but there hasn't been too much evidence to support the claim. Last summer she got quite serious with a rugby lug called Dylan but then E4 began their 24-hour coverage of *Big Brother* and he was history. She's currently got a crush on a chap called Gareth who's started popping into PhotoFinish, but despite having copied his phone number off the processing envelope she hasn't done anything about it. She says she's going to make a move next time he comes in but really I think her ideal relationship would be one where she and a minor celebrity got together once every six weeks for a photo shoot for *OK!* magazine.

As for me – when I say I've had it with love, I mean it. And I really think it's for the best because I can't take the way that one day the whole world seems dipped in gold and the next you're reduced to a blubbering pulp. Even before the Unmentionable One I hadn't exactly welcomed *amore* with open arms. It was more a case of grimacing as it twisted and contorted me – doing my best to keep a pleasant demeanour as my insides leaked acidic juices. I would tolerate relationships until they petered out, then shakily emerge and wait for the love toxins to leave my body and the alien personality traits (suspicion, jealousy, neediness) to settle back down to acceptable human quirks. After the last emotion-skewering disappointment two years ago I worked hard to give my life some equilibrium. Having Cleo around has helped enormously and now I'm so even-tempered I'm like a perfectly aligned spirit-level. The only thing that knocks me off balance is my mother, so I keep my encounters with her to a minimum.

'Don't you ever feel numb?' Cleo asked me a couple of months back and I had to admit that I do – most of the time, actually. I realize it's not ideal but it's got to be better than the alternative, hasn't it?

'Anyway, it's easy for your mum to be dismissive – she's already got the perfect figure,' Cleo decides.

'Yeah, what does she know about our suffering?' I grump, gloomily inspecting the floorboards.

'Do you really think Pamela Anderson has had a rib removed?' Cleo ponders, trying to cheer me up. She can spot one of my mother-induced sulks coming a mile off and has become expert at heading them off at the pass.

I take a closer look at the evidence in *heat* magazine then attempt to re-create her eggtimer waist using gaffer tape, while Cleo gets busy with her brown eyeshadow giving me contours I could only dream about.

We're just concluding a rousing rendition of *If I Said You Had A Beautiful Body Would You Hold It Against Me?* when the doorbell rings.

We freeze.

Our pose is absurd – Cleo twisting round to gauge the benefit of her manual bumlift and me hunched forward to create my most self-repulsing belly roll. We look like some feminist sculpture decrying modern woman's obsession with bodily imperfections.

The doorbell rings again. There's only one regular visitor to our flat but the pizza was delivered half an hour ago, so that rules him out.

My startled eyes search Cleo's for a solution. She mouths 'Ssshhhh!' though there's little chance of pretending we're not in with the lights on full glare and

Rod Stewart now serenading the neighbourhood with *The First Cut Is The Deepest.*

As the letterbox creaks open we drop to the floor like marionettes who've just had their strings snipped.

2

'Kimmy! It's me. Are you there?' a voice trills.

'*Mum?*' I hiss, cheek to grain with the floorboards.

'Can you let me in, darling – it's tipping down out here!'

'Just give us a moment!' I bluster as Cleo and I skid to the bathroom on loo-paper-bound feet. It's all elbows over the sink and inside-out dressing gowns as we attempt to scrub off our red crows' feet and cartoon lip-lines. As I lather frantically, Cleo goes for the Mrs Doubtfire face-in-cake-topping option, daubing herself with an oatmeal-nubbed clay mask. I decide to follow suit but the mask I spurt from a hastily grabbed tube has a gloopy gelatine consistency and provides zero coverage, just maximum sheen. The letterbox rattles impatiently. With an internal squeal I scurry back through the lounge and unlock the door.

'Sorry about that – we're just having a bit of a beauty bonanza,' I pant, securing my towel turban.

Mum eyes my freshly varnished face with suspicion. We've turned down every spa discount she's ever

16

offered so she knows there's no long-running tradition of Sunday evening pampering in this house.

'Cup of tea?' I say hoping to regain my composure in the kitchen.

'I told you I was dropping by tonight,' she says with a quizzical look. 'I don't know why you look so surprised.'

Oh God – that'll be the Sellotape hoiking my eyebrows up to my temples. I peer at my distorted reflection in the kettle and attempt to gently ease the tape off without giving myself a receding hairline.

'Camomile with lemon,' she calls after me.

I roll my eyes and reach for the PG Tips. Her quest for inner purity really gets on my nerves. She even puts filtered water in the kettle when she needs to fill a hot water bottle. Suddenly she's in the doorway.

'What's this?' she demands with a slight tremor in her voice.

I turn around and see she's holding up the New You Clinic brochure. I feel a chest-thump of panic – as much as I tell myself I'm my own person and don't care what she thinks, any hint of disapproval from her winds me.

'Oh that – nothing,' I cover masterfully, turning my back on her.

'Then why have you gone all pink?' she asks, moving closer so she can study my face.

'It's a self-heating mask,' I pout. 'I'm trying to encourage the natural oils in my skin. I've had a bit of a dry complexion lately.' (You don't get brought up by a perfume-squirting, product-pushing beauty counter assistant and not pick up some of the lingo.)

'Tell me you're not thinking of having surgery,' she pleads, looking stricken.

'Well, you're always saying I should make the most of myself,' I brazen, shakily sploshing semi-skimmed into the tea. If there's a way of making her feel somehow to blame, so much the better.

'Although it's really about making the *least* of yourself in this case,' blunders Cleo as she reaches for her Jamie Oliver 'Pukka Cuppa' mug. 'You could be seeing up to *a stone* less of your daughter in two weeks' time!'

Mum and I give her a 'not-helping' glare. She carefully puts the mug back on the rack and whispers, 'I'll be in my room if you need me.'

I brace myself for the onslaught of 'if you gave up dairy products you'd feel like a new woman' but instead Mum wanders back through to the lounge without saying a word. I watch her staring at the fireplace with glazed eyes and then, just as I am about to defend my decision and tell her I don't need her permission anyway, she says, 'I want you to come to Capri with me.'

I didn't see that one coming.

'I thought they'd already had the funeral . . .' I say, brow knotting in confusion.

'They have, but now Luca wants to buy my father's boutique and—'

'Who's Luca?' I interrupt.

'The shop manager. He's worked there for over ten

18

years. Twenty per cent of the shop is his and now he wants to buy it outright.'

'And the other 80 per cent is in your name?' I check as I edge on to the sofa.

'Yes,' she confirms. 'Dad left me everything to do with the shop, except the £5,000 petty cash which he gave to you.'

I didn't even think he knew he had a granddaughter but it's not the time to go into that now.

'Can't the lawyers just sort it?' I suggest. 'They managed fine with the rest of the will.'

'I'm not sure I want to sell,' she quavers.

Uh-oh. 'What do you mean?' I ask, levelly.

'I was thinking I might go out there and run the place myself.'

Is she mad? I'm incredulous. '*What?* It's got to be nearly fifty years since you were last there!'

'Forty-five.'

'I thought you swore you'd never go back!'

'My mother made me swear. Now she's gone . . .' She looks intently at her teacup. 'I don't want to leave it any longer.'

'But what is left for you now?' I don't understand.

'Memories,' she says defiantly. 'Memories I haven't been allowed to have since I was eleven.'

For a second I feel a flicker of sympathy for her. My mother has told me very little of her childhood but I know she was born on the Isle of Capri because for years I thought she was saying 'I Love Capri' and it became my singsong mantra. By all accounts she had a blissful childhood but then a couple of days before her

19

twelfth birthday her mother (Granny Carmela) discovered her husband Vincenzo (the dead guy) was having an affair – not just a fling, it had been going on for years.

In a justifiable rage Carmela grabbed three suitcases, two saucepans and one daughter and left for Cardiff the same day: one of her best friends had married a Welshman and she'd always promised to visit. From that day on Carmela severed all contact with Italy and even forbade the use of her native tongue in the home. Consequently my mother's knowledge of Italian is now sub-tourist level, as I now point out:

'You can't even understand the menu at Ciao Cymru!'

'Which is why I need you to come and translate for me,' she says calmly.

'Hold on!' I pull back. 'You can't have thought this through. Are you talking about giving up your job and moving out there permanently?' I reel. Mum has always lived so nearby. Driving me nuts but living nearby. The idea of her being based in another country . . . I shake my head. Not that I haven't wished it a few times . . .

'I'd like to give it a try,' Mum smiles. 'It would be a dream come true having my own boutique. I know all about fashion buying and window displays and sales—'

'In *Wales*,' I snort. 'It's a whole other world out there! Remember that week I spent translating for that poncey designer in Milan?'

'If you came with me, explained how things worked,

got me started, I'm sure I could make a go of it,' she says, ignoring my protests.

I look at the determined fifty-seven-year-old woman before me and wonder where she gets her energy from. And why none of it was passed on to me. I'm half her age and it all sounds like way too much upheaval. (Lately I've come to the conclusion that you have to accept change when it's forced upon you but why on earth would you go looking for it? It's so unsettling.)

'Don't you want to retire like a normal person?' I ask, finding it unfathomable that someone should want an alternative to all that guilt-free TV watching.

Mum sets her un-drunk tea down on the spray-painted side table.

'I'm not ready to give up working yet but I am ready for a new challenge. Now Teddy has passed away and I don't have a man to look after, I want to do something for myself.'

My eyes narrow – she's definitely been watching *Oprah* on her lunchbreaks.

'If I fail then I'll sell up and come home – no damage done,' she shrugs, adding: 'It's not like having surgery where you can't reverse the process.'

Oooh – pointed. I hold her gaze for a second and then sigh heavily. I suppose there's a price to be paid for my freedom. I've always said I'd be so much happier if she wasn't around to nit-pick and undermine me. It's just the tiniest things but they get to me so much; like I might be wearing a jumper I adore but all it takes is one of her classic 'Have you still got the receipt?' comments, and from then on every time I go

21

to put it on all I can see in the mirror is her look of disdain. (Of course it does make it easy to decide what to wear when we meet up. I like to be as aesthetically displeasing as possible to make her suffer.) I tried to do a bit of fashion sniping back at her one time, just to show her how it feels but the expression on her face when I said, 'That doesn't look as good as you think it does' told me I'd gone too far. I always wimp out because I feel guilty about being mean and I hate the prospect of any confrontation – I'd much rather leave things festering inside for all eternity. Perhaps her moving to Capri would solve the problem – it would be her decision to remove herself from my life so I wouldn't have to feel like I was abandoning her.

'How long would you need me for?' I ask cautiously. 'I've got work to do . . .'

'I'd pay you. This isn't just a favour. I want to employ you to translate for me and take a look at the business, talk to Luca, talk to the locals, help me make the right decision.'

'So if I said it wasn't going to pan out, you'd believe me?'

'Yes,' she says simply.

That's a first – she never asks my opinion on anything.

'How long?' She still hasn't answered me.

'A week, maybe two.'

Way too long to get my head around at the moment.

'Where would we stay?'

'I've found a beautiful hotel by the Gardens of Augustus. Hotel Luna,' Mum says dreamily.

'So no relatives?' This is key – I can't sustain the doting daughter routine for more than an hour at a time.

'No relatives.'

'And what you said before about memories – this isn't some kind of pilgrimage to rediscover your Italian roots?' I ask, sounding a tad more patronizing than I intended but really, I can't be doing with it if she's going to get all mournful about lost heritage and absent fathers.

Mum moves a sofa cushion closer to me and takes my hands. 'Come with me.'

I'm torn between duty and dread. Overlaid with the discomfort I feel when she touches me.

I think one of the key things that bound Cleo and me together was her confession that she cringes when her mother sits too close and gets too adoring. I'd never admitted I felt that way to anyone until she said it first. It seems wrong to shun parental affection when so many children are denied it but it's just the way we both feel. We've tried to rationalize it – our mothers carried us inside them so there is no such thing as too close for them – but we can't escape the feeling of being smothered.

'When are you planning to go?' I ask, wriggling my fingers to loosen her grip.

'Tuesday.'

'*This Tuesday?*' I panic.

She nods.

'Day after tomorrow Tuesday?' I double-check. 'I can't, I've got an appointment, I . . .' I stop myself from saying out loud I'll miss the final episode of *Ally McBeal!* even though it is high on my list of concerns. I can't cope with last-minute dashes any more. I like to have time to psych myself up and the prospect of being suddenly uprooted makes me feel slightly sick. I'm dug in deep here. I don't know if I want to come out of my bunker and squint at the sunshine.

'Think about it overnight and meet me for lunch tomorrow,' Mum says, getting to her feet.

Standing at the door she gives me a flesh-squidging squeeze and says, 'I'd do anything to have curves like you!'

'Well it could be arranged,' I begin. 'What's sucked out of me could be injected into you . . .'

She blanches and says, 'It's not funny, Kim. It's mutilation.'

'Body sculpting,' I counter.

'It's blood and scarring and –' she catches herself. 'Just come and see me tomorrow.'

'Okay,' I agree. 'Just one last thing . . .'

'Yes?'

'Can I have the clinic brochure back?'

Mum tries for a 'I don't know what you're talking about' expression but realizes she's been sussed and huffily reaches into her bag.

'You're beautiful as you are,' she insists, handing it over.

'You have to say that,' I reply, prising her fingers from the scrolled pages. 'You made me.'

24

3

I click the latch and watch my mother's feet turn left on the pavement outside our flat. I'm temporarily distracted wondering if anyone except my mother wears navy shoes when I hear Cleo scuttling into the kitchen behind me.

'Did you hear all that?' I ask, still feeling overwhelmed.

Cleo nods. 'What are you going to do?'

'Oh I don't know,' I whine. 'Is it my duty as an offspring to go? I mean, her dad has just died.'

'You know you'll feel guilty if you don't,' Cleo concedes.

'But is there any real point in me going? It'll just be like every other time we've been away – she'll dump me the minute she meets a fella. I mean, you expect that from your mates, but not your mum.'

After fashion, my mother's favourite pastime is men. She can't get enough of them. If anyone could get away with having a male harem it would be her. Even when a man knows he's not the only one she's seeing,

25

he'll keep coming back for more, such is her magnetism. Even if we're in a room of men all my age, it's her they become transfixed by. The more attention she gets, the more she shines. And the more she shines the dimmer I glow by comparison. I remember being at a nightclub in Nice with her on our last 'family' holiday. I'd been mesmerized by this man since we arrived and when he walked over to where we were I couldn't believe my luck. Until he asked my mother to dance. If there's one thing worse than being the ugly friend, it's being the less attractive daughter. I can still taste the bitter disappointment. As I watched them on the dance floor I couldn't stop the tears from flowing. She already had a boyfriend back home and it just seemed so greedy of her to be taking more than her fair share when I had no one. Especially when I knew the dance meant nothing to her. Half the time I don't think she even likes the men she flirts with, she just reels them in because she can.

Cleo joins me on the sofa. 'She's not going to have time for men, she'll have all the shop stuff to sort out.'

'Hello, Earth to Cleo? If my mother was on her deathbed she'd get off with the doctor *and* the priest.'

'And any non-blood relatives, you're right,' Cleo concedes.

'She always has time for men and in *Italy*, my God she'll have suitors sniffing around her like she's a particularly fragrant flutter of bougainvillaea.' I wouldn't mind but she always feels she has to go and marry them.

Granny Carmela only attended her first wedding –

to my father Huw – she said that it's the only one that counts. I went to them all, each time hoping in vain she'd come to her senses before the 'I do's were uttered. I really think the sermon should have been customized: 'till death – or another bloke – do us part', etc. There was one good man. He looked like David Niven and I absolutely adored him. He moved in when I was thirteen and I got to keep him as a replacement dad for nearly six years. Their split came without warning and it transpired that for eighteen months she'd been seeing some other man. l couldn't believe she'd led this whole other life without sharing any of it with me. When she explained what had been going on I felt like I didn't know her at all. And when she announced that she was moving in with the new guy I couldn't believe she didn't even ask me what I thought. Didn't my opinion or my approval count for anything? Didn't it matter that it affected my life too? That I'd be losing a dad all over again?

Apparently not.

That's when I stopped involving her in *my* life decisions. She used to try and wheedle things out of me but it was too late – I'd shut down.

'You know what else?' Cleo grimaces.

'What?'

'She'll probably try and set you up with some distant relative of Tiberius.'

'Agghhhh!' I bury my head in my hands. She's right. When Cupid laid down his bow and arrow in defeat at my love life, my mother took them up. She claims she's just trying to help but it looks a lot like gloating from where I'm standing.

'What would you do?' I ask Cleo.

She gives an impish smile. 'I'm thinking freshly prepared gnocchi, I'm thinking linguine with clams . . .'

'You'd go just for the food?'

'That's why most people go to Italy. Visiting the Sistine Chapel and taking gondola rides is just something to do between meals.'

I grin back at her.

'If you do go could you bring me back some extra virgin olive oil? And balsamic vinegar – Fondo di Trebbiano if they've got it, it's barrel-aged for eight years and—'

'What if you came with me?' I gasp. Oh my God – *brilliant*! That would change everything!

'I wish! But you know I have to give at least two weeks' notice at work.'

'Couldn't they make an exception just this once? I mean, there's practically been a death in the family,' I wheedle.

Cleo shakes her head. 'Julie and the Ape Man are both taking their holiday this week' – Ape Man being short for Aperture, I recently discovered – 'It's only me and the boss until next Monday.'

I rack my brains for some solution. There must be a way! Other than when we first met, we've never been abroad together. The closest we get is watching *Wish You Were Here* and whereas there was a time when I would have envied every trip, I now pick fault and say, 'Oooh, but imagine the jet lag!' or 'Injections – no

28

way!' Cleo's even started doing the same, muttering things like: 'Buffet food always looks better than it tastes' or, 'I'm not going anywhere where the women display their underarm hair'. Sometimes I feel bad about bringing out the xenophobe in her because she used to like the idea of discovering a new country and all its quirky habits and native delicacies, but she moved in with me at a point when I needed to believe that I would never have to leave the house again. I told her all the cock-ups and horror stories from my trips abroad and kept my amazing, inspiring, good-to-be-alive memories to myself. How can I blame her for wanting to stay wedged in our marshmallowy rut? It feels so sweet and safe.

'Oh Cleo, are you sure you can't come?' I say, wondering what it would take to change her mind.

'Yes, I'm sure,' she groans. 'Just because you've got to get all hot and bothered in a country with strange toilets—'

'That's France.'

'Whatever – someone needs to stay home and record all the TV you're going to be missing.'

'Doooon't!' I wail. I haven't missed a single thing Lesley Sharpe has done since *Bob & Rose* and Rob Lowe has got a romantic storyline coming up on *The West Wing*. . .

'It's like leaving friends behind, isn't it?' Cleo sympathizes.

I know she understands because she's even more of a telly addict than me. They tease her at PhotoFinish, saying she doesn't need a diary – she just scribbles doctor's appointments and birthdays on to her copy of the *TV Times*.

It's not true of course. We use *heat* magazine.

'Where exactly is Capri anyway?' Cleo frowns.

'Down near Naples. You just get a ferry across.'

'What's it like there?'

I think for a moment. 'I don't really know – it must be quite glam because the boutiques there sell all designer stuff. I know it was all the rage in the Fifties but Granny Carmela only ever bitched about Vincenzo's mistress.'

'The wanton Rosa?' Cleo remembers everything I ever tell her. She's the only person that really listens to me.

'Yeah,' I sneer. 'She never said much about Capri itself.'

'Let's look it up on the internet!' pips Cleo. 'Come on, that way you can make an informed decision.'

I reluctantly schlep over to the computer and watch Cleo busily click and scroll. I try to conjure up some of my former enthusiasm for going abroad but I just feel queasy with nerves.

'Well, that's it. You can't go!' Cleo announces.

'Why?' I gasp.

'It says here: "Walking around topless or with loud wooden sandals is not allowed outside swimming areas and beaches."'

I chuckle. 'What else?'

'It's titchy – just four miles long.'

'Nowhere to go to escape my mother,' I worry.

'Well, you could always take a ferry to Sorrento or

Positano – oooh that's where Marisa Tomei and Robert Downey Jnr go in *Only You*, remember?'

'Oh wow!' I feel a flicker of excitement and then quash it again. 'Look up the Hotel Luna,' I urge.

'Did you know the word lunatic comes from *luna*?' Cleo asks as she tickles the keyboard.

'As in howling-at-the-moon madness? Sounds perfect for us.'

'"Suspended between the heavens and earth ..."' reads Cleo. 'What a gorgeous location ...'

'Let me see!' I lean over her shoulder.

'And look, they have a view of the "Infamous Faraglioni" whatever they are.'

'They're rocks and it's pronounced Fara-lioni, the g is silent,' I tell her.

'Get you!' she teases. 'At least I know how to pronounce Capri properly. Someone said it at work the other day and I was like, "Actually, it's CAH-pree." Ever since you told me it should sound like "cat pee" it's really stuck in my mind.'

'You learn well, grasshopper.'

'My God look at all these fancy shops – Bulgari, Prada, Gucci ...'

'I told you,' I say feeling intimidated just by the names. I don't do glamour and I don't do labels and I think that people who do have got way too much time on their paraffin-waxed hands.

'I wonder what this Luca is like?' says Cleo, enquiring after the boutique manager.

'Too much aftershave, lots of gold jewellery, possibly

31

a little surgery around the eyes,' I surmise. 'Can you get Sky TV at the hotel?'

'No,' Cleo apologizes. 'But they do have hair-driers in the rooms.'

'It'll be one of those whirring hoover pipe things – they're about as much use as someone breathing on your hair.'

'You probably wouldn't need it anyway. According to this weather chart it was 85 degrees today. Sunny. Sunny. Sunny. Bit of a thunderstorm predicted for midweek but scorching from then on.'

'What's the weather forecast for Cardiff?'

'Rain. Rain. Rain. Partly cloudy with possible ray of sunshine midweek but hey, don't hold your breath.'

'Typical July, in other words.'

Cleo turns to face me. 'Looks like you've got nothing to lose and only freckles to gain.'

4

I arrive at Woodward's ten minutes early. Mum is with a customer so I skulk around the racks playing guess-the-price-on-the-tag like I used to do when I was a girl. I'm pretty spot-on with MaxMara but Ronit Zilkha beats me hands down. (Beautiful clothes, I'll admit, but at 'You've got to be kidding me!' prices.) I look over at my mum in Betty Barclay. Yet another member of staff is interrupting her to offer condolences. They look so upset. Do they know my mother hasn't seen her father in forty-five years? I guess it's still a loss. Maybe it's a good thing I'm telling her I can't go to Capri with her mid-way through her working day, that way everyone can rally round and it'll be forgotten by closing. I watch my mum put on a brave face and go back to showing her customer the belted jacket that goes with the apple green slacks she's sporting.

I can't look at my mother in a clothes shop without remembering shopping for a new grey pleated skirt for school when I was ten. As you may recall, kiddies' clothes are labelled with an age rather than a size but when the assistant asked my mum, 'And how old is

33

your daughter?' she leant close and said, 'Well, she's ten. But you can see what size she is.' She swears she wasn't alluding to my podginess but I've never forgotten that day. Fortunately she doesn't get the chance to give children complexes now, that's left to sixty-nine-year-old Mildred who could reduce Marilyn Manson to tears and a side-parting.

My mother's speciality is revamping divorcees. The bulk of them come to her with diminished confidence and puffy eyes full of 'Why did he leave me?' questions; two hours later they stride out of the shop reborn as a diva tigress. She always offers them a glass of champagne on arrival to make them feel spoilt and decadent then coaxes out of them what they are most afraid of – never attracting another man/what the neighbours must be saying/being conned into spending £2,000 on a new wardrobe – and sets to work. It's more than just the clothing. She gives them attitude. Sometimes they come in angry, determined to get big blonde hair and brassy barmaid clothes to celebrate their independence and show that no-good husband who's run off with a younger woman what he's missing, but then she shows them a classier alternative and usually within a couple of months they return saying that he's come crawling back. Nine times out of ten they don't want him any more, they just want advice on what to pack for the holiday they are taking to Barbados with their best mate. So maybe her job isn't such a joke after all.

Drawn by the glittering diamanté, I swish through the stunning creations in the evening wear section and realize that the only place I could feasibly wear such Oscar-worthy confections would be right here in the department store. Where else would I get to brush up against people wearing Christian Lacroix and Ben di Lisi? I haven't been anywhere more glamorous than Spar in months. Of course, they probably wear this kind of thing hiking on Capri.

I sidle back towards my mother and overhear her explaining how her customer is better suited to clean bright greens rather than muddy khaki or dark ivy. She certainly has a gift for colour-coding – rather like perfume testers with hyper-sensitive noses and food tasters with perceptive palates, she can really define a hue. It's never a red shirt but pillarbox or poppy or Heinz cream of tomato. Apparently there is a difference. And it matters. To her, anyway. As a girl, if I said something was yellow she'd ask me to be more specific: canary or egg-yolk or primrose? I'd look confused and say, 'It's not a bird or a flower, it's just yellow, Mum.'

I think my mother sees more colours in the world than the rest of us – she definitely missed her calling as one of those people who invents names for lipsticks. She gives full marks to Calvin Klein: 'Suede, ginger, adobe ... all good names for neutral colours!' and Clinique: 'Baby Kiss, Heather Moon, Amberglass – they really give a sense of the gentle sheen.' But according to her, Elizabeth Arden completely lost her mind with her Lip Lip Hooray collection: 'I mean, what possible colour would you imagine a lipstick called Wiggle to be? Or Romp?'

Just don't get her started on Urban Decay – she's

never quite recovered from seeing lipsticks named Stray Dog and Asphyxia.

Mum waves over at me mouthing, 'Two minutes!' I wave back, inadvertently catching my watch link in the delicate embroidery of a Ghost bolero. My God! If I can't even negotiate a department store, how could I possibly survive chi-chi Capri? My only snobbish gift is being able to identify a designer perfume at twenty paces. My mother brought me up on mini-samples and tested me every Saturday before she gave me my pocket money. The skill has yet to prove useful.

Normally when I meet my mum for lunch we go to the restaurant on the fifth floor but today she suggests the café over the road.

'You said you never wanted to go there again,' I say as she bundles me out of the side entrance.

'They've got a new chef,' she tells me.

'It's the décor you said you hated.'

'Well, metallic mahogany is in this season so I'm seeing it with new eyes.'

She's up to something, I can tell. I wonder if I'm too much of an embarrassment in my tracky bottoms? Last time she behaved like this she hijacked me into getting a haircut – invited Gianni to join us at the table and then frog-marched me up to the salon.

Mum sings along to Billy Joel's *Just The Way You Are* with no trace of irony as she helps herself to a plate of undressed salad.

I reach for a set of BLT sandwiches sprinkled with cress, wishing that she did love me as I am.

Wishing that I didn't feel like she's scrutinizing me every time I visit her. She stared too long at my eyebrows when I arrived. I'll be getting a 'little present' of a pair of tweezers before I leave.

'What would you like to drink?'

'Orange juice,' I tell the girl behind the counter.

'Oooh no, Kim. It's too acidic.'

'My mistake! I'll have a sparkling water,' I smile.

'Still is better for you.'

'Jeez, Ma! What harm is an air bubble going to do?'

'Your choice,' she shrugs.

I hate it when she does this. Most times I do the opposite of what she recommends so she has to sit and watch me poison myself but today I don't want to look like I'm being contrary because I feel bad about letting her down. 'I can't go with you to Capri,' I practise in my head. Just say it, I urge myself.

'I was thinking, about Capri . . .' she begins.

'Mum,' I cut in, voice wavering. It's so much easier when I'm translating. I don't have to take any responsibility for what comes out of my mouth.

'Mum,' I begin again, trying to sound assured.

'Gina! I've just heard, I think it's just awful!' A twister of talcum powder and chiffon swooshes into the café.

'It's okay, Monique, really,' my mum insists, looking uncomfortable.

'No it's not. He's a complete bastard. But that's men for you, isn't it?'

Blimey! Mum's obviously told Monique a lot more about her father than she's told me.

37

'He didn't have a choice,' Mum shrugs.

'That's rubbish!' hoots Monique.

I want to say, 'I'd like to see you argue with a heart attack!' but keep quiet.

'And to do it the same week your father dies. It's criminal!'

I'm definitely missing something.

'There must be someone we can complain to!' she persists.

'Really, Monique, it's fine. I'll talk to you about it later.' Mum gives her a distinct 'not now' look.

'Okay,' she says, simmering down. 'I'm in Hosiery today, come and find me before you go back up.'

'I will.'

I watch Monique collide with a young man in a Top Man suit, muffling him in fabric, and then turn to Mum and ask, 'What was that all about?'

'It's nothing!'

'It didn't sound like nothing,' I object.

'Oh you know – the shop manager has given Jesiré an extra square foot of floor space and Mondi are kicking up.'

'But why would that affect you?'

'Um . . .' she falters.

If I didn't know better I'd say she was going to cry. And my mother never cries.

'I'm just going to nip to the loo, darling. Why don't you pick out a dessert?'

Okay, something's definitely wrong. I look across at the department store hoping for a clue and spy one of Mum's oldest, Welshest chums emerging from the

38

revolving door. Darting out on to the pavement I call her name: 'Delia!'

She looks confused then spots me waving frantically from across the street. 'Kimmy!' she smiles as I join her. 'If you're looking for your mum she's already gone to lunch.'

'I know, I'm with her,' I say, motioning to the café. 'Um, she seems upset – has something happened at work?'

Delia looks shifty.

'What is it?' I ask, troubled by an unfamiliar pang of concern.

'Oh, you know – the manager has cut back her seasonal clothes allowance, which means she'll only be getting two autumn ensembles and—'

'Delia?' I place my hand on her knitted sleeve.

'She's been made redundant.'

'*What?* She's worked there thirty years!' I recoil.

'They say personal shoppers aren't essential staff members and—' Delia halts herself. 'The thing is, Kimmy, she didn't want you to know. Please don't tell her I told you.'

'I won't but—'

'Today's her last day. This trip to Capri couldn't have come at a better time, and the thought of running her own boutique has given her such a boost.'

I force a smile. 'I guess they can't fire you when you're the boss!'

Delia places a plump hand on my plump cheek. 'She didn't want you to feel pressured into going with her because you felt sorry for her. You know how she

39

always has to seem strong, that one. She doesn't want you to worry.' Delia pauses to take in my fretful face. 'God, I've really let her down, I should never have told you.'

'It's okay,' I mutter, still dazed.

'Anyway, she'll be fine on her own. She says she's looking upon it as a fresh start.'

'She's not going on her own,' I find myself saying.

Delia's eyebrows rise tentatively.

'I'm going with her,' I announce, trying to keep the surprise out of my voice.

'Because of what I've said?' Delia worries.

'No,' I lie.

'Good girl,' smiles Delia. 'That's super!'

Tears prickle my eyes. Delia squishes me into her cardi buttons and whispers, 'I know you're scared, *cariad*. She's scared too. But you'll look after each other.'

'*If Everybody Looked the Same (We'd Get Tired of Looking at Each Other)*,' Groove Armada inform me.

What is this? The Anti-Surgery Compilation Album?

I'm back in my seat in the café in time to watch my mother weave her way back to our table from the Ladies, fierce red lipstick daring you to doubt her feistiness.

'Soooo,' I smile. 'You were saying about when we get to Capri . . .'

Her whole face brightens like a spotlight has just picked her out of the crowd. 'You're coming with me?'

she says delightedly. Then just as swiftly a shadow of doubt falls across her face and she looks around the café for someone who might have swayed my decision.

'Turns out Cafiero's have got a big translation job coming up in September so it's a great chance for me to brush up on my Italian,' I tell her.

She seems relieved. 'Well, that works out wonderfully for both of us then.'

'Yes it does.'

'You know I could probably get Gianni to squeeze you in this afternoon . . .'

'Mum,' I growl.

'What?' she cries, faux innocent.

'Don't push it.'

5

See Naples and die. That's what they say. It's a phrase that's open to a number of interpretations and the more menacing ones spring to mind as a stubby, stubbly man blocks our path at Naples airport.

'You want taxi?' he growls up at us with such impressively shifty delivery he really should be pushing crack in a Quentin Tarantino flick. I ignore him and manoeuvre our luggage trolley to the exit, only to look back and see my mother's arm draped around his grubby sleeve. Before she has the chance to coo, 'My, what lovely syringes you have!' I yank her over to the official taxi rank. With all her experience of men you'd expect her to be able to instantly spot a wrong 'un but no, she has far too much faith in mankind. Lucky I'm streetwise. (Not that I've had much first-hand experience in foiling the bad guys but if you watch enough *Crimewatch* you pick up a few tips.)

As it happens the 'official' cabby switches off his meter halfway to Mergellina port and rips us off royally on arrival. I hand over the money with a pitiful lack of resistance. Mum is still fretting about what might have become of us had we gone off with the stubby, stubbly man. I tell her that we'd probably be at least 30,000 lire better off.

As we struggle with our luggage and try to get our bearings, I become aware that we are being eyed by a group of surly mariner types. Even though it's a public port I feel like we're on their territory without an invitation. They look as if they know something we don't. Something about the weather, for a start. Mum and I are in summer casuals (me considerably more casual than my mum) but they are buried under chunky navy cable-knits and heavy jackets. I become convinced they are either about to bludgeon us around the head or offer to carry our suitcases but they do neither. They just stare as we flounder around trying to locate our departure dock. I find the whole experience completely intimidating and scuttle along the jetty with my head down, whereas my mum responds by walking with an exaggerated sashay.

To transfer from Naples to Capri in style you would need a private boat – something pointy and speedy with gleaming chrome rails and a name like *Avanti!*. The £7 option is the hydrofoil. Having finally worked out which boat is going where, we teeter up the metal gangplank, jostle our suitcases into place and shuffle along to a window seat. As the engines start up we are handed plastic sick-bags. There's hardly a raging typhoon outside so this seems a little unnecessary to me but within minutes I am proved wrong. If the rhythmical lurching doesn't get you, the sound of the man to your left retching reconstituted prosciutto will.

My mother vomits noiselessly, just a gentle rustle of the bag as she ties the handles together in a bow. For a few seconds she looks forlorn – wan and vulnerable without her trademark challengingly-bright lipstick – and my hand hovers as I consider placing it on her back in that soothing, 'Poor darling!' way she used to do to me when I was off sick from school. But before I can make contact with her tangerine suedette another arm appears – one sheathed in oatmeal linen holding a glass of water.

'Prego!' smiles a man with platinum hair.

Jesus! She even throws up in an alluring way!

I decide to go for a walk. Make that a spasmodic arm-flailing stagger. I look like I'm in a Kate Bush video. With this being a hydrofoil there is no deck to stand on and no fresh air to breathe in, only the smell of the greasy engine. I can see the waves lashing outside but because I'm not being spattered with salt water it feels like I'm on a simulator, only the nausea is authentic. Lurching up to the front of the boat for the remaining forty minutes of this endurance test, I remember that apparently the best cure for seasickness is to stare at a fixed point on the horizon and sing loudly. Unfortunately the horizon is see-sawing and I think the dis-abled seamen and women have suffered enough without my singing. Instead I take deep breaths and swear I'll never leave dry land again. The Canadian couple beside me are already dreading the return journey. 'There has to be another way!' they wail.

I, for one, am swimming back.

44

I think of Cleo back home in Cardiff. 4p.m. She'll no doubt be trapped in a 'matt or gloss?' debate with a customer prior to her tea-break. I imagine how differently I'd feel if I was taking this trip with her. That would be a romp! Instead I feel a sense of trepidation . . .

At least Mum's covering all the costs *and* paying me a fee. (I feel a bit bad about that but she did keep insisting it was a 'business arrangement' and I'm only charging her a nominal amount – just enough to keep me and Cleo in belly chains when we get our new Britney-flat tums.)

Gradually the island comes into view. It's much greener than I imagined. And more dramatic: high angular cliffs at either end, slumping to a saddle effect in the middle, scattered with little white houses like tumbled stacks of sugar cubes. The hydrofoil reverses up to the dock in between a ferry and what looks like a big grey battleship.

'Marina Grande,' my mum sighs, smiling wistfully at Platinum Man. 'There were just a few fishing boats when I was a girl.'

'Well, it was nearly fifty years ago!' I begin.

She shoots me a look. Oh here we go. This lying about your age thing really gets on my nerves. If we didn't have identical onyx green eyes and a distinctive widow's peak hairline I'm sure she'd deny that we're related at all and try to pass me off as a friend or colleague. The killer part is all the 'You must be sisters' comments we get – highly flattering for her but seeing

45

as I'm thirty and she's fifty-seven just what does that say about me?

'Sorry – I meant to say thirty years ago, obviously!' I sneer, muttering, 'Or was it ten?' under my breath.

Platinum Man directs Mum's gaze away from the mob of tourists awaiting us on the dock, towards the shallow waters bobbing with wooden sailboats painted in primary reds, greens and blues. She smiles and squeezes his hand. I turn away, looking beyond the shore to the waterfront shops, trying to identify the dark burgundy building that stands out against its cream neighbours. I can just make out the word 'farmacia'. Must remember to purchase some sea-sickness tablets for the return journey.

When I turn back, Platinum Man is gone.

'Hotel Luna!' a voice rises above the maddening crowd.

'That's us!' yelps Mum, eyes darting every which way to locate the caller amid the jostle of luggage and elbows.

'We're never going to find him in this crush,' I despair, pogo-ing upward for a better view. Our hotel is unreachable by taxi and the thought of bumping our suitcases down endless dead-end cobbled streets is too much to bear. Suddenly the day trippers part and a man in a white captain's cap with Hotel Luna spelt out in twists of gold rope steps forward. He's wearing a navy blazer and looks exactly like Tony Curtis masquerading as the yachting playboy in *Some Like It Hot*.

Oblivious to our gawping he commandeers our suitcases and asks, 'Are you mother and children?'

'Yes,' I beam, chuffed that he has acknowledged the age difference, praying he realizes that I am the younger one.

Ticking us off his list, he directs us to the *funicolare* (a cross between a cable car and a tram) and says he will meet us at the hotel in 'alf an hour'.

We push through the chaos in a daze, passing tacky T-shirt shops and elegant white Fiat Marea taxis so boat-like they look as though they would sprout outboard motors if you drove them into the sea. At the *funicolare* kiosk we each pay 2,400 lire (about 80p) and board one of the creaky-clanky cabins. Just before the doors close a scurry of Japanese tourists join us, chattering busily. Then, as we start our ascent, one of them emits a hiccupy, nasal laugh.

Mum hoots, 'She sounds like a donkey!' and mimics her exactly.

I remain expressionless for the eight minutes it takes to scale the hill then, when the carriage is empty, I turn to her and say: 'Two things: One: Just because you don't speak Japanese doesn't mean they don't speak English. And two: Even if they *don't* speak English they are not deaf. If you copy a noise they have made they will hear it.'

She looks absolutely stricken and her hands fly to her mouth as realization dawns.

'I didn't mean to be cruel,' she flusters.

'I know, but imagine how you'd feel if you heard someone describing you as mutton dressed as lamb.'

47

She looks as startled as if I'd smacked her.

My hand smarts with guilt as if I had.

We proceed up the steps in silence, both flushed with regret.

I don't know where these snide remarks come from. It's as though my stomach fills with spite if I'm around her for too long, and every now and again some of it spurts out of my mouth. I thought the answer was to spend as little time together as possible, and it was easy when I was taking interpreting jobs abroad – she couldn't really keep track of when I was home and when I was travelling – but over the past two years I've had to make a lot of excuses. I feel bad about it but every time I think it'll be different and I make the effort to visit, it's not.

Gradually my mother's confidence returns and she starts pointing things out, getting caught up in flashbacks and exclamations of 'This was never here in my day!' and 'Oooooh, look at her outfit!'

Meanwhile I'm fascinated by the funny little buggies that go beeping by, laden with luggage. They're no more than a metal platform with wheels and a driver but Mum insists they're indispensable. 'Well, you can't get a car down these narrow lanes,' she explains, 'and even on the main roads tourists can't drive because there are no hire cars on the island.'

'It's like Toy Town,' I smirk as another buggy toots and requires us to flatten ourselves against a wall so it can pass. I turn to see if I can spot our luggage amid the Louis Vuitton and leather trunks and notice a dog has hitched a ride on the back step. He pants a smile in my direction as if to say, 'It's the only way to travel!'

'Via Emanuele! This is the one we want!' Mum exclaims, skipping ahead down the bustling boutique street.

She's in her element but I feel Ferragamo and Cartier sneering at me, reminding me how out of place I am among the seriously stylish. Then I notice a shop called Snobberie and concede a smile. At least someone here has a sense of humour. Forced to adopt a shuffling pace by a sudden surge of shoppers, even I feel the need to gawp at the window displays. Some of the gaudy fashions are a bit Meg Matthews-meets-Eurotrash but the jewellery stores are pure decadence: ludicrously flashy gems for people who've done tasteful till it hurts and now – having lost all sense of the real world – want attention-seeking monstrosities.

'What kind of person would wear that?' I grunt, peering at a brooch made up of gobstopper-size pearls encrusted with diamonds in the shape of a whale.

'Different fashion rules apply on Capri,' Mum shrugs.

It's almost grotesque to imagine how much such an item would cost (a darn sight more than my £5,000 fortune, that's for sure), not to mention all the better ways of spending the money.

'Look at this lovely picture of Sophia Loren from the Fifties!' Mum coos, peering in a shoeshop window.

I want to remind her that the authentic pronunciation of Loren is actually '*Lor*-un' as in Lauren Bacall not 'Lor-*enne*' but decide to keep my coin out of the criticism box a while longer.

'Nearly there!' Mum trills, gathering speed as we leave behind the heady mix of Gucci Rush and Kenzo Jungle and trot down a cobbled side-street that smells of warm buttery baking. At the bottom we're greeted by a cluster of postcard carousels and a stall offering freshly squeezed lemonade. Between the two is a sign for the HOTEL LUNA, hand-painted on blue tiles. We circumnavigate a German tour group and pass through a low gate. As we close it behind us we sigh with relief – there's definitely a feeling that we have escaped the marauding masses. The earth around our private rustic walkway is parched from the relentless sun but the plant life becomes more vivacious and colourful the closer we get to the hotel.

'What's that?' I ask, pointing to the series of bold sandy-coloured arches framing a large courtyard to our left.

'The Certosa di San Giacomo – it used to be a monastery. It's not actually part of the hotel but I think its proximity really adds to the tranquillity of the place,' Mum muses, inhaling the fragrant air with a contented smile.

I have to agree – though not out loud of course – that the Luna is a haven. 'Suspended between the heavens and earth,' I murmur as the hotel comes into view, remembering Cleo reading from the website.

We should be heading for reception but our feet instinctively divert us out on to the glorious sun-buffed terrace. Its weathered wicker chairs are dressed with cobalt blue cushions which, according to my mother, 'are the same blue as Delia's daughter's uniform – you know, Rhiannon, the one that works on the La Prairie counter . . .'

'Mmmm' seems an inadequate response to someone mourning the loss of a job they so dearly loved, so I chip in: 'Yes and if you look at those sofas in the bar you'll see they're the same buttercup yellow as the Clarins bibs.'

Mum smiles gratefully at me, forgiving my stilted delivery, and links arms as we stroll to the edge of the terrace. I wait a few seconds before disengaging limbs on the pretext of getting my camera out to snap the Faraglioni rocks that Cleo was so excited by.

As we stare across at the three imposing stacks of eroded limestone, a boat emerges from the low gully running through the middle stack, threading a ribbon of white froth around its base.

'There's actually a fourth rock you can't see from here,' Mum tells me. 'It's home to a colony of monarch seals. When I was a girl I used to fantasize that I might go and live there with them . . .'

'Don't suppose there's much call for makeovers in the seal community,' I attempt a joke.

My mother attempts a smile.

Then we fall silent, mesmerized by the water sparkling below us. It looks as though a fishing net woven from strands of pulsing, winking fairy lights has been cast over the surface.

I sneak a sunglass-shielded peak at my mum and wonder what memories are flitting through her mind

51

now. Did she ever paddle in the shingle below with her father? Or take a boat trip with Granny Carmela? I'm half tempted to ask but afraid of what I might unleash. I prefer to keep my mother at arm's length. Any personal revelations would make me feel uncomfortable. All the same, I feel that a nice daughter would probably say something sweet and appreciative at this point so I turn to my mother to say, 'Thank you for bringing me!' but as I open my mouth a baritone booms out, 'Buon giorno!'

We spin around to find a man greeting us with such an intrusively seductive look he doesn't so much undress us with his eyes as have a quick threesome.

'Is beautiful, yes?' he says, motioning to the vista but staring intently at me. As Mum gazes back out to sea, rhapsodizing over the vantage point, he leans closer and whispers, 'Bella,' with a post-coital sigh that makes me shiver. If I was with Cleo right now we would elbow each other then run around the nearest corner and squeal. But I'm not with Cleo, I'm with my mother and it's cringe-inducing to have a man look so hungrily at me in front of her. It's as if we're watching TV together and a sex scene has come on. I flick through my repertoire of facial expressions but can't seem to find an appropriate response: I don't have the sexual confidence to mirror his lust even if I wanted to, I daren't smile for fear of what it might invite, and if I look away I'll appear coy like some fluttery little pastel princess. What I really want is a look that says, 'I know your game, sunshine, and I'm not falling for it but, hey, thanks for playing!'

'Are you not feeling well, signorina?' he peers at me.

Ah. Didn't quite pull off the blasé look I was going for, then.

'Um, er . . .' I fluster.

'We've had a long journey!' says Mum, putting a protective arm around me.

'You would like coffee or perhaps a cocktail . . .'

'Oh no!' giggles my mother. 'It's a bit early! We're actually just about to check in.'

'You stay with us?' he looks wolfishly delighted. 'You are very welcome. I am Mario, I am bar manager. Please – let me present you to reception.'

And so we follow his highly polished patents across the marble floor: Mother with a click-clack of her Carvelas, me with a smeary squeak of trainer.

'Welcome to the Hotel Luna!' smiles the groomed, square-faced gentleman behind the desk.

I know Mum is waiting for me to make the introductions in Italian but suddenly I can't find the words.

She gives the manager an indulgent smile. 'My daughter speaks Italian but she is a little shy. Do you speak English?'

He nods adoringly at her, pityingly at me.

'We have a reservation – Gina and Kim Rees,' she continues.

'Si! Please I have your passports.'

There'll be no lying about her age to the hotel staff, I smirk to myself.

'This is your first visit to Capri?' he asks as we fill out the registration form.

'Er, well . . .' This time it's my mother's turn to look blank as a concise way to sum up our circumstance eludes her.

'It's my first time but my mother has been before,' I say, deciding to spare him the Rees/Desiderio family saga. Besides, on an island this size he'll probably hear the full story on the gossip grapevine before breakfast. Which, we're informed, is continental and served on the dining room patio.

'You have room 220, garden view. Your bags will be with you shortly. Enjoy your stay.'

On cue Mario appears in the doorway connecting the lobby to the bar, leaning on the frame in his black trousers and cream double-breasted jacket with all the insouciance of Bogart in *Casablanca*. We keep walking.

'No cocktail?' He looks dismayed, blowing his cool.

'Maybe later!' my mother chirrups, jabbing the lift call button.

'I make something special for you!' he tempts. 'I squeeze fresh strawberries . . .'

And anything else you can get your hands on, I think to myself as we contort to fit into the tiny *ascensore*.

These southern Italians may not be a tall people but what the men lack in stature they sure make up for in testosterone – it's as though the male gene is more densely present in them. Not something to be taken lightly: couple Italian men's presumption and persistence with British women's fear of offending and you've got a lethal combination.

'I will not succumb!' I tell myself.

No matter how grateful I am that Mario's flirting with me and not my mother.

6

The first thing I notice about our room is a grand-mother of a cut-glass vase displaying ten red roses. The buds are perfect teardrops and the stems are so long you could pole-vault with them.

'Do you think they've been left behind by honey-mooners?' I ask Mum as I gently tap one of the cat's claw thorns.

'No, they're fresh,' she asserts. 'And more of a claret than a true red.' As if that somehow makes them less synonymous with romance.

Personally I think some jaunty yellow chrysanthe-mums would be more appropriate for mother and daughter guests. Red roses, whatever the tint, can't help but taunt a person about the lack of a lovelorn suitor in their life. Not that I want a lovelorn suitor (you'd be forever tripping over them kissing your feet) but a girl can't help but have a quick fantasy about a man – not dissimilar perhaps to the fella in the captain's cap who met us at the port – brandishing a bouquet and crying, 'Ti amo!' for all the world to hear.

There's a knock at the door.

'Probably the suitcases,' says Mum, continuing to rummage through her toiletry bag.

I flush pink with expectation and rush to the door.

'Buon giorno – ho le sue valige!' announces the best-dressed teenager I've ever seen – swept-back hair and a dark navy suit. Cute, but no captain's cap.

'Where do you want the luggage?' I ask my mum, trying to cover my disappointment.

'Scusi! Sorry. I speak English!' he apologizes.

'That's OK, my daughter understands,' Mum smiles, motioning to me with her hotbrush.

'All'angolo . . .' I say pointing to the corner next to the roses.

He makes a great show of hoisting the suitcases on to a fold-out rack then painstakingly explains how to operate the automated blind, lock and unlock the safe, open the minibar, dial reception and adjust the shower nozzle. I usher him out of the bathroom with a tip before he's tempted to give us a demonstration of the bidet.

'Sweet boy,' Mum smiles after he's gone. 'The staff here seem very nice.'

I wonder who she's got her eye on. Better be the elderly manager.

Slumping in a chair, I kick off my trainers and relish the sensation of the cool tiles beneath my travel-weary feet. As I trace the emerald green serifs with my toes, Mum lays out her outfits on her bed. Or should that be her *side* of the bed. There may be two singles but you couldn't even fit one of the complimentary towelling slippers between them. I pray that if I start sleeptalking

I do it in Italian so she won't understand what I'm saying. Which reminds me . . . Using my gentlest 'just-in-passing' voice I say, 'Mum, I'd rather you didn't tell people that I speak Italian – I'll do it when I'm ready.'

'You just want to be able to eavesdrop!' she teases, hanging her clothes in the wardrobe in her ritual rainbow: creams-to-yellows-to-oranges-to-reds-to-pinks-to-purples-to-blues-to-greens.

'Well, it's what I'm trained to do,' I note, finally getting up the energy to unzip my suitcase. I listen to other people's conversations for a living. They speak, I repeat. It's all so passive. So frustrating. Just once I'd like to be asked my opinion.

There are times when I've been tempted to work my own theory into someone's sentence or even give a completely different interpretation to what they're actually saying, just to spice things up. I did it once in my first year as an interpreter at a business dinner dance – I had too much to drink in the name of lubricating my vocal cords and invented a whole new conversation, rather like that game on *Whose Line Is It Anyway* when they take a scene from an old movie and dub over the original dialogue with comical nonsense. Whatever I said did the trick: I went to the loo and came back and they'd left without me. I should have been offended but actually I was relieved – the dancing was just starting and I had images of a Kim sandwich merengue-ing around the dance floor, rather like that scene in *Dirty Dancing* where Patrick Swayze and Cynthia Rhodes are teaching Jennifer Grey the steps in the dance studio.

Realizing we have left the room key in the door I peer out into the corridor just as a stunning woman strides past in high heels and a white halterneck swimsuit. She's followed by a squat man with a sweaty bald patch carrying her beach bag and hat.

'Why didn't you tell me we had to be there at 6p.m.?' she hisses in Italian.

'I did! I told you yesterday when we were in Prada!'

The fool! Does he really think she'd be listening to a word he's saying when there are handbags involved?

Some people can't communicate properly even when they speak the same language. It's the same with me and relationships. The man speaks. I listen. Then I interpret his feelings back to him – same language, different words. Sometimes I want to scream from all the stuff I'm keeping in.

My mum moves around the room humming *A Woman's Touch* as she sets out her perfume and book on the bedside table. She's not doing anything wrong yet I get twitchy with irritation just looking at her. I take a deep breath but the room is still closing in on me. Leaping up I throw open the slatted wooden doors and step out on to the balcony in a blaze of white light.

Way after my eyes have adjusted I'm still finding the view overwhelming. Then I realize why – I'm used to a cameraman choosing the focal point for me. Now it's down to me to give meaning to the scenery and there's just too much to take in; my attention is being pulled in too many directions. I try and break it down into bite-size pieces: above me is a striped canopy – broad bands of green and white that co-ordinate with the room, thank God, it'll save my mum redecorating. Over to my right is the sea. It has a moody greyness to it now – my mother would probably match it to Air Force blue on her colour chart. The undisturbed water in the middle distance seems almost matt, like dried paint, then as the ocean meets the horizon it blurs to a paler watercolour wash so you can barely differentiate between it and the sky. It calms me to look at it. Beneath me are the lush hotel gardens extending towards the elegant pool and beyond that, the monastery. The rest of the view is crammed with a dazzling jumble of houses and hotels intermingled with cypress and poplar trees.

I lean over the edge of the balcony and peer at the public path – Via Matteotti – that leads to the Gardens of Augustus. Right now it could be mistaken for the underground platform at Oxford Circus during rush hour. Or more accurately Old Trafford prior to a big match. The noise coming from the groups of school-kids is incredible. They hoot and holler and yank each other's ponytails and bash into backpacks and hold conversations with classmates twelve people ahead of them, seemingly with invisible megaphones.

'They shouldn't be allowed here if they're not going to appreciate it,' Mum tuts, joining me on the balcony long enough to identify the source of the shouting.

Maybe they are, I think to myself. Maybe that is how they express their appreciation. I think I'd be pretty vocal if I came to Capri on a school trip. The furthest I ever got was Bristol, traipsing along Clifton suspension bridge in a bid to enliven our essays on Isambard Kingdom Brunel. (Naturally 3B were far more fascinated by the number of people who'd thrown themselves off it than with the design.)

The schoolkids continue with their anarchic *joie de vivre* and I envy them the defiant way they are destroying the peace. I wonder what it must be like to feel that it is more important to yell your guts out than to consider other people's feelings. It takes energy to make a big noise. I'm not sure I could summon up more than a bleat. To scream is to feel something. They wave their arms, they clap and sing, emotions unrestrained. These are not the kind of people you will find in some bogus 'finding yourself' class trying to have an organic experience beneath the strip lighting.

I watch an older couple pass the rabble with pursed lips, shaking their heads, and I just can't help thinking, Who's having more fun?

It's like the difference between people who swim in the sea and people who stay by the hotel pool all day. Pool people are expertly exfoliated and depilated. They have even tans, immaculate hair, designer sunglasses. They do lengths. (You can't quantify your swim in the sea. 'I swam out as far as *there!*') It's all chemicals, cocktails and cosseting. But then why would you consciously put yourself in the more troublesome situation? Go to the beach and you get sand in every orifice – you crunch for days, you shudder at the slimy squidging between your toes praying it's just seaweed and get tumbled by a tidal wave and cough up seawater and a slick of suncream. But at least it's real.

61

Not that I can talk. You won't catch me doing either any more. In the past I was a sea girl. Now even the pool seems like too much effort. I mean, I'd probably end up getting wet or something.

Suddenly I feel sulky and homesick. If I was sat in front of the TV I wouldn't be feeling like this. But here I feel as though I should be careering along to the Gardens of Augustus or exploring the monastery or running round exclaiming 'Ciao!' to everyone I meet. I want to be a force of nature! Why am I so limp? Why do I always feel so tired? Where did my oomph go? Perhaps that's one of the reasons I sleep so badly – I never exert myself. I am Sloth Woman.

This is why I stopped travelling: it makes you aware of all the possibilities in life and sometimes it's just too exhausting to even contemplate them. Anyway, adventure is overrated. It stirs up your dreams, your hopes, your expectations. It makes you feel things can be different, but in my experience you are left feeling even more disappointed than before. Right now I feel profoundly out of place, like I've been superimposed on the wrong backdrop. The only way to convince myself that I am a part of this new environment would be to touch everything – to shin up that palm tree and feel the rough ridges scrape my soles and the whiskers of frayed wood tickle my ankles, to run my hand along the fronds to see if they prickle or slice. And then jump in the pool and get water up my nose. But I won't dare to do either. There won't be any shinning or splashing. I'll just stay feeling numb wishing I was back home with Cleo and our biscuit tin.

That's it! Sugar! I need sugar! I haven't had any all day. I turn around to ask my mum if she fancies an ice-cream but she's fast asleep on the bed.

I creep over to her side. She looks so peaceful. And so neat: lying on her back, legs straight, hands loosely folded on her stomach in classic Sleeping Beauty repose, her slender body barely denting the mattress. I sigh as I scribble her a 'Gone for gelato!' note.

It's so much easier to love someone when they are asleep.

7

As I step out of the hotel I get a sudden fluttery thrill at being alone. I can breathe again. I don't know why I feel so suffocated around my mother – it's as if she sucks up all the good air, leaving me the murky toxins. Hmmm – such thoughts are probably considered sacrilegious in Italy where Mammas Rule, best I keep them to myself.

Or to Cleo . . .

'I don't think I can stand a whole week of her!' I wail, standing at a boxy orange payphone around the corner from the tobacconist. 'I just know she's going to try and foist half the clothes she's brought with her on to me!'

She always does that – pretends she's bought something and changed her mind about it, then offers it to me. (Like a personal shopper is going to accidentally purchase something two sizes bigger in a colour she never wears.) Her theory being that if I know she's bought it especially for me I'll refuse it on principle, but if it's just a little something casually wafted my way it might slip beneath the radar.

'Have you *ever* accepted one of her mock hand-me-downs?' Cleo ponders.

'Just that leopard-print fleece dressing gown – nothing that I'd leave the house in.'

'I bet she lays cerise designer outfits over your body while you're sleeping!'

'Don't!' I squawk.

Cleo chuckles. 'So what's it like, Capri?'

'Crowded, swanky, lots of weird men muttering "Bella" as they walk past,' I note, as a raven-haired stud does just that.

'Wow! I could live with that!'

'It's just so embarrassing,' I say, burrowing into the wall. 'How are you supposed to react?'

'How about "Grazie!" and a smile?'

'I don't want to encourage them!' I snort.

'Just how weird are they?'

'Well, it's not that they're weird *looking*, most of them are really handsome which makes it all the more suspicious . . .'

'What do you mean?'

'Well, why would a stunning man tell a girl like me that she's beautiful when the place is teeming with supermodels? It doesn't make sense.'

'Kim,' Cleo sighs.

'I'm not fishing for compliments here,' I assure her. 'I've been up since 6a.m., travelling for ten hours, I can't possibly look *bella*!'

'Maybe it's just like saying hello to them. If they see a man they say, "Ciao!" and if they see a woman they say "Bella!" '

I laugh. 'You make it sound so sweet!'

'Well, isn't it?'

'Not the way they look at you – it's so *carnivorous*! Mario – the hotel barman – it's like he's got X-ray eyes!'

'God, it's been a while, hasn't it?' Cleo muses.

'I feel like I've lost my nerve.'

'What I wouldn't do for a bit of male attention . . .' Cleo hankers.

'Are you sure you can't come out?' I plead. This could potentially be a riot if Cleo was here too.

'Don't tempt me! I'm sick of this job. I've just had some woman yelling at me because all her pictures had orange flares on them. She wouldn't believe that sunlight had got into her camera, even though I showed her the negatives.'

'Any sign of Gareth?'

'No,' she sighs. 'I was on the verge of ringing his number earlier, just to hear his voice, but everyone's got caller-display these days.'

'Stalking ain't what it used to be,' I sigh. 'Are you cooking tonight?'

'I fancied that Jamie Oliver prawn and pea risotto but it seems a bit pointless for one . . .'

'You could freeze my half – I'll be back in a week, sooner if I can.'

'Where are you going for dinner?'

'Don't know, but I'm just about to spoil my appetite with a massive ice-cream!'

'Have one for me.'

'Will do. I'll ring you tomorrow to see if Gareth's been in.'

'Okay, and try and collect a few chat-up lines for me – you're dealing with pros out there!'

The chic Bar Embassy on Via Camerelle tempts me with its bulgy cream cakes, glass tombola of croissants and tantalizing selection of smooshy ice-cream. Even the marble floor is like swirled chocolate and cream. A woman stands at the bar, handbag over her shoulder, nibbling a florentine in between sips of Campari. How come she looks so stylish yet when I do the equivalent at home (standing in front of an open fridge picking at the contents) it is considered so uncouth?

I step up to the ice-cream display, ogling the succulent patchwork of flavours.

'Sì, signorina?'

'Ummmmm,' I mumble, confused by the demands of my over-stimulated taste buds. 'Errrrrrrrr. . . .'

I'm paralysed by indecision. I hate it when this happens. I've lost hours of my life standing before the Ready Meals at Sainsbury's.

That pineapple looks good. What's lampone again? Oh yes, raspberry. I wonder what nougat ice-cream would be like?

The man behind the counter sees what he's dealing with, puts down his spatula and resumes cleaning the cappuccino machine. I could always get two scoops but then of course there's the problem of choosing compatible flavours . . . aaagghh!

A schoolboy enters the parlour, his shiny hair level

with my elbow. The man behind the counter picks up his spatula again.

'Dopo di te.' You go first, I tell the boy.

'No, no signorina. You are here first.'

'Really, go ahead,' I tell him. 'I can't decide.'

'Would you allow me to advise you?' His phrasing is so delightfully formal I can't help but smile.

'I know all the best combinations,' he boasts.

'He does,' agrees the man behind the counter.

'OK,' I concede. 'Go ahead.'

He studies me for a moment as if looking for clues.

'Cocco . . .' he begins slowly. I nod encouragement. 'Ananas,' he continues, eyes never leaving my face. 'And cioccalata!' he concludes with a confident cock of the eyebrow.

The man behind the counter presents me with a frilly glass piled high with coconut, pineapple and chocolate ice-cream.

'Quanto?' I ask the price.

'I pay, signorina,' the boy insists. 'It is my gift to you.'

My God they start young here! If there's a Casanova on Capri this has to be his son. I try to object but he's having none of it. As I take my seat on the padded banquette I hear him order caramello, vaniglia and lampone to go. Sounds good – perhaps I'll try that next time.

'And a double espresso.'

I look up in amazement. The man behind the counter is unfazed but tells him the coffee will be a couple of minutes because he's just refilled the machine. The boy shrugs 'Non c'è problema' and leans on the low lip of the counter like a scaled-down beatnik poet. I half expect him to light up a cigarette.

'You like?' he asks as I take a particularly filling-chilling mouthful of tropical bliss.

'Buonissimo,' I wince. 'You're good at this.'

'I know,' he nods.

'How old are you?' I feel compelled to ask.

'I bècame seven just one week ago!' he states proudly.

'And you drink espresso?'

'Noooo,' he scoffs. 'I take it to my father!'

'Oh!' I smile, loading my spoon with equal dobs of each flavour.

'How old are *you*?' he asks.

I normally say, 'Same age as Cameron Diaz!' but in this case I feel obliged to observe, 'Old enough to be your mother!'

'Are you a mother?' he asks, eyes widening.

'No.'

'Married?' he scowls.

'No.'

'Okay! Then you can be my girl!' he beams, strutting over to my table. 'My name is Nino!'

'Kim,' I say, shaking his outstretched hand.

'Look!' he exclaims, gleefully inspecting our clasped hands. 'We are like advert for Ringo biscuits!'

I look confused and repeat, 'Ringo?'

'Yes,' he insists, impatient to make me understand. 'I am chocolate and you are vanilla, you see?'

We interlock fingers – my milky white digits

69

alternating with his sheeny brown ones, chuckling at the piano key effect we create.

'Double espresso,' calls the man behind the counter.

Nino heaves a heavy sigh and says, 'I have to go', as if leaving for war.

'OK,' I grimace. 'Grazie for the gelato.'

'You're welcome,' he replies.

At the door he turns back. 'You will be here again tomorrow?'

I nod an eager yes. It's only after he's gone that I catch sight of the silly smile on my face and realize that I've just been pulled by a seven-year-old boy.

Back in the hotel room my mother is having an involved what-to-wear-to-dinner-on-the-first-night debate. With herself.

'I was thinking of wearing the bias-cut gold satin but I can feel a bit Oscar statuette in that. Perhaps cream would be better. More classic. But it could look a bit wishy-washy before I get a tan . . .' She holds the fabric up to her jawline, grimaces and turns back to the wardrobe. 'The hot pink palazzos are always fun but I'm never sure about trousers as a first impression and it is a Catholic country . . .' She scrapes a cluster of hangers along the rail muttering her *Better to be overdressed than under* mantra. 'This linen two-piece is too creased, I'll have to hang it in the bathroom for a few days.' She takes a breath and focuses. 'What I'm going for is understated, stylish, feminine. I always feel nice in the lilac. And I can dress it up with those amethyst drop earrings . . .'

Unsure how much longer this might go on for, I make a suggestion: 'We could pop down to the bar and see what everyone else is wearing . . .'

She looks up as though she is surprised to find me in the room.

'And then change if we're not in keeping,' I continue.

'Good idea,' she agrees, settling on the lilac.

My first night dinner policy has always been 'If in doubt, wear black'. But Mum is morally opposed to black. She thinks it's an unflattering cop-out. Unless you have 'winter' colouring, whatever that means. I can feel her eyes on me as I do up the last button on my mandarin-collared jacket.

'That looks lovely, darling,' she soothes.

I smooth the self-patterned satin, amazed she's letting me get away with a visit to the dark side.

'But why don't you wear this instead?'

I turn to find her holding up a plunging scoop-neck top. 'Give the waiters a thrill!'

'Mother!' I cry, sounding like Jane Horrocks in the Tesco's ads.

'Well, all they get is old people and couples,' she explains. 'I just thought . . .'

It comes to something when your own mother starts pimping for you.

Not that this would be the first time.

Just over two years ago – shortly after Granny Carmela died – my mother declared my love life to be in a state of emergency. I had sunk into an alarming depression

71

about not having a boyfriend (funny how now I'm older I care less, when in theory I should be more desperate) and even my ever-optimistic mother was forced to acknowledge that the good men of Cardiff were immune to my charms. So she decided that she would take me to Italy to find me an Italian count. Just like that. Her theory at the time was that only an authentic Italian could appreciate my heritage and unleash my latent Latin passions. Granny Carmela had always pooh-poohed this notion, saying that Italian men could never be the answer because they could never be faithful. In fact, if she had it her way none of her clan would ever set a toe on the boot again. So even with her gone, Mum and I felt a little guilty about taking the trip – her first to Italy since she'd left Capri at twelve. I kept putting it off but after a particularly pitiful Friday night down Chip Alley I was swayed by her conviction. I had to admit there was a certain logic to it. Let's face it, if you can't pull a fella in Italy then you need to check your birth certificate to see if you're really a girl.

We spent a week on Lake Garda (Count count: zero) and on our last day took an escorted day trip to Verona with twenty or so mixed-nationality tourists. In the afternoon our guide led us down Via Cappello and through an archway festooned with multi-coloured love graffiti.

'You remember those infamous Capulets and Montagues?' he asked, coming to a halt in a shady cobbled courtyard. 'This is Juliet's balcony!'

Smiling at our ooohs of delight he stepped towards a

life-size bronze statue and announced, 'Legend has it that one in every thousand visitors who touch Juliet's statue gets a new love!'

As the rest of the group sighed at the romance, I found myself propelled forward. Not by a higher force, but by my mother.

'Go on, touch her!' she urged as I regained my balance.

All eyes were on me. The guide motioned for me to go ahead, pointing out to the group how Juliet's breasts were shiny and golden from all the male hands that had groped her, whereas female lonelyhearts tended to be more respectful and fumble with the edge of her gown. Cringing at my mother's cheery 'She's desperate to meet someone!', I tentatively stroked Juliet's skirt. The worn bronze felt cool and silky. I touched it again. And then panicked that I had cancelled out the first wish so touched it a third time, much to the amusement of our group: 'Just how many new loves does she want?' they tittered.

Well I got a new love. But I think I should have read the small print on the statue. Of course he broke my heart, although I suppose by Juliet's standards I had it easy.

At least I got to live.

8

His name was Tomas and he was one of six sim-trans (simultaneous translators) employed for a week of international conferences in his native Sweden. (It was the usual set-up – we'd each have a booth at the back of the room, then take a language each to translate the debate and the delegates could tune into whichever language was appropriate to them.) As we were moving to a different location each day and the environment was integral to the project there was a certain amount of sightseeing involved and, as some-times happens on these work jollies, each delegate was allowed to bring a guest. Nine out of ten brought a wife or husband. The UK rep brought his daughter – a lovely food fetishist by the name of Cleo. She was just a year younger than me and we bonded over our passion for *Cold Feet* and our appalling taste in men.

Tomas was the first bloke I'd ever fancied who actually seemed like a good idea. He was strapping and strawberry blond and laughed all the time and everyone adored him. I loved that I could ask him something in German and he could reply in Japanese. I loved that he wore boots with big clompy heels even though he was already six-foot-four. I loved that every time he tried to pay me a compliment it would backfire horribly and he'd end up with a confused look on his face. Cleo was the first person I unveiled my crush to, mostly because she was convinced he was after me and nudged me every time he did something sweet. (One time I left my purse at the hotel and asked if he'd sub me the money for a choccy bar. He returned from the kiosk with twenty different bars. Another time I swapped our name badges and when I went to switch them back at the end of the day he said, 'Keep it on – I like seeing you wearing my name.')

It was all boding well and I couldn't wait for the gala dinner at Lake Siljan (held on the fourth night of the trip) because up until now evenings had been fairly sedate. When we spotted the outdoor heated pool at our resort Cleo, Philippe (lovely French sim-tran), Tomas and myself made plans to sneak a few bottles of champagne from the do and go for a midnight swim. I was so convinced by this point that Tomas liked me that I refused to be fazed by the excessive attention being lavished on him by Britta, the resort manageress. Apparently they knew each other from previous events and, as Cleo pointed out, 'She's offering it on a plate – if he wanted her he'd have had her by now.'

Dinner was a success, despite the fact that the Swiss delegate obviously couldn't hold his drink and had managed to offend every woman at the table, even the ones who didn't understand what he was saying.

After coffee and *pepparkakor* (ginger snaps) we were

75

officially off-duty so I walked up to Tomas, stepped on to his big black boots, just like little kids do with their dad, put my arms around his waist and let him clomp me back to the chalet. Following our enforced separation at dinner, flirtation was in overdrive. Tonight was the night – I could feel it.

'Come on you two!' urged Cleo, fluttering over from her chalet in a sarong.

Tomas ran off to change and I fretted about what to wear to cover up my cossie, settling in the end on a silk kimono.

'Ready?' I said, eager for the frolicking to begin.

'Let me just light this!' said Cleo, bending over the stove trying to ignite her ciggy on the electric oven ring but a full five minutes later the ring had barely a hint of pink and was giving her no joy.

'Why don't you go on ahead?' she suggested, sucking in vain.

'He's not there yet,' I said, peeking through the blind.

'Well, go and get him from his chalet.'

'Really?' It was all the dare I needed. I scampered barefoot across the grass brandishing two glasses of champagne and rapped on his door.

Britta answered.

'Ooh!' I gasped.

She looked at my two glasses.

'Soooo thirsty!' I exclaimed, knocking back both in quick succession. 'Are you coming to the pool?'

'We'll be along in a minute,' she said dismissively.

'We! *WE!?!*' I wailed to Cleo as we reconvened by the edge of the pool.

'It doesn't mean anything – she's a trog. Are you getting in?'

I contemplated the moonlit water. 'Yeah, probably best to before he gets here,' I decided. That way the bits of my physique I was most neurotic about would be shrouded in turquoise. I whipped off my kimono and sploshed into the water in under a second.

'Mein Gott!' a voice called from the other side of the pool. 'That's got to be the quickest disrobement I've ever seen! Just what are you trying to hide?'

It was the Swiss delegate from dinner. Didn't he realize that women are at their most vulnerable in a swimsuit? What was he playing at?

'Hey! You!' he called walking around to my side of the pool.

Oh marvellous.

'What's that thing you were wearing before you got in?'

'It's called a kimono.'

'*Kim-no-no* more like!' he roared. 'It's the ugliest bloody thing I've ever seen.'

'Thank you!' I smiled, courteously.

'What? I said I think it's hideous!'

'I know, it's so sweet of you to say that,' I simpered doggy-paddling frantically towards Cleo.

'This is not quite the *Blue Lagoon* experience I was hoping for,' I muttered.

'It's about to get worse,' she warned.

I followed her eyes to where Tomas and Britta were

77

settling on a rock on the other side of the pool. She was draped all over him like one of those bootylicious fly-girls fawning over a rap star.

'It's all her,' Cleo insisted. 'Look – he's not responding at all.'

'But he's letting her do it,' I sighed, feeling conned and foolish. I'd made it so clear I liked him and this is how he responds? I was obviously just another member of his fan club.

One by one, more people joined us – Philippe, a few tiddly delegates and a few kids sneaking out for some fun. I was desperate to escape, but knowing my exit from the pool would be about as far from Ursula Andress as you can get I decided to stay submerged until everyone had gone to bed. The resort's security guard had other ideas, however, stomping over to inform us that the pool was off-limits after midnight and yelling: 'Everyone out!'

'This should be good!' boomed Swiss mouth almighty. 'Let's all watch Kim!'

'Unbelievable! Is he the most twisted man in existence?' I asked myself, wishing I could borrow Halle Berry's bod for just sixty seconds of my life.

Luckily Cleo had a plan: she stood beside the steps with a giant towel, then hooted, 'Who's for a party back at Tomas's?'

The consensus of *YEAAH!* was all the distraction I needed.

'Thank you,' I whimpered, disappearing into the fluffy folds.

'Tell me that's just chlorine running down your face,' she said as we walked back to our chalet.

All I managed in response was a sniff.

'Right – you're going to get changed and we're going over to Tomas's for a drink,' she announced, exuding authority.

'I can't!' I protested.

'You can. The longer we stay there the less time she gets to be alone with him.'

I conceded a smile. 'Okay. I just pray Mr Congeniality isn't there.'

'What's his name again?'

'Jurgen something,' I told her, rooting in my case for dry clothes to change into.

'I think he fancies you!'

'*What?*'

'Really! I think he's just got a weird way of getting a woman's attention.'

'Cleo, you think everyone fancies me!' I laughed, wishing it were true about Tomas.

'Maybe they do.'

'Do you want to be my new best friend?' I asked.

'Er . . . .'

'No pressure!'

'No, I mean, yes! It's just . . .'

'The outfit?' I said, looking down at my crumpled combats.

'Yes.'

'I don't want to look like I've made any effort,' I explained.

'You don't,' Cleo assured me.

Over at Tomas's, everywhere he went, Britta went too – to the fridge, to the sofa, back to the breakfast bar where the rest of us were perched.

'So you decided to dump the kimono!' Jurgen cheered, walking in and helping himself to a whisky.

I was too weak to fight but Cleo stepped up.

'That T-shirt you're wearing . . .' she began.

'This?' he said plucking at his chest.

'Best colour for you?'

I hooted in delight, knowing for sure that we'd be friends for life.

'Tell you what – if she buries that kimono, I'll bury this T-shirt!' he offered.

'If you're wearing it at the time we could have a deal,' I replied.

But even that couldn't shut him up, so with a final glance at Tomas and the amazing limpet lady I went to bed, utterly defeated.

'How come you left the party so early?' Tomas asked me the next day.

I couldn't look him in the eye. 'Jurgen was bugging me too much.'

'You could have spoken to me.'

'You were *busy*,' I spat. Could I have been any more obvious?

Tomas looked regretful and returned to his post.

I spent all morning telling myself, Hah! His loss! He had his chance and he blew it! but by the end of the day I was really missing our banter. I wanted it to be how it was before Britta, so as we waved goodbye to her and her staff and left for our next location I decided: What the hell? She's stuck back at Lake Siljan, I'm only in Sweden for two more days. I'm just going to make the most of him while I can.

After draining a bottle of wine at dinner I apologized for being arsy all day and hinted at the reason why. When that didn't seem to register I just blurted it all out: 'I was jealous of Britta! I wanted to be with you last night. I can't take my eyes off you! I'm aware of where you are and who you're talking to everywhere we go. Twice I've gone to my room and told the wall that you are the most gorgeous, clever, lovely person I've ever met. I just wished you felt the same way about me.'

And he said, 'I do.'

And then we had that most wondrous of conversations where you say, 'I loved how you always ended up sitting next to me!' And he says, 'You think that was an accident – I was worried I was being too obvious but I didn't want to sit anywhere else. Did you notice that you were the only person I helped with their suitcase?'

By this time we were leaning on each other, stroking each other's hands but we still hadn't kissed. I'd stared at his mouth all week, wondering what it would be like to kiss him – his lips looked quite firm but when they finally met mine they were deliciously soft and I couldn't believe my luck when I got that sensation of falling as we kissed.

From that moment on, his attentiveness knew no bounds. He told me over and over again how beautiful

81

I was, seemingly baffled that I didn't share his entrancement with my face.

'What do you see when you look in the mirror?' he asked.

'I don't know,' I shrugged. 'But whatever it is, it isn't beautiful!'

The next morning he got up ahead of me and sneaked back to his room. When I stumbled to the bathroom ten minutes later I found, 'You are so beautiful!' squeezed in toothpaste on the mirror. He surprised me with treats and compliments right up until the last night, when he asked if I had an hour spare the following day before the flight.

'I might do, what did you have in mind?' I had grinned.

'I want you to meet my parents,' he replied.

Well, as it happened the family meet & greet didn't happen because the final session overran and we had to go directly to the airport but he travelled with me asking all sorts of vital last-minute checklist questions like, 'How do you cope with emergencies?' and 'Are you a cat or a dog person?' I faltered at the 'Do you like cooking?' because I really don't but didn't want to blow my chances of coming off as the perfect wife-to-be.

'I really like the idea that my wife and I would cook together in the evening,' he smiled. For a big bloke he was beguilingly soppy.

As for Cleo, she was beside herself with excitement. 'Oh my God! This is For Real! He's soooo in love!'

82

'D'you think?' It certainly looked that way.

'You should see the way he gazes at you when you're not looking! He's like a smitten schoolboy!'

'That's what he says! He says he's on a constant high and feels like a little kid again!' I blurted, then suddenly felt self-conscious.

'Oh Kim! You're so lucky. You're going to marry him and move to Sweden!'

'Don't be silly,' I scolded.

'Well, why not?'

And then it swept over me – a tidal wave of joy and love and possibility. This is it! This is my chance!

Back home in Cardiff, every time I'd worry that I'd been imagining it I'd call Cleo (who was still living in Sheffield at the time) and she'd reassure me that it was real. This time I wasn't deluding myself. I had a witness!

I also had emails.

He began with a simple: *When can I see you again? I am like a weakened storm without you.*

And rapidly progressed to: *Kim, I miss your beautiful face, that sexy smile and your soft heart that makes you such an incredible woman. You are so much that in a lifetime not even I would be enough to appreciate it. For once I feel I have the world at my feet just because you care about me.*

Initially my toes scrunched up with embarrassment – it was so OTT compared to the usual reaction I inspired in men. But his sentiments were so sweet and sincere, and seeing as I felt exactly the same way, I eventually decided that Tomas had been sent to me to make up for all the men who'd barely managed to say 'You're all right, you are!'

He always seemed to know exactly what I needed to hear: *I hope that your visit to your mum was okay. I wish I was there – I would like to meet her and tell her what a stunning daughter she has.*

He even made me laugh: *I am missing you and I am missing my self – since you have spoiled the Tomas, he thinks getting so much attention from you is normal. When this does not occur he thinks that a natural tragedy is going to hit Sweden. Now I have terrible problems with him – he regards himself as one of a few to be so handsome, he keeps on daydreaming and tends to think that the UK is not such a bad place . . .*

It was all the romantic escapism I'd ever wanted to hear: *Can we dance in the rain and fall in love, never to return to normal society and live forever happy in each other's arms?*

And he mirrored everything I felt: *I am lost! Wow – I wouldn't have believed this could happen to me . . .*

For once I was going to chick flicks and instead of blubbing at the endings thinking, 'If only . . .' I was shrugging, 'That's nothing – you wanna see how Tomas treats me!'

That almost daily sense of missing out wasn't there any more. I'd found someone who saw me as I wanted to be seen. It put me on such a high – I felt invincible! I stopped doubting that such dreamy romance could be real and decided to savour every one of his cyber-kisses. My mum was absolutely delirious. Nothing I'd achieved career-wise came close to the glow of pride I saw in her when I told her I'd finally met Someone. Both Cleo and she agreed: 'You have to go to him!'

Our work had conspired to keep us apart for five weeks, and the longer we left seeing each other the more nervous I became about potentially breaking the spell. But whatever my 'what if . . .' objections, Cleo always said the same thing: 'There's only one way to find out.'

So, despite being totally broke at the time (I'd blown my savings on a second-hand Volkswagen Polo the month before Sweden) I spent £350 on a flight to Stockholm.

I thought the worst thing that could happen would be that he'd smother me with too much love.

I was wrong.

9

'Buona sera!' Mario brightens as my mother and I enter the bar.

'Buona sera,' we chorus, hoisting ourselves on to a pair of velvet-covered bar stools.

'You are ready for your cocktail?' he asks, X-ray eyes boring so deep into me that even my liver blushes.

We nod and prepare to watch a master at work.

'Fresh strawberries,' he announces holding up two perfect heart-shaped samples. 'In Italy we say that the strawberry only taste good if you are in love . . .'

Mum leans forward and bites the strawberry he holds to her lips. Harlot! I take the one hovering by my mouth and feed myself.

'Well?' he says, eyes dancing between us.

'Delicious!' says my mother.

'A bit bitter,' I comment. 'But enough about me.'

'I will make it taste good for you,' he says, dropping the remaining strawberries into a blender.

I'm not sure if he means by adding sugar or having me fall in love with him. I feel a bit panicky, as though I wouldn't have any say in the matter. I can't really remember how this boy/girl stuff goes but I'm fairly certain I don't want to give up my Tomas-induced celibacy for Mario – in my limited experience it never feels like love with Italian waiters. More like an elaborate con. You start out thinking, I am *so* not falling for this – it's waaay too obvious! But they wear you down, first by looking at you with the kind of hammy yearning usually reserved for dogs trying to get you to sneak them a morsel of pork chop under the dinner table, then by kissing you like they are trying to fit their whole body into your mouth, tongue-first. If they are real pros they do something sweet or thoughtful that's very specific to your tastes so for a moment you don't feel as if you are on a conveyor belt with all the other suckers, you actually believe they've seen the real you. And to cap it all they have jealous strops that trick you into thinking you're having a full-blown relationship rather than a holiday fling so before you know it . . .

I study Mario as he gently stirs the champagne into the strawberry pulp without bursting a bubble. I couldn't fancy him, could I? I wouldn't even be asking that question if he didn't keep looking at me *that way*. But seeing as we're 50 per cent there (he's game) one has to check back with Heart HQ, just to make sure he's not on to something. He takes two small square cocktail napkins and sets them before my mother and me at a precise angle. No I couldn't, I realize with relief. All this finessing the drink is getting on my nerves.

'What do you call it?' asks Mum, finally getting her dainty hands on the glass of creamy pink fizz.

'I call it The Kim!' he says matter-of-factly.

My mother and I exchange a knowing look. 'And tomorrow it's called The Amanda and the night after that The Isabella . . .'

He gives a mock-affronted gasp.

We laugh, wish him 'Salute!' and take a synchronized sip. Mmmmmm. Bliss with a kick. Our cheeks flush instantaneously. By our second glass Mum has decided she's got the best 'dinner on the first night' outfit in the place (having ripped everyone else's ensembles to shreds – too Carmen Miranda frilly, too Kate Adie plain, too Anouska Hempel drapey). I've never seen her quite so embracing of her inner bitch and laugh until I snort. Mario looks mildly repulsed. I get the impression he thinks we need to soak up some of the alcohol when he offers 'Biscuits?' (pronouncing it bis-kwits so we can't help but giggle some more).

'You don't have any Ringos, do you?' I ask, remembering Nino.

'No,' he frowns.

'But you've heard of them?'

'Of course but they are sweet, I have only savoury.' He peels back a Tupperware lid and shakes a heap of bar snacks on to a plate.

'Mmmm, these green ones are flavoured with pesto,' notes my mum, popping a succession into her mouth. 'I used to have them as a girl.'

The white ones are like little knots of breadstick and

88

taste of nothing. Mum and I both reach for the last green one.

'You have it!'

'No, you!'

'No, I've already had more than my fair share.'

'But they're your favourite!'

Mario sighs heavily and opens the box again, carefully hoisting out only green ones with a swizzle stick. 'I only do this for you.'

It could be the booze but I'm starting to see a strong resemblance between Mario and the actor Jean Réno. 'From *Leon*?' he says, looking chuffed. 'He is very . . . masculine, yes?'

'Yes,' I say out loud. 'With a big nose,' I say to myself.

A waiter comes in carrying a silver tray, apologizes for interrupting us and orders 'Campari for Room 115'.

'She says I look like a movie star!' I hear Mario tell the waiter in Italian as he prepares the drink. The waiter looks me over. 'If only they could clone you, Mario, all the women in the world would be happy.'

'Ooh, we'd better go – I booked the table for 8.30 and it's gone that now!' Mum gasps, draining the last of her drink.

'You don't eat here at the hotel?' Mario looks dejected.

'Tonight we dine at Ristorante Faraglioni – how's my pronunciation?' Mum asks me.

'Perfecto!' I tell her.

'I see you later?' Mario scampers after us, pulling me

back. 'I finish at midnight. I make you a tour of island, yes?'

'Um, I, er . . .' I squirm.

'Very nice walk, I know a place . . .'

God! Where's the word 'no' when you need it?

'Get in line, Mario,' my mum butts in. 'I'm her tour guide tonight!'

I've never felt so in demand.

As we take an unexplored path out of the hotel I thank my mum for stepping in with Mario, confessing, 'I didn't know what to say – it's been a while since anyone asked me out.'

'I knew your Rees feminine wiles would kick in sooner or later!' she chuckles.

'I'm sure you mean that as a compliment,' I tell her.

'Of course!' she says, grabbing my arm. 'Look, I wanted to show you this . . .'

We stop outside a glass-fronted shop and look in at the myriad of silver cylinders, pipes and glass bottles lining the walls.

'Inhale!' my mother instructs. 'What can you smell?'

'Lemon,' I begin.

'Of course, this is Capri. What else?'

'Orange, peach . . .'

'Yes,' she encourages.

I take a moment. 'Sandalwood?'

'You always did have a nose,' she laughs, tweaking mine. 'Can you name the flowers?'

'Lily of the valley and . . .' I sniff again. 'Definitely jasmine!'

'Very good!'

'Is this a perfumerie?'

'Not just any perfumerie, this is the *Carthusia*!' she says grandly. 'Legend has it that in 1380 Queen Giovanna d'Angio paid an unexpected visit to the San Giacomo monastery—'

'The one over there?' I say, pointing back towards the hotel.

'The very same!' she nods, continuing, 'The father prior wanted to make the Queen feel welcome so he gathered together the most beautiful flowers on the island and made an arrangement for her. The water was not changed for three days and then when the flowers were thrown away, he noticed it had an enticing fragrance. He took it to the father alchemist and that became the first perfume of Capri.'

'That's lovely,' I say. But I doubt I'd want to bottle any of the stagnant flower water I've encountered.

'Your grandfather used to wear the man's fragrance,' Mum smiles, remembering. 'I would buy it for him every birthday. It was made from wild raspberry and marine oak. On the day that Granny Carmela and I left, I poured some on the cuff of my cardigan so I could smell it and think of him,' her voice quavers.

'Is that the little blue wool cardi you keep in the drawer?' I ask.

She nods.

I always wondered about that. It was so out of keeping with the rest of her things but survived every spring-clean and house-move.

'I'm starving, aren't you?' Mum says, jollying herself along.

Curiously, the Ristorante Faraglioni has no view of the infamous rocks, but it is on the road that leads to them. Via Camerelle also happens to be the most exclusive shopping street, home to Hermès, Tod's, Alberta Ferretti et al., and this is very much reflected in the richie-rich clientele. I secretly love that even competing with heiresses and supermodels my mother still manages to cause a stir when she walks in.

'Ahhh, buona sera, signoras!' The waiters clamber over each other in a bid to lure her to their section. A cuddly fellow by the name of Massimo triumphs, and makes a big show of indulging us with one of the exclusive outdoor booths.

As he sets a small vase of flowers on our table he smiles, 'From my garden!'

We laugh – as if. And then I notice that none of the other tables have flowers . . . He's just Cleo's type, I think to myself as he darts past the lobster tank into the kitchens: a sweet puppy-dog trapped in the body of a wrestler.

Ignoring the stigma attached to ordering rosé, we opt for a bottle of Lacryma Christi, which translates as 'Tear of Christ'. Not only is it the most poetic option on the wine list, it's also made from grapes grown locally, on the side of Mount Vesuvius. How cool is that? The pale pink lava is potent and instantly tops up our tipsy-factor. Which is just as well, because Massimo pours barely a trickle at a time. (I suspect it's a ruse to keep coming back to the table.) One by one the other waiters stop by to pay homage and, emboldened by drink, I too dare to smile back at them. It would seem my mother's flirtation is contagious. It feels weird at first, then oddly thrilling.

Mum seems to sense my tingles. 'Maybe you *should* take Mario up on his offer of a tour of the island!' she winks.

'You're kidding – would *you* go on a walk alone with him?' I ask her.

Silly question really. But I wonder if it's less to do with her being a slapper and more about sexual confidence in that she knows she could handle him getting out of hand. It's like Catherine Zeta-Jones managing to keep Michael Douglas at bay for nine months or so – the woman needs to share her secret. I wish she could teach me how to be sassy enough to say 'no' with dignity and command respect for it while still maintaining my allure. That's quite some knack. If I found myself at a remote beauty spot with someone as sexually upfront as Mario I'd be terrified. There would almost certainly be attempted border-crossing before I'd had a chance to check his passport and I handle situations like that so badly – I try and play it off in a jokey way, slapping away foraging hands with a 'naughty boy' reprimand when I really want to scream, 'What's wrong with you? How can you possibly think it's sexy to grab and scramble around my body like I'm a one-woman army assault course?'

'Are you ready to order?' Massimo smiles, still gracious though this is the third time he's asked.

'I'm sorry,' my mum apologizes, fanning him with her lustrous lashes. 'We keep getting distracted.'

I frown at the menu. I can't decide – vermicelli or trofie pasta? I need Cleo to talk me through. As I reach for my wine I catch Mum looking at me with a playful expression on her face.

'Penne for your thoughts!' she says, cracking up the minute the words are out.

I splutter with unexpected mirth, dribbling rosé down my chin. She emits a snort-shriek. It's the least ladylike noise I've ever heard her make and my shoulders shake as I try to control my giggles.

When we finally come up for air our eyes are streaming and our faces puce.

'Is everything all right?' Massimo asks, patiently waiting for the hysteria to subside, a small smile dancing on his lips. 'You need some water?'

'No water!' we scoff. 'Just more wine!'

Massimo looks delighted and instantly summons a second bottle.

'We'll order now!' I announce.

'You first!' Mum nods.

'No, you!'

Mum composes herself. 'I would love to have the champagne and pecorino risotto to start, followed by the monkfish.'

'So would I,' I decide, experiencing the unfamiliar sensation of going along with my mother.

'Bellissima!' Massimo grins deliriously.

As Mum chats excitedly about the prospect of visiting the shop tomorrow I become convinced that the elderly head of a party of twelve is staring at us. I suppose we have been rather loud. I wonder if he

94

thinks we're shockingly uncouth. His presumed disapproval makes me more giggly and I set Mum off again. Mid-screech, the elderly man appears at our table. The rest of his party are heading out the door.

He puts his fists on our table and booms, 'I just wanted to say, I think you are *wonderful*!'

Then he takes both our hands and kisses them.

Both!

I feel positively euphoric! Tonight I'm on a par with my mother, which pretty much elevates me to goddess status. Maybe this week isn't going to be so painful after all.

The attention levels go through the roof when it comes to dessert. We order profiteroles and as soon as the last smudge of chocolate sauce is gone, Massimo presents us with complimentary tiramisu. Next up is la torta Caprese – a dry almond cake. Even my sugar-phobic mother is relishing the treats. Once the dessert trolley is exhausted Massimo (and two other waiters) start plying us with limoncello – a pale yellow liqueur which the locals try to pass off as a delicacy but which I can confirm is in fact lemon-scented cleaning fluid, ideal for ceramic tiles and stainless steel surfaces.

'How can you drink this stuff?' I wince, wondering how to dispose of yet another measure.

'I always wanted to try it,' Mum reveals, taking custody of my glass. 'I was too young before – I'm going to make up for it now!'

When we ask for the bill, the owner himself brings it over, introduces himself as Giuliani, and thanks us for our custom.

'I don't understand it! Why are we being treated like celebrities when they see the real thing all the time?' I ask my mother.

She shrugs happily. 'I could tell you that it's because everyone else here is in a couple . . .'

'And we're the only women on their own? Gee, is that all it takes?'

'But actually I think it's just one of those nights when there's magic in the air.'

I smile. Could that be true?

Apparently someone wants to prove my mum right because just when we think it can't get any more sensational the one waiter who seemed immune to our charms sidles up to our table, leans over the candle and – in the sexiest Italian accent imaginable – flickers the flame with these immortal words: 'You are not women, you are *paradise*!'

Mum and I reel, incredulous. The limoncello may be heady but the compliments are truly intoxicating.

I'll remember this night for the rest of my life.

'Come on, I want to show you the Piazzetta!' Mum says, wavering to her feet as multiple pairs of hands reach to help her with her chair. 'The best time is before dinner – it's like a real-life catwalk – but even now you will see some sights,' she promises.

We're walking along linking arms and I don't even mind. I think I might be having a breakthrough. I feel like we're closer than we have been in years. I don't know if it's the fact that she was a pre-teen last time she was here that's got her all giddy or Mario's secret ingredient in The Kim cocktail, but either way, my mother is one cute drunk.

'What are all these men doing with cameras?' I ask, as we turn to stagger up Via Emanuele.

'They're like friendly paparazzi,' my mum explains. 'They take pictures of important visitors for *Capri Vip* magazine. They are never too intrusive so the stars don't mind – look!'

My mother guides me over to a photographic shop. The window display shows photographs of celebs at large on this very street: Dustin Hoffman, Nicole Kidman, Mariah Carey . . .

'Oh wow – Kevin Richardson!' I gasp.

'Who?' my mum squints.

'From the Backstreet Boys!' I say, pointing at the black-haired beauty.

'Mmm, very handsome,' my mum approves. 'Who's that with him?'

'His wife, don't rub it in!' I groan.

'He could pass as Italian. Let's see if we can find you a lookalike.'

Normally I'd run screaming but tonight I find myself laughing. If Cleo could see me now – about to go on the pull with my mother!

'Here we are – the world-famous open-air living room!' Mum beams as we take in the paved courtyard crammed with little tables and cane-backed chairs. I can't believe how co-ordinated everyone is. It's as though each couple or family was allowed to pick one distinct hue – soft caramel, silver-apricot, wear-once white – and then dyed everything they own to match.

It makes for an utterly immaculate ensemble: there's not a loose thread or ragged cuticle to be had. I have never before felt so profoundly lacking in jewellery.

'Here's a seat,' I suggest, darting beneath the canopy at Bar Tiberio.

'Hold on . . .' My mother scans the tables at the rival bars.

'Or is one bar more "in" than the others . . .' I tease, straining to see to if there's a Gucci gang facing off the Dolce & Gabbana contingent – belt buckles at dawn, etc.

'I'm just looking to see . . . *There!*' she says elatedly.

I follow her excited gaze, skimming across the froth of endless cappuccinos and discover – of course! – Platinum Man.

He gives my mother a ceremonial bow and beckons us over. Whaddayaknow? There are two free seats next to him.

All my boozy bonhomie evaporates in a second. All I can think is, 'I'm not enough for her. I've never been enough.'

10

'Kim, you remember Mr Hamilton from the hydro-foil.'

'Tony, please,' he says, shaking my hand and insisting she use his first name. How daring.

I try to be gracious but instead of a smile my lips tense into a straight-line Muppet mouth.

'Tony, this is my daughter Kim.'

He nods and coos, 'Well, aren't you girls looking radiant!' surprising me with an American accent. At least there's no misunderstanding what he's saying. One time my mother was chatting to this grey-Afro'd Jamaican man at a garden party hosted by one of her well-travelled clients when I bowled up with a trayful of rum punch . . .

'Ooooh this is your daughter,' he cooed in his patois lilt. 'She's a virgin!'

Mum and I looked absolutely mortified. I was twenty-five and not fooling anyone. Before we could even attempt a feeble 'I beg your pardon?' he repeated, 'Virgin! Virgin?' ever more urgently.

Suddenly my mother erupted with a triumphant,

'*Version!*' Adding with visible relief, 'You're saying she's a *version* of me!'

'Of course!' he replied, utterly bemused. 'You two could be sisters!'

I quietly passed out into the foliage.

Platinum Man raises a groomed eyebrow at the waiter. My mother opts for more limoncello, while I decide to order hot milk to give the impression that I'm winding down, ready for bed, might-drop-off-at-any-moment ... Unfortunately my Italian fails me and I ask for 'Latte fredo' by mistake and have to pretend I was craving a glass of cold milk. (No matter how many times I remind myself to see 'caldo' and think s-cald-ing hot, I think cold.)

Platinum Man toasts us with his Sapphire Martini and asks Mum how her first day back on Capri has been and whether she would like him to accompany her to her father's grave when she visits it for the first time. I'm indignant – 'That's what I'm here for!' I want to cry – but realize I haven't even offered. It seems to me he's got that nice, concerned, protective, 'Allow me' persona that so often turns into control freak when you get involved. I sit back and watch my mother talk animatedly about the vivid colours on the island and how just seeing the Faraglioni rocks again made her heart ache. She is indeed glowing but I can't tell whether it's because she's back on Capri or because she has a new admirer in tow.

Realizing that the majority of her lipstick has transferred to the limoncello glass she excuses herself to nip to the Ladies.

'So, does your mother always pick up strange men on hydrofoils?' Platinum Man joshes.

'I wouldn't say all of them have been strange,' I reply, straight-faced.

His face falls.

'No, you're the first,' I reassure him, adding under my breath, 'this trip.'

'Your mother tells me you're a translator . . .'

'Really? Translator is it this week?'

'Then you're not . . .'

'Prostitute,' I whisper, tapping my nose conspiratorially. 'She doesn't always like to tell people straight away.'

He pauses for a second. 'So, is this a working holiday?' I catch the glint in his eye and we both burst out laughing.

'This bodes well!' smiles my mother, returning to her seat.

'For what?' I ask warily.

'Kim,' she says, giving my hand a squeeze. 'You could be looking at your future father-in-law!'

It takes me a second to realize she's saying father-in-law not stepfather. There've been so many.

'My future father-in-law?' I repeat, blinking at Tony.

'Well, that was before I discovered that you are a prostitute,' he deadpans.

'Prostitute!' my mother screeches.

All the heads turn, though their bouffant hair remains facing forward.

Mother blanches. 'What do you—'

'Just teasing, Gina.'

She looks flustered and for a second I almost feel sorry for her. Almost.

PM turns to me. 'My son Tyler is joining me for a couple of nights next week. He's thirty-four, single, successful art dealer, properties in London and New York . . .'

'Does he look like you?'

He shakes his head. 'Sadly not, he takes after his mother.'

'Collagen lips, botox forehead?'

'I didn't realize you knew her.'

'We go way back.'

Mum looks confused but makes a brave bid to rejoin the conversation. 'I thought it might be nice if we all had dinner together . . .'

I sigh into my milk. 'If his son is just here briefly I'm sure Mr Hamilton would rather—'

'Oh no!' he anticipates my objection. 'Both my sons bore me stupid. I'd love it if you girls came along and livened things up a bit.'

'So there's a brother?' I say, thinking of Cleo.

'Morgan. But he's off the menu – married ten years. Tyler's the one.'

'So how come Morgan got snapped up and Tyler's still on the shelf?'

'Kim!' exclaims my mother, looking embarrassed.

'It's all right, Mum. I'm on the same shelf so it's not derogatory.'

'You want to know why Morgan is married and Tyler is not?' PM confirms.

I nod.

He takes a deep breath. 'Morgan is a bully. He likes having a woman around to lord it over and under-standably girlfriends kept dumping him. Then he met Angie. She'd been broke most of her life so he proposed, knowing how hard it would be for her to leave him and his money.'

'How romantic!'

'Isn't it?' PM grimaces. 'I don't think it's set a particularly good example to Tyler. He doesn't seem in any rush to settle down.'

Mum looks crestfallen. 'But when he meets the right girl . . .'

'Oh sure! Why not?' beams PM, giving my mum's knee a squeeze. 'So, Kim – what's your story? I'm surprised one of your clients hasn't wanted to take you away from it all.'

I smile. 'Well, there was this one really sweet pimp . . .'

'Oh Kim, stop it!' Mum pleads.

I'm obviously undermining her hard sell.

'But no one currently?'

I shake my head.

'She was engaged once,' Mum prompts, presumably hoping to prove that I'm not entirely undesirable.

'I think I've got the certificate with me somewhere . . .' I feign looking in my bag.

PM chuckles.

'Turn out to be a bounder and a cad, did he?'

'He was Swedish,' my mum contributes. As if that explains it.

A week before my flight to Stockholm the emails were as ardent as ever: *I cannot wait to see you – I want to show you to everybody!* There was even one gloriously impatient one that said: *Kim! Enough is enough, get back to Sweden now! Let's get the marriage behind us and start with the family!*

I rang him. He proposed. It was all so giddying and now I could be sure of his intentions, I just couldn't wait to get there. So it threw me slightly when he sent me an email two days before saying, 'Where are you staying when you get here?'

I'd always presumed I'd be staying with him. Especially since he appeared to be planning an exciting itinerary for us: *I want to show you so much, take you to places you only dreamed of where I can really get to know you. I have a spot in mind that I think you will like but of course the Sahara would be lush if I was with you.* I saw us cosying up in a series of B&Bs as we explored the area. Apparently he had a different take on the situation. But then why hadn't he asked the question before? And considering he was far more familiar with accommodation options in Stockholm, why hadn't he made any suggestions? Was it just a cultural hiccup? I couldn't work it out. Before that email I had felt so close to him. Suddenly I felt a stranger and I was too embarrassed to question him so I booked into the trendy Birger Jarl Hotel for the first three nights. (Hardly a cheap option but if it was to be our love shack I wanted to go all out.)

The night before my flight I was reassured by these words: *Just to think that tomorrow I will have you in my arms. Then I will inform the UK that you are a spy for a small revolutionary unit in Sweden and you will not be allowed to return*

for at least six months in which time you will become so
accustomed to me that you will only leave me for very short periods
of time. Something in the line of morning shopping.

Cute as a button.

The next day there he was at the airport twelve
times better-looking than I'd remembered, waving a
bunch of pink roses with an engagement ring strung on
to the ribbon. He swept me off my feet and swirled me
round and for that minute I was one of *those* women at
airports. I felt as though I was crossing over into a
romantic fantasy land that I wasn't even sure existed
until then. It was surreal having people look at me with
the same fascination I had with couples so ostenta-
tiously in love. I wasn't quite sure how to react – to a
degree it still felt as if I was looking from the outside in.

He led me to his car in a daze. I had barely slept the
night before from nerves and excitement and I wanted
to just crash with him at the hotel but he insisted we go
straight to meet his parents, who were waiting in a
coffee shop in a mall. I felt a bit hustled but was
flattered that he was so keen for us to meet. And it
went fine. I like other people's parents.

Now we could crash at the hotel. Roll around the
hotel bed. Fall properly in love. Only he had to get a
suit. For a wedding. On Saturday. 'Tomorrow Saturday?' I asked. He nodded. I didn't recall an invitation.

'So whose wedding is it?' I asked, as we began our
quest for something sleek and navy.

'I've never met them. It's actually as a favour to a
friend. Which is why I can't invite you – sorry!'

'Oh that's Okay,' I breezed. Feeling the opposite.

'Pale blue or dark blue tie?'

'Pale,' I said, channelling my mother. 'So, if you don't know the people that are getting married, why are you going?'

'This girl needs someone to go with.'

'You're going on a date?' I gasped.

'No. I've never met her before. I told you, it's a favour to a friend.'

'What friend?'

'My best friend, Henrik.'

Instantly I loathed him. 'Why can't he take her?'

'He's too young for her.'

'So it *is* a date!' I exploded.

'No,' he said, totally unruffled. 'They'd just look silly together. Anyway, he's engaged.'

'*You're engaged!*' I blustered, totally stunned by his logic.

'I gave him my word. It's not about her. It's about my friendship with him.'

I stood there blinking, trying to get my head around the concept. In a way I admired how he was standing strong. Was I over-reacting?

'Oh well,' I said, unwilling to have a massive stand-up row three hours after arriving. 'I guess it's just for a few hours in the afternoon . . .'

'It's an evening wedding.'

I gulped. 'So, basically, our first Saturday night together I'll be on my own?'

'I'll meet you after.'

'Oh.'

'I'm just going to try this on,' he said, holding up a pinstripe suit.

'Okay. I'm just going to pop across to the chemist to get some conditioner. I'll be back in five.' Phone. Phone. Got to call Cleo.

She thought he was out of order but decided to give him the benefit of the doubt. 'You can't let this ruin everything. Just let it go for today.'

So that's what I did. I pushed it out of my mind and I painted on a smile.

We went back to the hotel. Ordered room service. Drank wine. And fell asleep in front of the TV wearing the hotel bathrobes after some pretty fabulous lovin'.

When I woke up it was the dreaded day. At least the wedding wasn't until 6p.m. And I was seeing him after. I told myself things were going to be fine. We had breakfast, hung out and then he said he wanted to go to a mall out of town as he still hadn't got an outfit for the wedding. Shopping is so not my thing but of course I went along with him. It was quite a drive and when we got there he realized he'd left his credit card at his parents' house and he'd have to go back. No problem.

Then he said, 'My parents will be in, perhaps we could have lunch with them?'

'Er . . . Tell you what – why don't you go back and I'll wait here for you,' I suggested.

He looked concerned. 'Don't you want to be with me?'

'Yes. Yes! I was just getting a bit carsick. Just call me on the mobile when you get back. I'll probably be in the bookshop.'

At least I could look at the magazines. His parents were lovely but I just couldn't face them while I was feeling so tense.

'I'll be an hour . . .'

'That's okay,' I told him. 'I'll see you back at this entrance about 2p.m.'

There were kisses. Everything seemed all right-ish. I had a milkshake and some sluttish pastry. I flicked through the international magazine rack. I looked at Swedish hair products, wondering if they knew something the curl-tamers back home didn't and then I waited.

2p.m. came and went.

Then 3p.m.

'I'm not going to call. He's obviously just got held up.'

3.30p.m.

'Why hasn't he called me to say he's going to be this late? This place is driving me nuts!'

So it went on.

4.p.m. I cracked and dialled his mobile.

'Thank God it's you!' he blurted. 'My phone card is all used up. I couldn't make any outgoing calls!'

'Where are you?'

'On the way to the wedding!'

'WHAT?!?!' The shiny mall floor fell from beneath my feet and I plunged down a chasm of disbelief.

'I got the time wrong – I'm running really late. I'm on my way to pick her up now!'

I couldn't quite believe my ears. He was on his way

to her. Not me. He'd just left me at a mall in the middle of nowhere.

'I'm so sorry!' The first hint of an apology. 'You'll have to get a taxi back. I'll call you later.'

I hung up the phone. In a daze I dialled Cleo. Halfway through explaining what had just happened it hit home and I started crying. And crying. And crying. I didn't care about all the strange looks I was getting, I just couldn't control the sobs.

'I don't understand it – it doesn't sound like Tomas at all,' she said, close to tears herself.

She was right. He was like a different person. Distant. Secretive. I thought we were going to be in this thing together but it felt like another petty boyfriend/girlfriend game. What was going on? Why was this happening? Look for the lesson, my mum would say. The only thing I could come up with was: Avoid taking taxis in Sweden; they cost a *fortune*!

Back at the hotel I paced like a madwoman. I had to get away from this situation. I had to protect my heart from getting any more bludgeoned. I dialled the airline but then I pictured the look on my mother's face as I announced that the whole thing was off. I knew she'd think it was my fault. Maybe it was. Had I done something wrong? What? Perhaps I'd come off too narky about the wedding thing? But it was a wedding! Weddings are big deals. Who was this woman anyway that she thought it better to go to a family wedding with someone else's fiancé than by herself? Apparently she was an air hostess. Could things get any worse?

Of course.

He came to me after the wedding full of remorse. He said he'd been wrong, that he'd temporarily lost his bottle, that he was unnerved because he felt so strongly for me. He asked me to move in with him. It meant I didn't have to give up on the dream that he was the One and seemed to offer some security so I said yes.

For a month it was bliss. I'd even managed to get a couple of well-paid jobs which kept us in pickled herrings. But then the niggling doubts started creeping back. I'd been so preoccupied with the air hostess that I had forgotten about Britta. I was only reminded of her when he sent an email meant for her to me by mistake. A huge row blew up – it was far too flirty for my liking – but he assured me that even though she fancied him, he didn't find her remotely attractive – it was just an old habit, that's how they spoke to each other. It didn't mean anything. Cleo said, 'Why would he ask you to move in if he had something going with her?' I felt appeased but always slightly uneasy when he was tapping away at his beloved computer.

Then one Saturday I was due to be out all day on a job. He had the day off, and called me to say he was going to the supermarket, did I want anything special for dinner? I told him to surprise me. (Ahem.) Twenty minutes later I was informed that my job had been cancelled. I tried to call him back to say I'd meet him at the supermarket but his phone was switched off, so I decided to go home and wait for him. I unlocked the door and called his name, just in case he'd beat me back. No answer. I walked into the kitchen and filled the kettle. Out of the corner of my eye I noticed flickery-flashing from the study/lounge. I presumed he'd left the TV on and wandered in to switch it off. The screen was black. I turned around and saw the flashing was coming from the computer. I took a step closer. At first I thought it was internet porn – two naked bodies pulsing up on the screen in a series of obscene poses. I was disgusted and turned away, but then I went cold. Slowly I turned around. The man was Tomas. I waited, sick and transfixed until a picture configured showing the woman's face . . . Britta, open-mouthed in ecstasy. Shaking, I tore my eyes from the screen, praying it was all imaginary. Was my overly-suspicious mind pasting their faces on strangers' bodies? Then I noticed the wire trailing from the back of the computer to Tomas's digital camera. He'd left it to download while he was at the shops.

I clawed at my hair, trying to pull one last rational excuse from my brain. Could they be pictures from before we'd met? No. He was wearing the watch I'd bought him a week ago for his birthday.

I didn't know what to do. Then I thought of Granny Carmela. She didn't hang around for the humiliation: once she knew that Vincenzo had been unfaithful, she was gone. I had to get out before he got back. I pulled my suitcase down from the top of the wardrobe, called a cab, took as much as I could pack before the doorbell rang, left the rest. On the way to the airport I realized he probably wouldn't even miss me. At least Granny Carmela had my mother; she knew taking her away would hurt Vincenzo. I had nothing. I let him get off too easy but that was classic me. Never speaking my

111

mind. Running to avoid confrontation. I didn't even smash his computer. If I'd had the nerve I would have stayed and loaded a virus or sent the pictures to every one of his clients. There was plenty of opportunity for revenge but I wimped out. I just vanished.

I tried to wipe out all trace of him by slotting the engagement ring in the charity box for spare foreign currency at the airport but those images of him and Britta still flash in my mind two years on. And when any man tries to come close I just see his face in the frame and walk away.

When I told my mother she said it was a blessing that I found out before we got married. A blessing? Just once I'd like her to say, 'Poor you, it must have been devastating' instead, of 'never mind. It obviously wasn't meant to be.'

The only thing I agree with her about is that Cleo was the best thing to come out of the whole Swedish scenario. She took a sickie to come to Cardiff to comfort me as soon as I got back and the rest is history. Bless her, she was determined that the experience with Tomas wouldn't leave me a mistrustful and embittered old hag and did everything she could to balance his betrayal with stories of men being eternally faithful, often ringing me from work to read me some magazine article on 'fidelity being the new infidelity' or some nonsense. Gradually I managed to convince her that I was okay, that I felt entirely neutral – I just wasn't interested in buying into the love fantasy again. Pretty soon I stopped hoping for it. Then I stopped believing in it. Then I stopped wanting it. So that's me. I'm done.

The last thing I want now is a new love.

11

'Has it crossed your mind that this Luca might be gay?' I ask my mother as we approach Desiderio's the following morning. I'm still a little miffed with her for springing Platinum Man on me last night at the Piazzetta and can't resist the opportunity to rattle her cage.

'No.' She shakes her head, stopping to check her reflection in the shoeshop next door. 'Of course not.'

'Right,' I say, chewing my lip. 'So it could come as a bit of a shock to discover he's a transvestite.'

'What?' she gasps, whipping her head round to me. I redirect it to Desiderio's window where a tall man is smoothing the flared panels of his iced-gem motif dress.

'Oh my God!' My mother looks away aghast. 'He's not expecting us for another half an hour! Do you think he goes in early every morning and tries on all the—'

'Mum!'

'Oh God, I—'

'Mum!' I grab her by the shoulders. 'I'm just kidding.'

I push her closer so she can see that the man in question is in fact just leaning over a body frame displaying the dress: the way his head appears to be transposed on to the body of Gisele Bündchen is simply an illusion.

Mum expels a wobbly sigh of relief then starts giggling: 'Your grandfather always did say Luca had a way with women's clothing . . .'

As we approach the door, he looks up from his window dressing and offers us the first glimpse of his very untransvestite-like goatee. Mum gives him a 'coo-eee' wave and he responds with a nod of acknowledge-ment but his expression is unreadable. I had expected him to be in his late forties but unless it's true what they say about the youth-giving properties of olive oil, I'd be surprised if he's older than thirty-five. He's also atypically tall for the region – at least six foot – and dressed head to toe in black. I'm not sure if this is a fashion thing or a mourning thing or a convenient combination of the two but he looks stunning.

'Very Zorro,' Mum mutters as he unlocks the door.

'Signora Rees,' he says, addressing my mother. 'I am so very sorry for losing your father.'

She is momentarily thrown by his phrasing but gets it together to thank him and say: 'I know you must be feeling the loss also.'

'Ahhh,' he sighs as if in pain. 'This man, he give me chance when no one else would. He give me new life . . .'

I forget for a moment that this is real life and gawp as if I am watching someone share a heartfelt revelation on *Oprah* – you know when the camera zooms in and the whole screen is filled with their face? It's not the first time that I've felt a pang for a total stranger but this time there's something else, a kind of yearning . . . Could this possibly have something to do with the fact that Luca is utterly *beautiful?* His skin is sheeny sepia and he has the kind of eyes best appreciated by looking through a jeweller's loop – icy blue splintered with navy. When he returns my stare I feel both strangely alert and swimmy.

'You are Kim,' he says simply, a smile spreading across his face.

All I can manage is a mouthed hello and a shy handshake.

'Unfortunately she never got to meet my father, her grandfather,' my mother notes, steadying me with an arm around my waist.

'I think perhaps she carries something of him in her personality?' he suggests, still allowing me to marvel at his eyes.

I frown. What an odd thing to say – unless Vincenzo was a gormless mute. I haven't exhibited the merest hint of personality yet.

'Perhaps,' my mother concedes, tucking a stray curl behind my ear.

'And Gina, how is it for you to be back on Capri after so many years?'

'Wonderful. Sad. So many memories . . .' my mother sighs, lamenting: 'I wish we'd come years ago.'

116

'I wish that also,' Luca concurs, catching my eye.

I've got a horrible feeling that he shares my mother's instinctive need to mentally make over everyone she sees. He seems to be studying me far too intently. Perhaps he's never seen a man-made fibre up close before.

'The shop is just the same,' my mum smiles, brushing past the wooden display table in the middle of the room as she glides over to the gold velvet chaise.

'Vincenzo says style never go out of fashion,' Luca shrugs.

'Were you planning to make any changes?'

'Of course it is not solely my decision,' Luca defers.

'If it was?'

'Actually, no! I think if you want modern design you can go to Via Camerelle. But to me those stores are cold. Desiderio's has character. I believe in change only when it improve a situation.'

'I agree!' Mum cheers. 'Woodward's was always having re-fits just for the sake of it. You can be too sleek. I think it is important that the customer feels comfortable.'

'What do you think, Kim?' Luca turns to me.

I'm taken aback. It's been years since anyone asked my opinion.

'My daughter is not a big fan of fashion.' Mum attempts to let me off the hook.

'Please,' Luca urges me to speak. 'If this was your shop?'

'I'd maybe dim the lights a little,' I venture. 'But I like the smell of cedar.'

117

Luca smiles.

'It's very welcoming.'

'It is me!' Luca leans close so I can inhale.

'Oh!' I blush. 'Well, I guess you can stay!'

'Thank you,' he says with a little bow. 'Anything else?'

'No. You get new décor every time you get a delivery of clothes, don't you? It's like the leaves changing colour with the seasons – the tree they're attached to is supposed to stay the same.' Oop. May have gone a bit mad with my analogy, there.

Mum looks somewhat bemused. 'I've never thought of it like that before . . .'

'And Capri, what do you think of the island?' Luca asks, seemingly fascinated by my nonsense.

The telephone rings before I can attempt a poignant reply. I close my mouth and look down at the floor. Luca's feet are still facing mine. I look up and enquire, 'Aren't you going to . . .'

'Hmm?'

'The phone?' my mother reminds him.

'Oh! Excuse me, please,' he says stepping behind the counter.

'He's very handsome, isn't he?' my mum whispers to me as he confers in Italian on the phone. 'I bet he keeps all the women customers happy.'

I feel an unexpected jolt of jealousy. Of course every woman who enters the shop must feel as entranced as I do. It's his job to make them feel special. For a minute there I felt as if I was awakening to a beautiful new

118

morning; now I realize I'm just in a long queue to open the curtains.

'Bastardo!' he explodes, adding a string of unusual Italian curses.

My mother looks to me for a translation but I've never sworn in front of her and I'm not going to start now. He continues to rage down the phone. I find it surprisingly arousing even if he is arguing about ladieswear rather than world politics. I tell Mum the problem seems to be that the guy on the other end of the phone wants Luca to make a certain clothes order by 11a.m. which doesn't give him enough time to check out an alternative supplier or discover how much of a mark-up is being added. 'Basically he thinks this guy is ripping him off,' I conclude.

Luca replaces the receiver as if he's swatting a bug and then kicks over a tower of shoeboxes.

'Is there a problem?' asks my mother, mistress of understatement.

'Yes, my temper.' He slumps into a chair, seeming defeated.

Mum goes to console him but suddenly Luca's energy returns full-force and he starts ranting: 'I know he's giving me bad price. He sells to Allegra at the top of this street and I *know* they get better deal. And if they get better deal they will sell cheaper and claim my customers.'

I take a second to get up the nerve to say, 'Can't you just ask the other shop what they are paying?'

'This is business,' my mother tuts. 'They're not going to give away their secrets to the competition.'

'Not to Luca perhaps, but a customer could at least find out what they are charging,' I suggest.

Luca thinks for a moment. 'It would have to be a stranger, someone they don't know that I know. And I'm not even sure the stock will be there yet.'

'Kim could go and make enquiries,' my mother suggests excitedly. 'They don't know her and she's the right age group.'

He gives a 'yes, but . . .' grimace.

'What?' asks Mum.

'It's just . . .' he begins.

'Yes?' I encourage.

'Forgive me, Kim, but you don't look like the kind of woman who would be shopping for designer clothes.'

Ah. I can't argue with that.

'Unless . . .' begins my mother, eyeing the clothes rails.

'Oh no,' I retort. This is starting to smack of one of Mum's makeover conspiracies. I half expect Gianni to leap out from behind the till wielding his hairdressing scissors.

'We could . . .' says Luca, warming to the idea.

'No!' I stand firm.

'It would only be for half an hour,' wheedles Mum.

'I think she would look good in the Anna Molinari,' says Luca.

Bloody marvellous. It's been years since I've encountered a man this attractive in 3D and he turns out to be in league with my mother.

For a while they squabble over what I should wear – Mum, as ever, going for lurid colours and girlie-swirlie

120

patterns, Luca at least acknowledging that for someone 'so scared of looking like a woman' I should have something classic and understated.

'And plain,' I beg. 'I don't do beading or appliqué.'

'Neither do we,' Luca mutters, holding up a sleeveless linen shift.

'Can't.' I shake my head.

'Why not?'

'Dinner lady arms,' I reply.

My mother's head drops into her hands with shame.

'What is?' he frowns.

I wobble my upper-arm flesh. Always a turn-on.

'Ah!' he nods, moving on to a flimsy slip dress and cardi combo.

'No.'

'Why?'

'Knees,' I tell him.

'Knees?'

'Don't make me show you.'

'What about this?'

'Stomach.'

'This?'

'Bum.'

'Okay,' he says, holding up his hands. 'Let me think.'

He walks slowly around me. I have never felt more self-conscious.

'You have small waist.'

'Only in comparison to my hips.'

'Quiet please. You have good bones at the neck. Good cleavage . . .'

I flush with embarrassment. He doesn't miss much.

'We will go for tailored trouser suit, no shirt. Yes?'

I still can't get over the fact that he said 'Good cleavage'.

Mum nudges me.

'OK,' I say reluctantly.

'Please put this on,' he says, plucking an outfit from the rack.

'It's green.'

'No green. *Mint*,' he insists, adding, 'It will bring out the colour of your eyes.'

I hesitate.

'There is a fuschia pink one here,' says my mother, eagerly.

'Or lemon with orange lapels,' Luca taunts me.

'Mint it is,' I say, forcing a smile.

When I emerge from the changing room I find my mother gone.

'To the *pasticceria*,' Luca tells me. 'For cake.'

I raise an eyebrow. That's like me nipping out for a revitalizing shot of wheatgrass.

Now I am alone with Luca this ceases to feel like dolly dress-up. Instead I've entered some kind of fantasy where my fairy godmother turns out to be a hot Italian stud.

'How do you feel?'

Nervous, excited, tingling in places I'd forgotten existed.

'All right,' I fidget, 'but I'm not used to wearing anything so fitted.'

'Please stand straight,' he commands.

Gingerly I push back my shoulders and raise my head.

'Can you walk in high heels?' he says, noticing the trouser ankles slinking over my feet.

I give him a look.

'I didn't think so. No problem. I have sandals with thick sole. They will help. Now let go,' he says, prising my fingers away from the top of the jacket.

'It gapes,' I protest.

'Is sexy,' he says, stepping back to get an overview.

'Do you have a camisole or something?' I can't believe I've just said the word camisole out loud. Cleo would be choking with mirth.

'I could pin the jacket a little more closed if you like, and I have beautiful necklace that would cover most of this area,' he says, brushing my breastbone. I feel as if Tinkerbell fairydust has been sprinkled where his finger has traced my skin.

'OK?' he asks me. I look up at him stroking his goatee in contemplation and notice the contrast between the smooth brown leather of his hands and the light skin beneath his nails and wonder if he would take this much care *un*-dressing a woman. Or would he rip clothes from you as if they were held together with Velcro? Where *are* these thoughts coming from?

'Kim – shall I pin?'

'Oh! Yes! Go ahead . . .'

He takes a pin in one hand and reaches the other down the front of the jacket. I look up at the ceiling and try to control my breathing. Gradually my eyes

123

lower and take in the glossy tufts of his black hair, then the slant of his cheekbones and the ironed-straight-ness of his eyelashes.

'How long will you be staying in Capri?' he asks, hands still down my jacket.

'Um, about a week, I think,' I squeak. Offer to take me on a tour of the island, I wish inwardly.

'And you stay at the Luna?'

'Yes.'

'There!' he says, making sure the pin is hidden. 'Now the necklace.'

Luca fastens the clasp at the back of my neck and then carefully dabs the scattering of beads into place across my chest. His fingertips feel like the first soft splashes of rain on bare skin on a summer's day.

'Shoes!' he says, retrieving one of the boxes from the tumbled tower. 'Thirty-eight?'

I nod and he hands me a pair of wedge heels with silver criss-cross laces.

'Is it what you expected?'

'Well, I don't normally wear silv—'

'Capri. Is Capri what you expected?'

'Oh! I don't know . . . I guess it's better-looking than I thought it would be.'

'Better-looking?'

'Um, prettier, more picturesque,' I say, desperately trying to get my mind back on track. 'I've only really been to the Faraglioni restaurant and the Piazzetta so far.'

About that tour . . .

'It is a small island but it has many personalities,'

Luca observes. 'I'm sure you will discover them all. Now hair – I think is best we tie back, show your face.' I never wear my hair back but I'm way past resistance now. If he wanted to give me Beckham tramlines I'd let him.

Still facing me, he sweeps his strong hands into my hair. The last man who touched me was probably the postman as I took his pen to sign for a Freemans package so you can imagine the thrill. As he oh-so-gently smooths back the escaping curls I inadvertently let out a small moan of pleasure and have to quickly turn it into a cough.

'Are you okay?'

'Fine!' Nothing that a slug of limoncello wouldn't fix.

'Your hair has its own way,' he says, struggling to keep it pinned back.

'I know,' I sigh apologetically.

'No, is fantastic! Everyone who stay on Capri is so groomed, so smooth – they live so perfect.'

'You don't like perfect?' This bodes well.

'Perfect is good for models, for photographs, not for life.'

Maybe he doesn't have so much in common with my mother after all. 'Do you think you might be in the wrong job?' I ask him with a smile.

'I am not trying to make people look perfect,' he says defensively. 'Yes, I want my customers to look good and have confidence but I like to help them find something that feels effortless. I think you should forget about your clothes once you put them on.'

I relax my shoulders and tell my legs that they'll be back in their baggy cargo pants soon enough.

Luca brushes my cheek with his hand and sighs. 'You look lovely . . .'

I'm toying with the idea of accepting the compliment when he adds, 'You are ready to go under the covers?'

My eyes widen. 'Well, I . . .'

'I think he means undercover!' My mother rescues me as she returns with her bag of bogus goodies.

I turn to face her.

'Oh Kim – you look wonderful! It's so nice to see you in a colour, even if it is a pale one.'

I step in front of the mirror and gasp. I was sure I was going to look gargantuan but in fact I look like I left two stone in the changing room. I've got legs! I move my arm to check that it's really me. My reflection mirrors my movement.

'I look so grown-up,' I say, touching my new up-do.

'Sophisticated,' she corrects.

'Oh my God!' I laugh. 'I'm the daughter you always wanted and never had!'

'It's really wonderful,' Mum sighs, misty of eye.

'Take a good look,' I tell her. 'This won't be repeated in a while.'

'You don't like?' Luca looks crestfallen.

Actually I do, but I don't want Mum thinking this is for keeps.

'Handbag!' Mum blurts, grabbing a silver baguette from the display.

'Perfetto!' Luca approves her choice. 'Ready?'

'Sì, Agent Amorato!' I click my heels. 'Wish me luck.'

'Buona fortuna,' says Luca, kissing me on the cheek.

Turns out I could have worn high heels after all – I float all the way down the street.

It's only when I get to Allegra that the nerves bite. I'm never going to get away with this – my labels may be authentic but the person wearing them is a fake. They're bound to suss me in a second.

I go to turn back. No. I have to do this. I have to earn that kiss on the cheek.

I take a breath and push open the glass door, telling myself: I am rich, I am stylish, I know fashion. In order to avoid eye contact with the Sindy-sized girl behind the counter I pick up the first jacket on the rack and inadvertently balk at the price tag. Quickly trying to turn my raised eyebrows into a look of 'What an amazing bargain, I might get two!' I move on to an ivory silky number which slips off the hanger though I barely touch it. Bugger. Feeling rather hot I bend down to retrieve it from the floor and find myself staring at a pair of sheeny shins. 'Prego!' Counter girl bobs down on her kitten heels and smooths the top back on to the hanger with such reverence you'd think it was spun from Donatella's very locks. 'Grazie,' I say, unsure whether the shopping elite are chummy or dismissive to shopgirls.

'Are you looking for something in particular?' she enquires, standing protectively in front of her more delicate wares as if to say, Don't worry, Mummy's here. The nasty shopping lady can't hurt you now.

'Actually, I am – do you have the new Sarto range?'

'We just had a delivery today, it will be on display tomorrow,' she says, curtly.

'Oh, that will be too late,' I say, oozing dismay.

She gives me a pitying look and clicks back to the counter. I'm about to admit defeat when I hear myself venturing, 'Are you wearing Baby Doll by Yves St Laurent?'

She looks up, mildly intrigued. 'Yes, I am . . .'

'I love that fragrance,' I tell her. 'It's like glamorous candy – it suits you.'

'Grazie!' She can't hold back her smile.

'Oh well, thanks for your help,' I say, turning to leave.

She hesitates for a second, obviously trying to decide whether I'm worth the hassle, then hedges, 'What exactly are you looking for?'

I release my grip on the door handle. 'A dress,' I tell her.

'I'm not sure we have your size,' she says, eyeing my hips.

'I'm not just looking for myself,' I counter. 'I have a slim sister who also loves their stuff.'

She squints at me. Perhaps 'stuff' wasn't the most elegant choice of word.

'Let me see . . .' she says dipping out to the back of the shop. I take a breath and congratulate myself on getting this far. She returns with three plastic-covered dresses. 'Size 12 is the largest we have.'

'I knew I should have had that liposuction!' I half-joke. 'Um, I'll try the white one anyway.'

Reluctantly she hands me the dress, saying a silent prayer for the seams.

The changing room is tiny. A size 8, I'd say. Several dislocated limbs and unladylike groans later the dress is on.

'How does it look?' asks Baby Doll. Or Bambino Bambola as I like to call her.

Well, if you had a mirror in here I might be able to tell, I feel like saying. Instead I say, 'Ummm . . .'

'The mirror is out here.'

Of course it is. Out where you can fuss and fluff and tell me it's supposed to strain across the stomach and slip off my shoulder and convince me I look like a million dollars just before I part with a million lire. Well, this is payback time, I decide. Just try and tell me I look good in this!

I unclick the door and shuffle out into the shop.

Bambino Bambola swallows hard. 'The colour is good on you . . .'

I smile to myself. This is the first time I've been grateful for cellulite. It's worth having it just to see the look of revulsion on her face as she contemplates the way the clingy fabric highlights every ripple.

'How much is it?' I ask.

'900,000 lire,' she replies, still clearly stunned by my audacious display of feminine imperfection.

'And what else do you have in the range?'

She scrabbles for the jacket, hoping in vain that she can get me covered up before another customer enters the shop. '660,000 lire,' she says with an apologetic glance at the bony, bronzed signorina who has just come in.

'And the trousers?'

'They're a 10!' she practically squeaks, as if to say, Have mercy!

'For my sister,' I tell her.

'480,000 lire.'

Mission accomplished.

I change back into my original outfit and tell her I need to call my sister to check she hasn't already bought the trousers.

I'm out of the shop and halfway down the street when BB comes tottering after me yelping, 'Scusi!' My first thought is to bolt, but then I see she's holding up my handbag.

'Ahhhh, grazie!' I say, inadvertently undoing the clasp as I take it from her. The bag falls open to reveal nothing but scrunched tissue paper.

She looks at me.

I look at her.

'I forgot to check,' I smile brazenly. 'Do you take tissue paper?'

12

Back at the boutique, Luca removes the pin holding the jacket together as if he's performing surgery. Then slowly, seductively he undoes the buttons. As he slides the silky lining back off my shoulders he leans forward and hungrily kisses my neck. At least that's what I pretend happens as I change back to my everyday attire. In reality he's bellowing down the phone at the supplier man, challenging him on the prices and negotiating a new deal. Ah well, glad to be of service.

Mum, meanwhile, is assessing the book-keeping for the shop. Despite her minimal knowledge of Italian she seems to be finding her way around the figures. I sit next to her and translate the corresponding words, eyes flitting between the pages and Luca. He comes off the phone triumphant and says he would like to take us to lunch to celebrate.

'Wonderful!' says Mum, heaving another accounts book on to her lap.

'Everything is okay?' he asks, looking down at her notes.

'Yes, fine. But I can't find the books for this year.'

'Ahh, yes. I have them at home.'

'Do you live far from here?'

'You want I get them? No problem. Just twenty minutes, near Arco Naturale.'

'Oh, that was one of my favourite places as a child – those steps leading you down to another world.'

'You would like to come with me?'

'And leave Kim in charge of the shop?'

'Hey, after this morning's master class I could give Alberta Ferretti tips,' I boast.

'See?' he laughs. 'She knows her designers!'

'Why don't you two go? I'd love Kim to see the Arch and I could get more of a feel for the shop if I was here by myself.'

'But I wouldn't be here to translate for you,' I protest, mildly. (For once I'm not complaining about my mother's matchmaking.)

'Oh I doubt it will be too busy at his time of day. I'll get by,' she insists.

Luca seems happy to trust her and, after a quick lesson on the till says we'll be back in an hour.

'No hurry!' trills Mum.

The path Luca and I take is so tendon-twangingly steep I have to keep feigning amazement at the view just so I can stop and catch my breath. Fortunately the view actually is stunning beyond belief so I reckon I'm getting away with it.

'This is curious place,' says Luca, instigating our pit-stop for the first time to point out a walled garden littered with knitted dolls and weatherbeaten teddy

132

bears, sagging despite their bamboo stick back-straighteners. I get the impression that the owner just cracked one day, screaming: 'If I see one more picturesque olive grove, I'm going to kill myself!'

We continue on. Grumpy old ladies pass us carrying plastic bags of shopping, cursing the meandering tourists under their breath. Away from the town centre it does feel as though we are trespassing on their private lanes and I'm relieved to be legit-by-association, walking with a local.

As the gradient increases yet again I berate myself for not packing mountaineering equipment and breathing apparatus. This is hardcore. I pause and look upward – is that a supermarket at the top of the hill or a mirage?

'You like some water?' Luca asks.

'Yes,' I croak. I can actually feel trickles of sweat running down the back of my legs. Very weird sensation.

Luca jogs up to the *supermercato* and returns with a giant bottle of San Benedetto.

'You prefer *frizzante*, yes? Sparkling?'

I nod.

'Also your grandfather,' he notes.

'It sounds a stupid question,' I say, in between gulps of lukewarm fizz, 'but what was he like?'

'I carry for you,' says Luca, taking the bottle and motioning for me to walk on. 'Your grandfather was first of all a quiet man. But he sees everything. He feels everything.'

'How do you mean?' I ask, intrigued.

133

'By watching people, he understand them. He knows how they feel in their heart. He looked at me and he could see I was not bad inside.'

'Were you bad on the outside?'

Luca gives me a wry smile. 'Little bit,' he says, lifting up his shirt sleeve to reveal a tattoo of a panther slinking around his upper arm.

'Lots of people have tattoos,' I shrug. 'It's just fashion half the time.'

He stops for a minute, considering me, then turns and pulls off his shirt, revealing a torso writhing with images – daggers and unicorns and hearts intertwined with dancing flames and the swirling serifs of ocean waves. It's like a fantasy of adventures mapped out on his skin.

I motion for Luca to turn around and find myself immediately drawn to the beautiful dragon resting between his shoulder blades. I've always loved the idea of dragons – maybe it's a Welsh thing! I used to doodle them on everything and, up until a couple of years ago, I still lived in the dragon T-shirt my mum's only nice husband gave me when I was fourteen. I would have worn it until its last faded thread had unravelled if our neighbour's kid hadn't taken to playing Sisqo's *Unleash the Dragon* every time I nipped out to the newsagent.

I reach out and follow the mythical beast's tail into the dent that runs the length of Luca's silky brown back. Trying to stop my finger sliding down to the base of his spine is like trying to halt a toboggan that's pelting down an ice shute.

'Your grandfather watch me come out of the water

134

one day at Marina Piccola and he say, "I see you like to decorate your body." I tell him they are all my own designs and he says he has a job for me!'

'Did you know him before then?'

'Of course. Everyone knows Vincenzo Desiderio!'

'Because of what happened with my grandmother? Because he broke her heart and she left the island, taking his only daughter?' Woah! Where did that come from?

Luca is unfazed. 'This is small island. Everyone knows everything,' he says, replacing his shirt. 'Of course, some people judge him but he never judge anyone.'

'Not even himself?'

'You think he should?'

'Now you're going to tell me that in Italy it is acceptable for husbands to have affairs!' I roll my eyes, getting unnecessarily testy.

'No,' he says gravely. 'I am not. He cry his whole life to lose his daughter. And never to meet you.'

'His choice,' I say, refusing to feel any sympathy for him.

'He didn't know it would end like that. I make no excuse for him but also I don't accuse him.' Luca pauses and looks at me. 'You, you seem very angry . . .'

'I am angry!' I flush. 'I am angry that my mother inherited his wandering eye and that she was unfaithful to my father and because of that he left when I was nine and I never saw him again!'

Luca lets me simmer for a second. Wise man.

'And for this you blame your grandfather?'

135

'Not just him. I blame my mother too.'

'Oh.'

'Oh!' I mimic.

Luca smiles. 'You have always loved the right person?'

I'm not quite sure how to answer that so I say nothing.

'If you have then you are lucky,' Luca concludes.

'Love isn't really a major part of my life,' I blurt out.

Luca looks incredulous. 'To love is everything! It is breathing . . .'

'Not to me.'

'Why not?'

'It's just . . .' I scrabble for an explanation. 'Not everyone in Britain gets love.'

Luca starts to reply but a faint fluttering-buzzing sound we heard a few minutes earlier grows to a deafening, juddering roar. We look up and see a helicopter levitating above us.

'What's it carrying?' I ask, trying to identify the big rope-bound cube swinging beneath it.

'Washing machine,' says Luca matter-of-factly.

'What?' I hoot.

'It is best way to deliver something from the mainland to these high-up villas.'

'Luca!' a voice calls from down a side lane.

'Ciao Ricardo!' Luca shouts above the whirring blades.

'Ci potrebbe aiutare, per favore!' Ricardo beckons him.

Luca turns to me.

136

'I know, he needs your help,' I smile.

'It will just take twenty minutes.'

'That's fine, I'll go on ahead,' I say, pointing at the sign for the Arco Naturale. 'In fact, I've got a phone call to make.'

If I don't get the words 'Luca is a Love God!' out of my system soon I'm going to end up blurting it to his face.

'Okay, grazie, I catch you up. There is a green bench that looks at the Arco . . .'

'Green bench – I'll be there,' I tell him.

'Kim!' he calls me back.

'Yes?'

'You are alive. You deserve love.'

My heart dips as I watch him run down the lane. I take a deep breath and expel a tremulous lungful of air. What must it be like to be brought up in a culture where passion is expected, accepted, celebrated? Where you give free rein to your feelings rather than try and harness them. Maybe Italians see heartache as a part of life rather than something to be avoided at all costs. I've been here less than 24 hours and I feel my heart is daring me to take a risk. I'm not even sure I have a choice about whether to accept the dare any more. I think I said yes to it the second I laid eyes on Luca.

13

'Hello, PhotoFinish – say cheese!'

'Luca is a Love God!' I whoop.

'Sorry?'

'Oh Cleo! It's just so beautiful here!' I rave, extending the silver phone cord so I can take in the panorama.

'Who is this?'

'It's me, you fool!' How can she not recognize her own flatmate?

'*Kim!* What's going on?'

'I just had to ring and tell you – *You are not women, you are paradise!*' I mutter in a deep Italian accent.

'Have you been drinking?'

'Not since last night . . .'

I swiftly bring Cleo up to speed on the dinner at the Faraglioni restaurant with the never-ending dessert trolley and absurdly attentive waiters.

'*You are not women, you are paradise!*' Cleo repeats, delighted yet incredulous. 'That's the most outrageous line I've ever heard!'

'Brilliant, isn't it!' I giggle.

'I'd pass it on to my brother but I don't think you could get away with it in Sheffield.'

'Probably not,' I concede.

'They're in a different league, these Italian men,' Cleo sighs. 'They really do appreciate their women.'

I'm just thinking that the feeling is mutual when it slips out again – 'Luca is a Love God!'

'Who *is* this Luca?' Cleo sounds baffled.

'The boutique manager – Luca Amorato . . .' I sigh.

'You sound strange . . . *happy* . . .'

'Is that really so rare?'

'Well, yeah when there's a man involved!' Cleo decides. 'I thought he was supposed to be some slicked-back smoothie?'

'No!' I rally. 'He's all lean and tousled and *real*!'

'Real?'

'He's got this tiny scar on his top lip,' I moon. 'And the bluest eyes . . .'

'And you've known him . . .'

'. . . bout an hour and a half.'

I join Cleo's chuckles. 'I know! But he's just so gorgeous!'

'It must be the Italian accent – kind of like your homeland calling,' Cleo suggests.

If that were the case then Mario would have had me at Ciao! How do I convince her that Luca is the chosen one?

'He's like tiramisu personified,' I tell her.

'Ooooh, yum!' she enthuses, finally seduced.

'When he put his hands down my top . . .' I reminisce.

139

'*What?*'

'He was dressing me,' I hurriedly explain.

'Wait! Rewind! When did he *undress* you?'

I laugh. 'He didn't. I did.'

'You volunteered to take your clothes off in front of a man? *Never!*'

I take a moment to set the record straight.

'And now you're going to this beauty spot arch-thing to wait for him?'

'Yes,' I sigh. 'It feels like our first date or something.'

Silence.

'Cleo? Are you there?' I peer at the display on the telephone to check I'm still connected.

'Yes, yes. It's just . . .'

'Am I being ridiculous? I am, aren't I?'

'Oh God!'

'What?'

'It's that barking woman who always comes in wanting people erased from her photos,' Cleo hisses.

'Okay, I'll let you go. Good luck!'

I put down the phone feeling a bit guilty. I'm getting all the treats at the moment. Lucky that Cleo's one of those rare people who's genuinely happy for you if something good happens. Not that I've troubled her with too many joyous outbursts in the last two years. But who knows what I might have to tell her by the end of today . . .

The high-walled residential roads open out into dusty lemon groves and then, rounding a corner, I find myself confronted with what looks like a huge chunk of

Amazon rainforest transplanted on to a plunging valley. I peer into the intense, dense green. According to the sign, the steps to my right weave down to sea level and the Grotto of Matermania. A group of American tourists look daunted by the drop as they watch a panting conga line of red pulsing faces haul themselves up the last few steps. 'Is it worth it?' one lady asks. But no one has the breath to reply. The Italian guide tries to spur on his group by revealing that the grotto used to be *the* venue for ancient orgies.

'So maybe these people are not just exhausted from the walk!' he jokes.

One cheery Texan fellow tells him, 'You know, of all the guides we've had, you have the best English.'

'Yours is good too,' replies the guide, without missing a beat.

I leave them to it, passing through an open-air restaurant with the unappetizing name of La Grottelle to rejoin the path to the Arco Naturale. Each of the stone steps spattered with mustard-coloured lichen leads me closer to the green bench. I feel a thrill of anticipation and inhale: the air smells of sun-baked pine needles and musty dirt mingled with the bubble-gum and deodorant of passing tourists, their effusive shouting rivalled only by the squeaky-toy cheeping of the birds as they bounce from branch to branch. By my feet a tiny lizard starts-stops-darts across the hot cement paving like Morse code in motion. I follow him to a lookout ledge and am overwhelmed by the beauty that greets me: the stoically rugged A-shaped arch

141

stands proud against an infinity of aquamarine. I remove my sunglasses so I can be sure I am really here.

'Would you mind . . .?' A group of girls ask me to take a picture of them. They are English, three sisters, all giddy from the romance of the view.

'I have to bring James here,' announces Sister One. 'And if I can't get him here I'm going to marry him by proxy. This is the place!'

She's right. It is.

'I need *Him* to be here with me,' insists Sister Two.

'Him who?' says a perplexed Sister Three.

'The Him of my dreams!' sighs Sister Two.

I smile to myself. I know what she means. And better than that, mine's on his way. Oh God! Get a *grip*! I thought I'd stopped having dreams with a Him in them.

Crossing over to the other vantage point, I approach the green bench with reverence, slightly peeved to discover three camera-laden tourists sunning themselves there, eyes closed, leaving no room for me. Instead I lean on the railings, looking down to where the rock plunges into the sea, and watch an empty white rowing boat nodding in a pool of turquoise translucence. I tilt my watch away from the glare of the sun. Any minute now . . .

Turning towards the steps I try and spot a giveaway glimpse of Luca's clothing amid the foliage. The Californian surfer sandals teamed (unfathomably) with navy socks are swiftly dismissed, along with a pair of bronze ballet pumps, a straw bag that creaks and some top-of-the-range varicose veins. Leaning further back I see jumpers tied around waists, backpacks, baseball hats, a scrumple of maps. Further back still and I'm gazing up at wisps of white airbrushed across the truest bluest sky. Further back and . . .

'You fall in love?' Luca's upside-down face asks me.

I release my grasp on the railings and thud into his chest. For a second there I couldn't tell which way was up.

'I think everyone must fall in love with this special place,' he says softly.

'Mmmm,' I agree, wondering if he too can hear my heart thumping. 'I could stay here for ever.'

'You would like to live in Italia?' he smiles happily.

'I just want to live!' I find myself saying. What *is* going on? It's as though Luca emits a truth vapour instead of regular pheromones, and a part of me that has been gagged for years is finally getting the chance to speak.

'You don't live now?'

'I've wasted a lot of time,' I acknowledge sadly.

'Maybe you just conserve energy until now,' he says, optimistically. 'Maybe your new life begins today?'

What if he's right? I don't know what I did to deserve this second chance but I'm getting tingles. 'I just felt tired for so long,' I explain.

'Feeling tired is tiring,' he nods. 'And sometimes you can sleep for twelve hours and still not feel, you know, *perky*.'

I laugh at his choice of word. 'Yeah, what's that all about?'

143

'I think you have to have something you want to wake up for.'

'Have you got that?' I ask.

'Yes. I have two things. One of them is shop . . .'

Which my mother is trying to take away from you, I think, guiltily noticing the accounts book he's now carrying. 'And the other . . .'

'The other you will see at lunchtime,' he grins.

I study him for a second. 'It's ravioli, isn't it?' I tease. 'I've heard Caprese ravioli is the best.'

'It *is* the best,' he confirms. 'And where we are going is the best of the best!'

We amble back to the shop to pick up my mother (every silver lining has a cloud), and then head straight out to the restaurant.

The lanes burrowing off the Via Lo Palazzo may be grey and nondescript but at least they're downhill. We've shaken the tourists, bar a few frowning at the ceramic-tiled street name wondering how they got there and how they are going to get back to the shops selling unusually shaped limoncello gift bottles.

'We are here!' Luca halts at a wrought iron gate bearing the name La Pergola and waves my mother and me through to a secret garden with a stunning sunny vine-entwined terrace – trip up and you'd tumble all the way down to Marina Grande, splash out to sea and emerge from the water in Naples.

The potted geraniums lining the balcony are that creamy crimson-orange found on the Max Factored lips of little old ladies. My mother is currently wearing the 21st century gloss version. I always think it takes a certain amount of aplomb to carry off a bright lipstick. I've never felt sufficiently in touch with my inner diva to carry it off. I prefer a neutral pinky sheen, it always seem to taste better too. It's hard to believe that I was ever a fan of the trend for dead, flat browns and beiges. My mum was horrified and complained, 'What man would want to kiss lips that look caked in mud?' My particular favourite went on like smudged Caramac bar. It was so drying that sometimes flakes of skin would fall away from my mouth as I was speaking. No Parmesan for me, thanks.

Before we are seated Luca is beckoned over to the bar by a man with a bushy moustache. 'Excuse me, please!' he says, trading places with a waitress who sets down a basket of porous white bread and a bottle of gloopy green oil.

'Acqua minerale?' she asks.

'Sì,' I reply adding, 'naturale,' knowing how my mum feels about non-champagne bubbles.

I'm halfway through translating the appetizers when I hear a voice exclaim, 'Signorina Kim!'

Beside me is the manchild from the ice-cream parlour. 'Nino!' I laugh. 'We have to stop meeting like this – people will talk!'

He takes my hand and kisses it as though he's been taking lessons from Leslie 'Hellooooo' Phillips.

'Nino, I'd like you to meet my mother.'

'Hello young man,' she says, slightly taken aback.

'Hello old woman,' he replies with a courteous bow. Then, turning to me, 'You want for me to help with the menu?'

I grin. 'I think I'll be okay today. I'm told the ravioli is very good here.'

'Sì, the best,' says the miniature connoisseur.

'Are you dining alone?' I ask, picturing him in a cravat and smoking jacket, sending back the wine because it's corked.

'No, my uncle he owns this place. Also . . .' he says looking around the restaurant, 'I wait for my father.'

'The double espresso drinker?'

'*Ah!* He is here!'

I look up and see Nino collide in an affectionate embrace with Luca.

14

I feel like I'm doing arithmetic while holding my breath underwater. Luca plus Nino equals father and son. But who did Luca multiply with to create Nino? Fortunately my mum is here to cover my shock and say all the things I can't bring myself to. Like, 'I didn't realize you were married!' and 'Where's your wife?' For a moment I cling on to the hope that he might be a single dad but, no, there is a Mrs Amorato. She's currently away helping out with some sort of family crisis.

Even though I'm sitting down I experience a sensation of falling, followed by temporary weightlessness. The pain from every disappointment I've ever felt seems to be culminating here and now. Luca explains that she's been gone five weeks. He's not sure when she's coming back. I can't help thinking, What if she didn't? And that's not the kind of thought I'm used to entertaining.

To me marriage has always been sacrosanct – no trespassing. A big red STOP light, whereas some people merely see it as amber. They pause, 'Oh, married.

147

Darn. In that case I'll . . .' Not for me. Even if a guy has a girlfriend he is emphatically out of bounds. Which does rule out way too many men, I have to admit. Even my most honourable male friend (a therapist by trade) turned to me a few months back and said, 'It may have got to the point where you're going to have to steal a man from another woman.'

I must have looked utterly mortified because he retorted, 'I'm not suggesting you bump her off, for God's sake.'

But he might as well have been.

Nino is so demanding of my attention that I am able to avoid all eye contact with Luca without looking too obvious, I hope. On the outside I'm pretending I can't tell the difference between fusilli and radiatore pasta just to wind up Nino but on the inside I feel so flat and dejected I have to jab myself with an imaginary cattle-prod just to stay involved in the conversation. I didn't know I had it in me to be such a *girl*. Surely a man wouldn't have let his mind race so far ahead? It's not as if Luca even gave any indication that he liked me – I invented a whole scenario without even checking his availability. Why did I do it to myself?

I try and rationalize but realize my reaction to him was purely instinctive. I just got carried away with the giddy ecstasy of actually fancying someone again. The only really surprising thing is the magnitude of the sense of loss I feel, especially considering the whole thing has turned around in under four hours. But that should mean I'll get over it quickly, right? Don't people say it takes you half the time you were involved with someone to get over them? With any luck the sting will be gone by dessert.

Okay. It was unrealistic to expect to get over someone while you're sitting opposite them. I'll be fine once I've had a few hours alone.

'Will you come back to the shop now?' asks Luca, having settled the bill.

'Maybe later. I think I'll visit the grave this afternoon,' says Mum.

'Kim?'

'I'm going with her,' I reply, latching on to her excuse.

'Are you sure?' asks Mum.

'Of course – if you want me there.' I wouldn't normally be the obvious choice for a graveyard companion but perhaps today I'm suitably on the verge of weeping and pummelling the earth with my fists.

'I'd love you to come with me,' she says, squeezing my hand.

We're about to leave when the man with the bushy moustache – who turns out to be Luca's brother, Nino's uncle – comes over with a little plate bearing four foil-covered chocolates.

'Baci! Kim's favourite!' Mum whoops. 'Even I know *baci* means kisses. That's not a word you forget!'

Nino hands me his assigned chocolate. 'For you!' he says, as if presenting me with a diamond. I pop it in my mouth then lean my pale bulging cheek against his brown one and give him a tiny kiss. 'Thank you, Ringo!'

He gurgles delightedly at his new nickname then chases his uncle back to the kitchens.

'You can have mine, too,' says Luca, pushing his chocolate across the table to me. I murmur 'thank you' but don't pick it up.

Finishing his espresso, Luca reminds Mum of the best route to the graveyard and then we all push back our chairs. I'm first to the gate.

'You forgot your Baci,' says Luca holding out the silver and blue nugget to me. Now I know how Adam felt when Eve offered him a bite of apple. 'Don't you want it?' he looks searchingly at me.

I remember a sticker I once saw: I can resist everything, except temptation. I take a deep breath and smile: 'No, thanks!'

On the way to the cemetery my mother says she wants to stop off at the church where she used to pray with Vincenzo and light a candle for him. The romantic symbolism is somewhat diminished by the fact that the wax candles and long matches have been replaced by yellowing plastic sticks with flame-shaped lightbulbs at the top. You just put your money in the metal box and flick a switch. It's all so kitsch I can't resist having a go myself. I pop a coin in the slot and flick the switch but end up turning off someone else's candle by mistake and panic that I've negated their prayer. I put in another coin and try again. Now I feel like I'm playing a Vegas slot machine, only if you win this jackpot you get a miracle.

My prayer is that Granny Carmela's heart has healed in heaven. She died without ever getting over Vincenzo's infidelity. I still hurt thinking of Tomas and I only knew him for a couple of months. She was with Vincenzo for twelve years lavishing him with love, bringing up their child. Over and over again she'd describe their perfect love and then relive the agony of discovering that he had another woman. I remember sitting holding her softly wrinkled hand thinking, This is what men can do to you. And yet I still craved what she had before Rosa ruined everything. It was only when Carmela died that I decided to go after it. And look where that got me. Sometimes I think she sent Tomas to me as a warning.

I take a seat and look around me. The church is full of strange details – waxwork saints draped in purple and gold robes lending a Madame Tussaud's vibe, intricate gold carvings last seen in a Bangkok temple and paintings of religious figures with fairy-light halos like something from a Piers et Gilles picture. Leaning forward I notice a pretty stencilled pattern on the stone-slabbed floor and realize it is the light shining through the perforations of the confession box. I wonder if my mother ever ventured in there as a child. If she wanted to see a priest these days she'd have to tell him in advance so he could bring a packed lunch and a flask.

'AAAAA-AAAAA-OOOOO-AAAHHHHHH!' Unknown to us a twenty-strong choir has assembled for

151

an afternoon practice. As their voices soar up to the rafters, taking us on a brief flight, I see my mother tip her head back and blink. I've never seen her cry and it's not going to happen now because she's bustling me towards the door saying we should get to the cemetery 'Before . . . before . . .'

I open my mouth to try and help her out but I can't help thinking, Before what? He's not going anywhere.

'Oh look! There's a florist. Shall we buy something to put on his grave?' I pipe as we trip down the steps.

'Magnolia,' my mum whispers. 'He always loved magnolias.'

Watching my mother kneel beside the grave arranging the flowers I realize how little I know about her relationship with her father. Whenever Granny Carmela was badmouthing Vincenzo, Mum never defended him yet here she is looking lovingly at his headstone.

'Have you forgiven him?' I ask, knowing I haven't.

'Forgiven him for what?' she says, absently.

'His philanderings,' I say, realizing that I am indirectly attacking her for her own.

She looks up at me. 'He wasn't a runaround, Kim. There was just this one other woman – Rosa – his whole life.'

'How come he never married her then?'

'My mother wouldn't give him a divorce,' she sighs. 'It was her way of punishing him.'

I didn't know that. 'What if *she'd* met someone else?'

'She had no intention of letting that happen.'

'Because she was so broken-hearted, that's sad,' I muse.

'Because she was so bitter,' Mum counters. 'Which is sadder still.'

Lately it seems that all the onus is on the sinned-against person to set off on some voyage of self-discovery and get a new life the second they've been dumped, whereas very little is expected of the sinner – they just go on their merry way with the person they've been lining up for the last few months (or years). Yeah, yeah these adulterers are supposedly 'racked with guilt' at what they have done but the thrill of the new love has to exceed the queasy 'Am I wrong?' feeling or they wouldn't have done the deed in the first place. And really, just how much sympathy can you have for someone getting that much sex?

The person left behind, however, has a legacy of pain, rejection, anger, self-doubt, humiliation, mistrust, betrayal, etc. with no compensatory up-side, just an uphill battle to 'get over it'.

It seems strange that we are encouraged to admit that we all seek love and support the belief that love is the greatest thing/makes the world go round and so on then when it is snatched away from you you're supposed to accept the loss gracefully and move on. The whole system is messed up. If you want to shag someone else, at least have the decency to let your partner do the same.

I look at my mother. Her initial composure has crumpled with emotion, she actually looks in pain. At Granny Carmela's funeral she just looked relieved.

Maybe she feels she had more in common with Vincenzo than with her hyper-moral mother. Over and again she's had affairs. What is she looking for? What is missing in her that she thinks she's going to find in some man?

She never moaned about the husband she was married to at the time. Only afterwards would she say, 'Oh, well he made me feel so caged!' or, 'He had such a temper!' Well, if that were true then why didn't she dump him years ago? Because she would have been alone, that's why. Heaven forbid. So she waited, supposedly unhappily, until she could use the strength of an outside source. Interesting how it also gave the husband she was leaving someone else to blame. Instead of hating *her* he hates the man she left him for. And when the recriminations begin she has an ally to hide behind.

Cleo's parents are still married after thirty-eight years. They'd be marvellous role models if they didn't hate each other so much.

I sigh – where did all the true romantics go? Looking around me I take a moment to read the inscriptions on the gravestones and think: Here they are! Loving wives who gave their husbands sixty years of comfort and joy. Husbands who followed them to their final resting place just a matter of months or even weeks later, unable to live without them. Isn't that how it's supposed to be?

'Come on,' says my mother getting to her feet. 'I think we need one of Mario's killer cocktails.'

Back at the hotel, I'm in the bar and hoiked up on to the stool before I even notice my mother is no longer by my side. Bobbing back to the lobby I see her picking up a message from the reception clerk. I know before she speaks that it's from Platinum Man and that I'll be dining alone tonight.

'Are you going to have a cocktail before you go?' I ask.

'Yes but I think I'll get changed first. You go ahead.'

Mario pops his head around the door frame. 'Did I just lose my favourite customers?' he asks.

'No,' my mum laughs. 'Kim is coming in now and I'll have a quick one before I leave. You'll look after her tonight when I'm gone, won't you, Mario?'

'You are going out all night?' he says hopefully.

'No, I should be back before midnight!' she warns as she heads for the lift.

Mario offers me his crooked arm and escorts me back into the bar. 'You look a little sad tonight, I think we prepare a happy drink for you.'

I watch him tinkering around like a pharmacist trying to come up with a magic formula, all chinking bottles and spurting pipettes. Disappointingly there are no misty vapours swirling from the glass he sets before me.

'What's in it?' I sniff cautiously, wondering if the corner of my serviette could double up as a bit of litmus paper.

'Secret prescription. Drink,' he encourages.

I take a sip. '*Jesus*, Mario!' I splutter.

'I think perhaps a man upset you today, yes?'

'Maybe,' I concede hoarsely, adjusting to the blow-torch-blasting my throat has just received.

'Well, then you need something strong. Love is worst kind of pain!' He turns and replaces the various bottles of hardcore liquor on the shelves behind him. 'You want to hear my favourite song about love?' he asks me.

'Go ahead,' I encourage, knowing it's going to be some nonsense akin to moons hitting your eye like a pizza pie.

I'm not wrong.

'*The only fruit of love is the banana, the banana,*' Mario sings with a leery lilt. It would seem those are the only lyrics, you just chant them over and over. Sophisticated guy.

'*The banana . . .*' he taunts.

I roll my eyes and tell him I am going to watch the sunset from the terrace. 'And don't go singing that song in front of my mother, *please,*' I beg.

It's still hot outside so I find a shady spot and settle into one of the wicker chairs, dipping my tongue in the Happy Drink every minute or so. I'd say it was doing the trick – I feel hazy rather than melancholy – that is until a honeymoon couple stroll out on to the balcony all entwined limbs and intimate gazes. If Cleo was here we'd be making gagging noises and ridiculing them (God, I miss her!) but instead I feel as though it's another cruel display, like the red roses, showing me what I haven't got. I try not to look but I can't take my eyes off them. And I can't help imagining what it would be like to share such tender intensity with Luca.

I take a big gulp of Happy Drink but it just makes my eyes prickle with tears and I feel my heart pressing against my ribcage, straining to get closer, desperate to rub up against their love.

I look out to sea and take a deep breath – this sudden surge of loneliness is making me nauseous. Cleo's done a marvellous job of keeping it at bay for the past two years but out of the blue Luca appears and reminds me of what I'm missing. Just thinking of him makes my insides churn, as though a forgotten longing is returning.

'How do I look?' says Mum, twirling in her crinkly gold skirt and repositioning her embroidered shawl to expose her shoulder.

I tell her she looks beautiful. As ever.

'Not too much perfume?' she says leaning over me and wafting her hand around her neck.

'It's fine. Provided you're not sitting in the same restaurant as him!'

Mum goes to react and then smiles. 'You'll be all right, won't you?'

I hope so, I think to myself, knowing how weepy I can get when left on my own after a few bevvies.

'Your Bellini, signora,' says Mario, presenting my mother with her cocktail and taunting me by humming the instrumental version of the 'Banana' song in an insidious fashion.

'You would also like one, Kim?'

'Oooh yes, you have to try it – it's all peachy and delicious!' raves my mum.

157

Perhaps if I drink enough I'll bypass the teary stage and hit oblivion. 'I'd love one,' I tell him.

Mario returns minutes later with my drink and continues to hum as he clears the honeymooners' table of their drained glasses.

Finally, inevitably, he cracks. '*The only fruit of love is the banana!*' he sings, relishing the innuendo.

For a second I think we've got away with it as I watch my mum humming innocently along. Then Mario stops mid-ashtray-swap and turns to my mother, 'Your daughter – she did not want me to sing those words to you . . .' Pausing for effect he adds a plaintive, '*Why?*'

I'm trying to decide whether I can cause Mario greater pain with a cocktail stick or a pronged swizzle stick when my mother looks at her watch and says, 'Oh, I best be off. Don't want him to think that I've stood him up.'

I snort and mutter in Italian to Mario, 'Since when did a sure thing stand anyone up?'

'Your mother is easy?' Mario replies, also in Italian. 'You think she would sleep with me?'

'You're male, aren't you?' I laugh.

Suddenly my mother's drink goes everywhere. 'Oooh! Look at me! Nervous before my big date. Gotta run!'

And off she shimmies. Mario watches as her skirt flutters up to reveal a shapely calf.

'Forget it,' I tell him. 'It's too late to switch your attentions now.'

'You are jealous!' he says, delightedly. 'You want me for yourself.'

'I do want you,' I tell him, definitely tipsy now.

'You do?'

'Yes – I want you . . . to get me another drink.'

'Bellini?' he sighs.

'No, Secret Prescription,' I tell him.

His face brightens. Apparently all is not lost . . .

15

I open my eyes. Same view as when they were closed – darkness. I listen for breathing. Nothing. Slowly I move my left arm across the surface of the bedspread. (Or what the Italians call a bedspread. To me it is a tablecloth. They don't seem to go much for snuggly duvets over here.) My hand crosses over on to my mum's bed. I extend further – will the cool flatness continue or will I reach a warm mound? The bed is empty. I feel my way along the headboard and flick the bedside light switch. Empty and unslept in. I squint at my watch: 9a.m. Why do I feel so rough? I remember last night and fall back into the pillow with a thud. After my mum left I didn't eat dinner at all – just finished off Mario's pesto bis-kwits. And most of his alcohol.

In between serving other punters and dealing with waiter requests from the dining room he kept me company and wooed me with bar snacks. With the dish of assorted nuts he told me about the first time he went to pick a girl up from her parents' house: The father greeted him and offered him a drink. He accepted. On the table before him was a small bowl of pistachio nuts. He was so nervous he popped a handful into his mouth without removing the shells. The father watched Mario wincing with pain as the brittle casings clawed their way down his throat, and quickly handed him his drink. 'You know, in this house we eat them *without* the shells,' the concerned father told him, trying to make out that it was his quirky custom rather than Mario's *faux pas*. 'Oh I prefer them with the shells on,' Mario breezed, refusing to admit his mistake and throwing back another handful to prove the point. I laughed and told him it could have been worse – they could have been walnuts.

And then I had another drink. And another. Mario told me he would be shutting the bar at midnight and I must join him for a drink and then perhaps a walk. I told him I needed an early night. He told me I didn't. I liked his insistence.

'Now Kim,' he said, after appeasing a large group of Americans who were in Capri for a wedding, 'you know language. Please tell me a different word the British have for "sex", one that is not so rude as—'

'Shag!' I had interrupted him before he used this as an excuse to make me blush with a string of wham-bam-grazie-mam euphemisms.

'Shag?' he repeated uncertainly.

'Yes. It's more of a fun word,' I tell him. 'I think it's the nicest alternative.'

'Okay,' he nodded.

At about 11.30p.m. an Italian girl – slim, black hair,

gold jewellery – entered the bar. Mario introduced us then left us to chat. At first I thought she must be a local friend of his but it transpired she was a guest staying at the hotel with her sister, brother-in-law and their child. She was from Turin and told me how much more passionate southern Italian men were than the northern Italians she was used to. 'Mario is so *simpatico*,' she sighed, acknowledging his charm but admitting she was wary of him. I asked her why even though I felt the same way. She said that last night he had begged her to go for a walk with him. I removed the 'You're kidding – he asked me the same thing!' expression from my face and said, 'Oh really? Did you go?'

'No,' she shook her head. 'I like him but you know, men like Mario want more than to hold your hand. I cannot sleep with someone unless I love them. That is just the way I am.'

As she described the fairytale fantasy she's holding out for I felt strangely protective and annoyed with Mario for approaching her – she was too vulnerable, he was taking advantage. With me, it's a bit different. I'm already disillusioned. I think he can tell I have no luck with men, that I've lowered my expectations so much that an approach from him is flattering and gratefully received. I had been tempted to at least stay for a drink with him but after chatting with Paola I decided I should let him know it wasn't going to happen by ordering a hot milk. (Latte caldo, got it right this time.)

He protested 'It is still too early – I make you

162

another Secret Prescription!' but when I stood firm he talked me into having a dash of Cognac in my milk to help me sleep. (What I actually got was Cognac with a dash of milk. The prospect of sleep was looking good, I just wondered if I'd ever wake up again.) Paola had ordered camomile tea. It was the more virtuous option but hardly sophisticated as it looked like wee. Every time Mario went back to the bar he tried to catch my eye. He pulled faces behind Paola as if to say, She talks too much! and, I wish she'd go! And as lowly as this behaviour was, I was oddly gratified that I appeared to be his preference. I just hoped it wasn't because I looked like more of a sure thing to him.

Whether Paola wanted Mario or not, it seemed she had no intention of leaving me with him at midnight. At 12.05a.m. we made an unspoken sisterhood decision to leave at the same time. The frustration in Mario's face was a picture. As he walked us to the lobby he sneaked a hand around my waist, managing to worm his thumb beneath my waistband to touch my skin. You've got to admire his cheek. Leaning close he pressed the lift call button and then bid us 'Buona notte' adding, 'Sogna mi!' (Dream of me!). We giggled and shook our heads as the lift lurched to the first floor. 'This has been fun – maybe you come to Turin some day?' Paola suggested, giving me her card and a kiss on each cheek. I said I'd love to and marvelled at how quickly girls bond as I pressed floor two.

Stepping out of the lift, bedroom door in sight, key in hand, I was suddenly pounced on from behind and yanked into the laundry cupboard!

163

'*What?*' Cleo howls.

I've just regaled her with the whole story.

'I swear to God, I don't know how he got up the stairs so quick!'

'Did you scream?'

'I tried to but it just came out all muffled because—'

'He didn't gag you with a pillowcase?' gasps Cleo, getting overexcited.

'Nooo! It was muffled because he was kissing me! He started before I even realized it was Mario who had jumped on me.'

'Was he good?'

'No, awful – all ravenous and invasive. And he was squeezing me so hard I thought my spine would snap!'

'So what happened next?'

'I wrestled myself free and asked him what the hell he thought he was doing.'

'It's not like you to be so assertive.'

'I think it was shock. I sounded really outraged!'

'Good for you! Did he apologize?'

'Not exactly,' I pause to control a giggle. 'He said: "*I want to make shaggy with you!*"'

Cleo shrieks with glee. 'Noooooo!'

'Yes! Isn't that hysterical? And he actually wanted to come into the room.'

'What about your mum?' says Cleo, scandalized.

'Well he knew she wasn't back yet . . .'

'Yeah but potentially any minute – imagine her bursting in on you! I can just see him scrambling over the balcony to escape, getting his boxers caught on a prong!'

164

'That's exactly what happened!'

'No!' howls Cleo.

'No, of course not,' I chuckle.

'Were you tempted?'

'Only if there was a medical team and an osteopath standing by to tend to my injuries. I reckon you'd need to be a black belt to survive sex with that man.'

'Ooooh it sounds so passionate!' Cleo enthuses.

'Well, I'm sure Mario would be more than willing to oblige if you hopped on a flight. He's not exactly choosy.'

'Thanks a lot!'

'I didn't mean it like that,' I protest.

'Anyway, I can't leave now – there's been a Gareth-sighting!'

I gasp. 'Tell!'

'Well, I didn't see him but Branwen in Superdrug said he came in for some AfterSun and that he looked really brown so with any luck he'll be dropping off his holiday snaps any day now,' she pipes.

'Imagine if he wore a thong on the beach.'

'I wouldn't care – the more flesh the better. He's too delicious!'

'Maybe you should try the "paradise" line on him!'

'Oh God!' Cleo chuckles.

'Just think—' I begin.

'Hold on, that's the door,' Cleo interrupts. 'Must be the postman with the Freemans delivery, let me call you back.'

'Okay,' I say hanging up with a grin.

It's good to hear home. Being able to picture Cleo in

our front room is comforting. I wonder what she's ordered? Bet it's something for the kitchen.

I throw back the covers and swing my legs out of bed, mildly surprised to see that I'm still wearing last night's outfit. In the days when I actually had to leave the house to go to work this used to happen all the time – bootleg jeans, poloneck jumpers, zippy jackets, my bed has seen it all. Cleo would despair, convinced a restrictive belt or a hazardous hook-and-eye fastening would be the end of me. For a fellow slob-ette she's always had a very strict pre-sleep regime. The only time she's worn anything other than a 100 per cent cotton M&S nightie was when she unexpectedly ended up in bed with her old boss – she thought it would be less embarrassing if he didn't actually see her naked skin so she kept on her tights and black lycra 'body'. He went to bed with his best-looking member of staff and woke up with a ballet dancer.

The phone rings. Here's Darcy Bussell now.

'Hello, Luna Love Line, we are currently offering special rates at the hotel – half board accommodation and a shaggy from just 300,000 lire per night!'

'Sounds like a bargain,' says a male voice.

'Mario?' I say, mortified.

'No, er, this is Luca. From the shop.'

Even worse. I freeze, mouth open in a silent scream.

'Is Mario one of your regular customers?' he asks, finally.

'No! No! He's just the barman from downstairs . . .' This is looking bad.

'Ahhh.'

'Um, Mum's not here right now.' I wince, trying to sound normal.

'Okay, well just remind her that the boat leaves from Marina Piccola at noon.'

'Boat?'

'Unless you'd rather swim around the island?'

'Are we taking a trip?'

'She didn't tell you?'

'No.'

'Today we take you to the world famous Blue Grotto,' he says in his best tour guide voice.

'The sea's not rough, is it?' I worry, realizing I haven't even opened the shutters yet.

'Are you a bad sailor?'

'I'm just a bit hungover,' I understate.

'You went out last night?'

'Just to the hotel bar.'

'I can see I'm going to have to have words with your barman!' he jokes.

He's not *my* barman, I want to clarify but instead I just say, 'Mmm.'

'Okay, so see you at twelve o'clock.'

'Marina Piccola!' I say, trying to sound efficient and enthused.

'Marina Piccola,' he repeats.

I feel like he's about to say something else but he merely concludes with an 'Okay – ciao!' and puts the phone down.

I don't even breathe for a few minutes after I replace the handset, just sit looking slightly stunned. Finally I expel a whimper. I can't believe the effect he has on

167

me. If I never had any contact with him again I might have got away with it but now . . . I pull a pillow into an embrace.

The phone rings again.

'Hello?' I say cautiously.

'What's with the timid housewife voice?'

'Cleo!'

'Well, don't sound so surprised. I said I'd call you right back.'

'I know, I . . .'

'Are you all right? You're not, are you? What is it?'

'Luca just rang!' I blurt.

'The Love God?'

'Mmm,' I mumble.

'So many men—'

'Oh Cleo – he's *married*!' I wail.

'*NO!* When did you find out?'

'Yesterday lunchtime. About two hours after I spoke to you.'

'Why didn't you tell me, then?'

'I just felt so stupid . . .'

'Oh hon!'

I'm halfway through explaining that he even has a mini-Casanova for a son when the door opens and in sashays my mother wearing a white shirt tucked Katharine Hepburn-style into navy slacks.

'I've got to go,' I tell Cleo.

'Your mum's back?'

'Right.'

'Well hang in there and don't forget to switch on the invisible force-field around your heart.'

168

'Okay, love you!' I smile. 'Bye!'

'Do you like my outfit?' my mother brazens as I replace the receiver.

'Yes, it's great,' I tell her. 'House of Platinum Man if I'm not mistaken.'

'I wish you wouldn't call him that, his name is Tony.'

'I suppose I don't need to ask whether you had a good time . . .'

'Oh, Kim! He's just so wonderful,' she says sitting beside me on the bed, all pink-cheeked and peppy. 'Wouldn't it be amazing if we ended up having a double wedding – father and son, mother and daughter!'

'I'm not marrying you!' I protest. 'Surely it's illegal?'

'You know what I mean,' she tuts. 'Tyler arrives on Sunday afternoon. I said we'd have dinner with them in the evening.'

'Just like you said we'd go on a boat trip today . . .'

'Didn't I tell you?'

I shake my head.

'Oh. Well . . .' says my mother, heading for the bathroom.

'I thought we were supposed to be sorting out the shop, not going sightseeing,' I grouch.

'We can do both. Anyway, it was Luca's idea. He thought you might enjoy it.'

'Did he?' I brighten.

Mum has already started the shower and does not respond. But I pretend she says: We would have met him earlier only he had to go and file for divorce.

169

16

The sweaty, tetchy queue for the bus to Marina Piccola burgeons beyond the maze of railings at the depot and wavers obstructively down Via Roma.

'Forget it!' hoots Mum. 'We'll take a taxi.'

This seems an impossible extravagance – Capri's vintage stretch convertibles would make even the sleekest limo look Stringfellows-naff. Surely you have to be a Valentino or De Laurentiis to warrant travelling in such style? I catch my reflection in the gleaming chrome bumper. Oh dear. I wouldn't be surprised if the driver wrapped me in a pashmina for the duration of the journey so as not to ruin his image. For a second I think he's going to ask me to travel in the boot but he's just throwing his jacket in there. He greets us with a little bow. Judging by the look on his face my mother is well dressed enough for both of us and he waves us on board. I apologize to the ivory leather seat before I sit on it. ('Yes these are M&S pyjama bottoms not Fenn, Wright & Mason linen drawstrings, forgive me.')

I'm guessing this ten-minute journey is going to cost

about £100 and yet just seconds into it it feels worth every penny. The road to the marina is made up of hazardous hairpin bends and yet we glide along cooled by the gentlest of breezes so it feels like a sophisticated, slo-mo version of a rollercoaster ride. Finally I understand what people mean when they say life is not about getting from A to B as quickly as possible but enjoying the journey.

We swoop past sprawling villas seemingly painted with custard and calamine lotion, slowing at the corners to take in flowers with scarlet bristles exactly like bottle brushes and cacti scored with the faded beige hearts and initials of lovers. Watching the tumbling bougainvillaea blur into a magenta wash is the most serene experience of my life and when I discover the fare is actually the equivalent of £10, I slip the driver an extra £5 for allowing me to share such bliss.

'This place used to be a simple dock,' my mum tells me as we skip down the steps to the water, 'and the houses overlooking it belonged to coral-fishermen. Now look at it!'

I'm startled by the vivid cartoon colours of the beach huts – no weatherbeaten pastels here: the row along the raised concrete platform are all freshly painted citrus yellow and Granny Smith green, teamed with hot orange sunloungers. 'It looks like the stage set for a musical, doesn't it?' chuckles my mother. She's right – you expect swimmers to emerge in knee-length costumes doing choreographed leaps and squeals with beach balls. Unfortunately no one breaks into a number from *The Boyfriend* – this is more the Burberry bikini brigade – but there are a few swimcapped-heads, bobbing like gobstoppers in the water.

'Did you used to swim here?' I ask my mother.

'I preferred the cove just around the corner,' she replies. 'Follow me . . .'

We appear to be heading for the kitchens of the Ristorante Ciro but the sneaky side path opens out on to the cosiest pebbly beach. A low craggy arch wades a few feet into the sea, icy green water swilling around its ankles like mouthwash, throwing up a minty froth as it slaps the rock. I want to dive in, it looks so pore-tighteningly refreshing. Mum instinctively heads for the cluster of seaside shops, one selling pink cowboy hats and seashells sprayed silver. I hang back by the arch where a little girl is exploring the fuzzy flora, carefully dodging the spiky blades of aloe vera. It's only as she climbs down that I spy a diving school burrowed into the side of the rock, barely discernible but for the wetsuits hanging from the jagged ledges.

I slip off my shoes and tiptoe towards the water, noticing all the pretty chips of colour mixed in with the pale grey pebbles. It's as though someone has hurled their pottery out the window in a fight and the shattered pieces have created a random mosaic effect. I pick up one piece – rough terracotta on one side, smooth blue speckled with white on the other.

'It's like seeing stars on a sunny day!' says Luca, suddenly by my side, running his thumb over the flecks. The man is truly poetry in motion.

'Kim! Kim!' Nino a.k.a Ringo jostles me, as if aware

that he has his work cut out trying to get me to tear my eyes away from his father. 'I have present for you – look!'

He holds up a brown paper bag about the size of a shoebox. 'Open! Open!' he urges.

I unscrunch it and pull out a bumper packet of RINGO biscuits. 'Oh my God!' I laugh, feeling tearfully touched. 'Thank you!' I pull the non-edible Ringo into a hug. He squeezes me so tight our hearts bump and then says, 'Try one!'

'Okay!' I oblige, first reading the bright red lettering out loud: 'IL BISCOTTO-SNACK – Di Qua Bianco e di la Nero con Dentro tanta Crema Golosa!'

A custard cream and bourbon hybrid, I decide, munching happily.

'Kim, what are you doing? You've only just had breakfast.'

Meet my mother the Pleasure Killer. The woman with the unfortunate knack for bringing out the worst in me. Only I don't want Ringo or Luca to see my petulant, childish side so I calmly explain that they are a gift and won't she try one?

'Yes! Yes! You must!' insists Ringo. I watch with satisfaction, knowing that processed sugar is poison to her and she'll be convinced her teeth will rot unless she can find a toothbrush *now*!

'Everybody ready?' says Luca.

'I just need to pop to the Ladies,' says Mum.

'OK. Sophia is waiting by the rocks so we'll see you there.'

Oh no. *Oh no*! Not his wife. When did she get back? I

173

don't want to meet her. If she's beautiful I'll have the ugliest day of my life, if she's ugly it'll just bug me all the more because it'll mean there's an even stronger bond between them. All the same, please let her be ugly. Please. Please.

We walk up the steps beside the diving school, out on to a rocky jetty.

'This is known as Lo Scoglio delle Sirene, the Rock of the Sirens,' Ringo informs me. 'Is possible this is where Odysseus was tempted . . .'

How apt. But which one of these women enticed Luca down the aisle? Surely not the trampy blonde in a red leather jacket and mirrored Aviators? No she's with a Platinum Man double. The one with the high ponytail in shorts and sandals? No, she seems to be a diving school groupie. I follow Luca's eyes to a woman with waist-length hair sitting with her back to us at the furthest point. Everyone else is in pairs or groups, it has to be her. Moving closer, I prepare myself for the worst – I just know she's going to be a young Sophia Loren, Claudia Cardinale and Gina Lollobrigida all rolled into one. Another step and I'm near enough to push her into the water. She turns round.

She's seventy if she's a day! I recoil, stunned. She pulls me into an embrace. I must be mistaken, I try and twist my head around so I can inspect her neck for saggy skin but the liver-spotted hand that brushes my hair out of my face is all the confirmation I need. Holding me at arm's length she inspects my face.

I peer back at her thinking *how*? And then *why*? Why is she looking at me so fondly?

'I can see so much of your grandfather in you. And so much of your mother.'

I didn't even realize they had met. Surely they haven't?

'Is she here?' Sophia asks.

'She's just—' I begin.

'Sophia!' calls my mother, hurrying across the rocks to her.

'Gina! Your girl is beautiful!'

Mum gives me a look – pride mixed with 'I wish she'd do something with her hair'. 'Kim, I'd like you to meet Sophia Vuotto, one of my oldest friends,' she beams.

'Hey, watch who you're calling old,' laughs Sophia.

'So you're not . . .' I begin.

'Not what?' Sophia and Mum chorus, looking intrigued.

'Not, um, *related* to the Amoratos?' I say, gesturing over to where father and son are preparing the boat.

'No dear, I lived in the house next door to your mother when she was growing up.'

'Sophia was so glamorous, everything I wanted to be . . .'

'You were like a little sister to me,' smiles Sophia. 'I missed you so much when you went away.' She looks sad for a minute and then adds, 'When I saw you yesterday all the years flew away.'

Yesterday? My mother has truly missed her calling as a secret agent. I have no clue what she gets up to when she's out of my sight.

'The times we had together . . .' Sophia seems to be

watching an old cine-film in my mother's eyes. Then she turns to me: 'You see that beach club with the flags?' I nod. 'That is Canzone del Mare, Song of the Sea, former residence of Gracie Fields.'

'I doubt Kim even knows who she is!' tinkles my mother.

'Dame Gracie Fields? Born 9th January 1898 above her grandmother's fish and chip shop in Rochdale, Capricorn, known as "Our Gracie", signature tune "Sally", highest paid film star in the world in 1937, buried here on Capri in 1979? That Gracie Fields?' I deadpan. I knew that internet research Cleo and I did would come in useful at some point.

After a small stunned silence Sophia continues, 'Well, after the war she turned it into a bathing establishment and in the Fifties and Sixties it was the most fashionable place to be. Your mother and I would study the magazines and then swim out from here and see who we could spot. We saw Ingrid Bergman, Faye Dunaway, Elizabeth Taylor . . .'

'Tony Curtis, George Hamilton . . .' adds my mother, clearly more interested in the men even in those days.

'One time we even took my father's camera into the water with us and had to swim without splashing it,' Sophia recalls.

'Oh my God – you were pre-teen paparazzi!' I marvel.

'That's right!' laughs Sophia. 'Only I must have been in my twenties so I should have known better!'

'We were hoping someone would discover us,' my mother remembers.

'And make us into movie stars,' Sophia sighs wistfully.

'Or fall in love with us . . .'

For a moment they have my sympathy – their dream didn't come true. And judging by Sophia's incredible bone structure they were both pretty enough to think it might. I remember an episode of *Oprah* where the expert guest identified a beautiful woman's problem – she had fallen for the myth that pretty people get spotted walking along the street or lolling by the soda fountain and are promptly whisked off to Hollywood for a three-picture deal or offered a modelling contract in Milan. These things are supposed to just land in their lap. The beautiful forty-something never had a game-plan or a strategy to achieve her dreams because she thought her looks were enough and the rest would take care of itself, fairy godmother style. She wasn't so much bitter as bemused but the worst thing was you could tell that she was *still waiting* to see herself on the cover of a magazine. It fleetingly occurred to me that it must be very confusing to be stunning and not get the life you want because you must feel you somehow squandered your head start.

'Kim!' Nino's voice jolts me out of my musings.

'Yes, Captain Ringo!' I turn to salute my second-favourite sailor.

'Please, now you join us on board.'

We start up with a slow grinding putter, gathering speed as we head away from the beach and out to sea. Luca stands at the wheel, Ringo to his left, kneeling up on the seat so he can see over the top of the windscreen. The female contingent sit back on the cushioned seats, tilting further back with every knot-surge. Sophia laughs as the wind whips her long hair into an unruly upward swirl, creating a human candyfloss as the strands wrap around her face. Mum offers her a velvet scrunchie and ties a Pucci-print scarf around her own hair. Meanwhile I relish the tousled feeling – 'Bring on those comb-strangling tangles!' I've spent so long trying to live at the right temperature with the minimum amount of disturbance that right now it feels good to surrender to nature. I turn and reach over the back of the boat to let the whisked-up water race through my fingers. I used to love going to Penarth beach as a child. Why did I stop going? When did it start being too much of a palaver to take the twenty-minute drive there? I guess as an adult I thought I'd be swanning around some Caribbean resort. It was as though I was always saving myself for something better. And then when that didn't happen automatically, I let the whole thing slide. All the choices we are given as an adult and yet how few we explore. What do we do with our spare time? Watch TV. Sometimes I wish a few things stayed compulsory after school, like netball and art classes and psychology!

The boat jolts and my stomach lurches excitedly as we trip over a wave and thud down like a horse buckling after jumping a gate. I look over at Luca shaking the spray from his hair and flicking Ringo with the excess water. If he wasn't here would I be feeling so exhilarated? His presence definitely does something to me. I remind myself that he is married but part of me isn't convinced. It feels as if she doesn't exist. At least for today she doesn't . . .

'Everybody okay?' says Luca, turning to face us.

'Yes,' we smile back at him.

'Kim, you should put on some suncream, your forehead looks pink already,' fusses my mother.

I wonder if I'll ever stop feeling five years old around her. How do you respond to questions like, 'Did you want to spend a penny before you leave?' and sound like a grown-up?

'I'm fine,' I tell her.

'Have some of mine,' offers Sophia, handing me an expensive-looking tube with a gold lid.

'Sophia owns a beauty spa,' Mum tells me. 'She could have a look at your skin while you're here.'

Thanks a bunch, Ma.

'We have some lovely treatments, Kim, if you would like to try them,' says Sophia, kindly.

'They mostly just bring me out in a rash,' I deflect. 'But thanks anyway.'

'Of course my spa is not as high-tech as Hotel Palace Beauty Farm,' Sophia tells my mother. 'They offer thalassotherapeutic glycolic acid peels, ultrasound diathermies, Infrasnella . . .'

I doubt either Sophia or my mother would value my contribution to this conversation so I decide to leave them to it but just as I take a step towards Ringo the boat smacks over another wave and I skid forward, thwacking my funnybone on the throttle.

'Aaagghh, shit!' I blurt. 'Sorry, Ringo!' I hate people swearing in front of children. He doesn't seem to notice as he's busily kissing my elbow better and offering me his seat.

If only he were twenty-five years older.

'So you want just the view or also the tour?' asks Luca.

'I want everything!'

'Everything?' he says, giving me one of *those* looks.

'Both,' I say, trying to keep calm.

'Some people, they just like to look,' he explains.

'I guess it depends on who's doing the talking,' I say, sneaking a look at my mum.

'Okay,' he says. 'I begin . . .'

'Just the good stuff,' I interrupt.

He shoots me a look and continues, 'There are many grottoes around the coast of Capri—'

'Twenty! I can name them all!' pipes Ringo.

Luca gives in. 'Go ahead, Nino . . .'

'First we see Grotta Verda, that is the Green Grotto.'

Luca slows the boat so we can take in the kryptonite glow of the water.

'We pretend different creatures live in each grotto,' whispers Luca.

'This has got to be the Martian hideout,' I suggest.

'Sì, they have a timeshare with some leprechauns,' Luca confirms.

'Next is Grotta Rossa, the Red Grotto.'

I cover Ringo's ears: 'The prostitute hangout?'

'You want we drop you here now?' teases Luca. I flick his arm and nearly dislocate a knuckle on his bicep.

'Then Grotta Champagne . . .' Ringo continues.

Full of luvvies and It girls.

'Over near the Faraglioni there is Grotta di Forca.'

'A refuge for cutlery kleptomaniacs?'

'Fork is *forchetta*,' frowns Luca. 'Not *forca*.'

'I know,' I laugh. 'I'm just being silly.' I can't help it. I'm feeling quite light-headed.

'Of course, the most famous and most visited of all is the Blue Grotto – Grotta Azzurra!' trills Ringo. 'Is *magic*!'

'In the old days the locals avoided it because they thought it was inhabited by witches and monsters,' adds Luca. 'Now it is just tourists in there.'

'Are we going inside?'

'Of course,' smiles Luca. 'You are tourist. It is compulsory.'

17

Up until now we've only seen the occasional rival sailing vessel coursing by, but here at the entrance to the Blue Grotto there appears to be some kind of a floating boating convention. Big cruisers jammed with multinational tourists bear down on sleek yachts with slinky people who think they're in Duran Duran's *Rio* video. For some reason the people in the cheap seats are all bundled in sweaters whereas the yachtie-hotties sport only metallic bikinis – does being rich make you immune to the cold? Luca cuts the engine and steers us into what I presume is our position in the queue – second wave to the left.

'What happens now?'

'We have to transfer into the rowing boats. Only they are small enough to get through the opening.'

'Which is . . .?'

'There!' Luca points over to the base of the cliff face.

'That tiny gap? You're kidding!' Before my nerves can take hold Luca summons two rowing boats, explaining that we'll have to split up as each boat can only take three passengers.

'Put the old ladies in one,' says Sophia. 'Kim can squeeze the men.'

I'm liking Sophia more all the time.

'Will you be all right, darling?' Mum frets.

'I look after her,' Ringo reassures her. 'Please no worry!'

'Come on, Gina, this isn't *Titanic*,' Sophia groans. 'Get in the boat!'

The reunited friends giggle girlishly as they are rowed into their place in the queue.

'Now us,' says Luca. 'I go first so I can help you down.' In one move he drops into the back of the rowboat and reaches up for me. I'm less deft, lowering myself clumsily into his arms. I go to sit down but my movement destabilizes the boat and I shriek and spasm, wobbling the boat all the more, convinced we're going to capsize. Luca grips me tight and shifts me to the centre. 'It's okay.'

'Kim, you crazy!' laughs Ringo, springing to the front of the boat. 'See: I go first – is most scary place to sit,' he says heroically.

The gruff boatman begins rotating his oars and barks, 'Lie down!'

'What?'

'We have to be flat on the bottom of the boat,' explains Luca, shuffling his body down so his long legs slide either side of me.

'If you sit up you will lose your head – boof!' Ringo demonstrates decapitation by the grotto entrance. 'Also your hands – they will be sliced off if you hold edge of the boat. Must keep them inside!'

183

Okay, I am officially scared now. I look around for my mum and Sophia but they must already be in coffin pose and I can't see them.

'Lie back!' the boatman snarls.

I slump down, very aware that I am using Luca as a mattress. My back is flat to his chest and I try to lean as lightly as possible but don't have the stomach muscles to sustain the pose.

'Keep your head low,' Luca reminds me as he rests a protective arm across my collar bone. I tilt my head back and feel his goatee engage with the hair on the top of my head. My heart is hammering.

'Is it low all the way along inside, like a tunnel?' I ask, nauseous with impending claustrophobia and yet weak with lust. I wonder which of Luca's tattoos my shoulder blade is impaling . . .

'You will see . . . we're next.'

The boatman reaches out for the heavy chain that runs along the cliff and into the grotto, hauling us into place.

'It's rough today, Papa,' Ringo notes.

I crane my neck to see the water swell so high that it almost fills the tiny gap we're about to pass through.

'What happens if the wave rises up while we're going in?' I dare to ask.

'We will be smashed on the rocks!' says Ringo gleefully.

'Oh God!' I wail.

'These men, they know what they are doing,' Luca assures me, adding: 'You can swim, right?'

'What?!'

'Here we go,' says Luca. 'Keep down!'

I feel a rush of adrenalin as the boatman grips the chain, clamping his hands over and over and craning back in limbo pose as he thrusts us through the gap. It is like being sucked into the underworld. Or giving birth in reverse.

'Welcome to Grotta Azzurra!' Ringo cheers.

'We made it!' I gasp, giddy with relief, inching my way into a sitting position. The entrance is tiny but the grotto itself is a vast cavern.

'The width of the grotta is same as length of Olympic swimming pool – 25 metres,' Ringo tells me as my eyes adjust to the darkness. 'The length is 60 metres – same as indoor sprint track.'

I'm getting the impression that Ringo is quite the sports fan.

The boatman rows us deeper in.

'You like?' says Luca.

'Yes,' I falter, lost for words. It's beautiful, eerie, cool and yet I imagined it would be more dramatic somehow.

'Now turn back . . .'

I twist around towards the entrance. 'Oh my God!' I breathe, blissed out by the celestial turquoise wonderland that greets me. My eyes widen. My heart swells. 'How come it's so bright?' I blink.

'The sunlight, it passes through an underwater cavity and illuminates the seawater.'

'All natural? No tricks?' I ask peering for hidden floodlights.

'It is real magic. Give me your hand.' Luca entwines

185

his fingers in mine and plunges them into the water. Our skin chills to a luminous bluey-white glow. Reluctantly our fingers separate.

'Imagine swimming in here,' I say, reaching in up to my elbow. The water is invitingly pure and clear.

'It is said that Tiberius had a secret passageway connecting to his villa up above.'

'Wow, he could teach Hugh Hefner a thing or two,' I decide.

'Watch this!' calls Ringo, nudging the boatman. He takes his oar, slashes the surface of the water then flicks it upwards; the droplets sparkle like diamonds and sapphires suspended in the air. It is magical. I want to tell Luca, Now I know where they got the blue for your eyes! but instead I cry, 'Do it again!'

Luca ruffles my hair and I feel his breath on my neck as he laughs. Anything seems possible in here. I don't want to leave but already we are making our way back. 'O Sole Mio,' booms the boatman, trying to distract us from the fact that he's about to spit us back into the real world.

The water gets sloppy-choppy as we approach the bright triangle of daylight peeking through from outside. Worryingly, the closer we get, the smaller the gap becomes. Then a big wave sloshes in, blocking it entirely. I get a chill. Unless the water settles, there's no way out. Even the boatman looks anxious. We lie flat down on the bottom of the boat as instructed but after five trepidatious minutes feeling the water dancing dangerously high beneath us, we nervously prop ourselves up to see what's going on. Right now you couldn't even get an oar through the gap; a boat would be in splinters. I've always craved what people call a 'movie moment'. I just didn't expect mine to be a disaster movie. I practise holding my breath and curse myself for wearing white – everything will be on show when my drowned body is pulled from the water.

'Papa?' Ringo whispers.

'It's okay,' Luca reassures him. 'Kim?'

I only manage a whimper before the boatman croaks, 'Lie back!' and crosses himself.

This feels serious. My heart starts to pound as the boatman grabs the chain that will (in theory) yank us to freedom. He edges us forward. I'm toying with the idea of crying when I feel a surge and a whoosh and an almighty crashing of icy water slapping my skin and stinging my eyes. I'm drenched. But we're through. I struggle into an upright position, spitting salty water. The surrounding tourists cheer. Pushing my dripping rat's tail hair from my face I see Ringo pointing at me.

'Kim, I can see your—'

I slam my hands over my chest. It's not like I'm not wearing a bra but the bra I have on is white too and I can only imagine what's on view. I'm almost too relieved to be alive to care but hunch over to display some modesty as we row back to Luca's boat. Then I realize I'm going to have to let go of my T-shirt to board. Mum and Sophia look on with concern, towel at the ready. I use one hand to reach for the ladder and the other to try and prise the sopping wet cotton away from my skin. Not easy – it seems to be favouring the

187

shrink-wrap effect. It's all gone horribly Ibiza foam-party.

'Poor darling!' My mother wraps me up, covering my face as well as my body. 'I've got nothing for you to change into.'

'She can have my shirt,' offers Luca. 'She took most of the water and kept me dry.'

As Luca gets unbuttoned I peek out from the towel to watch my mother's face as he reveals his tattooed torso.

'Oooh,' she says. 'You're very colourful!'

'You can change down here.' Luca opens a hatch leading to a mini seated area.

I squelch down the steps and slide the hatch door closed behind me. It takes all my strength to de-sucker myself from the T-shirt and I stand topless and panting for a few seconds. Outside I hear more cheering. Presumably another boat has emerged from the Blue Grotto.

'Kim!' Luca rattles the hatch urgently.

'Er! Hold on!' I say, covering myself with the towel.

'You might want to close the curtains down there!'

I jerk round and find myself eye-level with a party of gurning guys hanging off a yacht so they can peer in the windows. I drop to the floor. Oh the shame! Surely there's some plug I can pull and go directly to a watery grave?

'Are you all right in there?' I hear my mum call. That's right, just draw more attention to me.

On the journey back I'm subdued but not exactly

miserable. My main source of comfort is Ringo – he's fallen asleep snuggled into my armpit and it soothes me to listen to his snuffly breathing and stroke his hot shiny hair. I look over at Mum and Sophia, still busily gossiping and reminiscing. I can guess at the gist of what they are saying from their expressions but the noise of the engine and the wind have created an audio cocoon for me and I'm grateful to be spared any obligation to join their conversation. A few times I look up to find Luca gazing down at me from the wheel. The increase in my breaths-per-minute is made all the more conspicuous by the resultant rising and falling of Ringo's head on my chest. I try and steady my breathing, afraid I might wake Ringo but he only moves once to drape an arm across my stomach. I take his hand and touch his small nails, smiling as I remember our first handshake. It's weird being able to be openly affectionate to the junior Amorato and yet feel sinful if I so much as brush Luca's hand while accepting a can of lemon soda from the cooler.

I try not to let my mind wander too far but reclining in the sun on his boat, wearing his shirt with his son using me as a pillow, I feel as though I am part of his life. And it's a beautiful feeling, even though it comes with an ache.

18

'Can you talk?'

'All clear, Cleo! Gosh, that's hard to—'

'Arrrgghhh!' she screams over me.

'What?' I gasp, stumbling back into the bed.

'Gareth came in today!' she says with singsong delight. 'I tried to call you earlier – where've you been?'

'Out,' I say, impatient to hear her news. My Miss Wet T-Shirt story can wait. 'Go on.'

'Well, it was about 5p.m. I was over by the lightbox, bracing myself for another Gareth-less day when in he walks, looking so golden delicious I sent a box of slides flying!'

'Where's he been?'

'I didn't get the chance to ask. He was in a real rush but he gave me one roll of film and said he'd be back on Sunday with a load of disposable cameras that he needs done in an hour. I reminded him we closed at 4p.m. on a Sunday and he said he'd be in after lunch. I can't wait!'

'But you don't work Sundays . . .'

'That's the whole beauty of it! I'm going to hang out until he comes in, then I'm going to fill out all his forms – I'm thinking at least six cameras so that's six different envelopes which should give me enough time to get him chatting.'

'What are you going to say?'

'Funny you should ask – I've got a few scenarios worked out, you tell me which sounds best.'

'Okay.'

'Number one: I casually say, "I've always wondered what people do in the hour it takes to get their pictures developed, I'm thinking of conducting a survey!" And then he'll laugh and say, '"I'm just going down the pub!"'

'How do you know that?' I butt in.

'Wait! So he says, "I'm going down the pub!" and I say, "Tell you what, I've got my break now – if you buy me a drink I'll get these done for you in thirty minutes."'

'Oo, I like that – flirty *and* exhibiting your professional clout.'

'Not too forward?'

'Not sure – what else you got?'

'I say the survey bit and he says, "I hadn't really thought – got any suggestions?" And I say, "I was just about to take my coffee break – I know a place that serves the frothiest lattes in town, I could show you if you like!"'

'Very Central Park!'

'Yeah, I'm not convinced. What about, "I'm going to River Island to pick out a jumper for my brother,

191

you wouldn't help me choose, would you? He's the same build as you . . ."'

'Utterly transparent device to get his kit off.'

'Oh.'

'Mind you . . .' I flash back to Luca dressing me in the mint trouser suit. 'It might just work.'

'I just want to be with him in a situation where there's not a counter between us!'

'Hey, what was on his film, anyway?'

'No beach shots – I guess they're all coming tomorrow – just a lads' night out.'

'Any mooning?'

'Yeah, total eclipse, but not him.'

'What are his mates like?'

'He's the catch, no doubt about it,' Cleo assures me.

'Did you recognize the bar they were at? Cos we could always stake it out . . .'

'What?' Cleo snorts.

'If you knew his regular—'

'You hate bars!'

'I hate queuing for a drink and not being able to find a seat and getting lager slopped over my suede jacket but if it was somewhere where we could perch on a bar stool and order a Bellini . . .'

'Well, the Drunken Dragon is dead on a Monday and they stock peach Bacardi Breezers, if that's any use!'

Reality bites.

'I think you should go for it tomorrow.'

'Really?' Cleo sighs, dreamily.

'Definitely. What have you got to lose?'

'Oh I wish you were here!'

I go to say, 'I wish I was too,' but the words don't come out.

'So how was Day 3 in hell?' Cleo asks.

I think of the zesty-zinging boat trip around the island, the magic and drama of the Blue Grotto, Luca ruffling my hair, Ringo sleeping in my arms, then meandering back to the Luna with Sophia and my mother to find cocktails waiting for us on the terrace. The sunset was incredible – great swirls and flourishes of pink and gold, as if an artist had taken over the skies.

'It was a real drag. Mum made me go to the dead guy's house after dinner so we could go through his personal effects,' I tell Cleo.

'At night? Spooky!' Cleo shudders. 'Find anything interesting?'

'Well, there was one thing . . .'

We'd been there an hour and I was counting my blessings that Sophia was with us so I didn't have to feign interest every time my mum began a sentence with, 'And this is where I . . .' or 'This was Papa's favourite . . .'

Vincenzo had got pretty much everything in order before he popped his hand-stitched loafers and it was up to Mum to decide what of the crockery, ornaments and sets of cufflinks etc. she wanted to keep. At one point I selfishly wished that I had as many tangible memories of my father as she had been bequeathed by hers. All I had was a Scrabble board and an old tie.

Mum came pretty close to tears when she opened a trunk and discovered all the childhood toys and books she'd been forced to leave behind. She took out one matted old bear and then said she wasn't ready to go through the rest yet. She was about to close the lid when I noticed a bulky brown-paper-wrapped package bearing the words ROSA MARESCA, 8 VIA TRINITA, RAVELLO.

I reached in and pulled it out. Mum looked concerned, probably fearing I would start channelling Granny Carmela and shred the package and its contents with my bare hands. But I had a better idea.

'I suppose we ought to see that Rosa gets this,' I said, calmly.

'Yes,' my mother agreed, offering to relieve me of it. 'We'll have it sent to her.'

I held fast. 'We don't know what's inside – it might be too precious to post. Why don't I take it to her. Ravello's not far, is it?'

Mum looked uncomfortable. 'Well, it's a ferry ride to Amalfi and then a bus . . .'

'I'll go tomorrow.'

Mum looked at Sophia and then back at me. 'Why would you want to do that, Kim?'

'Well, I get to find out what's in the package, for one!' Even with this flippant reply Mum could sense my real motive: 'I want to see if Rosa knows what she did when she had the affair with my grandfather. I want to see if she's sorry for the pain she caused.'

Mum closed her eyes and took a breath: 'You can't avenge my mother's heartache, sweetheart. It doesn't work like that.'

'It's got to be worth a try!' I said, faux-peppy.

What I didn't say was that I also want to know if the affair was worth it.

My mother sighed and let it slide.

'So, are you really going to go there?' Cleo asks, sounding utterly intrigued.

'Yup!' I tell her, eyeing the package on the chair at the end of the bed.

'Wow! Where's your mother now?'

'Gone to the Piazzetta for a coffee with Platinum Man.'

'At midnight? It's a bit late for being coy, isn't it? Why doesn't she just stay over with him?'

'She wants to be at the shop first thing tomorrow.'

'Are you going to wait up for her?'

'No, I was just about to turn off the light when you called. How about you?'

'Yeah, I'm going to have a bowl of Coco Pops to stave off the night starvation and then hit the hay.' I smile. This snack will be the first of many throughout the night. Her current weakness is Celebrations. Sometimes she kicks off her duvet in the night and wakes up covered in metallic confetti, giving a whole new meaning to the phrase 'sweet dreams'.

'Night then,' I yawn with a smile.

'Give me a call from Ravello.'

'Will do!'

I put down the phone, plump up my pillow and turn out the light. My mind is filled with fears about what tomorrow will bring and yet as I nestle down into the bed I burst out laughing in the darkness. I've just remembered my favourite Cleo/chocolate incident.

About a year ago she went to Bristol for the annual PhotoFinish conference and stayed up drinking with the dishy lads from the Bath branch, finally staggering back to her hotel room at 5.30a.m. By the time she'd performed her ablutions and changed into her nightie it was 6a.m. She then overslept so badly that the next morning she literally had to throw on her suit and run to the conference, no shower, nothing. As she took her seat the girl in the row behind tapped her on the shoulder and told her she had something stuck in her hair. It was the chocolate the maid had placed on the pillow! Now, with my mass of distracting curls I'd probably have got away with it but Cleo has poker-straight auburn hair, and though the chocolate had melted it was still half in its silver foil . . .

Anyway, it's unlikely to happen again as Cleo now eats everything within a two-mile radius of her bed, just to make sure she doesn't wake up with it stuck to her head.

I pull the covers up under my chin. God, I love that girl!

19

I've just had the worst night's sleep. I feel swampy-headed and leaden and grouchy. Not even the sight of last night's desserts on the breakfast buffet can cheer me.

My mother, of course, sprang out of bed with full-blown Julie Andrews *joie de vivre* and seeing her so 'perky', as Luca would say, is making me nauseous. I push away my crème caramel & cornflake combo and watch her scoop the last spoonful of mush from the skin of her baked apple. Everything is 'Delicious!' and 'Rejuvenating!' to her this morning. She turns her face to the sun and beams back at it. I just want to slump in a darkened room.

When I'm tired I just don't give a damn about anything. And my tolerance for my mother reaches dangerously low levels. When I tell her I'm convinced I didn't sleep one wink last night she responds with a cheery, 'At least you were resting!' I smash the shell of a boiled egg with excessive force. There is nothing restful about the teary-eyed hysteria you feel when you discover it's 4a.m. and you're the only awake person on the planet.

I was dozing quite happily until my mother got back from the Piazetta and then suddenly my pillow became a sack of unmixed concrete. No matter how much I battered and squished it I couldn't get comfortable. The more I told myself to relax, the more tense and panicky I became. I wanted to have a childish tantrum and stamp my feet. In fact I did do a quick number from *Riverdance* under the sheets trying to de-fidget my legs but it didn't work. I flipped from stomach to back, writhing as if I was wrestling an alligator. Finally I huffed to the bathroom, peered into my bloodshot eyes and angrily asked my reflection, 'WHY? Why can't I sleep?'

I suppose I did have a lot of stuff whizzing through my head after going to Vincenzo's house – not least wondering what my legacy will be when I die. Suddenly there seemed like a lot about my life that I wanted to change.

In the end I decided that if I was going to have to lie awake in the dark I would pretend I was in Luca's arms. But then I got all peeved and self-pitying over the fact that it would never happen for real.

'Okay, I'm just going to go and clean my teeth and then we can go,' Mum says, pushing back her chair and dropping her napkin on the table.

'I'm not coming to the shop today, I told you.'

Mum freezes for a moment and then sits back down. Looks like we're about to have that unfinished argument from last night.

'Kim, I—'

'I know you don't think it's a good idea but it's something I want to do.'

'I don't understand why,' she says, looking fretful.

'Look, I'm not doing this to upset you and I'm not going to cause a scene. I'm just going to drop by with the package.'

'She's seventy-three years old.'

'So?'

'I don't think she'll be prepared for you.'

'Good!' I smile.

My mother can tell I won't be budged. 'Where is it?'

I open my bag and show her.

'I just don't want you going over there upsetting yourself . . .'

'I won't.'

'Or her.'

I don't reply. I find it strange that my mother has no feelings of animosity towards Rosa. My only explanation is that she has been unfaithful too – they belong to the same anti-sisterhood. But I've never been the adulterer or the mistress. I'm still on my granny's side. I know that if she's looking down on me now she'd want me to go and challenge this woman and say the things she never got the chance to. I feel like I've been programmed for this moment from all those days of tea and Battenburg, listening to her relive her heartbreak, over and over and over. I listened so hard I felt her pain too. I felt the wrench as she left her husband just as I felt the wrench when my father left me. We understood each other.

199

'Will you call me after you've seen her?' Mum says, giving in. 'I'll be at the shop.'

I nod.

'Do you even know how to get there?' she suddenly flusters.

'Mario's written it all down for me.'

I get up and walk around the table to her, experiencing one of my rare pangs where I feel I should touch her. 'Just think of me as a delivery girl!' I tell her, placing my hand on her shoulder. 'Come on, what's your favourite line from *Runaway Bride* – you know when Julia Roberts scarpers from her wedding and jumps on a passing Federal Express van?'

Mum smiles faintly, 'Rita Wilson says, "Where do you think she's going?" '

'And your pin-up boy Hector Elizondo says . . .'

' "I don't know – but wherever it is she'll be there by 10.30 tomorrow morning!" ' she laughs.

I give her a quick hug. Now I'm on my feet I'd better keep moving. All I want to do is go back to bed but, having opened my big mouth, I'm now a woman on a mission. 'I'll see you later!'

'Seventy-three years old,' Mum reminds me as she waves me off.

I know you are supposed to feel sorry for someone because they are old, but I think it's all too easy to make excuses – it's too late, they're no longer accountable, they're too frail. I've decided I'm going to knock on this woman's door and say, 'Sorry Carmela couldn't make it. She sent me instead.'

And then, when she's done crossing herself, I'm going to listen to what she has to say.

'Wait!'

I'm savouring the last few moments of unobstructed movement in the hotel grounds before I have to swim against the tide of tourists heading for the Gardens of Augustus, when a voice halts me. I turn around to find Mario waving me down. 'I take you to the Marina Grande on my bicycle!' he calls.

'I don't think this would fit on your handlebars!' I say, grabbing my *sedere* (a.k.a. bottom).

'No, is motorbicycle, of course!' he says, now level with me.

'Oh. It's very kind of you . . .' I falter.

'I know.'

'But there's no need, I can get the *funicolare*.'

'You afraid?'

'Of your driving? Of course!'

'No, I am like little old man, I promise.'

'Shouldn't you be working?' I thought he had poolside duties during the day.

'It's my break.'

I study him. He doesn't look nearly so wolfish by day. 'Come on then,' I give in.

'You have to hold me very tight,' he nudges me as we head up Via Federico Serena.

I roll my eyes but I'm smiling. Every girl should have a Mario – an attractive man who flirts relentlessly with little or no encouragement.

'I am sorry if I offend you with the kiss in the laundry,' Mario says, doing his best to look remorseful.

'That's okay,' I say, dismissively. I'd rather not relive that awkward tussle.

'You're not angry?'

'No,' I say casting a glance down Via Longano as we pass. I wonder if Luca is at work yet.

'So tonight, maybe we can go for walk at midnight?'

I stop, hands on hips, mock indignant. 'How long is this going to go on?'

'What?'

'*You know!*'

'You mean me trying to make shaggy with you?' he says, unable to keep a playful twinkle out of his eye.

'Yes,' I say, trying to look stern.

'Until the day you leave.'

'Really?' I laugh.

'Yes, of course. I must keep trying.'

'Why?'

Mario thinks for a moment and then shrugs, 'That's just the way it is.'

'Oh.'

'This way please,' he says, motioning me to the left.

I step off the kerb and nearly collide with a scooter. The driver swerves dramatically and screeches to a halt. Mario bellows a few fine Italian expletives at him even though it's my fault. All rather embarrassing, especially when he removes his helmet and it's Luca.

Instant butterfly action.

'Kim! Are you all right?' he says, abandoning his scooter and leaping to my side.

'Are you?' I ask, checking that there's still just one scar on his lip.

'Don't worry about me,' he says, placing his hands on my shoulders. I think he's trying to soothe me but it's having the opposite effect.

Mario grunts.

'Er, Mario this is Luca,' I say, presuming he's waiting for an introduction. 'Luca this is Mario . . .'

'The barman!' Luca concludes.

'Yes,' I smile nervously, watching the two men eye each other with profound suspicion. 'I'm going to Ravello today – he's giving me a ride to Marina Grande.'

'That's where I'm going,' Luca grins. 'I can save him the trip.'

'No!' says Mario gruffly. 'It is no problem.'

'Really, I am happy to take her,' says Luca, wheeling his scooter towards me.

'My bike is bigger!' protests Mario.

I shake my head. 'Look, Mario, I may as well go with Luca, I don't want you to get into trouble at work.'

He scowls at me for a second before giving an overly carefree, 'Okay, ciao!' and turning on his heel. I watch him merge with the Piazzetta crowd, feeling horribly disloyal. Mario did offer first but Luca's right here with his bike and after all, he is, well . . . LUCA!!

20

I climb on the seat behind Luca, unsure of where to put my hands. As he rolls us into position I casually rest my palms on my knees like I do this sort of thing all the time, but as soon as the engine revs I instinctively clutch at him. My hands are now on his dark denim hips. That's not right. We're not doing the conga. As we gather speed I lean forward, shrinking behind his back but still resist wrapping my arms around his torso – I don't want to look too opportunistic and I know I'll cling too tight. Perhaps I can grab hold of the seat in front of him? I shunt forward, reach around him, find a nub and place both hands on it. We swerve slightly as we take a corner.

'Er, Kim . . .'

'Yes,' I say, pressing my face against the wind so I can hear him.

'That is not safe place for your hands.'

He looks down. I strain around and see that I am gripping his crotch. Oh my God. I snatch my hands back and latch them on to his shoulders as if I'm some kind of koala bear backpack.

'It was very nice, but . . .'

Oh-God-Oh-God. I scrunch my eyes tight, intending to stay in mortification mode for the rest of the journey but when we slow to allow a bus to pass he reaches back, takes my right arm and straps it around his waist. I tentatively add my left. He pats my interlocked hands, 'Now you are my safety belt!'

I let my head rest on his back, relieved and delighted. I'm not going to have to spend the rest of my life with a puce complexion. Everything's going to be all right.

When my mother and I snaked down to Marina Piccola in the cab, it was all high walls, hidden villas and tangled vines. This view has its arms flung wide! Every corner we take offers a breathtaking new vantage point revealing the layers of lemon groves and higgledy-piggledy houses staggering down to Marina Grande. My grouchy tiredness breezes away as we glide along the road. Who'd have thought that going 20m.p.h. could be so euphoric? We pass a cab bearing two older women with faces hoiked up from matching facelifts and I think to myself that I've gone one better than them – I've got a heart-lift.

'This is as far as I can take you,' says Luca, pulling up just shy of the marina. It's market day and the stripy-canopied stalls are heaped with the kind of man-made fibres and Constance Carroll make-up that you simply wouldn't think would be tolerated on Capri.

I let go of Luca and step off the bike. Immediately I feel disorientated and disconnected. I want to climb straight back on and wrap myself around him again, it felt so good. I take a breath and try to shake off the yearning.

'Thanks for the lift,' I chirp, trying not to look at his groin. Did I really go there? 'You're a good driver,' I add.

Hmmm. Not something you ever expect to say to an Italian.

'You're a good passenger,' he responds. I love his voice. So smoky and sensual. I experience a small shudder of lust. I wonder if I should apologize for groping him? Then again I'm not in the least bit sorry so I guess it wouldn't sound sincere.

Luca retrieves my bag from the lock-box on the back of the bike. I squish the escaping parcel back down inside but he's already seen the label.

'Are you going to see her?' he says, looking deep into my eyes.

I'm wary of his response but nod. 'Do you think it's a bad idea?' I ask.

'Bad? No. You wouldn't do anything bad, would you?'

'No,' I say. Is he asking me or telling me?

'You are just listening to your heart.'

'Never a good idea!'

'It's the only way to live,' he insists.

'Is it?' I ask.

He stares back at me. Are we still talking about my visit to Rosa?

I heave my bag on to my shoulder. 'Well, I'm listening to my heart but I'm not sure I understand what it's saying!' I joke. 'It wouldn't be the first time I've got the translation wrong.'

'The heart has many voices. Sometimes they speak at the same time. You choose which one you listen to.'

I look at him. 11a.m. Not a whiff of limoncella on his lips. 'How do you mean?' I frown, intrigued.

'We say people have a big heart or a warm heart or a cold heart . . .'

'Or a brave heart like Mel Gibson? Or a simple heart like the Three Degrees?' I say, babbling from embarrassment.

He gives me an 'if you like' shrug and continues, 'It makes it sound like we've been assigned a certain model. But you can't label a heart like that. A heart is capable of many emotions. It has many parts. People say "follow your heart" but it can pull you in more than one direction.'

This could explain the internal tug-of-war I feel when I'm with Luca.

'Your heart can want something and be afraid of it too,' he says, seeming to read my mind.

'Afraid of the pain it might feel?' I query.

'Yes.'

'So which part of your heart feels the pain?' I ask, morbid as ever.

'All of it. That's why it hurts so much.'

I peer at Luca, wondering what his story is. It's obvious he's had sadness and conflict in his life but I get the feeling he's mastered it. He seems in harmony with his heart. As for me, my heart has got some kind of death wish and I'm constantly trying to talk it back down from the ledge.

'Make sure you visit Villa Cimbrone while you are there,' Luca urges me, climbing back on to the bike. 'It is not far from Rosa's house.' He starts the engine. 'You know Greta Garbo?'

'Well, not personally . . .' Why oh why do I say these things?

'She used it as a secret love nest, I think you will like it.'

Hearing the words 'secret love nest' formed by Luca's lips is almost too much to bear. Suddenly I don't want to board the boat. I want to spend all day mooning over him at the shop. I have to stop him revving off. I reach out, inadvertently clipping his wing mirror. He looks up at me expectantly but self-preservation swoops in just in time. I give a cheery 'See you later!' wave and throw myself into the throng of schoolkids elbowing each other over the sparkly hairclips.

On the steamboat I count the hats on deck to keep from obsessing about Luca: eleven baseball hats, three sun visors, two canvas cloches, one bizarre wicker affair and a cowboy hat with a turquoise beaded band. Well, that occupied a few minutes at least.

For the majority of the blissfully leisurely journey there is no land in sight and I feel contentedly cut off from the world. However, as the mainland appears, I get a flutter of nerves. Amalfi is a jostle of tourists and as I make my way along the jetty I nearly get caught up in the surge for the boats taking trips to the Grotto Smeralda – the Emerald Grotto. After the magic of the Grotto Azzurra it's a tempting option but not why I'm here.

I cross the road to the al fresco bus station. If only waiting for buses back home involved ice-cream parlours and sea views. I gaze upwards and survey the green mountain twisting up the sky – that must be Monte Lattari, I tell myself. Somewhere up there on a small escarpment is Ravello. And somewhere down a side-street is Rosa the temptress, the ruin of my grandmother's life.

Feeling rather intrepid I look around for the appropriate bus to take me there. Blue, Mario said. It can't be this one though, surely? It has the SITA logo but ... Suddenly a display banner flashes the words RAVELLO and SCALA in electric orange – it is. Blimey! I wasn't exactly expecting to be travelling next to a woman with a basket of lemons on her head but equally I'm not prepared for this smart air-conditioned coach (complete with curtains and snazzy carpet-covered seats) offering to take me on a journey of twenty-five vertically challenging minutes for just 60p.

I board feeling like I'm getting the bargain of the year. The young blonde girl in front of me, however, is convinced this 7 kilometre trip is going to cost her her life. She cannot bear the sight of the plummet-to-your-death lushness of Dragon Valley and fixes her eyes on the dainty yellow flowers peeking from the rockery-style walls on the inside of the road. After ten minutes' mechanical mountaineering she seems to be calming down, but then she catches the driver using just one hand to steer while yawning excessively, and becomes hysterical again. Considering the road has all the random loops and squiggles of a swirl of chocolate sauce on a whippy ice-cream, she could well have cause for concern. It doesn't help matters when he answers his mobile phone – 'Pronto!' – while negotiating a precipice. At this, the poor girl becomes so distraught she wraps her head in the curtain and remains that way for the rest of the journey.

It's all worth it when we get to the top. The view looking down over the vineyards and trellises leading to the beaches of Maiori and the Gulf of Salerno is what postcards were invented for. I gawp, brimming with wonder at Mother Nature, then remember my mission and take out the map Mario has inked on a cocktail napkin. Standing in the main piazza with the church to my right, I take Via Dei Rufolo to my left. Here we go! For a second I wonder why I'm facing my grandmother's demons rather than my own but then I remind myself that I'll have plenty of time with my mother when I get back to Capri.

I'm only a couple of steps along the road to Rosa when I find myself veering into a ceramic shop. I can't tell whether I'm deliberately putting off the confrontation or genuinely interested in purchasing a pair of hand-painted olio & aceto bottles for Cleo, but either way I waste a further fifteen minutes dithering over a Parmesan dish. Then I spot a photograph of Ray Liotta with his arm around the proprietor. It's all the persuasion I need to buy all three items, though I instantly regret the extra weight in my bag as I begin striding up a shallow but taxing flight of stairs. I'm making reasonable progress (if you forgive the splintering of my knee joints and sweaty upper lip) when I hear male grunting ahead of me. Young grunts, middle-aged grunts and a been-smoking-since-I-was-ten wheezer.

Rounding the corner, I discover the reason – five men struggling down the narrow lane with a piano. It probably began life as a grand but now it's an upright, sucking itself in to avoid being bashed. It still only just fits: elbows are gashed against the rough stone walls, feet stumble down the uneven paving and they seem to be building momentum. I flatten myself against a doorway to give them passing room but they swerve through an archway before they reach me. I step forward and peer after them. They set the piano down with a thudding twang and chorus of '*Cretino!*' addressed to the young man who let go too soon. I catch his eye and scurry on as his voice chases after me with the words 'Concerto – questa sera 9p.m.!' Interesting. I would never consider going to a piano concert at home but it seems so appealing in this setting – up a back street, amid the peeling-pillared cloisters. Shame the last ferry back to Capri leaves at 6p.m.

Onwards and upwards, I'm feeling the burn from the increased gradient but decide to push through the pain barrier as Via Trinita is in sight. A few more paces and my thighs start trembling – agony! When will I learn to carry a bottle of water and a spare pair of legs? I'm dizzy and I want to rest but her sage-painted door is in sight. I surge for the finishing line.

When I look up the door is gone and a woman stands in its place.

21

I'm rooted to the spot, shocked to discover that the been-smoking-since-I-was-*five* wheeze is my own. My head throbs mercilessly. I can't take another step. The only escape would be to roll back down the hill.

The woman examines my face, looking bewildered. 'G-Gina?'

So much for the element of surprise. I hadn't counted on her clocking the family resemblance so swiftly. I try to speak but only a seal-like honk comes out.

'Momento!' she says, reappearing seconds later with a glass of water. I glug it back between pants.

'Thank you!' I manage huskily.

Hold on. This is not going according to plan. I'm supposed to be intimidating and superior, not quivering and grateful. I try to release my icepick-like grip on the door frame but my vision is swamped with swirly silver light and I reel into the wall.

'I think perhaps you need to sit down, Kim.'

Kim? *Kim*? How does she know my name? Did Luca tell her I was coming?

'It is Kim, isn't it?' she asks gently, leading me into her sitting room. 'Gina's daughter?'

'Carmela's granddaughter,' I say pointedly before collapsing into a soft damson armchair.

She gives an 'Oh I see' grimace before graciously offering more water.

'I'm fine now,' I tell her, though I am still disorientated.

She lowers herself on to the edge of the sofa, never taking her eyes off me. 'You have your mother's—'

'Hairline,' I interrupt.

'Also the—'

'Eyes,' I say with a Gee, never heard that before! sneer.

'Eyes, yes,' she confirms. 'At least the colour is the same.'

What does she mean by that?

Her eyes are darkest conker brown framed by liquorice lashes. Her mouth is feathered with lines but still forms a pretty pink Cupid's bow. She must have been stunning in her twenties. No wonder Vincenzo was lured.

'Go ahead,' she says, giving me a patient look.

I look blank.

'You want to ask me something?'

All this second-guessing me, she's throwing me off my game. I'll show her. 'I've brought you a parcel. We found it when we were going through Vincenzo's things,' I tell her.

I pull it out of my bag and hand it to her. She places it on her lap and lovingly smooths out the crinkles in

214

the brown paper wrapping. I wait for her to open it but she just sits there running her finger over Vincenzo's handwriting. It's only her name and address but it seems to spell out a secret love code to her.

As her eyes become glassy with tears it occurs to me that maybe I'm the reason she's holding back. 'Would you like to be alone to open it?' I ask, sitting forward, ready to leave.

'I know what it is,' she smiles, studying me for a moment as if she's deciding whether to reveal herself to me.

I wait. Afraid to move. I don't feel the antagonism I was expecting to feel. At the moment I just feel intrigued.

'It is a wedding dress,' she says simply.

'Your wedding dress?' I ask, realizing how little I know about the woman sitting before me.

'It was bought for me but I never wore it.'

'Did Vincenzo buy it?'

She nods. 'In Milan. Every year he asked Carmela for a divorce and every year she said no.'

With good reason! I snort inwardly.

'Then one day he came back from a fashion-buying trip and he said he had found the perfect dress for me. He said that even if Carmela would never grant the divorce she could not deprive us of the moment when we could look at each other and know that we were man and wife in our hearts. He wanted me to put the dress on but I could not do it.'

'Because of the guilt?' I suggest.

'Guilt?' She looks confused.

I summon the spirit of Carmela and force out the words, 'You must have felt guilty for breaking up his marriage.'

Rosa blinks at me. Instantly I feel uneasy. Now she's ready to tell.

'Do you want to hear the truth?' she asks.

'Your version of it?' I challenge.

'I tell you what happened and you decide.'

I nod. It's what I've come for, after all.

She settles back into the sofa. 'I met Vincenzo when I was sixteen years old. I loved him the first moment I saw him and he loved me. But he was hot-blooded. I would not sleep with him. I knew he was the only man for me but I wanted everything to be perfect so I told him that we should wait. He agreed but he would get *so* . . .'

I raise an eyebrow as she searches for a euphemism.

'*Hot,*' she sighs. 'One day we argue and he goes back to Capri and finds the girl who is always trying to tempt him, always telling him he should be with her and not with me. She is older and . . .'

I feel a horrible sense of foreboding.

'. . . that night she give him what I would not,' Rosa looks down at her black lace cuff. 'The next day he comes back to me. He confesses and he cries. I cry. But I forgive. He says he will never see her again. Four weeks later she tells him she is pregnant.'

My heart is thumping. 'She . . . ?'

'Carmela,' she confirms.

My thoughts collide as they try to order themselves:

216

Carmela was the temptress. My mother was conceived on a one-night stand.

'Vincenzo has no choice – he leaves me and marries her.'

'Did he love her?' I say, grasping at straws. 'At all?'

'He tried to. She said she loved him enough for both of them. She always wanted him and she got him but she was so afraid to lose him she would cling so tight . . .'

I've been brought up with such a different version of the story: Carmela was blissfully married to her one true love and Rosa deliberately destroyed their union. 'She said you . . .' I don't finish my sentence.

Rosa looks at me but says nothing, kind enough not to say, 'She lied' out loud.

'So what happened then?'

'We did not speak for five years. I felt that if this was the way life had to be then he should be committed to her, and he felt I should try to make a new life for myself. It was hard,' she sighs. 'Then one day I was visiting my good friend Rafaella in Positano and we were shopping and I saw him at the end of the street. By the time that we drew level I knew that nothing had changed for me – he turned my heart to gold all over again. In a way I did not even mind the ache I felt when, after just a few words, we walked on because it proved to me that our love was eternal. I knew then that the feelings would never go away and that I would always carry my love for him. It was not something to forget or let go of, it was something to be treasured.'

I look at Rosa, amazed she could be so philosophical when fate had been so cruel.

'Didn't you cry?'

'Of course!' she laughs. 'Against how I felt when I was with him I was only half alive all those years but you know, you get used to it. You think maybe you exaggerate in your head how good it was when you were together and then you see him again . . .' she sighs, looking luminous with love: 'And you know that it really was that high and that bright.'

I can't help but smile too.

'It was only a day after Positano that he came to my door.'

I look at Rosa expectantly.

She nods. 'It began again. The Gods decide. For me there was no one else.'

I sigh. In a way it seems right that they were reunited. Then I feel a pang of disloyalty to Carmela. Every day they were together Vincenzo would have to go home to her and lie.

'He wanted to try and keep his promise to both of us,' Rosa explains. 'It was not easy. He was trying to be everything to three women in his life – to Carmela, to me and to Gina. He wanted to be the perfect father. Gina is what kept him going in our first years apart.'

I swallow hard, picturing my mother as a little girl.

'I think we should have some tea,' Rosa suggests, getting to her feet.

'Do you have any limoncello?' I find myself asking.

'It is yellow poison!' she cries in disgust.

'I know but—'

'I have something better. Stronger,' she says, opening a cherrywood drinks cabinet.

'*Stronger?*' Now I'm afraid.

'Grappa,' she says, handing me a small glass of clear liquid.

I take a slug. My body shudders and my face contorts. 'Back home we call this meths!' I croak.

'Is good, yes?' Rosa pours a glass for herself and returns to the sofa.

'Does my mother know any of this?' I ask. 'You know, that you were her father's first love?'

'I don't think so.'

'Didn't Vincenzo ever try to tell her?'

'At first, things happened so fast. When Carmela found out that he had been seeing me she started to pack straight away. It did not take her long – it was as if she always knew the day would come.'

Poor Carmela. I wonder if she was ever really happy, even when she was with Vincenzo.

'And at the marina Carmela allow Vincenzo no time alone with Gina to say goodbye.'

'But why didn't he . . . I mean . . .' I try to think of what he could have said to make my mother understand.

Rosa shrugs. 'He knew that Carmela needed 100 per cent of Gina's support at that time and he did not want to make things complicated for her. He thought it best to wait until they had both calmed down but then of course once Carmela left he had no way to contact Gina.'

For the first time I imagine the situation from

Vincenzo's point of view and I feel a sadness seep through me.

'The first he heard from Gina was eleven years later – she wrote to tell him that she was getting married.'

'To my father?'

'That's right. Then of course she sent him a picture when you were born – every year she like to send a picture of the two of you together on your birthday.'

'Did she ever send pictures of my father?'

'A few at Christmas.'

'Did she tell Vincenzo why he left?'

Rosa gives a sympathetic smile. 'She wrote and told him that she understood why he had done what he did – even though she didn't really know the full story – and for the first time she gave an address to write back to.'

'So why didn't he?'

'Oh he did.'

'She told me he never contacted her!'

Rosa sighs. 'Carmela found his letter when she was babysitting you one night. She became hysterical. Poor Gina, she was so torn. She wrote back to Vincenzo and told him she would continue to write to him but he must never reply.'

I never knew my mother had made such sacrifices for Carmela. She never seemed that sympathetic to her misery. But then maybe sympathy wears thin after nearly fifty years.

'Did he keep her letters?' I ask.

'Oh yes. Every one.'

'I didn't see them when we were going through his things.'

'He keeps them—' Rosa stops to correct herself, 'he *kept* them at the shop. Most likely they are still there in the desk.'

'Why would he keep them at work?'

'Luca – you know Luca?' she asks.

My stomach flips. 'Yes,' I say holding my breath.

'He used to like Vincenzo to read them to him.'

'Why?'

'He always wanted to travel. He loved to hear the stories of this bold girl who would have all these adventures in different countries – Germany, Japan, Sweden . . .'

'M-me?' I stammer.

'Of course – who else? I think he had a little crush.'

'On *me*?' I'm incredulous.

'To him you were like an explorer. You went to the places he dreamed about.'

I take a moment to try and view myself as a bold adventurer. It just doesn't wash – I suppose my trips could *sound* jet-set but in reality they were just jobs. It's not as if I ever got to see much of the country I was in, though I would have liked that. In the beginning I used to get so excited about visiting somewhere new that I would negotiate with the booker to get a flight back a few days later than everyone else. After they'd gone, I'd check out of the Holiday Inn or whichever could-be-anywhere hotel we were in, and find somewhere small with a bit of character so I could really get a taste of the culture. Those were good days. I always came back full of stories. Now I come to think of it, my friends were pretty impressed that I'd found my way around Berlin or Cannes by myself. I seemed to have a charmed existence. But then the jobs became more plentiful and there just wasn't time. Initially I took to sneaking out for night tours of the city but pretty soon I got into the habit of staying in the hotel watching cable like everybody else. What a waste.

'Why didn't Luca travel himself?' I ask Rosa, fantasizing about bumping into him on a bridge in Prague . . .

'He didn't have those kind of opportunities. Luca ran with a bad crowd. Bad boys, bad girls. People going nowhere. But in his head he would, have adventures, dream . . . you have seen his body?'

'Yes. Well. I mean. You know, on the boat . . .'

Rosa smiles. 'His body is painted with his imagination. Each tattoo is like a promise to himself.'

'What kind of promise?' I ask, remembering unicorns and hearts.

'A promise to keep believing that there is magic and love in the world. He had some dark times.'

'And then he met his wife,' I venture, torturing myself with the idea that she somehow saved him.

'And you met Tomas.'

'*What?* I can't believe you know about him!'

'Your mother wrote and told Vincenzo that you had finally met someone who loved you nearly as much as she did.'

'She said that?' I blush.

222

'Yes. Luca was crazy-jealous!' Rosa laughs. 'Vincenzo used to tease him.'

'Oh no!'

'Not to be cruel – Luca said himself he was being foolish! He couldn't understand why he spent so much time thinking about someone he had never met.'

My blush deepens as I reflect back on our first meeting and the way he looked at me. No wonder there was a sense of familiarity and insight in the way he spoke to me. He's known me for years.

Suddenly I feel sick. If only I'd come to Capri sooner!

'It didn't last with Tomas,' I protest helplessly, hopelessly.

'Of course, Luca was married by then anyway.'

'How did he meet his wife?' I ask.

'He went over to a club in Sorrento with some friends. I think she was the first British girl he had been with.'

'She's *British*!' I screech. 'His wife is British?'

Rosa looks slightly taken aback but I can't control myself: 'Who is she?' I bark.

'Tanya,' she shrugs.

'Tanya? *Tanya*?!?' I squawk. I had her pegged as a Carlotta or Estella.

'She was working as a travel rep.'

I roll my eyes, flumping back into the armchair with an aggrieved wail.

'More grappa?' Rosa offers.

I don't reply. I'm still inexplicably outraged.

'I bring the bottle,' Rosa decides.

22

I'm sitting amid Rosa's lace and trinkets trying to work out why the fact that Luca's wife is British has thrown me so much. Is it because it makes it all the more real that she could have been me? In a way Tanya was a substitute for me. I feel sick. Why didn't I get here sooner?

'I was about to go to the piazza for lunch but now you are here I could prepare some pasta, if you like?'

My 'That would be lovely' response is drowned out by an enthusiastic stomach snarl. 'Can I do anything to help?' I add, shyly.

'It takes minutes,' Rosa says. 'Please sit down.'

'How come there were no pictures of you at Vincenzo's house?' I ask, sliding on to one of the blue wooden chairs by the kitchen table.

'I took them all away,' she says, filling a pan with boiling water. 'When I heard your mother was coming over, I did not want to upset her.'

'Did you know her when she was a girl?'

'I met her just a few times but of course Vincenzo talk about her all the time. She was very brave girl.'

'Brave?'

'Always cheerful on the outside even when she was worried or sad.'

'What did she have to worry about?' I ask. The way Mum tells it, her childhood was idyllic.

'It's not so easy to have your parents fighting all the time . . .'

'Carmela said they never . . .' I tail off, remembering I've been fed a majorly edited version of my grandmother's relationship with her husband. 'I don't think my mother ever gets depressed now,' I note, trying to look on the bright side.

'Then she has perfected her mask,' Rosa smiles.

My face falls. Is it possible that my mother experiences inner turmoil? That she too gets scared and lost? I fret for a minute and then dismiss the notion – the only concerns my mother has is what to wear and 'Will he call?'

'Parmigiano?' Rosa offers as she places a tangle of spaghetti in front of me. I accept a generous sprinkling. We eat. It's *delicious*. Rosa smiles at the oily orange lashes on my chin and offers me a second helping. Afterwards we share a nectarine and she shows me photos of her and Vincenzo. The difference in the expression on his face compared to the pictures I've seen of him with Carmela is marked. With her there was a sense of formality and what I can now identify as trying-too-hard tension. With Rosa he has a look of serenity and devotion. I feel more sorry for my grandmother than ever now. She thought she'd won when she married him but she must always have

225

known he loved Rosa more. That's got to be hard to live with. In a way the best thing she did was leave the island. If only she could have let go of Vincenzo and moved on instead of letting her feelings for this man dominate her whole life.

I pick up a picture of Vincenzo relaxing on a bench with a cat sprawled belly up by his side. He must have been in his thirties, Luca's age, when it was taken. I feel like I'm seeing him as a man for the first time. It's only now I realize how handsome he was and acknowledge that my head would have turned in his direction if I'd been alive then. I look into his kind eyes.

'He looks so wise!' I say. 'I wish I'd met him.'

'He was often with you in his thoughts,' Rosa tells me.

It's strange to think that these two people I'd never met would speak of me, that my name was said out loud in Capri long before I arrived here. Stranger still to think that Luca . . . I look at my watch: 4p.m.

'You have to leave?' Rosa asks. I nod, though it's going to take a combination of tenacity and old-fashioned exertion to extract myself from the embrace of Rosa's sofa.

She peers out of the window. 'The weather does not look good. I hope you do not get easily seasick.'

'Actually I have to go up to Villa Cimbrone before I catch the ferry. I promised Luca . . .' Suddenly I feel embarrassed saying his name out loud.

'You must hurry then before it rains. It is just five minutes more up the hill.'

'For you, perhaps! You must have legs like an

226

Olympic athlete living around here,' I say, shaking my head.

Rosa laughs, affectionately cupping the side of my face in her hand. Her touch is so light and un-needy. 'Thank you for coming here today, I am so happy that we met.'

I want to say the same but feel a strange twist of guilt as though Carmela is watching me. Instead I swig back the last of my grappa, give a rasping, 'Cin Cin!' and head for the door.

'You never did marry Tomas, did you?' Rosa asks, stopping me in my tracks.

'No,' I say turning back. 'I never married anyone.'

'When you do—'

'If,' I interrupt.

'When,' Rosa insists. 'You will need this.' She holds out the brown package to me.

'What? No, no I couldn't!' I protest, backing away.

'Please, I want you to have it,' she insists.

'Really Rosa, I can't take it. It means so much to you.'

'I have beautiful memories, I do not need a dress I will never wear.'

'But I'll never wear it! And I don't mean because of the marriage thing, I just . . . well, I wouldn't fit in it for one thing.'

Rosa tuts. 'I am an old lady now so I shrink but at your age I was same size as you.'

'I don't think so,' I splutter.

'Trust me. I am a woman. A woman who spent her

227

life with a man in the fashion industry – you think I can't tell what size you are?'

That shuts me up.

She holds the package out to me again: 'I don't have a daughter. I don't have a granddaughter. But today I have you. And I would like to you accept my gift.'

The tears well up. I wasn't prepared for any of this. I frown and falter and then my eyes spill over into a sob.

Rosa catches me in her arms and holds me tight. 'Is that a yes?' she asks.

I nod into her shoulder, bristling my hair against her blouse.

'Good. You can open it the day you kiss your true love!'

The walk to Villa Cimbrone takes me twenty minutes. I have to stop twice en route to get some control over my breathing. And my emotions. Resting against a wall overlooking a vineyard of dusty black grapes I feel a warm ache from the affection Rosa has shown me. Then I become weak with yearning to have what she had with Vincenzo. It's been a long time since I was around a real-life relationship that inspired me, I've always despaired of my mother's partners (although Platinum Man does show some promise) and I'd certainly given up even hoping that true love would find me. Now the longing for it spreads through me like a forest fire.

Then again that could be the grappa.

Continuing through a wrought iron gate and down a path with a leafy blanket thrown over the wall to my right and vivacious palm trees thriving in the gardens to my left, I come to a halt at the bottom of a short flight of steps. At the top is a vast doorway, big enough for a carriage to pass through. Perhaps once it had grand castle gates but now it is boarded with greying planks of wood, with a smaller door set like a panel in the right-hand side. It all seems very *Alice in Wonderland* though I realize the small door is actually full size as I pass through. Into another kingdom . . .

The villa itself is a big block of sandy stone with a pointy parapet, crenellated turret and courtyard spilling over with creeping vines and historic curios. I can't help wishing Luca were here with me so we could stroll hand in hand like the other visitors with their pac-a-macs and guidebooks, taking alternate breaths of the rose-scented air.

There's more than one route around the gardens but I'm instinctively drawn down the 'Alley of Immensity', a low-walled avenue which appears to stretch like a runway into open sky. Ceres, goddess of the harvest, greets me at the end and directs me through an arch to the most striking vista I've ever seen: a long, broad balcony with seven proudly aligned marble busts silhouetted against regal mountains and an indigo sea. We're so high that a plane flying by appears to be at the same level as us. This is the Terrazza dell'Infinito – the Terrace of Infinity.

I walk up to the first bust and inspect his face. The once smooth marble has worn away leaving a pocked complexion with a gritty texture, as though he has been moulded from sugar or fine sand. A blotch of lichen has given his cheek a yellowy-orange birthmark and a charcoal moss has smudged his toga with a random pattern. Peering over his shoulder I see stepped vineyards and trellises encircling the contours of the hillside like layers of lace on a petticoat. On the more curvaceous corners it more closely resembles the wavy ridges of an oyster shell. There can't be any easy way to till that soil. And how do you go about building a house on raggedy slopes like these? You'd have to employ stuntmen·as well as construction workers.

I give Beppe, as I call him, a wink and move on to the next bust – a woman with a pout and an up-do. Then the next. Bless, erosion has left the poor chap with a broken boxer's nose. The other busts (one with parted lips and a cobweb spun between them, another with the naturally occurring grey streaks in the marble looking like veins on his neck) are busily posing for photos with tourists, complaining slightly about the conditions. (They've got a point – today's overcast skies can't do them nearly as much justice as an opulent blue backdrop.)

I'm moving towards the end of the balcony when a startling series of popping explosions – like a gunshot, whip-crack and car backfiring all in one – throw everyone into confusion. The words 'What was that?' echo down the balcony in at least four different languages. 'It sounded like a bomb,' opines the Scottish gent beside me. Then a threatening rumble of thunder reverberates around us and a jagged dagger of electric-white lightning fractures the now dark purple sky.

Everyone scurries for cover as the rain starts. Except me.

Finally some weather to reflect my mood.

I step up to the edge of the balcony. The sea below thrashes angrily. Forget the hydrofoil, we're going to need an ark to get back to Capri. Which reminds me – I was supposed to have called my mum hours ago. If she wasn't worried then she will be now – all behind the mask of course, not letting anyone see.

Five more minutes enjoying the storm and I'll head back.

Making sure my wedding dress package is protected from the rain I walk alone to the very end of the balcony. In this dim light the soldier bust looks a little like Luca, something about the mouth . . . I take a step closer. If I stood on tiptoe I could kiss him. Could he count as my true love? I reach up and gently touch his cold white face and run my fingers along his clearly defined collarbone. If he were real I would be able to feel his breath on me now. I look at his mouth again.

Just one kiss . . .

23

Out of the corner of my eye I sense movement at the other end of the balcony and swivel round. My stomach flips before I even consciously identify the moody grey shape moving towards me.

'I think that sculpture was about to kiss you!' Luca laughs.

'And you had to barge in and ruin the moment!' I mock-curse, praying he won't notice how the raindrops sizzle and hiss as they hit my furiously blushing skin.

'Oh! I didn't realize you *wanted* him to,' says Luca, feigning awkwardness.

'Are you kidding? This is my dream man – disembodied and with a broken nose – isn't that every girl's fantasy?'

'Okay, then I leave!' He pretends to go.

I laugh. 'No, you can stay.'

'No, really – I have to go *schleeck*!' he makes a throat-slitting motion with his hand.

I laugh, feeling strangely flattered. Gee, you'd cut your head off for li'l ol' me?

He steps forward, placing his hands on my shoulders. 'Kim, you are soaking.'

'I think it's the rain,' I tell him.

He rolls his eyes. His beautiful blue eyes.

'Are you going to tell me why you're here?' I ask. 'You know – of all the balconies in all the world . . .'

He tilts his head to one side and looks directly at me. 'I am here for you.'

My heart stops.

'Your mother . . .'

Instant dismay.

'My mother . . .' I repeat suspiciously.

'She was afraid for you – the storm is coming and they cancel the ferries. She ask me to come over on my boat and make you safe.'

Make me safe. I like that.

'I'm sorry to put you out!' I apologize.

'Put me out?' He sounds confused.

'Non voglio disturbare,' I translate for him.

'It is not a problem. Tonight your mother looks after Ringo and I look after you.'

'Tonight?'

'We have to stay here in Ravello. The sea is too rough to sail.'

I feel a rush of adrenalin. The situation seems both dangerous and enticing.

'Of course, if I'd known you had –' he nods towards the bust I was about to kiss, 'Salvatore here to protect you . . .'

'Actually, I think I might prefer Fabio,' I say, pointing to the next bust along.

'No,' he objects. 'Fabio is no good. He has bad hair.'

'He stands head and shoulders above most men I know!' I joke. Badly.

Luca ducks in between the two busts and mirrors their pose. 'How do I compare?'

I study his jutting jaw and high-rise cheekbones and tell him, 'I think the sculptor who worked on you was . . . what's the Italian word for amateur?'

'Genioso!' he deadpans.

I go along with him. 'Whoever created your face was a genius!'

He beams at me.

'Kim?'

'Yes?'

'Can we get out of this rain?'

He takes my hand and we hurtle down the Alley of Immensity – the wisteria twisting around the pergola offers us occasional shelter but by the time we reach the villa we are sopping. There is something so liberating about not cowering from the rain. I want to stand out in it and let it teem over my face and body but Luca pulls me into the shelter of the cloister.

If this was a movie we'd be kissing now. Instead he says, 'Did you know Villa Cimbrone was once owned by the same man who designed Big Ben?'

'No!' I laugh. 'Are you serious?'

'Yes. His name was Lord Grimthorpe – that is his coat of arms.' Luca points to the heraldry in the courtyard and continues: 'He was a Cambridge graduate who became a lawyer and then president of the British Horological Institute.'

234

Luca's command of English amazes me. Even I can't say 'horological'.

'As in clocks?' I clarify.

'Yes. He bought the villa in 1904 and he enrich the gardens with temples and statues and medieval antiques . . .'

'What's that?' I ask, pointing at a stone wall-carving featuring seven spooky faces.

'The Seven Mortal Sins,' he says. 'Would you like to stay here?'

The segue throws me. Would I like to stay in Greta Garbo's secret love nest with the sexiest man I have ever encountered? My eyes widen. 'Y-yeah! That would be amazing!'

'Wait here, I go ask if they have rooms available.'

I'm slightly disappointed to hear the 's' on the end of the room. The grappa and the rain and the running have got me giddy. I smile delightedly and spin around on the spot, filled with anticipation.

But Luca returns looking glum. 'Nothing,' he sighs. 'We must go into town.'

I try not to look too disappointed and brace myself for another drenching. We are just heaving open the gate when a voice cries, 'Signor!'

A woman beckons us up to the main building. 'One couple leave us in an hour. If you return in two hours I could let you have their room.'

'We need two rooms,' he reminds her.

I find myself emitting a reticent, 'Ummm . . .'

Luca turns to me.

'We could, you know, um . . . it would be so incredible to stay here and if perhaps . . .'

'It has two beds,' she announces, putting me out of my misery.

Luca turns back for my approval.

I nod.

'We'll take it!' Luca smiles.

'Come back around 8p.m.'

'Grazie mille!'

Luca takes my arm and leads me through the gate. 'I think you are a different Kim to the one I meet on Capri. Perhaps you tell me what happened to you today?'

So I do.

Not all of it, of course.

I don't tell him that I have discovered that a boy called Luca once had a crush on a girl called Kim.

I call my mother before dinner to reassure her that I have neither drowned nor sent Rosa to an early grave. She's relieved on both counts and delighted to hear that we are staying over at Villa Cimbrone.

'You were so lucky to get two rooms,' she notes. 'It's such a special place it's normally booked up months in advance.'

I don't correct her. I can barely think the thought that I'll be sharing a room with Luca, let alone say it out loud. Even so, I'm relishing the fact that our evening has no end. It feels good to know for certain that he won't spring a 'Well, goodnight!' on me and

236

jump into a cab, leaving me feeling miffed and adrift with unfulfilled longing.

So many times I've felt cut short on dates. You know that feeling when you are hanging on someone's every word and being as charming and attentive and seductive as you possibly can be and you are convinced a kiss is imminent and then they suddenly pull the rug from under you by saying they have to get up early for work the next day or run to catch the last train. Whatever exit excuse they choose you know that if they felt the same way as you they would stay up all night irrespective of the consequences. As they get up to leave you either do the 'Me too! Must dash!' thing and summon all your bravado to scoot through an uninspired farewell scene before blubbing your way home on the bus; or you get clingy, begging them to stay for one more drink and daring yourself to make a last-minute lunge. Ugh! I hate that feeling as your dignity slips away and you scrabble to turn things around, anything but acknowledge that there is not going to be a happy ending. You may well be seeing them at the office coffee machine tomorrow but it still feels like this is your Only Chance to make something happen.

Well, I don't have to face that tonight with Luca. He's going to see me through until the morning. I won't be lying alone in my bed wondering what went wrong. I'll be lying there next to him, loving knowing that he's right there, not going anywhere. Nothing has to happen. Nothing *can* happen. Nothing must happen. But the thought of spending all night with him is making me deliriously happy.

*

The rain is still coming down as though whole bath-tubs of water are being tipped from upstairs windows so we duck into the first restaurant we come across. The waiters don't seem to mind that we are dripping on their floor, in fact one by the name of Eugenio seems particularly keen on mopping me dry. 'You are rainbow!' he exclaims, dabbing my face. 'Your clothes have the water but your smile have the sunshine!'

I positively beam at the compliment and when the *maître d'* shows us to the cosiest nook in the place I feel like a honeymooner. I love the fact that we must look like a couple. A man and a woman sitting down to candlelit dinner – hardly a remarkable sight and yet for me it is a rare pleasure. It's always been take-aways in front of the TV rather than 'Table for two, preferably the booth'. I could count the number of romantic dinners I've had in my life on the prongs of a fork.

Over a feast of garlicky bruschetta, orange-flavour noodles, swordfish, rughetta and sublime melone gelato, Luca asks me about my travels and relishes my descriptions of foreign foods and fashions. I think about how exciting it would be to explore a new country with him. He has such an enquiring mind, such an eye for detail. I've been on holiday with two boyfriends and the closest either of them got to taking a day trip was swimming to the deep end of the pool and back. I'd go off exploring on my own and come back full of stories and encounters and I'd be lucky if they could even tell me how many beers they'd had since I'd been gone.

'Limoncello?' the waiter offers as he clears our

dessert plates. I'm already in a smoochy haze from the red wine I swore I would resist; anything more would just push me over the edge.

'Do you have grappa?' I ask.

'Sì, we have three kind – Verduzzo, Chardonnay and Rebbolla.'

'One of each!' Luca decides for me.

I slump down on the table at the prospect of feeling even more swimmy and squint up at Luca, trying to bring him into focus. 'Do you know my all-time favourite scene in a movie?' I slur.

'Tell me.'

'It's in *The Pink Panther*. David Niven has got Claudia Cardinale drunk on champagne and she is flat-out on this leopard-print rug with her head resting on the animal head and she complains that she can't feel her lips, and . . .' I trail off, suddenly embarrassed.

'Yes?'

'And he kisses her until she can,' I say in a small voice.

Luca smiles. 'Can you feel your lips?'

'Yes. They are buzzing,' I tell him, prodding them with my fingers.

'Just let me know if they go numb.'

I perk up. What does that mean? Does he mean . . . ? Did he just . . . ? A twister of desire swirls through my body. How do I respond to that? I search for something subtly seductive to say.

'So, what's your favourite drunken movie scene?' I blunder, ruining the moment.

He thinks for a second.

'Have you seen *Come September*? Is old movie with Gina Lollobrigida and Rock Hudson, made 1961.'

'Is that the one where he comes over to Italy to find that his butler has turned his private villa into a hotel?'

'Exactly!'

'Remind me,' I egg him on.

'There are two American school groups staying – one of boys led by Bobby Darin and one of girls—'

'Led by Sandra Dee!' I recall.

'Rock is determined to keep them apart so the boys try to get him out of the way by getting him drunk. They think they can out-drink him because to them he's old man but he obliterates them! He is the victor but once again he loses what he really wants...'

'Which is to spend the night with the lovely Gina!'

Luca nods. 'So he wakes up all frustrated with this hangover and his butler brings him special drink which he says is "*Perfect for the morning after ...*'

'*... when there hasn't been a night before!*" ' I complete the line and we chuckle together.

'Do you watch a lot of movies?' I ask as Luca pushes the final drop of grappa over to me.

'Yes, I like to. It is way of travelling in your mind. I have not had so many adventures as you but I go to the cinema and I enter another world.'

I smile. Everything he says sounds so romantic.

'Did you know Rosa was in a movie once?' Luca asks me. 'Just a small part. Italian movie ...'

'Really?'

'Yes. Vincenzo was so jealous because the lead actor

was completely infatuated with her but at the time he could not object because he was married to Carmela.'

'So what happened?

'She said no to the actor. She was always true to Vincenzo.'

'It must have been very difficult for her,' I venture. 'Being so in love with him yet having to accept that he was with another woman.'

'It is sad story, yes? Also for him – a man in love with one woman his whole life, but married to another.'

Luca and I look at each other.

'Shall we get the bill?'

24

'Cleo?'

'Yes.'

'Is that my dearest darlingest master-chefest flat-mate?'

'You're not drunk by any chance, are you, Kim?'

'Mmm-huh!' I confirm.

'Good girl!'

'I'm more than drunk, I'm *grappa-d*!' I exclaim.

'You're what?'

'It's this liqueur. I'm going to bring a case-full back. They make it from distilled grapes and—'

'Kim!' Cleo cuts in.

'What?'

'You're drunk and you're not crying. This can only mean one thing!'

I cup my hand over the receiver and murmur, 'I'm about to spend the night in Garbo's secret love nest with Luca!'

'Oh my God!' Cleo shrieks.

I shriek back.

'How did this happen?' she asks.

'It's fate, Cleo! Do you think it counts as infidelity if they loved you first?'

'What are you talking about?'

No time for the full Rosa saga so I cut to the chase: 'Just tell me if I should—'

'Go for it!'

'*Really?*'

'Yeah – I've been thinking about this – remember back at the Arco Naturale Luca said he had two things to get up for in the morning?'

'Yeah . . .'

'They were the shop and Ringo. Not *her*. No mention of his beloved wife!'

'Well, I suppose he's not literally getting up for her at the moment cos she's not here,' I reason.

'Maybe they're having a trial separation.'

'D'you think?' I brighten, feeling reassured.

'Anyway, what do you mean he loved you first?' she bleats.

'He's coming back from the loo,' I hiss. 'I've got to go!'

'Kim, tell me!'

'Byeeeeee domestos goddess!'

'Domestic!'

'Domani!'

I clunk down the phone and slide over to Luca.

'Ready to go?' he asks.

'Yup!' I beam.

We step outside and discover the rain has abated, leaving a clear sky and clean-scented air.

'And now for the climb!' says Luca, contemplating the road leading back to Villa Cimbrone.

I take a deep breath and stomp up determinedly but within seconds I look like I'm walking in treacle. Every foot forward requires excessive effort.

'You walk like an old lady!' Luca teases.

'I wish!' I laugh. 'The old ladies round here skip up these hills!'

'It's true,' Luca acknowledges.

'I feel like I'll topple backwards if I straighten up,' I say, explaining my hunched posture.

'I help you,' says Luca, dropping behind me. He places his two hands firmly on my back. 'Now walk!'

I take one step. And then another and another. With Luca taking care of my body weight I only have to worry about my feet. All at once I'm turbo-charged! After a few minutes I experiment with leaning back into his hands. He groans with the strain. I am practically horizontal when Luca releases me for a second and then catches me in his arms. We fall about giggling and tumble on to the pavement.

Quietening down, we hear the soft strains of a piano.

'Wagner,' Luca notes.

'The concerto!' I gasp, looking at my watch. 10p.m.! It started an hour ago but it's still worth it. I clamber to my feet, hauling Luca up from the pavement. 'Come on!'

We surge up the hill, round the corner and then compose ourselves before tiptoeing into the open-air courtyard. Every face is turned towards the pianist, utterly rapt, and we creep in unnoticed.

'I'm not sure I can stand upright!' I whisper, swaying unsteadily as I realize all the seats are taken.

'We lean on this wall . . .' Luca says, taking my hand.

All through dinner I felt such a need to touch him – even if he brushed my arm reaching for the balsamic vinegar I'd feed off the sensation. It all seemed so tantalizing. Now I get the pay-off – the wall is gritty and dirty so he places his back to it then manoeuvres me so that I am leaning back against his chest. It reminds me of reclining on him in the Blue Grotto boat, only then I was tentative, practically trying to levitate above him. This time I relax into his body, loving the security of his arms around me. Now he is my seatbelt.

The music is beautiful. As I listen my limbs go slack and my heart feels suspended in space. It's all the more poignant for knowing that Wagner partly composed *Parsifal* right here in Ravello. On the sad notes I feel as if a great weight is pressing down on my chest. My hand creeps up to my heart and my eyes prickle.

I'd forgotten just how powerful music can be, triggering emotions whether you like it or not. You can't choose how you respond and it's impossible to quash a feeling once it hits. Some songs seem to stretch and twist your internal organs and induce an almost suffocating swimminess. *Pray* by Take That gets me every time. And *I'm Like A Bird* by Nelly Furtado. But most killer of all is *Starmaker* by the Kids from Fame. I mean it! If the Backstreet Boys re-recorded this it would finish me off altogether.

Cleo's got far cooler music tastes. For her it's *Yellow* by Coldplay.

'What was that?' asks Luca, his face next to mine.

I look at him blankly.

'You said something about the stars.'

My hand flies to my mouth. 'Tell me I wasn't singing!' I beg.

He smiles.

Oh the shame! We're at a classical recital and I'm dubbing Coldplay over the tinkling ivories.

He ruffles my hair and leans his jaw on my shoulder. 'Are you warm enough?' he asks.

'Yes,' I sigh, snuggling into his centrally heated embrace. He just feels so comfortable. So safe.

I only become conscious of the sexual tension between us when the concerto ends and everyone files out, leaving the prospect of going to our room at the villa at the forefront of our minds.

We linger, looking up at the stars, seeing how they shine for us, until Luca finally speaks.

'Are you tired?' he asks.

I frown, undecided.

'Do you want to go to bed?'

I raise an eyebrow.

Two entirely different questions, I think you'll agree.

The Villa Cimbrone receptionist leads us to the intimate sanctuary that will be our room for the night.

'This is Viola,' she smiles, setting a candle on the dainty bedside table tucked between the two singles, 'Enjoy!'

I run my hand along one of the ornate headboards and then gaze up at the softly-stencilled ceilings.

'Which bed would you like?' Luca asks.

Whichever one you're in.

'I don't mind,' I reply.

Luca shrugs, sits down on the one nearest to him and starts to unbutton his shirt. Much as I would love to stay, preferably with a video camera, I feel awkward and bumble out on to the balcony. Below is the cloister where we huddled in the rain. Above – 'Luca!' I gasp. 'Look at the moon!'

He appears in the doorway wearing only his black trousers – a cross between a matador and a member of the Red Hot Chili Peppers. His tattooed torso always comes as a surprise to me. Until now I've been distracted by the designs, but with nature's dimmer switch in effect I can really appreciate his sculpted physique. Just looking at him makes me shiver.

'Are you cold?' he asks.

Before I can reply he dips back into the room and reappears flourishing a bedcover like a cape. He wraps it around my shoulders and our hands touch as he brings the fabric round under my chin. He doesn't let go straight away. I only have the nerve to hold his gaze for a second – the grappa has blurred the world yet Luca is hyper-defined.

'These clasped hands?' I say, pretending to be studying his tattoos, not the definition on his stomach.

'It is a prayer for my dear friend Corrada, he died too young. I promised myself, no more fighting.'

He twists around to look at his right shoulder blade.

247

'This garland is for my mother – she chose the design!' he twinkles.

'It's beautiful,' I say. You're beautiful, I think.

'So, which one was your first?' I ask, trying to keep the shiver out of my voice.

'This,' he says, showing me the raggedy dagger slashing through the silk of his shoulder. 'I was fifteen.'

'Gosh – I didn't think Capri was the kind of place to have teenage tattoo parlours!'

'It's not. I had this done in Napoli. It's where I was born.'

'So how did you end up here?'

'I was in plenty of trouble,' he muses. 'My mother, she was very worried and she begged my father to take charge of me for a year.'

'And your father lived on Capri?'

'Still does.'

'Oh.'

'It didn't really work out when I came over. We had never met before and—'

'Never met?'

'Yes. He left my mother when she discovered she was pregnant. She marry another man, have four more children with him . . .' he shrugs. 'I was thinking of going back to Napoli when I met Vincenzo – my other father!' he laughs.

'On the beach at Marina Piccola?' I remember.

'That's right,' he smiles. 'I got my last tattoo a few months after meeting him.'

'Which one?'

Luca turns his back and flexes the dragon between his shoulder blades. My favourite.

'Does it have a special meaning?' I ask, moving around so I can see his face.

He looks shy. 'I tell you another day.'

I'm intrigued but the sight of the taut skin over his hipbone distracts me and I find myself stumbling back into the room on the pretext of getting some water. Preferably thrown in my face.

'Can I get you something?' I call, trying to keep the lust out of my voice. I have to sober up!

Shrugging the cover off my shoulders I shake it out over the bed. There's a clunk and I don't figure out what's going on until smoky yellow flames leap up from the bedside. I scream, Luca hurtles in, snatches the cover off the bed and stamps it into the tiled floor. I grab the fallen candle and blow it out before it does any more damage. Or, rather, before I continue to use it as a tool of destruction.

'Are you okay?' Luca feels his way through the shadows towards me.

'Yes,' I whimper, heart thumping. 'Is it ruined?'

'Don't worry about it,' he says, pulling me into his arms, stroking my hair.

I wonder if it's a sign – '*You're playing with fire! Beware!*' – but it's too late for caution.

My face is against his shoulder now. He smells so wonderful. I turn my head just enough so that my mouth is touching his sheer skin. I breathe in and as he breathes out, I can feel the warmth of his breath on the tip of my ear. His fingers weave between my curls and

249

find the nape of my neck. Finally, gradually, tentatively I dare to tilt my face towards his. Our eyes connect long enough to say 'yes' and then our mouths meet and we're set adrift on a swirl of kisses. My heart begs to join in. I let it. And as the kisses deepen I feel myself melting into him . . .

25

I wake up in the cinder-free bed, unsure which limbs are mine and which are Luca's. The only thing I'm certain of is that I'm desperate for a wee. I don't want to enter 'morning after' territory just yet so I extricate myself from his embrace in slow motion, as if I'm playing a game of human pick-up sticks. Once out of bed I feel naked. I *am* naked. I grab the other bedcover off the floor and shuffle into the bathroom. Sitting on the loo I inspect the damage – there's a big black-edged hole towards the top left-hand corner, but not far enough over for it to be tucked out of sight. I'll definitely have to confess to the hotel, I just pray it's not some hand-spun heirloom, or that will be my £5,000 inheritance up in flames. If there's any change I'd happily blow it on renting this room out for the next few weeks.

Gradually an understanding of what has happened steals over me. I can't help but smile as I relive Luca's tender looks and never-ending kisses, and I emit an elongated sigh as I conjure up the sensation of his touch. Oh God – what a completely gorgeous man! I kept promising myself that I wouldn't sleep with him but my clothes seemed to come off of their own accord. The whole thing was so smooth and natural. Normally I feel like I'm out of sync with a man – as though he's got his job to do and I'm not being quite as accommodating as I might be – but with Luca the whole thing was seamless. And it just felt *so good*.

I hear voices from next door's bathroom and my stomach dips. The real world is already waking up. I push aside my first twinge of guilt and tell myself I must never have any regrets. Then I gulp back one of the mini bottles of mineral water by the sink and congratulate myself on being the kind of person who carries a toothbrush wherever they go. Not having been further than the post office in the last year it was beginning to feel redundant in my bag but it's going to come into its own right now.

I reach around the doorway and drag my bag into the bathroom. I have to remove Rosa's brown paper package to get to the contents and I chuckle thinking of her – if she could see me now! And then I imagine the fright I could give Luca – imagine him waking up to find me sitting on the bed wearing a wedding dress! I wipe the smile off my face, wondering what his wife wore to their wedding . . . Oh God, it's all so hopeless.

I panic. And yet . . . I've still got this thrill of delight chasing around inside me. And a sense of misplaced pride. In a way it meant *more* to me because he's married. It's all too easy for single men to make overtures and appear to mean it, then they flake and you realize they weren't that interested in the first place, just going through the motions. With Luca it was a big deal. He must have really struggled with himself over this. And I know it's wrong but I'm secretly chuffed because the fact that he's married and he's a decent guy and he *still* kissed me must mean he really, really wanted to. I'm getting a kick from the very thing I've despised in other people all my life. Worse than that, I know that I want more. And even though it might be the worst possible thing to pursue I can also feel a sense of inevitability. It's possible he'll wake up with a hangover and consider it nothing but a drunken aberration but deep down I know it's going to happen again. The question is: Who will make the first move?

I feel a delicious dread of anticipation as I give my teeth a vigorous de-grappa-ing scrub and peer in the mirror. My hair is flattened on one side, major Afro on the other. Not that different to how I wore it all yesterday, then. My chin looks like a pink ping-pong ball from the abrasion of his goatee. It'll start peeling tomorrow but for now I relish the hot tingle because it reminds me of all the industrious kissing we had to do to get it that way. I decide I'll have a quick inch-deep splash in the bath to freshen up but as I turn on the tap it begins squeaking and juddering so I quickly wrench it back to the off position before any water splurges out. I skid back to the doorway to see if I've woken Luca. He's turned over but his eyes are still closed. I look at his beautiful face. I don't want this to be over. He moves again. I start fretting – what if he gets up and behaves like nothing happened? I couldn't bear it. I scamper to the edge of the bed, loosening the bedcover toga so I can swiftly drop it and slip in beside him but before I get the chance, he stretches and squints up at me.

'Buon giorno!' he smiles sleepily.

I grab the bedcover to my chest. 'Buon giorno!'

'Mmmmm, you look beautiful!'

I try to flatten the springier side of my hair but he looks past me and points at the dressing table. I turn my head to discover my entire rear reflected in all its gluttonous glory in the mirror. Squealing I grab the covers and bind my bum, exposing my chest in the process, crying out in frustration and embarrassment. Luca chuckles to himself, watching the fumbled mummification. He's just reaching out to me when there's a knock at the door.

We freeze.

It's my mother. I just know it! She's taken the first ferry and come to make sure I'm all right. How are we going to explain *this*!

'Colazione!'

Breakfast! Thank God!

'Venire!' Luca calls.

I look down at the big burn in the bedcover, positioned like a target on my stomach. Panic! I try to make it to the bathroom but the cover is wrapped too tight around my legs and I slip on a flap of material and thwack on to the floor, whacking my elbow as I land. Aaaggghh! The door opens. I'm lying flat out, stomach down on the floor, wincing in pain. A woman with a large wooden tray surveys me. I can't risk moving and exposing the burn so I simply relax and

254

rest my cheek on the cool tiled floor and smile up at her. She looks over at Luca with concern.

He shrugs back as if to say, Well, she's got a point, it's got to be 80 degrees outside!

Stepping over me she offers to set breakfast out on the balcony.

Luca approves. As soon as she steps outside I slither into the bathroom on my belly, kick the door closed behind me and pull myself into a sitting position using the bidet.

Then I put my head in my hands and wait for the nightmare to end.

'Kim?' There's a light rap at the door.

I don't respond.

'She's gone!' says Luca in a whisper.

'I don't care!' I blurt. 'I'm too embarrassed – I'm not coming out!'

Luca doesn't reply. Instead, a minute later, he backs into the bathroom carrying the entire tray of breakfast goodies. He looks for a place to set it down. The sink is uneven, the bidet too low . . . But it's a perfect fit midway along the bath. 'I'll take the taps,' he says, helping me to my feet. Then he hesitates. 'You might be more comfortable in a towel.'

He hands me one and then turns away. I know he won't look. No need really – he's already seen everything. Once I'm securely wrapped I tap him on the shoulder. In one move he swoops me into his arms and slides me into position at the smooth end of the bath.

'Okay?'

'Yes,' I say, not knowing whether to be more stunned that I'm about to eat breakfast in an empty bath or that he picked me up without grunting.

He steps into the other end of the bath and slides his legs outside of mine. 'Coffee?'

I nod.

'Cornetto?' I know that's Italian for croissant but it amuses me anyway. I lean forward and take a piece from his fingers with my mouth without my usual self-conscious squirming.

'Baci?'

I lean forward again and kiss him, gaining a raspberry jam pip from the experience.

'At last a smile!' he says triumphantly.

I tear open a plastic pouch of honey with my teeth, scooch forward and squeeze it on his shoulder.

He looks at me with wide eyes, then twists his lips. 'Hmmmm . . .' he says, digging his knife in the jam and flicking it at me. It splats on my arm.

I tear off a piece of gooey Danish and throw it at him. He catches it in his mouth. I laugh.

Things go downhill from here. Coffee is spilt, eggshells are shattered, sachets of sugar are shaken into hair and cream cheese is smeared Adam Ant-style across noses . . .

Eventually, the tray is set aside, the tub is filled with bubblebath and the noise of the taps is nothing compared to our shrieking and giggling.

We continue in absurdly high-volume high spirits as we dance out of the villa into the blinding sunshine two

256

hours later. Pausing by the main door Luca points to a plaque honouring 'La Divina' Greta Garbo and her elopement with Leopold Stokowski. I squint at it, imagining the names Kim Rees and Luca Amorato in their place.

As we veer off, chasing each other around the sundial in the rose garden, we are shushed by a middle-aged couple. Luca apologizes for disturbing them with a sincere look on his face, but I can't wipe the grin from mine – I've just been shushed and tutted at like those rowdy schoolchildren on their way to the Gardens of Augustus that Mum complained about on our first day at the Luna. My inner child has been awakened and it turns out she's hyperactive. I want to see all the things I missed in yesterday's storm – the Temple of Bacchus, the Crest of Mercury, the stone seat with the D.H. Lawrence inscription, the bronze statue of David, the marble statue of Flora, goddess of flowers – all at once! And I can't wait to get to the Terrazza dell'Infinito to view the marble busts in the glorious sunshine.

'Have you got a camera?' Luca asks as we lean over the edge between our good friends Salvatore and Fabio.

'Somewhere in my bag,' I say delving into it. I pull out the brown paper package and set it to one side.

'You didn't deliver?' Luca frowns.

'She said I could keep it,' I explain.

'And you don't open it?'

'Well, she said . . .' I stop myself from repeating, '*You can open it the day you kiss your true love.*'

Instead I say, 'I know what it is.'

Luca looks inquisitive.

'It's the wedding dress Vincenzo bought for Rosa,' I tell him. 'She never wore it, obviously.'

'And she gave it to you?'

'Yes!'

'That is wonderful.'

'I know. Would you like to see it?'

'Of course! But please don't open if you're not ready,' he says, eyeing an elderly lady in a baseball hat and trainers joining our end of the balcony.

'I am,' I tell him. This is the perfect spot, even if we're not totally alone.

I take a breath and smooth the brown wrapping. I am just about to slide my finger under the tape when I stop, look up at him and say, 'Luca – kiss me!' He obliges with the perfect kiss – tender and heartfelt and sexy – and I know for sure that this is the right moment to see what might one day be my wedding dress.

26

The dress is softest cream satin with a diamond-shaped sprinkling of crystals at the waist and a twinkling around the hem. The long sleeves are sheer with a sheeny ribbon winding its way from each shoulder to the wrist. The skirt is crumpled but Luca shakes and smooths it with his expert touch, then he holds it up to me with a misty look in his eyes and sighs, 'You will look like a *principessa* when you wear this.'

Grabbing my camera, he snaps me before I can say, 'Where's my tiara?' then turns to the old lady in the baseball hat beside us and says, 'Would you mind taking a picture of us?'

She looks reluctant for a second but agrees. We do one grinning like fools and the other exchanging the lightest kiss. Then she takes out her camera and asks Luca to snap her beside Salvatore. She tells us she's from Califonia and that she just had to do the Amalfi Drive because friends told her it's the Italian equivalent of the Pacific Coast Highway.

'How does it compare?' I ask her.

'Well, I thought the cliff road through Big Sur was perilous but this . . .' She shakes her head.

'I've heard it's pretty twisty-turny all the way . . .'

'It's not the road, it's the drivers,' she rallies. 'These Italians are crazy!' She glances at Luca. 'No offence.'

'None taken!' he smiles.

'I was just in Rome and you'd think they use red lights for decoration!'

The photo-tag continues when a Dutch honeymooner taps Luca on the arm and asks him to take a picture of him with his new wife at the other end of the balcony. As I watch him I feel such adoration. I can't believe he feels the same way about me. My fingers trace the crystal beading and I think of Vincenzo and all the love that went into choosing this design.

'You know, you shouldn't let the groom see the dress before the wedding, it's bad luck,' the American lady advises me.

'The bad luck has already happened,' I tell her in a rush of unwarranted frankness. 'He's already married to someone else.'

She looks stunned then gets to her feet. 'You people have no respect for the sanctity of marriage!' she spits. 'How can you be so brazen? So cruel? Do you not have any feeling for the wife?'

I blink in disbelief at what I have unleashed.

'Do you have any idea what it's like to have your husband cheat on you?' Her voice quavers.

Obviously she does, I realize with regret.

'You disgust me!' she concludes, stomping off,

shooting a filthy sideways glare at Luca as she returns to the gardens.

I look down at the ground. I've done the thing I swore I never would. Committed the act I've despised in everyone else, especially my mother. I've crossed over, become an accessory to an adulterer. Until now I held my head up high, so high I never really looked down at the reasons why these things happen. Of course, everybody's at it now. It's hardly an arrestable offence. Besides, she doesn't know the full story. I try to dismiss her words but can't stop the self-disgust seeping through me. I can make a million excuses but she's right. I have no respect. Not for the sanctity of marriage. Not for Luca's wife. Not for myself.

'Are you okay?' Luca asks, kneeling beside me.

'It's just the hangover kicking in,' I say, swallowing.

'There is a little café bar just here,' he says, pointing behind us. 'We get some water?'

'Okay,' I nod, taking his outstretched hand.

Always punishment after pleasure. I feel smacked down, like a child joyfully making mud pies and then berated for messing up her clean clothes.

From the café's belvedere, set a level below the Terrazza dell'Infinito, I follow the road winding down to Amalfi in a trance.

Luca sets the glass before me and says, 'Do you want to talk about this?'

I look up at him. Just looking into his eyes fills me with calm. And love. 'Is this wrong?' I ask.

261

He looks down at the table and then back at me. 'Does it feel wrong?'

'Not when I'm with you,' I say.

'Kim, I—'

I put my hand to his lips. I don't want to hear about his relationship with his wife. I don't want to hear excuses. I don't want to face the reality until we have to. If this is the only time I'll ever have with him I want to enjoy it.

He kisses my fingertips.

'Can we look around Amalfi before we sail back to Capri?' I ask.

He nods, brightening, 'We will be tourists. We can even send a postcard!'

I wonder if I'll be able to find an appropriate one – *'Having a lovely time on the Isle of Denial . . .'*

On the way back to Ravello's main square we're beaten to every picturesque spot by yet another bride and groom posing for photographs. In the Gardens of Rufolo alone there are three sets of newlyweds vying for the prime backdrop. I feel like jumbling up the brides and assigning them a different groom just for the hell of it. Imagine how different their lives could be.

A member of the most extravagantly attired wedding party asks me to move out of their shot. I step aside and study the coiffed, gilded women in the group and for the first time I want to be that glamorous. I'm in yesterday's clothes and though I washed my hair it was probably a mistake to use the hotel's body lotion as a substitute for frizz-taming serum.

In our secret world at Villa Cimbrone I felt so happy

I didn't mind what I looked like. Now I feel shabby, cheap and profoundly not *de rigueur*. I'm almost tempted to slip into Rosa's wedding dress. At least then I'd feel in keeping with everyone else.

'Here is the bus,' Luca announces as it reverses around a tight corner. From my seat I take in the locals going about their business – even the OAPs are into 'peasant-chic'.

'Are there many clothes shops in Amalfi?' I ask, trying to sound casual.

'You want to shop?' Luca sounds intrigued.

'I just wondered, you know, if you have much competition here?'

I'm not fooling anyone.

'Here is different kinds of clothes.'

'Less designery?' I say hopefully.

Luca smiles. 'You like simple, yes? Comfortable?'

I nod. 'No mint green trouser suits.'

Luca rolls his eyes. 'It is funny, your mother, she is so in love with clothes and you do not enjoy them at all.'

'It's just that she was always dressing me up like a doll when I was a girl. Too many bright colours, too many bows.'

'So you show your independence now by wearing these masculine, what is that word, like "loose"?' he says tugging at his shirt.

'Baggy!'

'Yes, very *baggy* clothes.'

'I did try some other "looks" once but she always made me feel like I'd got it wrong.'

263

'It is just a question of finding your own style.'

'I don't think I've got one,' I admit.

'Of course, everyone has one. You have just given up too early in your search! It is not either/or – you know, what you wear now or what your mother would have you wear. Besides, you would not feel comfortable in what your mother would choose for you because it would get you too much attention. For her it is okay, she likes to be looked at. It is part of who she is.'

He's right. I'd far rather blend. Unfortunately I've come to the wrong place for that. If I ever did stray from the house in Cardiff no one looked twice at my low-slung jeans and hooded cardis. On Capri everyone is so groomed and garish I can tell they're thinking that my luggage got swapped with that of a teenage boy.

'Even if I did miraculously "find my style" I don't think my mum would stop criticizing my appearance,' I decide.

'You could let her dress you one day. Let her do your hair, your make-up. Just for fun.'

'Fun?' I squawk, realizing too late that Luca is joking. 'Dressing head to toe in hot coral with matching lipstick and nails is not my idea of fun!'

'It might be interesting actually,' Luca muses. 'If you eliminate the thing you say she pick on the most, she might only have good things to say to you!'

'I doubt it. She'd just start on something else.'

'You don't know that.'

'Hold on! Why should I change just to suit her?' I say, suddenly outraged.

Luca grins at my delayed defiance. 'What you have to realize is that she thinks she's being helpful.'

I raise an eyebrow.

'Think about it,' Luca continues. 'All day long she tells people what suits them and what doesn't and they are grateful. That's her job! People pay money for her opinion. And she's giving it to you for free.'

'And you expect me to be grateful for that?' I snort. 'Or perhaps you're suggesting I should *pay* for her insults?'

'Don't you see? She's *not* insulting you. She's trying to help you. It's what she does!'

'I wouldn't mind if it was occasional,' I explain. 'But it's all the time, *every* time. I might not have seen her for three months and I'll be telling her my news and I can still tell she's thinking "A shimmery highlighter on her cheekbones would make all the difference . . ." or "I've got a pair of earrings that would pick out the khaki in that combat pattern beautifully!" ' I huff and gaze out the window.

'Just once I'd like to walk into a room and feel that she sees *me*, not what I'm wearing.'

Luca puts his hand on the back of my head and leans close.

'And maybe just once she'd like to walk into a room and feel that you see *her*, not the woman you blame for your parents' divorce.'

I whip my head round, shaking off his hand. What kind of talk is this for a bus ride? Never mind the fact that we've just embarked on a torrid affair. Not that I really know what torrid means but I'm sure there's not meant to be any psychoanalysis involved, or comments that make you feel like you are falling backwards into a chasm.

I grip the plastic bar in front of me and stare ahead. That's it! I'm not talking about my mother any more. It obviously makes me sound like a complete bitch. Goddammit! Even when she's not here she ruins things!

I try and concentrate on the view but a thought keeps weaving back into my head.

What if he's right?

I sit in silence for as long as I can and then turn to Luca. 'I don't want to talk about her any more,' I assert.

'Okay,' he concedes.

'Only . . .'

'Yes?'

'Do you think . . .' I pause, trying to find the right words. 'Do you think I make her defensive? Is that what you're saying?'

'Honestly? I don't know what I am saying. I don't have all the answers, I just say what I see.'

'And what do you see?'

Luca takes my hand. 'I see two people who aren't showing each other who they really are because they feel criticized by the other one.'

'But I don't criticize her like she criticizes me, do I? What have I said?'

'Kim, for a person who doesn't say much you say an awful lot.'

'What do you mean?'

'Even when you are silent you are speaking. And the resentment . . .'

'I'm full of it!' I blurt, feeling exposed. 'I feel it all the time. I don't know how to get it out of me.'

I clutch at my T-shirt. 'It's such an ugly thing, don't you find it off-putting?'

Luca leans forward and kisses the tip of my nose. 'I'm distracted by all the other stuff.'

'What stuff?'

Luca's eyes roam seductively around my face. I feel a flutter of lust.

'The good stuff,' he says simply.

And then the bus jolts to a halt.

'Amalfi!' cries the driver.

27

As we alight from the bus I take in my surroundings – people trying to push on board before the previous trip's passengers have disembarked, unescorted female visitors being asked 'Where you from?' by every local male they pass, students who could do with indicator lights for their backpacks, old Italian men sipping espresso oblivious to the bustle around them, highly tanned bus drivers looking like movie stars in their pale blue shirts and wraparound sunglasses . . .

Everything is just as it was yesterday. Everything except me.

Yesterday I arrived ready for a confrontation with Rosa. Now I have nothing but admiration and real affection for her.

I thought I might spend an hour at Villa Cimbrone. I spent all night.

I walked up the hill feeling morally superior and down the hill holding hands with a married man.

And if all that wasn't enough, something happened on the bus: the acidic, sneering resentment I feel towards my mother was challenged. I didn't deny it.

Why would I? I've always felt perfectly entitled to resent her. But this time was different. This time I felt ashamed. And I realize now that it's not the resentment clawing into me, but me clinging on to the resentment for dear life. I'm afraid of *not* being angry with her. Because if I stop blaming my mother I have to start asking awkward questions like: Even if her affair was so painful for my father that he couldn't face my mother again, why couldn't he face me? Did he use it as an excuse to get away? Why did he never get in contact? Not even a birthday card . . .

I'm falling . . .

Luca catches me. 'It is very hot today. We get you a sunhat. Worst taste one we can find!'

I smile, revived by his touch and relieved to be led to a sheltered back street away from the crowds.

'And as a consolation prize for making you upset on the bus—'

'You didn't!' I protest.

He gives me a look.

'OK, you did but in a good way.'

'As a consolation prize, when we go shopping I will let you dress *me*, any way you want.'

I grin, thrilled at the prospect of giving Luca a make-over-the-top. 'Even one of those ripply-knit Missoni cardigans?'

He shudders. 'For you, anything!'

We find a little row of boutiques and I start rummaging through their wares with a vigour I have never before experienced in a clothes shop. For every piece of exquisite tailoring there's an item you can't believe survived the 1980s – shiny cycling T-shirts, Miami Vice thin lapels, Spandau Ballet peg-pleat trousers – it's all here.

'So what are next season's trends for men?' I ask, making myself dizzy by flicking through a rail of psychedelic shirts too fast.

Luca rolls his eyes as if to say, I'm not falling for that!

'No really, I need to know so I don't accidentally pick out anything that's about to have a fashion revival.'

'Well,' he begins, dubiously, 'Autumn/Winter is about military, epaulettes, anything retro . . .'

'How old do clothes have to be before they become retro?' I ask.

Luca goes to speak then catches the glint in my eye. 'Velvet will be big,' he continues, ignoring my non-sense, 'and anything with fur detailing.'

'Does it count as fur-trimmed if your cat has slept on it?' I tease.

Luca gives my neck a mock-strangulation squeeze.

'I have one serious question.'

Luca raises an eyebrow.

'You know double-breasted suits . . . ?'

'Yes?' he says warily.

'Is it possible to get double-waisted trousers? You know – for the larger man?' I chuckle in delight as Luca manhandles me out of the shop.

We continue on our quest, practically crying with laughter as we force each other to commit crimes of fashion. It's enormously frustrating to me that Luca looks good in practically anything, except perhaps pastels – a-*ha*! As I attempt to search out something in sherbet lemon he settles on a flouncy straw hat with a big lilac flower for me, and then cracks up every time he looks my way. It's all right for Sarah Jessica Parker – she wears the most fright-night things on *Sex and the City* and gets called a style icon. Cleo and I watch with jaw-dropping awe at some of the designer-jumble-sale things she wears to first dates and are repeatedly astounded that the men she's meeting don't hide under a bar stool when they see her walk in. (Unless of course she's wearing one of her 'tits on toast' dresses, as Miranda calls them. Then her appeal is clear.)

I smile as I watch Luca rifle through some gimmicky cufflinks. In the past when I've been with a man, I've been conscious of making an effort all the time, of trying to be entertaining or alluring or interesting, as if I'm auditioning for them. I'm always wondering what they are thinking, specifically what they are thinking about me. I study them, trying to fathom them out. No wonder I find relationships stressful – I'm always 'on'. I don't know if it comes from being used to providing a service: when I'm translating my function is clear but when I'm on a date I never really know what I'm supposed to do. I very rarely relax and go with the flow. I think back on my past relationships and now it hits me: if part of my problem is that I'm always seeking approval, then it makes sense I end up with men I don't respect. That way if I don't get their approval it's no big deal – it doesn't really matter because they're obviously not The One.

271

It's different with Luca. He hasn't exactly given me an easy ride but it's okay because I know he wants to lift me up, not tread me down. He's only being honest and he's not holding back his love for when I'm perfect. I feel accepted. There are no fines for my excess baggage and already that's making me want to dump a lot of it.

'I think this might be it,' Luca says, swishing back the changing room curtain. I recoil. It's perfectly horrible – skin-tight silver T-shirt with a mock-turtle neck, a frantically patterned waistcoat and tapered peacock-purple trousers with a belt buckle the size of a CD. He looks like a Chippendale about to hit Tiffany's nightclub singing, '*Everybody Wang Chung Tonight*!'

'Wait! Let me take a picture!' I beg.

'No rush, I'm keeping it on.'

'*What?*'

'I said I'd let you pick out an outfit for me.'

'I thought you just meant to try on, I . . .'

'I don't mind. It's you that has to walk with me.'

'There's always a catch, isn't there,' I sigh.

I watch with amazement as he removes the tags, pays for the outfit and rolls his own clothes into a bag. 'Are you really going to do it?' I ask.

'Just watch me!' he says, stepping out into the street.

There are one or two double-takes and the odd passing snigger but overall Luca's defiant stride (plus the fact that a few choice tattoos are on show) seems to deflect undue attention. Ready for lunch, he takes me to his favourite pizzeria. We sit by the wood-burning stove and order the largest pizza on the menu with

272

every available topping. When it arrives twenty minutes later it is so obscenely outsize I could cut a hole in the middle and wear it as a poncho. I don't say this out loud though, in case Luca challenges me to do just that.

We talk about the shop. I ask how he feels about the possibility of my mother keeping Vincenzo's majority share of the business and running it. He admits that at first he was very disappointed. 'But then when you came to Capri two things changed.'

It's always twos with Luca.

'One – I liked your mother and I like what she wants to do with the shop.'

'I didn't think she wanted to change anything?'

'Exactly!' Luca grins.

'The other thing is that meeting you has reminded me of all the other things I want to do. The things I want to show Nino . . . Maybe I would be too restricted if I owned all of the shop.'

'Why since meeting me?'

'Well, you have travelled so many places. Tokyo, Zagreb . . .'

'That was years ago.'

'But you still have the memories, yes? They will be with you for ever.'

'Yes but it was work. I'm not sure it counts as an adventure, which is what you seek, right?'

He shrugs.

I think for a moment. Maybe I have done more than I realize. I think back to a few of the more unexpected

273

things that have happened on my trips and consider that maybe he's right, maybe I have had a taste of life.

'I bet you pictured me differently,' I suggest.

From the letters, Luca probably thought I'd be some gorgeous cosmopolitan huntress like Bridget Hall in the Ralph Lauren *Safari* ads – all golden freckles and sleek tawny hair, not my ghostly hue and Medusa mane.

'I didn't have to guess. I saw the photographs your mother sent.'

'You knew what I looked like and you still—'

I'm thinking: You knew what I looked like and you still fantasized about me! but I can't say that. I'm not supposed to know. I wouldn't know now if it weren't for Rosa.

'Still . . . ?' Luca prompts.

'Dessert?' the waiter intervenes.

'You've got to be kidding!' I blurt. I could hibernate till spring feeding off the pizza we just ate.

'Maybe we have some in the square later,' Luca suggests.

The waiter hands us the bill. I wanted lunch to be on me but Luca seems to adhere to that strange Italian custom that men should always pay. I encountered a similar 'problem' with the only other Italian man I've dated. It was five years ago. I was twenty-four, he was twenty, just over from Abruzzo working for the winter in an Italian restaurant in Cardiff. I met him on his last week (typical!) and we went for a drink four nights running. First night he paid. Second night I said it was my turn but he said no. Third night I tried again and still he said no. I said it was ridiculous and demanded an explanation. He said, 'I am the one who asks you out, I should pay.' So I said, 'OK: How would you like to come for a drink with me tomorrow night?' He said he'd love to. I arrived at the pub, purse at the ready and still he refused. I was exasperated, '*Why??*' I complained. 'I thought you said I could pay if I was the one who did the asking.' 'Yes,' he said. 'But I am so happy that you asked me for a drink that I would like to celebrate by paying.'

We kept in touch for a while but then things just petered out. I still think of him fondly – he didn't seem the type to cheat. I don't think he'd be able to afford to.

Our plans to wander inside the amazing cathedral are scuppered by a wedding in progress. Instead we sit in a little café facing it and wait for the procession to emerge. It's like having front row seats at the theatre. I tell Luca about the time I went to see an off-Broadway show called *Tony & Tina's Wedding*.

'New York!' he sighs.

I am jet-set. It's official.

'It starts in this church hall and you take a seat as if you are part of the congregation. You can't tell who's audience and who's an actor until they start heckling the bride and groom in these New Jersey Italian-American accents,' I tell him. 'Then, after the ceremony you go on to the reception in this nightclub. They lead the way down the street and to passers-by it looks like a real wedding party – it's surreal. You actually get fed too – chicken cacciatore, pasta marinara and wedding cake for dessert! There's even a champagne toast, all included in the ticket price but you can go up to the bar at any time and buy more, just as if you were at a normal reception. There are mock fights and affairs exposed and tears and then dancing and Cousin Mikey will ask you for a slow dance and some mad uncle wants to do the Macarena.'

Luca laughs. 'Did you dance?'

'At first you try so hard not to catch their eye and pray they won't pick on you but once you're up there they can't get you to sit down! It feels just like a real wedding reception, in fact it comes as a bit of a shock when they say, "Show over, goodnight!" You just want to carry on . . .'

'Good memory?'

'Oh yes!' I beam.

Luca nods.

I tilt my head. He's right. I'll have that memory for ever. And this. I am never going to forget sitting here watching the most spectacular fashion parade spilling out from the cathedral in the afternoon sun: *Godfather*-groomed men in sleekly tailored suits, women parading their richest fabrics in the most jewel-bright colours, long black manes tamed in chignons with starched velvet bows. The bride, in glittering lace, pauses at the very top, then begins her descent. We count the steps along with her – fifty-seven in all, and her train covers at least thirty of them.

Along with a trio of yelping kids and two chunky-kneed women in shorts we scamper up the wide stone staircase and flirt with the idea of sidling into her wedding photos.

'Do you believe we get more than one life?' Luca asks, watching cousins and nephews embrace.

'I think so,' I reply, uncertain. 'But only one life as we are now.'

'Maybe next time I'll come back as him,' Luca says pointing at a squat, round-bellied man.

'I'm coming back as her!' I say, selecting a gazelle-legged model type.

'Can you see those two together?' Luca asks, sounding concerned.

I smile and snuggle into his arm, then let him pull me on to his lap as he sits back on to the step. Pushing back his hair, I gaze into his eyes. He smiles at me. It's weird having a secret thought while actually locking eyes with someone. There seems to be an element of risk involved, as though they might be able to read your mind. I wonder if Luca can tell that I'm thinking, Promise me that in your next life you'll marry me.

At 5p.m. we step aboard his boat and head back to Capri. Luca teaches me to steer and then freaks me out by leaving me to drive solo while he jumps out to the front deck of the boat on some kind of daredevil death-wish mission. I'm convinced he's going to skid off into the sea and then, in a bid to swing back and rescue him, I'll shred him with the propeller blades. Consequently I get quite shrill in my insistence that he climb back on board.

The temperature drops the further out to sea we go.

At first it is a relief after the stagnant heat in Amalfi but when the slap and bluster of the winds gets a tad too vigorous Luca rummages in the cabin and offers me a sweater. It's a dark grey cashmere V-neck, adding to the general mismatched absurdity of my outfit. I put it on. Luca says he likes that I'm wearing something of his, and I couldn't be happier. Every part of me just wants to keep going but all too soon Marina Piccola is in sight.

'Maybe tomorrow we go to Punta Carena and see the lighthouse?' he offers.

I grin delightedly, thinking, We get a tomorrow! This isn't the end!

'I would *love* that!' I tell him.

I am about to steal one last kiss when I hear, 'Papa! Kim! Papa!' coming from the shore and see a mini Ringo pogo-ing on the jetty.

We wave back with vigour. It's good to see him. I feel like part of the family. As soon as we're level with the decking I scramble up and give Ringo a big legs-off-the-ground hug. (His legs, not mine. If my legs left the ground I'd crush him in a trice.)

Ringo watches impatiently as Luca cuts the engine and leans over to moor the boat. 'Papa, Papa!' he urges, dragging him into an upright position. 'Look who's here!'

I don't even need to turn round. I can tell by the look on Luca's face that he's just seen his wife.

28

'"*What in God's name are you wearing?*" That's the first thing she said to him!'

'After how many weeks apart?' gasps Cleo.

'Five!' I tell her.

'Nooooo!'

'Yes! And the worst thing was I thought she was talking to me because I was wearing his sweater!'

'I bet that didn't look good.'

'Well, not with my combats,' I concede.

'I mean, it must have looked bad to her – like you two were a bit familiar.'

'That's what I thought so I tried to take it off really quickly but just got all tangled up with my hat.'

'You never wear hats!'

'It was part of the bad taste wardrobe we were compiling . . .'

'You two must have looked a sight!'

'We did! Oh Cleo if it wasn't so tragic it would have been funny – all these chic Mediterranean yachting types and us dressed like we'd lost the plot in TK Maxx!'

'Was anyone laughing?'

'Just Ringo,' I tell her.

'Bless him!'

'I was desperate to say something nice to appease her so I told her how adorable Ringo is and she just snapped back that as far as she was aware his name was Antonino or Nino for short, not Ringo!'

'Bitch!'

'I know.'

'Did they kiss?'

'No, it was pretty strained. I don't know if that was because of me or whether it would have been like that anyway.'

'Has he told you what's going on between them?'

'No, nothing. And I deliberately haven't asked.'

'So what does she look like?'

'Hideous!'

'Really?'

'Well, hideous in a stunning ice queen way. When Rosa said she was a travel rep I was sort of hoping for an 18–30s perm with a scrunchie, over-plucked eyebrows . . .'

'Berry lip-liner with frosted pink lipgloss,' Cleo interjects.

'Acrylic nails.'

'Ankle chain.'

'And a packet of fags,' I conclude.

'And what you got was?'

'Lady Victoria Hervey,' I groan.

'Blonde?'

'Very,' I affirm.

'Just as a female villain should be. I don't know why
Servalan and all the Wicked Witches had black hair. In
life all your enemies are blonde. Tell me she opened
her mouth and out popped Kathy Burke.'

'She's actually quite posh. All very angular. Absolutely no bottom whatsoever.'

'Maybe that's why he was so delighted by yours.'

'Oh *don't*! I can't believe he saw it in daylight. It
makes me shudder just to think of it.'

Cleo chuckles and then gets serious. 'Are you going
to be all right?'

'Yes,' I tell her. 'It's weird but at the moment I'm on
such a high I feel like nothing she could do could
compare to our time together.'

'Yeah, flammable bedcovers, food fights in the bath,
slow kisses in a speedboat – she's got her work cut out!'

'Oh Cleo, it was the *best*. I can't wait to be with him
again.'

'Are you sure there's going to be a next time?' Cleo
cautions.

'He said he'd take me to the lighthouse.'

'That was before he knew his wife was back.'

My adrenalin seeps away. Now I feel wobbly.

'D-do you think—'

'I don't know,' Cleo sighs. 'I don't want to be a
downer but it's not going to be easy, is it?'

I felt so invincible when I first saw Tanya. Now the
reality of the situation is hitting home.

'I just hope he doesn't confess,' Cleo adds.

'Oh my God *no*! You don't think he'd tell her?'

'You know how incredibly stupid men are about

these things. It sounds like she's sussed you guys already so she'll go on and on and on at him. He might crack.'

'Cleo! Stop it!'

'Just be prepared for a quick getaway – that's a small island you're on. Nowhere to hide.'

And few places to meet in secret, I fret.

'Still, you've only got two more days and then you can put some distance between you and the scene of your last goddamn crime!' yelps Cleo, paraphrasing *Thelma & Louise*.

Two days? This can't be happening. Suddenly everything seems to be slipping from my grasp.

'Kim? Are you still there?'

'Ask me if I'm going to be all right again,' I prompt.

'Are you?'

'Noooooo!' I wail, moving out of the way of two elderly sun-worshippers climbing the steps up from the beach.

'Ooop! Excuse me you dropped this,' I say, handing them their bottle of Factor 4.

'Grazie!' they nod.

'Hey – tomorrow's the big day,' I say, grateful for the memory-prompt. 'By this time tomorrow you might've had a mini-date with gorgeous Gareth!'

'Oh God, I'm so nervous! What if he turns me down flat?'

'Come on, you have to keep the faith,' I say, trying to sound chipper. 'I mean, law of averages, one of us has got to have a happy ending, right?'

Neither of us is convinced but we make peppy, 'Yeah, course!' noises anyway before we say goodbye.

I put down the receiver and look at my watch. The Amorato clan should be gone by now. I didn't want to get into sharing a taxi with them, it was bad enough just walking along the jetty listening to Luca ask Tanya about her trip. I felt like I was spying on his other life.

I walk up the steps to the bus terminal. Ten minutes until the next departure. No queue. I don't feel like looking at postcards and fishing nets so I wander into the small white church next to the bus stop and take a seat on one of the wooden chairs. The perfect peace is disturbed by some heavy panting. I look around and watch a large shaggy-coated dog lumber in, claws clicking on the tiles as he approaches the altar. He turns back to give me a 'Whadda you lookin' at?' stare and then drops to the floor, obviously relieved to be out of the sun. I leave him to it and spend the bus journey back to Capri town trying to stop myself imagining what Luca is doing and saying right now. It's okay, I tell myself. They'll just be having dinner. I don't have to feel sick with jealousy until bedtime. Don't think about that. Just switch off. Get through the night and you'll see him tomorrow at the shop.

It's going to be fine.

I look at my watch again. Fourteen hours. I'll see him in fourteen hours. I can do it. I can do it . . .

'Mum?' I call, as I open the door to our hotel room.

'Kim! You're back!' She hurries towards me, arms outstretched, then hesitates: 'That's an interesting hat.'

283

'Not you too.'

'Not me too, what?' she asks, clutching me to her.

'You should meet Luca's wife Tanya, I think you two would have a lot in common.'

'Oh I already have,' she says, releasing me. 'She came into the shop today looking for Luca.'

'When did she get back?' I ask, trying to sound light.

'This morning. She was hoping to surprise him but I guess he surprised her!' Mum chortles. 'At first I think she was a bit concerned about him spending the night with you but I told her that once she'd met you she wouldn't be worried any more.'

'Thanks a lot!'

'I don't mean it like that,' Mum tuts. 'I said that she'd be able to tell straight away that you weren't the kind of girl to get involved with a married man. I told her how much you disapprove of that kind of thing.'

Mum's eyes flicker for a moment and I can tell she's thinking: How much you disapprove of me.

I feel a pang and pull her back into my arms, feeling the need to comfort her. And to hide my face from her.

'Mario was very worried about you last night,' Mum says, resuming her hair-tonging. 'We should go and have a cocktail with him to show him that you're back in one piece.'

I sigh. I can't face getting all dolled up for dinner. I'd do anything for a microwave meal on my lap in front of the telly.

'Just have a quick change and we'll eat in the hotel and then have an early night. How does that sound?'

'Don't you have plans to be with Platinum Man?'

'I told him I wanted to be with you tonight,' she smiles. 'Besides, we're seeing him tomorrow. Tyler is arriving in the afternoon and we're meeting for dinner at their hotel at 9p.m.'

My face falls. I'd forgotten all about this ridiculous set-up.

'It's going to be lovely. I thought maybe you and I would go to the Quisisana for pre-dinner drinks first, then we can say we graced both of the island's five-star hotels in one night!'

'Great,' I say, failing to muster any enthusiasm.

'Come on – quick shower and spruce and we'll go downstairs.'

Absolutely nothing is going to happen with Tyler and yet I feel strangely disloyal to Luca at the prospect of a dinner date with him. It also means that my whole evening is going to be taken up with awkward small talk and embarrassing innuendoes from my mother, leaving no chance for me to sneak off to be with Luca, presuming he could do the same. I think I might develop a mystery affliction and cry off; that way I'd be here if he called. There's no point in me going out. I don't want to think about anything else but Luca. I want to stay with the memory of him. The feeling of him . . .

'Kim!'

'What?' I snap, annoyed to be interrupted mid-memory. Then I remember the conversation with Luca on the bus to Amalfi and open the bathroom door with a smile. 'Sorry, Mum, what did you say?'

'Just checking that you're getting in the shower – it's after eight!'

'I won't be long!' I chirrup, returning to the bathroom and reluctantly removing my hat.

Twenty minutes later we emerge from the lift. Mum is immediately waylaid by the hotel manager so I continue into the bar.

'Ahhh! Welcome back!' beams Mario. 'We missed you.'

I hop up on to the bar stool with a smile. It's strangely comforting to see Mario. 'I missed you too!' I lie.

'So how did you like Ravello?'

'I think it's the most beautiful place on earth,' I grin.

'Even in the rain?'

'Absolutely!'

Mario gives a grudging nod.

'Your mother tells me that the shop manager came to rescue you . . .'

I try not to look guilty. 'Yes.'

'Hmmmm,' Mario eyes me with suspicion. 'I think perhaps he likes you.'

'He's married,' I tell him, trying to throw him off the scent.

'That means nothing,' Mario shrugs. 'I'm married.'

'You're married?' I gawp.

'Well, I have the same girlfriend for ten years so it is same thing.'

I'm slightly stunned. He's just so blatant in his advances it hadn't occurred to me that he would be in a long-term relationship.

'Does she know what you're like?'

'What I am like?' Mario looks quizzical.

'Does she know about the other women?'

'She knows that I love her and that I won't leave her.'

'And *do* you love her?'

'Oh yes,' he asserts, and for the first time I see sincerity in Mario's eyes.

I'm confused. 'So why all these other women?'

'It's always nice to touch new skin,' he tells me. 'To . . . Signora!' Mario greets my mother as she enters the bar.

I look down at the drink Mario has prepared for me and sink it in one. Doesn't anyone fall in love and stay in love with one person any more? It felt so special with Luca at the time but now I feel like I'm just part of this sordid party where people move around like bumper cars and get it on with whoever they happen to collide with.

Somehow I get through dinner and the night. There is so much I need to talk to Mum about but for now I'm only interested in ticking off the hours until I see Luca again.

In the morning I skip breakfast and tell her that I want to take a few pictures of the Piazzetta before the crowds arrive but in truth I just want to get to the shop before she does so I can have a few moments alone with Luca.

As I walk down Via Longano I feel sick with anticipation. I'll be able to tell straight away how he's feeling: If his eyes twinkle and he kisses me I'll know nothing has changed and it's going to be all right. If he arrives with a furrowed brow and a guilty look then I'll know that he's had a hard night and is feeling conflicted. If he's cold and avoids eye contact then I'll know that he has resigned himself to having no more to do with me and that he wants to pretend it didn't happen.

I try the shop door. Locked. I tap on the glass. No response. I can't sit on the step, I'll look desperate, so I pace up and down the street, pretending to look in the other shop windows. Fifteen minutes pass and still no sign of him. At 9.15a.m. my mother appears.

'Did you get what you wanted?'

I look blank.

'The pictures?'

'Um, it was a bit misty but I think so.'

I follow her into the shop but I can't settle. 'Shall I go and get coffees for everyone?' I offer.

'It's just you and me today,' she replies. 'Luca rang to say he's taking the day off.'

'Why?' I blurt.

'He wants to spend some time with his wife.'

29

'Did he actually say that?' I whimper.

'Say what?' Mum looks up from her inspection of a pomegranate-pink blouse.

'That he wanted to spend the day with her?'

Mum looks at me strangely. 'No, not exactly but she's been away for over a month so I'd imagine they'll have some catching up to do.'

I lean against the door frame.

'Are you all right?' she asks.

'Yes, um, I'm going to get one of those pastries with the cherry jam inside, is there anything you want?'

'No I'm fine, but don't go too mad – we'll be having a big meal tonight.'

I stumble out of the door feeling panicky. I can't do it. I can't last another 24 hours not seeing him, not knowing . . . Tears spring into my eyes. This is awful! I feel tricked. I got myself through the night thinking I would be seeing him this morning and now he's not coming I feel I might go mad. I'm not the kind of person who can shrug these things off and say, 'I'll talk to him tomorrow.' Tomorrow might as well be a year away. I'm not sure I'm even going to make it through the next hour with all the impatience and frustration fighting for supremacy inside me. I hate that it's so out of my control. I hate not having any say on the subject: he doesn't show up for work and that's it, I don't get to see him. I could probably find his phone number at the shop or Mum would have it but I can't risk calling so I'm just left dangling. I lean against a wall and try to calm myself. I despise this aspect of my personality: the over-emotional over-reactor. But there's so much at stake here.

As I continue down the street a couple pass me on the verge of a vicious argument. I watch them sniping at each other and consider that perhaps Luca isn't having an easy time of it either. A new feeling washes over me – empathy for him. I'm not here to add to the aggravation in his life. I want to be his haven. I'm not going to freak out. Okay. One step at a time. Starting with the cherry pastry.

When I return to the shop Mum is hanging up the telephone.

'That was Sophia!' she grins. 'We've decided – today is *Treat Day*!'

'Is it?'

'I've booked us in at the spa after work so we can get pampered in preparation for dinner tonight.'

My facial expression obviously isn't conveying enough unbounded joy so she tries again: 'I'm going to

290

have a luxury mani-pedi and get my hair set. What would you like?'

I think for a moment.

'Do they do massages?' I ask.

'Of course!' says Mum, apparently delighted to get any kind of response from me. 'Would you like one?'

Under the circumstances I think it's essential that I be physically pinned to a table so I can't run off to the Arco Naturale on the off-chance of bumping into Luca. 'Actually I would,' I say, surprising myself.

'Well, they've got all different types – Ayurveda, shiatsu, lymph drainage, sea salt, synchronized four-hands . . .' she reads from the brochure.

I want to ask which one is the best antidote to female hysteria but instead I opt for the sea salt scrub because it sounds the most vigorous and I need to know that the masseur can restrain me if I try to escape.

'Wonderful!' beams my mother. 'And perhaps they could—'

I give her a stern look.

'Well, we'll just see if you feel like having anything else done when you get there.'

'It's my hair, isn't it?'

'No, no, well . . . yes. I know you like it unruly, I just thought that maybe for tonight but no – it's fine.'

'I'll think about it,' I sigh. Perhaps Luca is right and it's her way of showing her love. 'Anyway, I'm going to get started with Grandad's office – I've only got today and tomorrow to get things sorted.'

My mother puts down the spa brochure and blinks

at me. 'That's the first time you've called him Grandad.'

I hesitate then say: 'Well, Rosa told me some things. In fact—'

Suddenly the door springs open and in bursts a thoroughbred fifty-something last seen on the 'bystander' pages of *Tatler*.

'Darling you have to help me!' she cries. 'The wretched airline lost my suitcase – Gawd knows when I'll get it back! I desperately need an outfit for lunch at Canzone – something stunning because my arch-rival is dining with us! – then a swimsuit and a sarong for the yacht, a dress for dinner and something cosy to slip over my shoulders when the temperature drops. The concierge said you'd be able to help.'

Before my mum can speak she adds conspiratorially, 'Actually he told me to ask for Luca but I'd much rather a woman helped me. These Italian men are so distracting!'

Mum smiles, about to enter her element. 'Why don't you take a seat while I pick out a few things. I'm thinking soft golds for the day, so pretty with your colouring, and in the sunlight you'll easily out-glow your rival! In the evening, we'll go for drama. This midnight blue with the chiffon sleeves is wonderful . . .'

Even with my mother's ability to instantly match a person with an outfit this could take some time so I decide to get started in the office. I'll tell Mum what Rosa said later.

I stand before Vincenzo's rosewood roll-top desk. All

the account books have been accounted for and Luca has an up-to-date contacts book so it's just a matter of checking through the old paperwork and throwing out most of it. I wheel myself up to the desk in the big wooden chair and wonder if this is where Vincenzo would have read my mother's letters to Luca. Where would he have sat? Perhaps he'd bring in the stool from behind the till. Or maybe perch on the stack of fashion magazines and telephone directories in the corner.

I pick up what looks like a leather-bound writing set but when I open it I see it is actually a photo frame. On the one side is a picture of my mother aged about eleven, arms around Vincenzo, smiling proudly at the camera. She seems to be saying, 'This is my dad!' I'm guessing it was taken the summer before she left – it was probably one of the last pictures he had taken with her. On the other side is a picture of me aged five, sitting on my mother's lap. I know I'm five because it's my birthday. My legs are like two short stacks of dumplings sticking out from an excessively frilly dress. My hair is Shirley Temple meets Macy Gray. No wonder Luca got a crush on me – who wouldn't? I set the frame on the top of the desk and imagine my grandfather sitting here, gazing up at his girls, the girls who became women he would never meet.

In the shop I hear a shriek of laughter and a cry of, 'Well in that case I'll get two!' I have to admit my mother does have a way with the customers. Although she is still undecided about whether to stay, I'm beginning to think it is actually the smartest choice, at least for the summer. Maybe Delia and Monique could come out for a few days to visit – she'd love that.

I pull open the little drawers one by one. Cracked biros and elastic band balls in one, testaments from satisfied customers in another – we'll keep those, maybe get them framed for the office. I open a notebook with the used pages folded down into triangles and covered with graffiti serifs. I do that, I think to myself. I wondered where I got it from.

Top of the desk tidied, I push the chair back and open the doors beneath. Two shelves. Two long boxes, previously containing knee-length boots. I ease the first one off the shelf and remove the lid. It's tightly packed with envelopes filed in date order from as far back as April 1967. I recognize my mum's handwriting on the first envelope, and the second which is dated February 7th 1972 – just two days after I was born. I shuffle to the end of the box. The letters go right up until two weeks before Vincenzo died. Wow. Over thirty years of letters, all from my mother. My hands are shaking as I take the first one from the box.

Questa lettua e lungo dovuta. Mi sposo domani e mi si spezza il cuore che tu no sarai qui per darni via.

(This letter is long overdue ... I'm getting married tomorrow and it breaks my heart that you won't be here to give me away.)

I don't understand. It's in Italian. Then again, I suppose the language would still be logged in her

294

memory after twelve years. And it is just a few lines. I read on. She's talking about my dad.

His name is Huw Rees, he's ex-army, now working for the Post Office and I'm going to try and love him for ever.

I rifle through to the middle of the box and pull out another letter. August 1990. She's telling Vincenzo about my A level results and how languages are really my thing. In Italian. I pull out another nine years later – it's the one about my engagement to Tomas. Again, in Italian. My heart starts pounding as I reach for the last letter in the box. I close my eyes before I open the envelope. Please let it be in English. My hand shakes as I open the pages, 'Sorry to hear you are not well . . .' ITALIAN. My mother has understood everything everyone's been saying – including me. I get hot at the memory of the nasty quip I made to Mario about her being a sure thing – no wonder she sent her drink flying, I would never have said it to her face.

I jam the letters back in the box and step back from them, wishing I didn't know, wondering what it means. Why did she lie? For years she's claimed she can barely remember a word of Italian and the whole reason I'm here is because . . . I stop. The whole reason I'm here is because she said she needed me to translate for her. I scramble to my feet and peer into the shop. She and Bunny Polo-Ascot are still at the tailored trouser suit stage, trying to find the most complementary shirt.

Another two women enter the shop. I ask if they need any help. They're just browsing. I step back into the office and close the door behind me. Kneeling beside the box I take a deep breath and pull out the letter from the week that I was born.

The lights are dim on the ward and some mums are reading, some have headphones on and some are already sleeping but I couldn't sleep without writing to tell you my news, Dad – or should that be Grandad?! Two days ago, my beautiful daughter Kim came into the world, just in time for lunch!

How appropriate!

I'm loving being in hospital, believe it or not. (Do you remember the fuss I made when I broke my ankle clambering around Tiberius's villa, and had to stay in for a week?) I think this must be what boarding-school would be like – I feel like I'm in a dorm but with all first time mums and new babies. There is a big, stern matron who has a heart of gold really, and makes me feel very safe. Today she chose your granddaughter as the demonstration baby when the nurse taught us how to bath a baby properly. Of course she performed brilliantly – perhaps she'll be an actress!

Well, it turns out I'm not so spotlight-friendly after all but I do remember how much I loved the water. I used to paddle and splash till I was a pruney. I still love the water now, even if I never go swimming any more.

We are allowed to have the babies in little cots by our beds at set times between visiting hours, and then at night they all go to the main nursery together to make sure we get a good night's sleep, so we don't know if they cry – just as well. I pick Kim up straight away when she's here, holding her in my arms like the most precious treasure.

I feel an unexpected pang of emotion.

Huw can't wait until she can speak but I want to hold on to every day as long as possible. If you ever felt this way about me I know you must have missed me as much as I've missed you over the years. Nobody really tells you what to expect, do they? Did you too have this feeling of overwhelming love? Dad, at this moment in time I must be the happiest girl in the whole wide world – I feel I could burst, I'm on Cloud Nine!

My eyes well up. I can't help thinking: She's talking about me! I did that – I made my mum that happy!

I grab another letter. Summer of '76. There's a note to '*See pic of Kim at beach*'.

Dad, I just marvel at my daughter at times – only four years on this planet and she is so knowing. After lunch yesterday I took Kim to the beach to tire her out ready for a good night's sleep in a strange bed. She's never been to a big hotel before let alone a vast beach and seems to treat it all like an adventure. We'd just settled ourselves on the blanket and she was off – heading for a much more interesting family further up the beach, without even a glance back at me! I left her for a while, as they gave me a not-to-worry wave, but after ten minutes I went over. They thought she was wonderful and very entertaining and I had the devil of a job to get her to come back with me. How about that? I thought, when she grows up will she be like this – so independent and sociable – or is every child trusting and curious, eager for life?

I *was* bold. My mother saw me as an adventurer when I was just four years old. I'm stunned. And dismayed – how did I let the last two years slip by being so cowardly? Hiding from the world?

There's going to be a show on Wednesday for little children staying here so I shall look forward to watching her reaction. Kim is developing a wonderful sense of humour and I love to hear her laugh. She must take after you, I remember you had a very special laugh . . .

I thought my mother and I were so different but all this time we've both been desperately missing our dads. Not that either of us would admit it out loud.

I pluck randomly from the box.

Happy Birthday, Dad! Are you still wearing Carthusia Man?

My eye is immediately drawn to the word Huw a few lines down . . .

. . . it's coming up to Kim's twelfth birthday and I know that the best present I could give her is a visit from her father but I have tried everything to find Huw again and no one has a forwarding address. His old friend Clive thinks he may have moved abroad—

I didn't know about this. I suppose Mum didn't

mention it because she couldn't find him – she wouldn't have wanted to get my hopes up. I wonder where he could be – whether he now lives in one of the countries I have visited. Maybe I've always been unconsciously looking for him . . .

I read on:

I know how much Kim misses Huw and I can't bear that I'm the cause of her heartache. I know you understand that it's the last thing I wanted for her. If I'm honest, I'm not sure I've done the right thing marrying again so soon but I wanted to try and create a family home-life again. It felt like such a responsibility bringing Kim up on my own. I didn't think I was doing a good enough job and I thought she would grow to love Roger but then I think of how I would have felt if Mum had tried to replace you . . . You were always so wise, Dad. What should I do? I know we can't speak but even being able to write these letters to you helps me think . . .

I never knew Mum worried like this. She was always so bright and buzzing and breezy. I thought it was just me who fretted and got down. Apparently beautiful people feel pain too.

I continue my trance-like perusal of the letters. The one about me leaving for university and Mum missing coming home to the smell of burnt toast and the heap of coats and bags at the bottom of the stairs, gets me all choked up. And then there's the whole span of years talking about my overseas jobs. So much of her news is about me. If I didn't know better I'd think she was really proud. And there's no mention of my hair. She

299

talks about what I do. All the times I thought she wasn't really listening ...

Then there's the exchanges of ideas about fashion. I had no idea she was so amazingly informed – she uses in-language that means nothing to a non-trade person such as me. Suddenly I realize I've never thought of my mother as talented or clever or ambitious, partly because clothing is not something I take seriously and partly, I guess, because I've always just thought of her as being my mum, so working her way up at Woodward's just seemed like a hobby – her real job was bringing me up. The arrogance of me! She makes me her utter priority and in return I show no interest in her life outside being my mother.

I feel dizzy. Leaving the letters scattered on the floor, I stumble through to the shop where Mum is just waving off the two browsers, now laden down with bags and shoeboxes.

'When you're good, you're good!' Mum beams as she turns back to me. The expression on my face causes her to do a double-take. 'What is it, love?'

'Quanto hanno speso?' (How much did they spend?) I ask her.

She goes to answer and then stops herself. 'What was that?'

'Quanto hanno speso?' I repeat.

The smile on her face fades. 'You found the letters.'

I nod.

'I wondered where they were. I thought I might find them at the house. Sophia was going to look after them for me . . .' She takes a deep breath. 'I owe you an explanation.'

'I owe you an apology.' I beat her to it.

Mum looks thrown. 'If you mean for reading the letters, I don't mind—'

'It's not that, but thank you for saying it's okay – I'd love to read them all some time.'

'Of course, but what is it?'

I flip the shop sign to CLOSED and lead her to the velvet chaise. Part of me just wants to pretend it never happened but I know I have to say my piece.

'Mum, I'm sorry that you heard me say those cruel things about you. I feel horrible about it. I didn't mean it, I was just feeling left out.'

'It's all right,' she says, taking my hand and giving me the courage to look her in the eye.

'I don't feel that way any more. I feel . . . I feel very lucky to have a mother that loves me as much as you do.'

I can barely see her through my tears. I've never said anything like this to her before. She looks suitably stunned and then her eyes spill over and she pulls me into her arms. 'I'm sorry that I lied,' she whispers, stroking my hair.

'Why did you?' I sniff.

She removes a tissue from her cuff, gently dabs away our tears, and sighs.

'It began even before you were born. As you know, Granny Carmela said she didn't want any more Italian spoken in the house once we got to Cardiff and for a while I didn't want to hear any because it made me

301

miss Dad and my friends. But then not hearing it just made it worse. I used to get Italian books from the library and hide them under the mattress and then, much later, when videos were invented I'd get out Italian films and just revel in them. I'd even sneak a look at your Italian homework! So many times I wanted to join in when you were practising for your oral exam but you were so loyal to Carmela and I didn't want to upset anyone.'

'I can't believe you were so convincing, even with the restaurant menus when we went out.'

'Well, it became my secret game. I know it sounds mad.'

No it doesn't, I think to myself. I've played those games too.

'So you didn't really need me to come here with you, did you?' I ask. I think I know why she insisted on it, but I need to hear it from her.

'Oh Kim, I know you say you're happy living the way you do and I was trying so hard not to interfere but then when I saw the plastic surgery brochure . . .'

I look down at the floor.

'It just seemed so wrong to me. All the amazing things you've done in your life, all the things you still have to do and you want to use the money to . . .' She can't even say it. 'I thought maybe if I could remind you of the true beauty in the world, you might start to see it in yourself.'

'I'm so glad you brought me with you,' I tell her. Adding in a small voice, 'But it's hard to think of myself as beautiful when I'm sitting next to you.'

'Oh come on, you know how much effort goes into getting me looking like this!' Mum laughs, dismissively.

'You think *I* should make more effort, don't you?' I want to get to the bottom of this once and for all.

She sighs. 'I know it's fashionable to dress down, it's just when I look at someone as pretty as you I can't understand why you don't want to reach your full glorious potential! That's all. I'm sorry if it seems like I'm criticizing you. You don't take it that way, do you?'

'I used to,' I tell her. Up until a day ago, in fact.

'Oh darling. I just want the best for you – of *everything*!'

There's a rattle at the door as a customer tries to get in, not noticing the sign. Mum turns to me. I give her a 'let her in' nod.

'Are you sure?' she says, clasping my hand.

'Yes, go ahead,' I reply, kissing her cheek. 'I've got some reading to catch up on.'

30

'He didn't show!' Cleo complains.

I know the feeling. No Luca. No Gareth. What are we doing wrong?

'I think he might have gone to Snappy Snaps – they've got a special offer on – the bastard!'

'Hold on – he's still got to pick up the lads' night out pics, hasn't he?'

'Yes . . .'

'Well, then – even if he had taken the disposable cameras to Snappy Snaps he would have come back to collect them.'

'I suppose so . . .' Cleo pouts.

'He must be ill.'

'D'you think?'

'Definitely! It's delayed Thai flu or Delhi belly or malaria—'

'Branwen thinks he went to Cornwall.'

Ah.

'Maybe he's broken his leg.'

'Doing what?' Cleo laughs.

'Rushing to get to you!' I tell her.

'So you think he'll be back?'

'Of course. You've just got to be patient.'

'I've just ordered a massive Rustica pizza with extra artichoke to cheer myself up. It always works when you're here but it just feels really sad on my own,' Cleo confesses.

I think of the last pizza I ate – not out of a cardboard box on my lap but by a wood-burning stove in Amalfi. This isn't right. Cleo should be out here too. 'Are you sure you can't get a few days off work and come out here?' I venture.

'I couldn't afford it even if I wanted to,' she replies, bleakly.

'There is the small matter of my £5,000 inheritance . . .'

'Don't you dare! That's sacred. I saw this divine cropped top in Hennes yesterday and the thought of one day being able to wear such a thing is what's keeping me going! Anyway, tomorrow's your last night so there's no point.'

My stomach does a queasy loop.

'Unless you're thinking of staying on,' Cleo says nervously. 'What's happening with Luca?'

'No idea. He didn't come to work today,' I sigh. 'But I've got it bad, Cleo. Worse than Tomas.'

'Really?'

'Really,' I say, laying myself on the line.

'Well, I guess there are two ways of looking at this,' Cleo decides, sounding authoritative. 'One, which would be your standard "He's married – walk-away-Renee" bit . . .'

'The right thing.'

'But the right thing very much depends on your perspective. The right thing might be for you two to be together.'

'But how can I know that for sure?' I whine.

'Well, there's only one way to find out.'

'What exactly am I supposed to do?' I flail.

'Anything! Everything!' she exclaims. 'When you think about it, it's a bit lame to say, "Oh, he's with someone else. I give up." All fairy stories have insurmountable odds that have to be . . .'

'Surmounted?'

'Exactly.'

'Yes but isn't this a bit like Snow White trying to nick Prince Charming off Cinderella?'

'Well it's either that or end up with another Dopey or Sleazy.'

'Sneezy,' I correct.

'Bless you!'

'Oh Cleo!'

'What?'

'Oh, I don't know,' I humph, defeated. 'Shouldn't I be holding out for my own prince, not someone else's?'

'Your prince got waylaid by Rapunzel. I'm sorry to have to tell you but he's not coming.'

'Don't say that!' I wail.

'Are you seeing him tonight?' Cleo asks, cutting to the chase.

'No, I've got to go on this hideous blind date dinner thing with PM's son.'

'Oh my God! You've never had so much men-action! Are you going there now?'

'No, first I've got a massage ...' I trail off, feeling guilty again.

'Oh. I think I'm just going to watch a video and have an early night.'

'Right.'

There's a moment's silence. Suddenly I feel we are a million miles apart.

'Well, at least think about what I said about going for it with Luca. I know it's in direct opposition to your morals but neither of us have exactly been rewarded for being good,' she reasons. 'Maybe it's time we started being *bad* ...'

I hang up the phone and sit in contemplation for a moment. Every time I reach for something solid and familiar it changes form: my sweet best friend is talking about being bad, my dry-eyed mother is crying and most bizarrely of all, I'm going to a beauty spa.

Until now my cellulite had seemed merely porridgy, but as my mother and I enter Sophia's seaspray-scented world I feel as though my skin has been stuffed with gnocchi. I'm convinced alarms will start to wail and I'll be raced into a treatment room on a gurney. Instead we get right up to the desk before the young girl on reception looks up from her book – probably some engrossing tome on free radicals and expensive ways to combat them.

'Welcome to Issima!' she smiles up at us with poreless skin.

'Grazie! I am Gina and this is my daughter Kim. Sophia has booked us in for some treatments.'

'Ah yes. Sophia will be back in five minutes but we can get you started straight away. Please ...' she motions for my mother to join a petite, highly polished brunette in her nail booth.

'See you in a couple of hours!' Mum winks.

'Please take a seat,' the receptionist tells me. 'I can begin with you when Sophia returns.'

I sit down feeling like I have a double-dental appointment rather than what is supposed to be an indulgent pampering session.

'Would you like some tea? We have a range of healing infusions.'

'Um ...' I hesitate.

'I choose for you.' She peruses the jars. 'I think you try this one for emotional balance.'

Is my weakness that obvious?

'It contain damiana, clover blossom and motherwort which is good for the heart.'

I take a tentative sip. Marvellous. I'm cured!

'You are having the massage, yes?'

'Yes, salt scrub,' I confirm.

'Perhaps we also put a little soothing compress on your eyes,' she suggests. 'We take away the pink, then no one knows.'

Her kindness nearly sets me off again.

'Can you do the same for my mother?' I gulp. I don't want to be reminded of her tears when I next look at her, it's just too heartbreaking.

'Sì, of course,' she agrees, moving back to the desk and setting her book to one side.

'What are you reading?' I ask, knowing I'll get nervous and bolt if we slip into a polite silence.

'*The Dead Zone* – Stephen King,' she says, holding up the book.

'You like horror stories?' I gasp.

'Oh yes! *Misery* is my favourite – when Annie Wilkes takes the hammer and—'

'Chiara!' Sophia growls from the doorway, 'are you scaring the customers again?'

'No, I—'

'Sometimes I think she'd be better off working in a morgue, you know, doing the make-up on the dead bodies.'

'One day . . .' sighs Chiara.

'In the meantime, you can give Kim her massage. Oh! That didn't sound right,' Sophia apologizes.

'No, it's fine,' I tell her. 'She wants gruesome, she's got it.'

Sophia laughs. 'Enjoy!'

I follow Chiara. 'I'm not joking, you know. I really do have the most horrible lumpy thighs and bottom.'

'Oh, you have nothing to worry about,' she appeases me, showing me into a private room. 'Everyone thinks they are worse than they are. You are not so bad.'

'You haven't seen me yet,' I mutter. People never believe me until it's too late. Oh well, I've tried to warn her. I can't be held responsible for her screams.

Chiara hands me a paper G-string. 'This is for you!'

She's got to be kidding. I've seen bigger eye patches. No robe?

'I'll leave you to get changed.'

Apparently not.

This is far more nerve-racking than undressing for Luca. At least then I could distract him with kissing and wriggling. Now I'm just going to be lying there, utterly open to scrutiny. There's not even a sheet to crawl under on the massage table.

When Chiara returns, my T-shirt, knickers and bra are gone but I've hoisted the elasticated waist of my skirt up under my arms so it's a kind of boob-tube-cum-smock.

'Um . . .' she says contemplating me.

Up until now it would seem I've been doing a passable impersonation of a size 12 but my true identity is about to be revealed.

'Okay, you want me to lie on the table without . . .' I tug at my skirt.

'Yes, please,' she smiles. 'You have nothing to worry about.'

I drop the skirt and make a clumsy transition to the table.

For a second she is silent. Then she says, 'So, you don't do *any* exercise at all . . .'

Great. What a comfort it is to know that I am *not* one of those women who makes a fuss about nothing. All those silly girls who pinch a millimetre of flesh and wail, 'I'm so fat!' Pah! You thought I was exaggerating about being unfit and overweight? Nooooo! I was telling the truth. See! What a triumph.

I scrunch my eyes shut and try to not to visualize what she's seeing and touching. At least this scrub has a gritty texture. If it were an oil or a sheer cream she'd

310

be able to feel every pimple and ripple of flesh. I become aware that she's wearing surgical-style gloves to apply the gunk. Paranoia strikes – I hope that's standard procedure, not personal revulsion.

Back done she asks me to flip over. Somehow I manage to get salt in my mouth in the process and develop a raging thirst.

As Chiara places the cooling eyepads on me, I want to suggest she does the same for herself. Don't masseurs normally just expose a morsel of you at time? It just feels so exhibitionist to lie here naked bar the Post-It note knickers. It would have been worth all the pain and potential scarring of liposuction to be lying here with a flat stomach and a pert bum. I knew I should have gone ahead with it. As Chiara wraps me in cellophane I confide that I was contemplating surgery.

She shakes her head. 'As a beautician I could tell you that you could lose a few stones but as a woman I will tell you something else.'

'What?' I ask.

She leans close to my ear. 'Men love this shape!'

I peak out from my eyepad and giggle. 'Really?'

'And do you know what men's all-time most favourite shape is?'

'No, tell me!'

'Naked!' she laughs. 'That's all that really matters to them!'

She putters around with some pots. 'I think we give you a quick face mask while you are cooking.'

'Chiara?'

'Yes?'

'Is there anything you can do with my hair?'

'I can do nothing.' She shakes her head.

'Oh, fair enough, I know it's a bit wild.'

'No, no, I can do nothing but Antoinetta can. She is the hairstylist.'

She finishes applying the yummily scented mask and says, 'I will make you an appointment with her now. Just relax for ten minutes and think of naked men!'

Instead I wonder at what point I might actually come to terms with my looks. At what point I will accept that there isn't really an alternative. I think in a way I have been biding my time, presuming that at some point I'd get something better, that with or without the aid of surgery I would be given the option to morph into Beyoncé Knowles. What I am realizing now is that it is going to get worse from here on in – I'm getting older and if I don't like how I look now I'm going to like it even less in ten years' time and then I'll look back and kick myself for not being grateful for the lack of crinkles I once had. I decide it's about time I learned to love myself, gnocchi-knees and all.

All the same, when Chiara returns to unwrap me I am thrilled to see she is bearing a floor-length robe.

I shower, washing my own hair for expediency, then present myself to Antoinette, who turns out to be a fantastically patient woman, coaxing and separating each curl until I go from my usual 'finger in an electrical socket' look to glossy spirals like Julianna Margulies from *ER*. I love it.

As for my mother's gushing reaction, you'd think I'd

just emerged from a chrysalis. Just wait until she hears what I'm going to say next.

'Mum?'

'Yes my darling girl!'

'Have we got time to nip back to the shop?'

She looks at her watch. 'Just about – did you forget something?'

'No, it's just . . .' I say, stringing it out. 'I was wondering if you could pick me out something to wear for tonight.'

She's so happy she drops her cup of colon-cleansing tea.

31

There's a woman in the Krug bar of the Quisisana Hotel wearing a peach sequinned dress. I still can't quite believe that it's me.

The fact that my mother is wearing a copper satin slinkfest is making me feel all the more sorbet-girlie but I have to confess that I'm tickled to have taken Luca up on his dare to let my mum dress me. Luca . . . I take a deep breath and push away the queasy feeling I get when I think of him. I so desperately want to be with him. Even the thought of going 3 kilometres up the road to Anacapri for dinner is making me fretful. I need a drink. Miraculously two flutes of champagne appear before us.

'From the gentleman at the bar,' the waiter informs us.

'This bodes well!' beams my mother, raising her glass at her wrinkly suitor. I twist around trying to do the same but end up sloshing fizz over my skirt.

'Oh Kim!' says my mother, discreetly handing me a napkin. 'Don't worry, it'll dry out by the time we get to their hotel.'

I look forlornly at my glass. What a waste of Dutch courage. I gulp back the rest before it evaporates.

'Just think, Tom Cruise might have drunk from that glass!' my mum giggles. 'He's stayed here, and Jean Paul Sartre and John Belushi.'

I'm just picturing the scientologist, existentialist and hedonist getting drunk together when my mum leans close and whispers: 'We've only got a few minutes here but I just wanted to make sure we had a drink together in case all your time is spent with Tyler from now on.'

'Mum!' I groan. 'It's not going to happen! Please don't get your hopes up . . .'

'I can't help it. I've got a good feeling about this one.'

I sigh. I'm tempted to tell her about Luca. Not the rude bits but at least how I feel about him. She might even be able to give me some good advice – she must have been in this situation a fair few times in her life . . . Instead I say, 'I'm not really in the market for a—'

'Jet-set millionaire bachelor?' she twinkles.

I look at her. She's utterly incorrigible. 'Okay, I'll be nice but please promise you won't talk me up in front of him or make any comments about how good we look together.'

'Spoilsport!'

'I mean it! It's embarrassing enough as it is.'

'Okay. I'll behave. Let's just have one more glass and then be on our way.' Her eyes rove the room. 'Now, who shall we get to pay for this one . . . ?'

I get in a bit of a tangle trying to clamber out of the

taxi at Piazza Vittoria in Anacapri. I'm not used to transporting this many metres of fabric with me. Mum tries to help by giving me a gentle tug but falls back into a rack of touristy T-shirts. 'D'you know, I think I might be a bit tipsy!' she says, regaining her balance.

'It's the third one that did it!' I note, grateful now that I spilt so much of my first glass and therefore still have my faculties.

I follow my mother up a flight of steps and along a walkway, then pause in front of a vast oblong of blue glass framed by white concrete. 'That's the hotel pool seen from beneath,' she tells me. On cue a pair of long bronzed legs start treading water before me.

'I bet she's been to Leg School,' Mum muses.

'Leg School?'

'Oh, it's this special course they offer at the hotel's Beauty Farm – Sophia was telling me about it. Some people spend a whole week getting their legs wrapped in medicated bandages and lying in these shallow tanks of seawater – Kneipp vascular something.'

I look bewildered.

'Something to do with lymphatic drainage and varicose veins,' she says absently.

'Do you think that's why PM is staying here?' I tease.

Instead of defending him she giggles and grabs my arm. 'Actually, he's here because he heard that Liz Hurley and Julia Roberts stayed here, though not together, obviously.'

I was feeling quite glam up until this point but if I'm

316

going to have to compete with media vixens and movie stars . . .

'They've got this Megaron suite with servants' quarters and its own private swimming pool,' my mother informs me, swaying slightly. 'But the best bit is this: if you're lying in bed in the master bedroom there's this button you can press and the panel on the ceiling parts so you can kick off the covers and let the sun flood in on you before you're even fully awake.'

'Or gaze up at the stars at night,' I sigh, imagining being entwined with Luca.

We round the corner to the entrance of the hotel where water spills over a sink-size shell into a marble trough lit by a dozen twinkling tea lights. As we step into the cream dream of a lobby, Mum watches me take in the smooth low arches, endless off-white sofas and ankle-height tables swathed in coarse ivory cotton, then tells me she is nipping to the loo to check her lippy. Gradually the details come into focus – the tarnished gold of the chandeliers, the pale orchids and potted grasses, the cordoned-off antique carriage missing only four footmen, two poles and a princess. I had presumed the Hotel Palace had the edge with PM because it was easier to pronounce – I mean, try saying Quisisana after you've had a few – but it is an entirely different experience of five-star luxury. Whereas the Quisi has a formal grandness this décor inspires an 'Ooooh, I wish my home looked like this!' yearning.

Mum returns and links arms with me as we approach the bar. 'I know most women like to be late so they can make an entrance and keep the man on his

317

toes but I always like to be five minutes early so I can get a good spot . . .' She surveys the room – again extreme cream but this time with contrasting darkest wooden tables (the weight and clunkyness of cellar doors), waist-high pewter lanterns and enormous unframed canvases displaying bold contemporary art. (I'd be interested in art-dealer Tyler's take on the painting of an upside-down woman sliding down an angry red backdrop hung above the bar.)

'Okay, they'll be entering from the lobby so if we sit . . .' Mum manages to walk in an impressively straight line to the furthest corner, '*here* then we'll be able to get a good look at Tyler as he walks towards us.'

A waiter appears the instant we make contact with the sofa. My mother opens her mouth but I beat her to it by ordering mineral water for us both. She looks peeved but I know she won't be able to keep her promise to lay off the matchmaking if she has any more champagne. From our prime spot we watch a man approach the bar wearing a honey-coloured suit so perfectly co-ordinated with the décor he is barely distinguishable from the furnishings. He accepts a box of matches and lights his cigarette. The flame illuminates his amber eyes. Now if that was Tyler things would be looking up. But no, he's waving to someone out on the terrace and glides across the room to join them. There's not a woman in the place that doesn't glance in his direction as he passes. Our eyes return to the doorway.

'How serious are you about PM?' I ask.

'As serious as you can be about a man who lives in Atlanta.'

'What does that mean?'

'Call me old-fashioned but I like my men to live in the same country as . . . oop! Here they come!'

Platinum Man looks as elegant as ever in a slate grey suit, white shirt and lavender silk tie. He flashes us a smile and puts his hand on the shoulder of the man to his side. A man in a Nehru-collared shirt with a gold pin at the neck and a lurid red, gold and black waistcoat. A man with pudgy pocked cheeks. A man with a moustache.

My mother is working overtime to hide her dismay. 'You must be Tyler!' she charms him, extending her hand.

'No, ma'm. I'm Morgan. I'm afraid the good-looking son already got snapped up!'

Ye gods and little fishes – if he's the good-looking one!

'Tyler said he'd meet us here, he had to send a fax.' PM looks around the room. 'Ah! There he is!'

We follow PM's gaze past half a dozen sheath dresses shimmering on the terrace until it settles on the amber-eyed stud from the bar. 'That's Tyler!'

I like to think I'm the only one who heard my mother sigh, 'Thank God!'

32

This isn't my first dinner date with a millionaire. About nine years ago I met a stinking rich sports promoter when I was a student doing bar work. He took a shine to me – despite the excessive froth on his pint – and invited me to dinner. Knowing he was financially advantaged I began mentally grappling with an excess of cutlery and dodging low-flying champagne corks before we even arrived at the restaurant. So when his Rolls-Royce purred to a halt outside Pizza Hut I thought it must surely be a joke. (This was pre-Stuffed Crusts so there was simply no excuse.) But no, he parked up and strode towards the door. I was loath to leave the refined leather seats of the £50,000 Roller for a plastic-coated banquette but tried to look on the bright side – it was Saturday so at least we didn't have to suffer the indignity of an All You Can Eat buffet scuffle. As I was a poor student at the time I managed to convince myself that he'd brought me there so I wouldn't be intimidated by my surroundings. However, the flicker of hesitation on his face when I offered to pay my share of the bill made me less certain – he

320

was clearly the type of guy who would tot up his order on a group bill rather than split it evenly, just because he didn't have a second cappuccino or cheese on his garlic bread.

There are many flaws you can overlook in a millionaire – shrivelled, sagging skin (especially in the wheelchair-bound over-90s), suspect arms deals, appalling taste in yacht interiors . . . but stinginess? You wouldn't expect a bodybuilder to make you carry the shopping home from Sainsbury's or a barman to skimp on pouring you a vodka, would you? Perhaps he'd lived hand-to-mouth as a child, I reasoned. Or perhaps it was me: I've never been one to inspire 'treat her like a princess' behaviour in a man. Well, I may be a cheap date but I draw the line at what is essentially a fancy cheese and tomato sandwich (I didn't dare order extra toppings on my margarita).

Miserly behaviour is a real passion-killer for me, so I must have looked stricken when, ten minutes after leaving Pizza Hut, we pulled up outside a dingy B&B. Most millionaires would have shacked up at St David's Hotel & Spa. The place should have had a skull & crossbones on the sign instead of a star rating.

I made it clear that there was no way I was snuggling up in a stained single bed with him and he said he'd drive me home. On the way he began telling me of the recurring nightmares he'd been having about being locked in a prison cell. Before I could indulge in any amateur dream analysis he added that this was principally because, until recently, he had been locked in a prison cell.

My mind raced – I'd put the overpowering after-shave fumes down to heavy-handed macho dumbness but was he actually attempting to asphyxiate me with Old Spice? I was rigid with anxiety. There's something about being enclosed in a car with a convicted criminal that makes you want to get intimate with a speeding pavement but before I did any rudimentary stunt moves I just had to know what he was banged up for . . .

'It was a bank job,' he sighed. 'Just a small branch but it went wrong.'

Now I've seen enough films to know that bank robbers are good blokes at heart but more than anything I was relieved that his crime didn't begin with 'm' and end in 'urder'. I cheerily asked if he wore a balaclava on the job. He looked impatient at my insensitivity. Somehow the evening still ended with a snog. He left the next day for a world tour. A month later he phoned and told me how he'd flown his private jet to the Caribbean and cruised Australia's Gold Coast on a yacht. So when he mentioned a weekend break my thoughts turned to Paris, Rome, New York . . . I should have known better. 'I was thinking, you could come and visit me at home in Newcastle.'

He'd mentioned that he was back in Cardiff in a couple of weeks so I told him I'd wait until then – I couldn't bear the thought of going to make a cup of coffee and discovering his kitchen was entirely stocked with sachets nicked from service stations.

This time I arranged to meet him at the Armless Dragon, planning to woo him with a bit of traditional

Welsh fare. It's reasonably priced but he walked in and broke out into a none-too-fetching sweat. When he kissed me hello I noticed he was trembling. My new hairdo had clearly wowed him.

'I don't like the look of this place,' he muttered in my ear. 'Let's find a nice plate of pasta.'

We trailed the streets for over an hour comparing prices, which is quite absurd because it's unlikely you'll get stiffed for more than £7 for a plate of tagliatelle wherever you go. When it came to it, I paid the bill because I couldn't bear the angst on his face when the little saucer arrived with the folded receipt. By the end of the night I had cringed so much at his penny-pinching I had a newly toned physique. And when he offered me a lift home in his flash new sporty motor (so that's where the money goes) I said I'd rather make my own way home, thanks. He insisted he drive me. I firmly declined and headed for the taxi rank.

'At least let me pay for you to get home,' he offered. I conceded.

He reached into his pocket and handed me ... £1 bus fare. I kid you not.

You've got to read the small print if you get involved with a millionaire. At the moment I can't tell which way Tyler is going to go. The hotel is super-flash but it's his father's choice. I'd say he's spent a few bob on his suit but he's in the art world, he needs to look good.

'Shall we have some champagne?' he asks, motioning for us to take a seat.

'Oooh yes, that would be lovely!' my mother coos.

He turns to the waiter and says the magic word, 'Cristal!'

We're talking £100 a bottle in an off-licence in the UK. I dread to think what kind of mark-up it gets in a five-star hotel. That's what I like to see – a millionaire that behaves like one.

At PM's suggestion we take the champagne through to the restaurant.

'Welcome to L'Olivo,' the *maître d'* greets us. 'Table for five?'

'Unless you're joining us!' Mum giggles.

I wonder if PM sensed she needed to start soaking up the alcohol pronto?

The *maître d'* weaves us through the squat pillars and potted palms to a cosy table matched with three fabric-covered armchairs and a two-seater sofa.

'Would you two gals like to take the sofa?' PM offers.

'Thank you,' I say, sitting back into an ivory embrace.

'I'd actually prefer one of the chairs for my back,' Mum says, playing the 'old lady' card for the first time ever. 'Why don't you join Kim, Tyler?'

Mmm-hmm. It's begun.

'I'd love to,' he smiles, inadvertently depressing my seat cushion as well as his as he sits down so I tip into his arms.

'Oop,' I blush, trying not to claw at his expensive suit.

'Your daughter doesn't waste much time!' Morgan taunts.

324

'She gets it from her mother!' Mum laughs, before realizing that she's just called herself a slapper.

'We Hamiltons are hard to resist,' PM winks, getting her off the hook.

'Rich men often are,' Morgan mutters. Surely he can't be so blatantly insinuating that we're a pair of gold-diggers? We'll see about that . . .

'I'd like to propose a toast to the new owner of one of Capri's oldest and most exclusive boutiques!' I say, raising a glass to my mother but keeping my eye on Morgan.

'You own one of the shops here?' he looks startled, as predicted. 'That must be pretty lucrative.'

'I hope it will be!' Mum smiles, sipping her champagne. 'It's like a dream come true for me – I've always loved fashion!'

'What woman doesn't,' Morgan groans. Oh good, sounds like his unfortunate wife is at least milking him for all he's worth.

'Mr Hamilton?' a waiter approaches our table.

The three men chorus, 'Yes?'

'Mr Tyler Hamilton?'

'That's me!' Mr Amber Eyes raises his hand.

'There's a call for you from New York, signor. They say it's urgent.'

'Please excuse me,' Tyler addresses the table. 'I'll be just a few minutes. Do go ahead and order without me.'

I return to perusing my menu but Morgan isn't done quizzing my mother just yet. 'So, do you have any actual business experience?' he asks.

Do you have any actual manners? I want to squawk, noticing the look on Mum's face.

'Thirty years in the business, isn't it, Mum?' I nudge her. (I've knocked a few years off to keep her around the fifty mark but I'm sure she won't mind showing her age to shut him up.)

'That's right,' she says, raising her glass to me. 'I've worked my way up from the Almay counter and loved every minute of it.'

'So, you're a shop assistant made good. Well, good for you!' Morgan cheers.

Patronizing git. I suppose it's been quite a stretch for him to go from silver spoon in his mouth to, er, silver spoon in his mouth.

'What line of work are you in, Morgan?' Mum somehow manages not to take offence.

'Finance, but I won't trouble you with the details,' he shrugs.

Apparently he thinks us 'gals' wouldn't understand.

'Boring, is it?' I find myself saying.

PM chuckles to himself. 'Kim has an unusual sense of humour, Morgan. You better keep on your toes!'

'My job is not boring,' Morgan pouts. 'It's just that a lot of people find my success intimidating.'

'Really?'

'Yes,' he nods, head heavy with self-pity. 'As Bette Midler says, "The worst part of success is to try finding someone who is happy for you." '

'Are you a big Bette Midler fan?' I raise an eyebrow.

Morgan scowls at me. 'Another of your jokes?'

'I just wondered.' I shrug, adopting my most

326

innocent expression. Suity prats like Morgan always hate being associated with anything remotely gay and I love nothing better than tripping that switch.

'Perhaps we should go ahead and order.' PM beckons the waiter with classic diplomacy.

There's much salivation as we make our choices: red potato gnocchi with prawns and marjoram, mint-spiced baby squid with green bean salad, chive-scented turbot with candied tomatoes, laurel-scented beef sirloin with anchovies . . . Last to order is Morgan, with a fittingly poisonous selection – orecchiette with scorpion fish ragout followed by rabbit loin in crust of pork cheek. Pork cheek?! I shudder.

'Are you ready for the wine list?' the waiter enquires.

'Give it to me,' Morgan demands. 'If Pop chooses we'll end up with something that still has the locals' toenails floating in it!'

I look up in disgust.

'You're not the only one with a sense of humour!' Morgan rallies.

Hilarious, I think.

'Oh here he is – the golden boy.' Morgan fanfares Tyler's return. 'A tip for you, Kim – never mess with my brother's hair. His halo is his trademark.'

His sun-kissed blond flicks do indeed enhance an already glowing complexion. Mum gazes at him with girlie adoration but it's too late for her – she's already assigned to PM a.k.a. The Man with the Golden Son, I snicker to myself. Whoah! This champagne is potent!

'Everything all right?' PM checks.

'Yeah, they just want me to go to Verona earlier than planned,' Tyler explains as he returns – carefully – to the sofa. 'I'm going to have to leave tomorrow.'

'Oh no!' Mum cries out in genuine dismay.

'I have to go meet with a new artist,' Tyler informs us. 'He's kind of temperamental and his agent has just told my boss that it's Tuesday or not at all so . . .'

'Couldn't you stay one more night?'

'I've got a whole bunch of preparation to do out there. I haven't even seen his latest exhibition yet.'

'Did you say Verona?' Mum asks.

Tyler nods.

'We've been there, haven't we, darling? Do you have a translator working with you?'

Could she be any more obvious?

'Yeah, they should have one booked. I just hope they'll be able to switch days too.'

'Well, if not, you know that Kim—'

'Verona's really lovely,' I speak over her.

'I've never been before,' Tyler tells me, slightly cigarettey of breath.

'Be handy to have someone who knew the city . . .' Mum keeps plugging away.

'Have you been, Morgan?' I ask in desperation, trying to get the conversation tacking in a different direction.

'I'm not really into that olde-worlde stuff.'

'He thinks art is overrated,' Tyler sighs.

'I guess some of the classics are okay but this guy you're seeing out there—'

'Alessandro.'

'He's into abstract art, right?'

Tyler nods.

'I'm afraid I'm with Al Capp on that: "Abstract art is a product of the untalented sold by the unprincipled to the utterly bewildered." ' He takes a moment to look smug before adding, 'Give me a beach and a quality hardback and I'm happy.'

'Oh yes, you're going to Sardinia after this, aren't you?' Mum is successfully diverted.

'Yeah, we've been every summer for the past three years. I just found Bermuda was getting too cliquey.'

'And now you've fallen under Italy's spell,' Mum says proudly.

'I like the country, not too keen on the people.'

'And yet they speak so highly of you,' I snort inwardly.

PM looks embarrassed. 'I think you might want to retract that remark, son. Gina is Italian.'

'I thought you were British!' he barks, accusingly.

'No, born on Capri, lived here until I was eleven and then moved to Cardiff.'

'Oh,' he says. 'Well, it's really the Italian *men* I object to.'

Now I'm getting offended on behalf of Luca.

'They're just so goddamn lecherous with the women,' he continues, despite the fact that a very Italian waiter is currently topping up our wine.

'Maybe the women like it,' I suggest, catching the waiter's eye.

'Nobody with any class likes to be ogled like that.'

I go to say, 'I do!' but instead simper, 'I'm delighted

329

to hear you have so much respect for women.' I bet his poor bullied wife Angie would beg to differ.

'Scorpion?' the waiter returns with the first starter plate.

'Morgan,' we chorus.

For the past hour an ever more garrulous and obnoxious Morgan has dominated the conversation. It's all 'as Nietzsche said . . .' and 'Mark Twain put it this way . . .' Relentless quotations. Tyler has barely uttered a word. I can see now why PM said his sons bore him stupid. Even my mother has tired of indulging Morgan and telling him how marvellously well-read he must be to remember all these clever lines. I wonder how someone as fun as PM could have such a pompous son.

'Do you have a favourite quote?' PM asks me as we pause to consider the dessert menu.

'Oh – you have to give me a second to think,' I admit. 'What about you?'

'Always be nice to your children because they are the ones who will choose your rest home – Phyllis Diller.'

Mum and I laugh.

'What about you, Gina?' PM asks my mother.

A sad look passes over her face. 'People need loving the most who deserve it the least,' she says wistfully. 'John Harrigan.'

Following our emotional afternoon at the shop, her words seems all the more poignant. I sigh to myself, wishing I could love her more.

'Tyler?' Mum smiles, batting the question over to him. By the look on her face I can tell she's hoping for something romantic.

He doesn't disappoint. 'Love is a fire. But whether it is going to warm your hearth or burn down your house, you can never tell.'

Wow. I can relate to that.

'Who said that?' Morgan frowns.

'I don't know, I think it was some singer or actress, I can't recall.'

'Very impressive, bro,' Morgan snorts.

'Surely the words are more important than who said them?' I venture. 'Otherwise we'd just be sitting here listing names—'

'Woody Allen, Coward, Yeats . . .' PM demonstrates.

'And where's the fun in that?' I conclude.

Morgan just rolls his eyes and says, 'Mine would be—'

'Hold on, we haven't heard Kim's yet,' Tyler interrupts.

Morgan huffs like a petulant child.

'Kim?'

'Nothing that is worth knowing can be taught – Oscar Wilde.'

'Quite right, you've got to experience things for yourself before you understand them, haven't you?' PM agrees.

I meant it as a dig at Morgan for flaunting his highbrow education but PM's comment has mirrored it right back at me. Am I coming to understand my

331

mother because of what I'm experiencing with Luca? I don't get to follow this thought any further because Morgan is now ready to take centre stage. But instead of some pseudo-intellectual twaddle he grabs a passing waiter and booms, 'This wine is corked! It tastes appalling!'

The waiter tries to speak but Morgan launches into a poncey, show-offy, monologue about how such a wine should have a long, velvety finish when this is short and bristly, how the tannins aren't softly rounded but positively square – on and on and on.

All the while the waiter is shifting from foot to foot looking increasingly distressed. Finally he gets to speak: 'Non parla Inglese!' he blurts.

'Oh well, isn't that just typical!' Morgan roars, looking around for the *maître d'*.

'Scusa,' I quickly tell the young boy in Italian. 'This man is mentally retarded and I can only apologize. If you would be so kind as to remove the wine and bring a fresh bottle that would be wonderful!'

'Ahhh, grazie signorina!' He bows, gingerly removing the glasses from the table, careful not to get too close to Morgan.

'Five-star hotel and the goddamn waiter doesn't speak English!' Morgan sneers.

'I think he was just what you call a bus boy,' I tell Morgan, trying to control the hot angry feeling burgeoning inside of me.

'Your favourite quote?' Mum says, seeming aware that if Morgan makes any more anti-Italian remarks

I'm going to storm the kitchen and grab the sharpest *mezzaluna* I can get my hands on.

He opens his mouth to speak and then halts to watch a lavishly dressed older woman take a seat at the small round table near us. Her sole dining companion is her fluffy Shih Tzu dog. My heart goes out to her. Before I met Luca I was beginning to think that I would end up like that.

'Ha-ha! I've got a great one!' Morgan bellows. 'August Strindberg: "I loathe people who keep dogs. They are cowards who haven't got the guts to bite people themselves." Ha-ha-ha!'

The fact that this Strindberg fellow was a *Swedish* writer is the final straw for me – when the Shih Tzu doesn't turn round and bite Morgan I decide to do it myself.

'What about people who haven't the guts to *speak* for themselves?' I spit.

There is a stunned silence. Morgan glowers at me.

'I have a quote for you, Morgan. Ralph Waldo Emerson, American philosopher and poet. He said: "I hate quotations, tell me what you know." '

He opens his mouth to retaliate but I get to my feet and say, 'Honey, I can put you down in six languages so unless you've got a witty comeback in Croatian, forget it!'

And with that I strump out of the dining room.

Pausing to catch my breath in the lobby, I realise that I'm shaking. I can't believe I said that! I can't believe I called Morgan 'Honey'!

'Kim!' Mum hurries up to me.

'I'm not going to apologize.' I stand firm.

'I'm not going to ask you to,' she grins. 'I thought you were wonderful. So did Tony!'

'He's not angry?'

'Only with Morgan for being so rude.'

'Oh.'

'Will you come back to the table?' she asks.

'I'd rather go back to the hotel,' I admit. I'd be far too embarrassed to return now.

'Do you want me to go with you?' Mum offers.

'No, I'll be fine,' I smile. 'You stay. I'll see you later.'

She looks a bit sheepish.

'Or tomorrow,' I add. 'If you're planning to stay over . . .'

'I have got a spare outfit here.'

'Well then, I'll see you at the shop, 9.30a.m.?' I do my best to sound breezy.

'If you're sure . . .'

'I'm sure,' I say, giving her a peck goodnight. 'Please thank whoever is paying for dinner.'

'I will,' she says, looking at me with affection. 'Good-night, darling. I'm very proud of you.'

My heart experiences a little squeeze.

'Night!' I wave as I exit.

I take the path leading past the pool – no feet flippering past this time – and approach the steps leading down to the piazza.

'Hey wait!'

Before I can turn around Tyler is upon me. He

grabs me by my upper arms and plants a kiss on my mouth.

I gawp at him, stunned.

'Sorry, I just had to do that!' he pants. 'I've tried for years to get the better of him but that was perfect. You're amazing!'

My eyes rove the paving slabs, as I try to recover.

'Please don't go,' he says softly.

'I have to,' I tell him.

'No, you don't,' he smiles.

'Well no, I don't have to,' I concede, 'but I'd prefer to.'

'We could celebrate!'

'I'm tired,' I tell him, feeling shy now it's just the two of us.

He contemplates me for a second. 'Okay then, I'll escort you. It's the least I can do.'

I shift awkwardly. 'I'll be fine, really.'

'No, I insist.' He turns and nods to a cab driver leaning against his vintage green and yellow Fiat Marea.

At Capri Town I urge him to stay in the cab and return to Anacapri but he says he's seeing me to the Hotel Luna even if he has to follow five paces behind me all the way there.

When we finally get to the gate Tyler is distracted by the Certosa di San Giacomo.

'Oh wow – you're right next door. You know I was actually here earlier today.'

'Really?'

'Yeah, they have an exhibition of Diefenbach

paintings in there. Pretty grizzly stuff. I'd say we sneak in but it would probably give you nightmares.'

'How bad is it?' I ask, intrigued.

'Very dark, in both senses of the word,' Tyler explains, luring me into the Certosa grounds as he talks. We take the tree-lined track to a lookout point that offers a perfect view of the Hotel Luna. I feel a sense of pride as I look at the hotel. It really has proved to be such a haven.

'It's a great location,' notes Tyler. 'Our rooms at the Palace don't have a view as such. Which is yours?'

'Second floor, about halfway along,' I say, pointing. 'Overlooking the gardens and the . . .'

Oh my God.

'And the sea?' Tyler finishes the sentence for me.

'Um. Yes. I've got to go,' I babble as a sting of adrenalin zings through my body.

'Wait!' says Tyler as I begin striding away from him.

'I've just remembered I've got to make a phone call,' I say quickening my pace.

'Here, you can use my cellphone.'

'No, the phone number is back at the hotel. I'm sorry, I've really got to run, bye!'

Luca is at the Hotel Luna. I just saw him coming out of the lobby. I have to get back there before he leaves. Please let him wait, please let him be gazing out at the Faraglioni when I get there.

With a pounding heart I tear past the gate and up the hill, pushing myself through the wheezing and the pain. If I blow this, if I miss him . . . it doesn't bear thinking about. I run faster, feet pummelling the dirt, then the pavement and finally the path to the hotel . . .

33

I spin around. There's no one on the terrace, no one in the gardens. I skid through the lobby and smack into the reception desk.

'Was there . . . ?' I puff at the night concierge. 'Did someone . . . ?'

'Yes, signorina. A gentleman call for you. You have just missed him.'

I close my eyes, wretched. 'Did he say where he was going?'

'No, I am sorry.'

'Did he leave a message?'

'Not with me.'

I'm crushed.

'But he did have a drink in the hotel bar. Perhaps Mario . . .'

'Thank you!' I blurt, dashing through to the lounge.

'Heyyyyy, Kim! Where have you been all night?' Mario greets me.

'Did you see Luca? Did he leave a message?'

'I'm fine, thank you for asking – *molto bene*,' he grunts.

338

'Please, Mario. It's important. Tell me everything!' I command.

'He was here for maybe half an hour, he had two Peroni . . .'

'What did he *say*?'

The night concierge pops his head around the door before Mario can answer: 'Signorina, there's phone call for you. Is gentleman. Would you like me to put it through to the bar?'

'Yes! *Yes!*' I squeal.

It rings. Mario hands me the phone.

'Hello?' I gasp.

'Kim?'

'Yes?'

'It's Tyler.'

My heart plummets.

'I just wanted to make sure you're all right.'

'I'm fine,' I fake. 'I'm sorry I had to tear off.'

'Did you get through to whoever it was?'

'Um, actually I just missed them,' I say, forcing myself to accept that Luca has vanished into the night.

'Oh. Well, I hope it's nothing too serious.'

'So do I,' I say, wondering what Luca had come to tell me, what he had to say that couldn't wait until the morning.

'Maybe I'll see you tomorrow?' Tyler suggests.

'Maybe,' I reply, not really paying attention.

'Are you playing hard to get?' he laughs.

I snort. If he only knew that I'd just given myself cramp and shin-splint trying to get to Luca in time. I'm not exactly the 'playing hard to get' type. 'I'm sorry, I have to go – the barman needs to use the telephone,' I say, pulling a face at Mario.

'Okay, well, sleep well and . . . it was really great to meet you, Kim. I look forward to the next time.'

'Mmmm,' I muffle.

'I guess you can't really talk in a busy bar, huh?'

'No,' I lie. (There's only one guest over by the far window and he's absorbed in a book.)

'Okay, *laku noc!*'

My jaw drops. He just said goodnight in Croatian.

I guess there's more to Tyler than colour co-ordination and a whopping bank balance.

Mario replaces the phone then sets a glass in front of me. 'Grappa,' he says. 'On me.'

'Thank you,' I sigh, feeling utterly defeated and bewildered.

'This Luca,' he begins. 'He has a wife but he wants you?'

'I don't know,' I shrug.

'I don't think it is so normal to visit another woman at midnight.'

'I don't know what's going on. She just got back to Capri yesterday. It's complicated.'

'You want to talk about it?'

'To you?' I laugh.

'No, to his wife!' he snorts. 'Yes, to me!'

I study Mario for a second. I already snubbed him once over Luca when I accepted his scooter ride to Marina Grande. Wouldn't this just be rubbing his nose in it?

'I don't think so,' I tell him.

340

'Come on, try me. After this gentleman leave I am finish for the night. We can be private.'

I consider the alternative – sitting alone in my room fretting.

'Okay,' I tentatively accept.

'I have to bring in the cushions and the tablecloths from outside. You wait here.' Mario opens the door to the terrace and starts to stack the cobalt cushions. Once he's amassed a dozen or so he flips the pile on its side and carries them between his hands like a big blue concertina.

'Do you play any instruments?' I ask him.

He gives me a quizzical look. 'You are a very strange girl, Kim.'

I chuckle to myself and decide to help him clear the tables.

'No, you are guest!' he protests.

'Please, I'd like to help!' I wheedle.

He rolls his eyes and I roll the tablecloths. Having a practical function is an effective distraction from my inner angst. As I carry the bundle inside I see the lone book-reader getting to his feet and dropping a 1,000 lire note on the table as a tip. That's about 30p. Gee, Mario will be able to retire after tonight. The book-reader walks behind me as I dump the cloths on the bar stools.

'Don't give him all your money!' the book-reader smirks, implying – I presume – that Mario has got me wrapped around his little finger.

'Too late, I've already written him into my will!' I reply.

Cheek! All at once I feel quite protective of my relationship with Mario. I'm sure to the book-reader it looks like another silly Brit falling for an Italian waiter but to me this is starting to feel like a real friendship. I think about how I'd be going half crazy now if I were alone, eaten up with frustration at having missed Luca all because I was dallying in the moonlight with Tyler. Suddenly I get chills – if I could see Luca, then maybe he could see me – *us*! Maybe that's why he left. I run out on to the terrace and try to locate the lookout point but it is nestled in shadow. I sigh with relief. Mario herds me back into the bar, locks the doors and dims the lights. Normally this would make me nervous but this isn't about him getting a shag any more. If I didn't know better I'd think he actually cared.

'First of all,' says Mario, stripping off his cream jacket and black tie and pulling on a casual sweater. 'He didn't confide anything in me so I can't solve any mysteries for you, but it seems to me that this thing between the two of you must be quite serious for him to risk slipping out in the night, yes?'

And so we begin our amateur analysis of the situation. We discuss the possibility that he needed to warn me about something (like a rampaging wife) but then he could have done that over the phone or left a note. And the fact that he didn't leave a note means that it was either something too delicate to write down or that he didn't want anything incriminating in print. I tell Mario that we already have some highly incriminating photographs. He suggests I wait until I get home to get them developed, just in case the people working in the camera shop are in some way connected to Tanya. I start to tell him that my flatmate works in a photo lab but he pulls me back on course and asks me what I want to happen next with Luca.

I tell him I just want the chance to be alone with him again. He asks me to think beyond that. I tell him I can't – obviously us being together is completely impractical, not to mention immoral. Mario tells me that sometimes people come together for a reason but only for a brief amount of time. I agree but I find it almost impossible to get my head around the concept of letting Luca go. How can I not fight for this? He's married to someone else but he feels more 'mine' than any man I've ever been out with. And I am more sure of him than I have been of anyone else. Yes, everything about our circumstances is conspiring to keep us apart but there's no doubt in my heart that this is the man I am supposed to be with.

'Oh dear,' is all Mario has to say to that.

We call it a night at 2a.m. It has been a great comfort talking to Mario, he's been surprisingly level-headed and sympathetic. And I only had to bat him off me twice.

34

I awake at 10a.m. After wishing away the hours until I see Luca again I'm actually late for the shop opening – I could have been with him half an hour ago! I leap out of bed and then stumble backwards; champagne, red wine, grappa – will I never learn? I move slowly to the bathroom as a new kind of nausea infuses my body – nerves. Suddenly I'm not in such a hurry. Until I see him, I can still have hope. I stand in the shower longer than necessary, then slowly dry my hair, taking the time to use the miracle hair product Antoinetta gave me. I try and compose myself, telling myself that whatever happens I can cope. I will always have the memory and I will get over it. But somehow I still feel entirely at his mercy.

On the way I stop and look in shop windows at the designer sunglasses, bejewelled compacts and raggedy coral necklaces.

Then Desiderio's comes into view. I take a long, deep breath, adopt a breezy demeanour and stride forward.

'There you are!' trills my mother as I enter the shop.

No sign of Luca.

'I was beginning to think you weren't coming.'

'I overslept,' I explain.

'Did you have any breakfast? Luca's just gone to – here he is now.' Mum hurries to the door to help him unload the coffees and pastries. 'I'm starving,' she laughs. 'I think I've still got quite a bit of alcohol to soak up!'

'Hello,' he smiles, looking sweet but wary.

'Hello,' I reply, amazed at how relieved I am just to see him again.

'I was just telling Luca about what a mad night we had! You'll be pleased to hear that Morgan will be well on his way to Sardinia by now, Kim.' Mum takes a gulp of cappuccino and then continues, 'I was thinking this morning how funny it is that you clashed with one brother and got on so well with the other. Tyler is absolutely smitten. He couldn't stop talking about you. He wanted to know if you were seeing anyone.'

I feel myself blush slightly and try to convey to Luca that it's not how it seems.

'I thought he was such a gentlemen to see you back to the hotel,' Mum continues.

Is that a flash of jealousy in Luca's eyes? He's certainly dismantling those cardboard boxes with undue vigour.

'I wished I'd got back earlier, a friend of Mario's was in the bar,' I say.

Luca stops shredding and looks directly at me.

'I would really liked to have seen him.'

Mum looks concerned. 'Kim, I think you'd better

have some of this tramezzino with me.' She hands me half a multi-layered sandwich. 'Anyway, he wants to take you to lunch today.'

'I can't!' I blurt.

'Don't be silly. Of course you can – I told him to call by the shop at one o'clock.'

'But I've got to . . .' I search wildly for an excuse.

'Watch Nino play football,' Luca rescues me.

'Yes!' I say, latching on to the excuse. 'I can't let him down – I promised.'

'Since when?'

'Since we got back from Ravello,' I lie. 'He's playing against a school from Naples.'

'I'm sure he'll understand. Tyler is leaving for Verona this afternoon, so it'll be your last chance to see him.'

'It's my last chance to see Ringo play.'

'Well, I know which I'd rather do,' she mutters under her breath. 'Are you going too, Luca?'

'I said I would go for an hour at lunch.'

Mum takes my hand. 'You're not really going to blow this, are you?'

I give her a steady look.

'I don't understand you, Kim. Tyler is special. You won't get too many chances with a man like him.'

'He's not my type,' I say simply.

'Not your type? He's everyone's type – handsome, rich, interested in you . . .'

I don't reply.

'So, just what is your type?' she asks, completely exasperated.

I sneak a look at Luca. 'It's not really a question of type,' I say, contradicting myself. 'It's about how someone makes you feel.'

Mum sighs. 'Will you talk some sense into her, Luca?'

'I don't think I can,' he demurs. 'I like what she is saying.'

It's a good hour before Luca gets me alone long enough to say he'll meet me at the top of Monte Solaro at 1.30p.m. I express my concern about the proximity of the mountain to the Hotel Palace but he says it's fine and besides Tyler will be down in Capri Town by then. Presumably he's chosen such a touristy hot spot because there is little chance of locals observing us together but I worry that we won't be able to really talk with so many people around. If only we had the time to take his boat and find our own private grotto.

At 1p.m. I leave the shop, squeeze through the crush of tourists in the Piazzetta and board the little orange bus bound for Anacapri. As we climb the dramatic cliff road, passing paint-scrapingly close to the oncoming traffic, I look down towards Marina Grande and spot the island's main football pitch. It must be the most glamorous location in the world. The length of it is aligned with the edge of the coast and from this height there appears to be no barrier between the side of the pitch and the sea – kick the ball beyond the white sideline and it'll become a bobbing buoy. Judging from the cluster of dots at the top of the pitch the game looks to be very one-sided but at least the redundant goalie at the other end can amuse himself by gazing out across the sea to the Bay of Naples. If he had a pair of binoculars he could probably see San Paolo Stadium – once home to Maradona. Talk about an inspiring view!

I wonder which of the animated dots darting around the pitch is Ringo, then I experience a twinge of guilt for using him as an alibi ... He's so innocent. Sometimes being an adult feels so corrupt.

As the bus continues on up the road and passes the Caesar Augustus Hotel I remember Mario telling me that he plays five-a-side football at the tennis courts just up from here. Teams from various hotels and restaurants get together for tournament play-offs after work, sometimes kicking off as late as midnight. For an island with a reputation for hedonism it also offers such simple pleasures.

Two more minutes up the road and here we are: Piazza Vittoria. This is only my second time in Anacapri yet that sets me apart from just about every day tripper that crowds the steps. I weave through a group on a cruise excursion and purchase my chairlift ticket. As I queue at the barrier I look up the mountain – the final incline looks perilous. Before nerves can claim me, I am summoned by the two men co-ordinating bums and seats and told to stand on the red circle painted on the ground. As the chair rounds the enormous wheel they slide me back into the seat, press the security bar across my waist and I lurch forwards and upwards. I grip the metal frame with both hands, snorting at a sign forbidding swinging on the chairs. As if. The drop may be no more than 50 feet but that's still quite some bruise-potential.

Then something strange happens . . . almost instantly my tension vanishes and an overwhelming sense of serenity flows through my body. I thought this would be like a spine-jiggling fairground ride but it is smooth and graceful, silent save the gentle ticking-whirring sound as the cable passes over the cogs of the occasional pylon. Beneath my dangling feet pass neatly trimmed gardens followed by a flourish of ferns, fig trees and nobbly vines, then bigger bushier trees with furry green pom-poms the size of tennis balls. Mid-way up the mountain I glide over an eccentric sculpture garden a-jumble with treasures – there's a grey gnome with a beard of what look like glass fruit pastilles, a stone monkey proffering a platter of real bananas and a mosaic bird bath crammed with ceramic miniatures, all set amid a muddle of pink and yellow flowers. A hairy-backed man pads around sloshing water on his plants, seeming oblivious to his aerial intruders. Over to my right are the rooftops of Anacapri, white and flat and angular like a jumble of shoeboxes. Beyond is the sea, extending into a hazy navy infinity. The sense of bliss I feel is positively transcendental.

After a final stretch of rockier terrain I reach the top. My heart starts to dance. He could be ten chairlifts behind me or already here. I scamper up the steps and reel at the realization that I am now at the highest point on the island – 589 metres high according to the American student reading from his guidebook to his three buddies.

349

'Man, do you think this is what paradise looks like?' one ponders.

'For sure!' the others agree.

They look like the kind of boys who would only be impressed by free tickets to see Limp Bizkit or Blink 182 so I think they're probably right.

In fact I know they are because Luca is walking towards me.

35

He's still mine! I beam as Luca thuds into my chest, wrapping his strong arms around me and nuzzling my neck. Euphoria and relief intermingle as his kisses welcome me back home.

'Now we dance!' he announces.

I feel his hands interlock with mine and slowly begin to raise my arms.

'Tango?' I frown, trying to guess his next move.

'No, tarantella!' he says with a twinkle. 'It is local dance. I teach you.'

We could have sat and quizzed each other – me about his wife, him about Tyler – but instead he invites me to dance. I like his style!

'Now this dance is typically *vigorous* but we do it in slow motion . . .'

As our faces draw level he closes his eyes for a second and shakes his head imperceptibly as if to say, 'This is too hard. Don't tempt me.' In return I look at him wide-eyed with wanting, unable to disguise the wonder of what I feel for him.

'It is said that the origin of this dance come from the

bite of the tarantula spider – its victims are typically women and the trance the poison sends them into is cured by frenzied dancing.'

'Maybe I don't want to be cured,' I grin as he sways and rocks me.

'Normally there is mandolins and guitars and tambourines. Today we only have the drum of my heart!' He pulls a face.

I giggle up at him. I never knew what it was like before to have such an easiness with someone who with one look can take your breath away.

After the dance, we roam the mountaintop, gawping at every dazzling view. Our brief time together is nearly up but we still have not broached the subject of 'What next?'. I know it's going to alter our mood but I can't hold back any longer.

'Luca – do you know tonight is my last night?'

He looks shocked. I guess not.

'I was wondering, would there be any chance we could . . .' I tail off as he shakes his head.

'Tonight I will be in Sorrento. A woman Tanya used to work with is getting married. We leave at 6.30p.m. . . .' He looks vexed.

'Oh.' I'm crushed.

'I am sorry, I did not know until this morning, it was planned months ago.' He heaves a weary sigh and takes my hand.

'Then this might be our last chance to be together, alone?' I quaver, suddenly feeling panicky and pressured.

He kisses my hand and for a moment we sit in silence.

'Unless . . .' he begins.

Ask me to stay. Ask me to stay.

'Yes?' I say.

'Tanya has her sister coming out this week. It is possible I might have some time then,' he sighs. 'But I cannot ask that.'

'Ask what?' I egg him on.

'For you to stay. It is not fair. I do not know what I can offer you.'

My mind races with possibilities. 'When does she get here?'

'I think Thursday.'

Today is Monday. That would just leave Tuesday and Wednesday with minimal or no contact with Luca. Could I get through that on the semi-promise of some time together on Thursday? I could probably change my flight for a fee. My mother wouldn't mind if I stayed. She might be *surprised* but . . . I turn and stroke his face. The thought of leaving him makes me nigh on hysterical. I have to stay. It's the only way. I just wish it didn't leave me feeling so vulnerable. Am I setting myself up here? I flashback to Tomas and Stockholm. Sod it! I'm broken-hearted either way. At least if I stay there's the chance of being with him, even if it only allows us the chance to say goodbye properly.

'If it's okay with my mother, I'll stay,' I tell him.

'Yes?' he says, face brightening. 'I don't want to make things difficult for you.'

'I know,' I say. 'I just can't leave you – yet.'

He pulls me into his body and we sit entwined, watching the speedboats streaking patterns in the sea. I try and register every second of bliss with him so I can recall it and savour it during our time apart. As I snuggle into him I slip my hand down the back of his shirt and get a peek of the dragon tattoo he was so mysterious about in Ravello.

Tracing my finger along the shimmering scales, I say, 'Can you tell me what the dragon means now?'

He smiles down at me, looking abashed. 'I feel a little silly . . .'

'Oh go on, tell me!'

'It is a *red* dragon.'

'Yes,' I frown.

He sighs. 'I got it because I wanted something that reminded me of you.'

I scrabble to sit upright.

'Gina used to say the dragon from the flag of Wales was like your good luck charm, your pet . . .'

'You're making this up!' I laugh. It's true about me and the dragon but surely he wouldn't have gone so far as to get a tattoo.

'See here?' he says, pointing to the tattoo. For the first time I notice a tiny K on its claw.

'You are my travel muse!' he laughs. 'Your grand-father knew how much I wanted to see the world and so when Gina would send letters about your journeys he would read to me,' he confesses, unaware that I already know this. 'I used to dream that you would one day visit Capri and we would sail away on an adventure together.'

Pure delight spreads through my body. 'Why didn't you tell me before?'

'I thought maybe it would be too much,' he says, still squirming slightly.

'No! I love it!' I say, snuggling into him.

He begins stroking my hair. 'I have wanted to be with you for such a long time, Kim.'

Tears spring to my eyes. When he kisses me I feel like I'm floating. I've wanted to be with him my whole life. I just didn't know it until I met him.

Somewhere a clock strikes 2p.m. We have to go back to the real world. I don't mind. Our bond is unbreakable. I'll do whatever it takes to be with him.

We walk hand in hand to the chairlifts, then I wave him off feeling as though I could stretch out my arms and fly down the mountain beside him.

Once the metal hook of his chair reduces to the size of a paperclip I slot into my own. This time I carry my shoes on my lap and let the buttery-soft breeze caress my feet. It feels incredible. A black cat darts across the path below me. I wonder if it's still considered lucky if I am suspended above him?

Halfway down the mountain I see a red-faced tourist in a khaki fishing hat coming towards me on the up-side of the chairlift loop. So blasé is he about the ride that he's actually reading a newspaper! It seems crazy to me – how can he have this abundance of beauty around him and be buried in monochromatic news-print? Doesn't he want to truly experience his sur-roundings? I pity him. And then I pity myself. Or at least the old me. I wonder how many times I've scurried head-down to the newsagent and walked home buried in a magazine, busily reading my horoscope or a soap plot-line when I could have taken a diversion through the park or smiled at passers-by like I'm doing now. I don't care how dippy they think I am. I've got a lot of smiling to make up for.

I'm still smiling when I reach Piazza Vittoria, even when my bus pulls away seconds before I reach it. There's a payphone right by the bus stop so I call Cleo, bursting to update her on Luca. She laps it up and then demands the full story on PM's son, cooing and gasping and giggling in all the right places.

When I'm done she asks, 'Are you sure you've got the right one?'

'What do you mean?

'Well this Tyler sounds a dream.'

'Listen, if a man doesn't have at least part of my name tattooed on his body I'm just not interested!'

Cleo laughs. 'You don't know, he might have all sorts under that honey-coloured suit!'

'Yeah, but he's not Luca,' I say simply.

'But what if there was no Luca, would you have liked him then?' she persists.

'Honestly? I probably wouldn't have believed my luck, but I don't know about actually feeling anything for him because all my feelings are tied up with Luca – it's too late to divert them now!'

Cleo sighs. It's not a sigh of disapproval exactly but . . . 'I just don't want to see you hurt again,' she tells me.

'I know it looks bad but I feel like I've got to go a little bit further with this,' I say, wanting her to understand that this is destiny, not some holiday fling. 'In fact, I'm thinking of staying on a few more days.'

'Oh,' she says in a small voice.

'Tanya's sister is coming here on Thursday which should mean we get the chance to scamper off somewhere together.'

'Thursday,' Cleo muses.

I feel a pang of guilt. 'I feel bad, leaving you . . .'

'Don't be silly!' Cleo tinkles. 'I was just thinking Julie at work has got her birthday drinks on Thursday – should be a right laugh.'

'I thought she was a Libra?'

'No, no, Cancer,' she breezes.

'The thing is, I know he's married and I can't have him 100 per cent, but the high that I get when I'm with him . . .' I'm filled with bliss thinking about it. 'I just want to make the most of it while I can.'

'Whatever happens you know I'm here for you,' she reassures me.

'Thanks, hon!' I don't like her ominous tone but then it's hard to predict a happy ending – there's no easy way for Luca and I to be together.

'And if I might make just one suggestion?' Cleo says, sounding chirpier.

'Yes?'

'Keep Tyler on as back-up!'

I roll my eyes. 'Cleo!'

'Is it too late to catch him before he leaves?'

'Kim!' a male voice cuts into the conversation.

'Tyler!' I gasp, startled. Where did he spring from? Did he hear . . .?

'I'm just getting a cab down to the marina,' he says motioning to a taxi driver loading his suitcase into the boot. 'What are you doing here? Your mother said you were at a football match.'

'I . . . I . . .'

'Sorry – am I interrupting a phone call?' he asks, noticing the receiver clasped in my hand.

'Um . . .' I try to form a sentence but can't find the words. Whatever impression he had of me being a killer wit is well and truly obliterated now. 'I'm just . . .'

The taxi driver leans on his horn.

'I've got to go but I'm so glad I saw you, I wanted to give you this.' He hands me a tiny package.

'What is it?' I ask.

'A present.' He smiles before giving me the gentlest kiss on the lips. 'Goodbye!'

'Did he just kiss you?' Cleo screeches.

I muffle the receiver with my hand and watch him climb in the taxi then turn back to give me a final wave as he shrinks down the hill.

'Kim! Kim! Are you there?' Cleo's voice squeezes through the gaps in my fingers.

'Oh my God!' I breathe, still feeling caught out.

'What did he give you?'

'Hold on, I'll open it,' I scooch the receiver into the nook of my neck, open the bag and prise open the box within.

Set against rich blue velvet are a pair of pearl studs

encrusted with miniscule diamonds, clustering together to represent the continents around the world.

I'm stunned and feel a twinge of guilt. Have I snubbed Tyler? He's been so kind but what can I do? He doesn't even come close to Luca.

I describe the earrings to Cleo.

'That's it! I'm coming to Italy! Things like that never happen here.'

How I wish Cleo could call in 'un-adored' to work and come to Capri. But until Gareth shows up to collect his pictures I know there's not a hope of persuading her.

'I've got to go,' I say regretfully, 'my bus is here.'

'All right, just keep me updated,' Cleo replies, adding: 'God, by the time you get back you're going to have so much to catch up on – *Ally McBeal*, *The West Wing*, *Home Front*, *Hollyoaks*, *Top Ten TV Sisters*, *Celebrity Bad Hair Day*, I've taped them all and there was a one-off thriller with Caroline Quentin . . .'

Images of the TV shows flash through my mind as I sit on the bus bound for Capri Town. Is that all I have to go back to? Videos of other people's lives, other people's relationships, other people's hairdos? The couple in front of me are rattling on about their trip to Pompeii: 'All those people going about their business, suddenly freeze-framed for eternity,' muses the wife. I imagine myself back home in my old life in Cardiff – if a volcano erupted I would be immortalized melting over the sofa with a TV remote in one hand and a copy of *heat* magazine in the other. Just thinking about it suffocates me. I press my face to the open window,

359

gasping for air, then we round a corner and the whole of Capri splays out before me. How can I leave this splendour?

I don't want to go back.

Ever.

36

'So how was the football match?' Mum asks when I meet her back at the hotel room.

'It was a draw. Two-all,' I reply, turning away so she can't see my face.

'That's interesting, Luca said they won,' Mum frowns.

'Oh. Well, maybe a draw is considered a win here,' I bluster.

'He said they beat them three-one.'

I bite my lip.

'Do you know what's even more interesting?'

'What?' I give her a furtive glance.

'Tanya said they lost five-two.'

I go cold. 'Tanya?'

'Yes, she came by the shop about half past four.'

'Oh.'

'She said she didn't see you at the football pitch.'

My heart starts pounding. 'Well, I . . .'

'And I'm guessing from the look on Luca's face that he wasn't there either.'

My eyes widen.

'And no, I didn't land him in it, if that's what you're worried about.'

I expel a wobbly breath.

'Is he the reason you want to stay on?'

'What do you mean?'

'Kim, it's okay – I'm not exactly in a position to disapprove of such things, am I?'

She's got a point but even so . . .

'I don't want a big confession,' she tells me, opening the wardrobe to pick tonight's outfit. 'I don't know why I didn't see it sooner. Poor Tyler didn't stand a chance.'

I sit down on the bed and try to collect my thoughts. I want to blurt out, 'It's not what you think!' or 'What we have is special!' but it sounds so clichéd.

'Just give it some thought before you get in any deeper,' Mum advises as she gets swallowed up by the scented steam billowing from the bathroom.

I've never before discussed the intimate details of any of my relationships with my mother. (And by intimate I mean the emotional ups and downs, not the physical stuff. That's never going to happen.) So when we sit down to dinner and I find myself struggling to keep myself from talking about Luca, I know something has changed. For the first time I'm desperate to have her give me some advice on how to cope with what I'm going through. I tell myself it would be a waste not to pick her brains, considering all her expert knowledge on conducting affairs, and – come the main course – I dare myself to broach the subject.

'So, do you think that if you do stay on at the shop

362

you'll continue to work with Luca?' I ask, slicing my escalope.

'I don't see why not,' she shrugs. 'I think we work well together.'

I take a sip of wine.

'I hope it hasn't made you feel awkward – you know, knowing . . .'

'Not at all.' Mum shakes her head.

She's not biting.

I don't know where to start. This is so important to me, I don't want to fluff it. 'I really like him,' I say simply.

'I know, darling.'

'I think he feels the same way,' I hedge. 'But it's difficult . . .'

Mum sets down her knife and fork. 'I know you hate me interfering so I won't.'

'Oh no, please do!' I yelp.

Mum looks taken aback.

'Oh Mum, I'm feeling so out of my depth. I want to be with him more than anything but I just don't know how to make that happen. I don't know if I'm saying the right things or acting the right way – I don't know whether to fight for him or let him come to me or—'

Mum places her hand on mine and says, 'It's okay.'

I look up at her. I've been desperate to hear that it's okay. Or if it's not okay now, that it will be.

'To a certain degree it's out of your hands. I mean, you may be ready to move forward with this but it takes commitment from both of you to make it happen.

363

And even if he wants to do that, his circumstances are pulling him in the opposite direction.'

I slump, hating to be reminded of Tanya.

'The hardest thing is not getting caught up in the circumstances yourself. It's not easy when you find someone you want to really get close to and for your own survival you have to keep something back.'

That's just how I feel! I'm totally ready to surrender myself to Luca but I can't let go with things as they are. I'm trying to bide my time but already the waiting is driving me nuts.

'I do trust him,' I tell her.

'And I think he deserves your trust. But at the same time, it doesn't mean you won't get hurt. Even if that's the last thing that he wants to do.'

I heave a sigh.

'There's no simple answer. All the situations I've been in have required different tactics.'

'Tactics?' So there is an infidelity manual after all – I knew it! 'Have you got any tips?' I ask hopefully.

Mum thinks for a moment, possibly trying to find a match in her affair repertoire so she can relate to my situation.

'The danger is to give them everything on a plate,' she advises. 'On the one hand you have to be there for them whenever they can fit you in because otherwise you won't see them at all, but on the other hand that can be very demoralizing. You have to find a balance or you go crazy.'

I concentrate hard on what she's saying, almost wishing I could take notes.

'He must not become everything in your life.'

Bit late for that. 'But I'm only here for a short time,' I complain.

'That's probably a good thing. He can't take it for granted that you're going to be around. Of course it also means he's always got this voice in his head telling him that you're going away – that you'll leave him anyway . . .'

'Oh no!'

'I don't know him well enough to even guess what's going on in his head but I'd say he's a serious young man at heart and he'll be giving this whole thing just as much thought as you.'

I prod at my fruit salad dessert. Hardly acceptable comfort food. 'What do you think is going to happen?' I ask, nervously.

'I don't know,' Mum shakes her head. 'You have to take it one day at a time. And focus on the good stuff – treasure it. Don't let the rest of it get you down.'

'And don't let him become everything in my life,' I repeat, finding that concept the hardest to get my head around.

'Shall we have a cappuccino in the bar?' Mum offers.

We sit over by the window so we can speak privately without Mario pulling faces at us. We've pretty much exhausted every 'What if . . .' scenario with Luca and now I'm daring myself to tell my mother why I'm so smitten with him. In the past I never raved about boys I liked because I was afraid she'd say something to spoil it but now I can't help bragging.

'I can see it in your face when you talk about him,' Mum smiles. 'You don't need to say anything.'

But I do.

I tell her how ordinarily I spend my relationships (if you can even call them that) wondering what I'm missing out on, what other couples are doing and do they know something I don't?

'But none of that crosses my mind with him!' I smile. 'He has all my attention and every minute I spend with him I like him more. I can't get enough of him!'

Mum beams back at me. 'It's a good feeling, isn't it? I remember when I first met Huw . . .'

For the first time since my father left, Mum tells me about their courtship. It never occurred to me until now that she might miss him as well.

We're just debating whether to risk sharing a grappa when the phone rings. I look over at Mario and he beckons to me.

'Who is it?' I mouth, leaning on the bar.

'Tyler Hamilton for you, signorina,' he announces.

'Hello!' I say, taking the phone.

'How did you like the earrings?' Tyler asks.

'Oh they were beautiful – thank you!'

Mario looks up from his lemon slicing. I turn away feeling guilty – he must think I'm getting it on with every man in Capri but him.

'I'm glad you liked them. Listen, I want to ask you something,' Tyler cuts to chase.

'Yes?' I say, nervously.

'There's a problem with the translator they've assigned me and I need a replacement by tomorrow afternoon. I was wondering if you would consider saving the day – well, saving three days actually. We'd begin in Verona and then go on to Rome to meet with Alessandro's agent to seal the deal. Obviously we will pay for your travel and expenses, plus the fee of £300 a day.'

I do a quick calculation – not of the money but of when I would be back: Thursday night at the earliest, more likely Friday – that's eating into my time with Luca. I begin doodling frantically on the notepad Mario has pushed my way.

'Unfortunately I need a quick response,' Tyler apologizes. 'Can I call you back in ten minutes for an answer?'

'Yes, yes,' I say, glad to have the chance of a few minutes to recover. 'I'll speak to you in ten.'

'I hope the answer's yes,' he says, softly.

I replace the receiver.

'What now?' says Mario.

'He wants me to go to Verona to translate for him.'

Mario gives me a knowing look.

'Do you think it's a line?' I ask him.

'Of course. Do you think you are the only person in this country who speaks English and Italian? *I* could translate for him!'

'Shall we send you instead?' I laugh.

Mum scurries up to the bar, sensing intrigue.

I explain that my first instinct is that I can't leave – it might unbalance what I have here: but she and Mario are in favour of making Luca wait – 'Give him a chance to experience what you are going through.'

I tell them that seems cruel.

They disagree. 'It will make him want you more,' Mario tells me.

'Plus it will keep you occupied for Tuesday and Wednesday,' Mum says, predicting how stir crazy I could become.

'But what if I come to my senses while I'm gone?' I gulp, getting myself in a frenzy. 'I don't want to do the right thing this time! I don't want to go back to how I was feeling before.'

Mum gives me a meaningful look, 'You won't.'

'But what if Tyler . . .' I crumple.

'If you truly love Luca nothing Tyler can do will change that,' Mum assures me. 'And if you have this time away from Capri you'll come back surer than ever of your feelings.'

I'm not convinced. I think of calling Cleo to ask for her opinion but I already know what she'd say.

'What have you got to lose?' Mum asks.

'Luca,' I say.

'You won't lose him.'

'But I won't even have the chance to explain properly.'

'You can write him a letter. I'll give it to him tomorrow.'

'You mustn't let him know that I've told you about us!' I panic.

'I won't. But I'll also make sure he doesn't think anything is going on between you and Tyler.'

'Really?'

'Yes.'

I think for a moment. Even setting aside my doubts about leaving Luca there's the whole issue of spending three days alone with Tyler. I barely know the man – a dinner where he hardly spoke, an unexpected kiss, a pair of earrings and a walk around a monastery in the moonlight haven't given me a firm take on his personality. I suppose it's not like going away with a total stranger because he is PM's son. And it is business, I reason. But it's all a bit awkward if he's really as keen on me as Mum would like to believe. What if he's angling to mix business with pleasure?

'You've got about a minute to decide,' Mario informs me, looking at the clock.

I can't do it. I can't leave. What if something happened to me and I never got back?

The telephone rings.

'What did you say Luca admires most in you? Your spirit of adventure! Do it!' Mum urges.

Mario picks up the receiver. 'Yes, she's here.'

'Hello?' I croak.

'So, what's the verdict?' he says, cheerily.

I look at Mario – he nods. I look at my mother – she smiles encouragement. I look down at the notepad where I've doodled a dragon. I guess there's only one way to feel worthy of being Luca's travel muse.

I take a deep breath and blurt 'I'll do it!'

37

Today feels like a new beginning. I woke up with the sun and watched it stretch its rays across the sky, casting a golden light over the arched rooftops and spiky palms of our balcony vista. Instead of my usual grogginess I felt wonder and anticipation.

Just a few hours earlier I had clung to the mattress, daunted by the prospect of the six-part journey that lay ahead, let alone what awaited me when I got there. But when I finally set myself in motion, I experienced an excited *I can do this!* surge. And as I ticked off each aspect of the journey – the *funicolare*, the ferry, the taxi, the plane, etc. – my confidence grew and I felt a sense of achievement: 'Look at me! I am an adventurer, just like Luca says!' I thought I'd lost my nerve and my nous. I haven't! Maybe this was meant to happen – if there had been any hope of a few stolen hours with Luca I would never have left Capri but seeing as that wasn't going to happen, this trip could be the best diversion.

Verona is the most elegant of cities – tall rice-pudding-coloured buildings with long shuttered windows, wrought iron balconies and red-tiled roofs. Even the lowliest quarters have frescos on the walls. Nothing is garish or modern. No frantic horn-honking or arm-waving. Just a harmony of narrow streets and highly coiffured old ladies emerging from cake shops with beautifully-wrapped packages.

As my taxi rolls into exclusive Corsa Porta Borsari I spy Tyler outside the hotel, waiting to greet me.

'How was your journey?' he says, opening the car door for me.

'Wonderful, thank you!' I say, rummaging for my purse as I climb out.

Tyler halts me before I part with any lire and ushers me inside so I don't have to witness anything as sordid as money changing hands. I look back to thank the driver and check he has my suitcase but it is already in the care of the porter.

I gasp as I enter reception: the dark wood, luxuriant floral displays and ye olde silverware puts me in mind of a medieval banquet.

'Wow, how did you find this place?' I coo.

'Easy – it's the only five-star hotel in Verona,' Tyler shrugs.

'It's like a private palazzo.'

'Yeah, very quaint.'

Is that American for small? As I check in I notice they have just twenty-seven rooms. Preparing myself for the possibility of having to sleep upright in a decadent broom cupboard, I follow the porter up the stone staircase, gripping the twisted red rope last seen cordoning off royalty from the plebs.

As it happens, my room is a good-size square with an almost Provençal feel to the bold yellow floral and red-check furnishings, deliberately at odds with the dark timber and raspberry-sluiced walls bearing ingeniously displayed antiques. (Imagine two vertical beams with a heavy gold picture frame between them. There's glass in the frame but instead of protecting a painting it's shielding an antique vase.) As I take in all the other details – the oriental rug, a picnic-style tablecloth, three elderly walking sticks in a rack with a further five painted on the wall beside them! – I can't help but feel something is missing ... like a bed! The porter 'Ahems', opens an adjoining door and shows me into the wood-panelled bedroom. At the head of the double-cream double bed is a lacy canopy and beneath that a coat-of-arms fresco. (I half expect to find a groovy little chainmail number hung in the wardrobe.) As Tyler inspects the brushwork on the fresco, I cross the terracotta-tiled floor and step out on to the tiny leafy balcony. Sadly no Luca pining for me below, but the next-best thing – a *pasticceria* window crammed with the most exquisite sugar-dusted tortes and biscotti.

'It's beautiful!' I smile back at the porter.

'One more room ...'

I've got a suite! I've got a suite! I sing to myself as he leads me to the bathroom. Suddenly I'm in Caesar's Palace: black tiled floor, walls of peach marble with a gold mosaic border running throughout, a whirlpool bath and one of those outsize showerheads that's like having your own personal raincloud pound down on you. I'm just thinking that I could mount an exhibition called 'Showercaps of the World' when Tyler says, 'This do you?'

'Yeah!' I enthuse, looking over his shoulder for the porter.

'He's gone.'

'I didn't ...' I say, reaching for my purse.

'I did. You don't have to pay for anything when you're with me.'

'Oh. Thank you.' I'm already feeling like a kept woman.

'Listen – I've got to make a few more calls to New York so you just settle in and I'll meet you in the lobby in an hour, how's that?'

'Perfect!' I smile, relieved that he's in business mode.

As he shuts the door behind him I look at my mini suitcase. It'll only take me ten minutes to unpack and change for the meeting. I wonder ... I lean out of the sitting room window and peer down the street, catching sight of a winged lion atop a towering column. That looks familiar. I turn back to the room and dial reception.

'Buon giorno! Can I help you?'

'Hello, yes, could you tell me how far we are from Casa di Giulietta, please?'

'Certainly signora, it is no more than five minutes' walk from here. If you would like directions, I would be happy to show you on our complimentary map.'

'Great! I'll be down in a second, thank you.'

I feel a flurry of excitement at the thought of skipping out and then emit a growl – I've got some

373

unfinished business with Juliet. Then again, maybe I should be thanking her – perhaps she realized what a mistake she'd made giving me a new love in the form of Tomas and sent Luca as compensation! How things have changed since I was last here – all tense and wretched and embarrassed by my mother's over-zealous attempts to find a man for me. I wonder who she would have put me with if she could have summoned her ideal at the time. An Italian Tyler? I suppose he fits most people's dream criteria. How strange that I should find myself back in Verona with him. Juliet is definitely up to her old tricks, I need to have a word.

I'm just two steps along the street when a priest swishes by me with a designer shopping bag and steps into a chauffeur-driven Mercedes. Only in Italy. Even the policemen look like they've been styled by Armani. I pass two as I progress down Via Cappello, one frowning into his police radio, the other laughing into his mobile phone.

I'd forgotten that Juliet's house was set in the main shopping area: you can get engaged and get your elopement outfit within minutes. Shops aside, it doesn't look like much has changed since her day – even the road surfaces trundled by public transport are not tarmac but mosaic-style cubes of stone and the pedestrianized Via Mazzini has pink marble underfoot. (Quite a contrast to the chipped paving slabs ingrained with dirt and chewing gum back home.)

I pause for a second and then step through the entrance arch ... The graffiti seem brighter than I remembered – layer upon layer of names and hearts marked in lipstick, Tippex, spray paint, nail varnish and glitter glue over score upon score of engravings – some of which you can only read when the sun shines on them and fills the grooves with light. I take a step closer, reading the lovers' messages: 'Eros and Nicky Forever', 'Il Sole, La Luna – Audry + Stefy', there's even a rather formal 'Mr and Mrs Reeves'. I wonder how many of these couples are still together. 'Ich liebe ein Mädchen, und sie ist so wunderschön.' My heart swells and I sigh at the rainbow of Ti amos. All this love. Dare I be a part of it? There are no tour groups at present, just a few stragglers under the balcony and a man posing for a photo with Juliet's statue (grabbing her breast and biting her shoulder, the old romantic). If I'm quick I can etch seven letters and a plus sign. But where do I squeeze 'Kim + Luca'? Even the drainpipe and the knotty-barked tree in the courtyard are dense with inscriptions. I step into the doorway beside the gift shop (not sure how a heart-shaped kitchen scourer rates as a token of eternal love). This feels more private, secret even. I take out a felt-tip pen and, trembling, write our names on the door frame next to a bubblegum heart. Emboldened by no one calling me a vandal, I add, 'Together in our hearts' in tiny writing.

'Romeo, Romeo! Wherefore art thou Romeo?' Interesting. I've never heard Shakespeare in a Japanese accent before. Every nationality seems equally besotted with this tragic tale. Suddenly the courtyard has become a bustling Benetton ad so I wander across to the family home musing how Juliet Capulet is a neat little rhyme, rather like me being called Kim Simms or something.

At the bottom of a creaky staircase there's a red glossed postbox where visitors are invited to insert their love letters. Every year the city of Verona chooses the author of the most romantic letter and invites them and their beloved for a romantic weekend as guests of the city. I wonder how the letter I left for Mum to pass to Luca would compare?

Dear Luca, I realize you are going to have to eat this letter once you've read it, so I'll keep it brief or you'll get indigestion! As Mum has probably explained by now, I have taken a three-day translation job with Platinum Man's art-dealer son, first stop: Verona. Much as I'd love you to get jealous, there is zero need. Every second of every day I am going to be wishing that you were with me. I might even set fire to a bedcover in your honour!

I'm at the Gabbia D'Oro tonight, and when I retire I'm going to imagine that you are waiting for me in my hotel bed – feel free to join me in your dreams.

Longing to be with you again in a Villa Cimbrone-kinda way, your Romeo-less Juliet.

I scrapped a good many soppier 'parting is such sweet sorrow' versions before deciding I should keep it light and jokey. It's not that I thought my true feelings would scare him off, it's just that there's still that horrible feeling lurking within me that Luca could turn around and say, 'I'd forgotten how much I loved Tanya – since she's returned we've got so much closer.'

I don't want to make a complete fool of myself by talking as if we have a future together. Obviously things are a lot more complicated now his wife is back. He doesn't need to have me making presumptions or threatening to glug vials of poison if we can't be together. I guess I just have to bide my time. But it's hard to keep my feelings in check – I long to be able to let them spill over. No wonder people are so enamoured of Romeo and Juliet. Few people today are prepared to live so wholly at the mercy of their hearts.

Flicking through one of the books on display I read a translation of Bandello's pre-Shakespeare account of the first time Juliet saw Romeo: 'And love . . . touched her so at the quick, as for any resistance she could not make . . . and felt no pleasure in her heart but when she had a glimpse by throwing or receiving, some sight of Romeo.'

Sigh. I pay the small entrance fee and ascend the stairs. The large open-plan rooms all have wooden floorboards except the area beside the infamous balcony which is chequered squares of marble – ideal for games of human chess. Beside the fireplace there hangs a 16th century R&J-inspired painting. It seems traditional enough – Juliet leaning over her balcony in flowing robes – only one small difference: her breasts are fully exposed. Obviously her Romeo needed a bit of extra encouragement to climb up.

I feel nervous as I approach the balcony itself, as though Juliet's spirit might enter my body. If ever there was someone who knew about loving the wrong person it is her. I make a wish as I step forward, not for a new love this time but for Luca and me to have the chance to fulfil our heart's desire.

As I emerge into the sunshine a cheer goes up. Looking down to the courtyard below I see a cluster of faces gawping up at me, waving and calling, 'It is my lady; O it is my love!' Well, that's what I wish they were calling. It's more a case of, 'Oi Juliet!' and 'Don't jump!'

I scurry back inside, taking a moment to flick through the visitors' book and smiling at the many 'Leonardo – ti amo!' messages. There's even a proposal and an acceptance in Spanish. Taking the pen I decide to make a written dedication for some other lovers – 'Gina & Platinum Man' and 'Cleo & Gareth.' As I press a kiss on to the page I decide this would be a good time to get an update on my best friend's 'developing romance'.

'Cleo! Guess where I'm calling from?'

'An ice-cream parlour if you've got any sense.'

'Juliet's balcony in Verona!' I whoop.

'They have a phone on the balcony? I don't believe it!'

I groan. 'Not the balcony itself, I'm just by the entrance to the courtyard. It's beautiful – all tumbling vines and cobblestones.'

'Is Tyler with you?'

'No, he's making calls back at the hotel. I'm meeting him in about quarter of an hour to go to this artist's studio.'

'How's it going with him?'

'Well, I only saw him briefly but I don't know, there's something about the way he is with the hotel staff. He doesn't say thank you or look them in the eye—'

'That's probably because he's only got eyes for you!' Cleo interrupts.

'Yeah, right!'

'Does he tip them?' she asks.

'Oh yes, he even came to my room with me so he could pay the porter.'

'Big tip?'

'Well, I caught a glimpse of what he gave the taxi driver and it looked like quite a chunk. But that could just be because he hasn't got the hang of the money.'

'Give the man a break!' Cleo hoots. 'It's like you're looking for faults. Anyway, what do you think his minions would rather have – hard cash or a smile?'

'I know, hard cash, but he could do both.'

'Not asking for much, are you?' Cleo sighs. 'Do me a favour – every time you think he's behaving in a dodgy way, play devil's advocate and give him the benefit of the doubt. You could be getting him all wrong.'

'I'll try, but my mind keeps zooming back to Lu—'

'OH GOD! OH GOD!'

'What?' I jump.

'It's him – Gareth – he's coming in the shop,' Cleo squeaks with fast-forward urgency.

'Don't put the phone down!' I beg. 'Leave it out so I can hear.'

Cleo makes an anguished 'oh all right then' noise

379

and obliges. A second later she emits a breathless welcome, 'Hi!'

'Hi!' he replies, sounding cheery. 'I finally rounded them all up – nine disposable cameras.'

I hear a clattering as he unloads them on to the counter.

'Great!' says Cleo, with a rustling of envelopes. 'One hour?'

'No, tomorrow's fine – I'm not in so much of a rush now.'

Oop, that's foiled Cleo's pre-rehearsed lines. Will she be able to come up with a new angle on the spot?

'Oh. Okay, well they'll be ready about the same time. Does that fit in with your lunch hour?'

She's still trying to work the hour concept into the conversation, gotta love her for trying.

'I don't really have a lunchbreak as such, so no worries there. Any time before 3p.m. would be great.'

'Okay. Matt or gloss?'

Why didn't she ask him what he does? She's either biding her time or lost her nerve.

'What do you think?' he asks.

Ooh, that's promising – seeking her opinion . . .

'Well, if they're going to be handed around I'd go for matt cos gloss can get quite fingerprinty.'

Is that a technical term?

'Okay, matt it is.'

'Border?'

I'm guessing that he's raising an eyebrow now.

'They're back in fashion,' Cleo informs him. (With a playful twinkle, I hope.)

380

'Oh well then, it's a must. I'd hate to have unfashionable photographs!'

I stifle a snigger. He sounds nice.

'Narrow or wide?'

'Narrow, I s'pose,' he says, uncertainly. 'God, it's getting like Starbucks in here! I don't remember having this many choices last time I came in.'

'Well, not everyone gives as good service as me.'

Nice touch of innuendo, Cleo.

'Size?' she sleazes.

Excellent Graham Norton-esque follow through!

'Grande! No normal, whatever!' he laughs. 'I'm just glad I didn't do anything panoramic – oh, that sounds rude!'

Cleo giggles. She's so in there. 'Any extra sets?'

'Wow, I think my head is going to explode. How many pictures would that be altogether?'

She's good with her sums is our Cleo, wait for it . . .

'486 – if they all come out!'

'Hey, are you doubting my photographic skills?'

Banter. Definitely banter. She's going to be on such a high after this.

'Dost thou love me?' A female voice. Not Cleo's. I spin around and see a couple of costumed actors dressed as Romeo and Juliet leading a parade of tourists, projecting quotes as they walk. I muffle the phone against my jacket but Juliet spies me and – wouldn't you know it? – she's one of those breed of street performers who think it's hilarious to humiliate passers-by. Tugging the phone out of my hand she loudly recites: 'If thou dost love pronounce it faithfully!'

I wrestle it back to my ear. 'Where's that coming from?' Gareth sounds confused.

'Must be the radio,' Cleo covers.

Juliet grabs the phone again. 'Or if thou think'st I am too quickly won I'll frown and be perverse, and say thee nay, so thou wilt woo!'

I snatch it back, much to the amusement of the tourists.

'It's Shakespeare, isn't it?' says Gareth, sounding intrigued. 'Part of Juliet's balcony speech when she's wondering whether she should've played more hard to get. I did that at uni. Well, not her speech, obviously . . . I think it's coming from that phone.'

'What? No, couldn't be! Erm . . .' (Then into the phone:) 'Hello? Hello?' Cleo blusters.

'*Sorry!*' I hiss.

'No, nothing there,' she assures him.

'I thought you had a live link to fair Verona for a minute there!' he chuckles.

I hear Cleo's nervous laughter and then a click.

Ah well, it's got to be a talking point for them – you know, 'Do you believe in playing hard to get?' 'Is there a Romeo for every Juliet?' or 'How do you fancy spending eternity together in a tomb with a view?' That kind of thing.

38

Swapping my trainers for sandals I skip down the stairs to the hotel lobby to meet Tyler.

'You are Kim Rees?' the young woman behind the reception desk addresses me.

'Yes,' I confirm.

'Signor Hamilton will join you in the Orangerie shortly. He waits for just one phone call.'

'Okay. Um. The Orangerie?'

'Please, let me show you,' she says, emerging from behind the desk. 'My name is Camille, I am general manager here.'

'Nice to meet you,' I smile, shaking her hand. She's about my age with clear green eyes, enviable curved cheekbones and long, soft brown hair wound into a bun.

'This is your first visit to Verona?' she asks.

'Actually, I was here just over two years ago, with my mother. She adores it here.'

'Also my mother,' Camille smiles. 'She is originally from Florence but she choose Verona to open this hotel.'

'Your mother owns this place?'

'Yes,' she smiles. 'She always love antiques and design and this became her dream.'

I think of my mother and her dream of the boutique. Suddenly it seems unthinkable that she could give it up and return to Cardiff.

'Was it a hotel when she bought it?' I ask.

'No, a residence. She destroy it completely and rebuilt with her own style.'

I take in the quirky details in the Orangerie – the pineapple-based lamps, the tablecloths featuring pheasants and Dobermann dogs, the bird cage with two red, gold and green parrots. (I feel they should probably have Jamaican names but they are, of course, Romeo and Juliet.) I comment on the banjo-jazz music.

'She has a very strong personality,' Camille smiles. I nod knowingly as she confides with a twinkle, 'It is not always easy to live close to someone who is so volcanic!'

'How long have you worked here?' I ask, always fascinated by other mother-daughter double acts.

'About twelve years – since it opened. In the beginning I was a student and I wanted to leave college to come work here but my mother said I must first finish my education.'

'Were you studying the hotel trade?'

'No, political science!' she laughs.

'Oh!' I grin.

'In the beginning my mother set me to work as a chambermaid. I clean the toilets, everything, for I must prove that I really want to work here.'

'Really?'

'Yes, I have worked all the jobs – housekeeper, in the breakfast room, front desk – I think it helps to keep in touch. I don't want to just sit in an office.'

'Your mother must be very proud of you – does she tell you that?' I wonder out loud.

'Absolutely not!' Camille laughs. 'But my mother is a great businesswoman,' she observes, proudly. 'And now that I work with her, I see also Giuseppina Marani, the woman, not just the mother.'

I look at Camille with delight and admiration – she has made a conscious decision to celebrate the positive and it has given her great warmth and composure. I decide that Camille is my new role model and wonder if I have time to give my mother a quick call and tell her how proud I am of her wanting to run Desiderio's.

'Sorry to keep you waiting, Kim.' Tyler gives me the benefit of his diligently-flossed smile.

Darn, I'll have to call later.

'No need to apologize,' I tell him as Camille dips back to reception. 'I've just had a lovely chat with the general manager, she's—'

'Great – shall we go?' he cuts me off.

There it is again. Total lack of interest in other people. How can he get by doing his job with so few social graces?

The cab takes us over the Ponte della Pietra crossing the meandering Adige river, and into the poorer Roman Theatre district. The journey is a matter of minutes but when I say, 'We could have walked' Tyler

385

looks at me as if I'd suggested we hop all the way. He's definitely the type of person who drives to the gym to go on a running machine.

'Is there anything I should know before we start?' I ask as we approach the studio.

'Not really, just don't look too impressed by his work or he'll get ideas about raising his price.'

I can't be sure he is joking.

'Are you actually discussing money with him today?' I ask. I hate haggling.

'No, this is just a sweetener – the business will come with his agent in Rome. The important thing is that he likes me enough to trust me with his work. I don't think he's had too many other offers so it should be fairly straightforward.'

I feel a flutter of nerves. It's been a while since I did a job that involved interacting with real live human beings and this Alessandro sounds a little bit unpredictable.

As Tyler presses the buzzer he reassures me, 'Just be as calm as you were with the waiter at the Hotel Palace and you'll do fine!'

I feel a flush of pride – he noticed!

There's a growly, shuffly noise the other side of the door and I have visions of it being opened by some kind of hairy-hunched trog. Instead the man who welcomes us in is clean-shaven (of chin *and* scalp). He just happens to have a dreadlocked dog at his feet.

'Tyler Hamilton, pleased to meet you. This is my translator, Kim Rees.'

'Non parla Inglese!' he snaps.

Looks like I'm on.

Prior to our meeting with Alessandro, I had thought Tyler relied so heavily on his looks to make an impression that his charm would only work on women and gay men. However, the second we enter the studio he speaks with such impassioned expertise about the work that surrounds us that it's a stretch for me to do his prose justice in the translation. His amber eyes are sparkling like I've never seen before – except perhaps when he gave me that rather rash kiss as a reward for slapping Morgan down. It's almost as if the smell of the oil paints and turpentine have awakened an alter ego in him. Alessandro responds accordingly. Especially when Tyler talks of the lucrative deals he's made with other artists around the world – including one in Zagreb last year, which explains his ability to say goodnight in Croatian.

I look at the daring paintings and wonder how much my £5,000 would buy. Considering Tyler is so rapturous, I could probably just afford an autographed palette.

'You must stay for dinner,' Alessandro insists. Only his dog seems unconvinced, as if he knows that would mean less scraps for him.

'I wish we could but we are dining with friends of my father,' Tyler says regretfully.

First I've heard of that.

Alessandro looks dismayed but Tyler quickly flatters him: 'Alessandro, it's been a privilege to see your latest painting at such a tender stage and I very much look forward to displaying the finished work in deserved glory in a New York gallery a few months from now.'

Alessandro gives a small bow of gratitude, shakes our hands and shows us to the door.

Tyler is on such a high when we leave that he actually suggests we walk back.

'That was amazing!' I laugh, scurrying to keep up. 'I had no idea you were such a fan of his work.'

'Oh his stuff's okay – nothing I'd have in my own home,' he shrugs.

I lose my footing for a moment. 'All those things you said . . .'

'Just doing my job. You get to know what they want to hear. But it still gives me a kick when I know I've nailed it!' he says, looking smug. 'We're going to make a lot of money from his paintings.'

Is that all he cares about?

'You were great, by the way. I always think having a woman translator helps soften them up a bit.'

I try to play devil's advocate, as Cleo suggested, and wonder if this is just bravado. Could it be that Tyler feels he has to talk down his appreciation for abstract art – perhaps because Morgan has ridiculed him so consistently?

'And an *attractive* woman translator . . .' Tyler gives me a wink.

'What's this about dinner with your father's friends?' I ask, hoping to sidetrack him from any further compliments.

'Oh, nothing, I just didn't want to have to spend hours with Alessandro. When you've got them on your

388

side you don't want to risk offending them in any way. Always best to keep these things brief, I feel.'

'So where are we going?'

'Bottega del Vino,' he mispronounces. 'Got a recommendation from a colleague in NYC – it's notoriously atmospheric.'

As promised, the place is buzzing with animated conversation and the occasional crash of plates from the kitchen. Everyone seems in high spirits apart from a sulky teenager eating her risotto one grain of rice at a time. As we are led to our white-draped table, I wonder which came first – the mustard yellow walls or the fug of cigarette smoke? Fortunately the exceptionally high ceilings mean it is still possible to breathe.

Each table is set with the appropriate number of elongated champagne flutes, and no sooner have we settled in than a waitress fills our glasses with fizz – how civilized is that?

'Salute!' I toast Tyler. 'Here's to signing the contract with Alessandro!'

'Here's to you and I making a great team!' he replies.

My sip of champagne becomes a gulp and I quickly hide myself behind the menu.

'Some of this stuff is weird,' Tyler shakes his head. 'Cod stewed with milk and anchovies?'

My stomach has already churned at the prospect of polenta with lard or, worse still, tripe with Parmesan.

'Arrabbiata is the hot sauce, isn't it?' Tyler checks with me.

'Yes, *arrabbiata* actually translates as "angry",' I tell him. Angry sauce!

He looks faintly amused. 'Do you know what you're having?' he asks.

'Probably the Bigoli all'Anatra.'

'English!'

'The thick spaghetti with duck sauce and a salad, I think. You?'

'Parma ham followed by the deer fillet with sweet red wine and wild fruit,' he concludes, closing the menu.

'They've got a massive wine list, haven't they?' I marvel, looking up at the chalked blackboard. 'Palazotta, Santa Cristina, Vertigo – I guess that's what Kim Novak would order!' I joke.

No response from Tyler.

'You know, from the Alfred Hitchcock film . . .' Luca would know what I mean, I huff. Then I hear Cleo nagging me to give Tyler the benefit of the doubt. Perhaps there's something more current I can make a quip about. I read on, 'Reynella Shiraz, Albion, *Bradisimo* – Jennifer Anniston's favourite vintage!'

A faint smile. I wonder what it would take to get this man to laugh. He obviously doesn't take after his father.

'Sooo,' I begin. 'Do you see much of your mother?'

'Why do you ask?'

Interesting. Looks like Tyler might have as many mother-related issues as me. *As I used to have*, I think with a smile. I suppose it'll take a while to fully grasp that she's no longer the enemy.

390

'No reason, other than your family seem to be scattered around so many different states, I wondered how often you got to see her, that's all.'

'Well, it's a fairly short hop from New York to Miami, when I'm there,' Tyler shrugs. 'But I don't visit as much now that she's remarried.'

'Don't you like him?' I ask.

'Put it this way, he's had more surgery than she has.'

Hmmm, this might explain why Tyler is supposedly attracted to someone as natural/flawed as me. Weird to think that I'd probably be on an operating table right now if I hadn't come to Italy.

'Um, I know someone back home who's thinking of having surgery,' I begin. 'What do you think makes people do it?' I'm curious to hear Tyler's take on this.

He shrugs. 'In my mother's case, she was a former Miss Florida and I think she spent too long comparing herself to how she looked the day she was crowned. She has this big, framed picture of herself in her dressing room. I think it's time she took it down.'

Tyler pauses while the waiter pours our wine into a pair of glasses so bulbous you could fit a grapefruit in them, and then asks, 'Has your mother gone under the knife?'

I shudder at the expression, almost feeling the incision.

'No way! She's totally against it. Never will. Anyway, she doesn't really need to.'

'That's irrelevant half the time. My mother looked great, she just didn't look twenty any more.'

'And now she looks like a middle-aged woman who's had surgery?'

'Exactly,' Tyler sighs. 'All my mother's friends are at it too, but it's funny, I don't know any of them that look better for it.'

It's different with facial surgery, I tell myself. Surely he wouldn't begrudge belly-reduction? But what if Cleo and I became addicted and moved on to chins and cheekbones? Just as well the cost is prohibitive and we're running short on dying grandparents to fund such projects.

'My mother has dodgy taste in men too,' I tell him, trying to find some common ground.

He raises an eyebrow.

'Other than your father, of course!' I squeak. 'He's a gem.'

Mercifully my blunder is forgotten as the waiter chooses this moment to arrive with our order. Even though I have a plate of piping hot pasta and a salad with enough rocket to stuff a pillowcase, I can't help asking, 'Could we get one of those?' as the next table is presented with what looks like a plate of shredded red cabbage – one of my passions.

'You like to try?' Our waiter looks enthused.

'Yes please!'

Minutes later he returns with a heaped plate. I tuck in but the taste that greets me is unfamiliar. I try to place it – 'Weird, it sort of tastes like bacon ...' I frown.

'Excuse me,' I beckon the waiter and whisper, 'What is it?'

'Horse meat,' he announces, zipping on his way, leaving me to gag and Tyler to collapse with laughter.

So that's his idea of funny, is it? I have a feeling four hours at the opera should wipe the smile off his face.

When Tyler first mentioned that he was taking me to see *La Traviata* after dinner, I was stunned. The Verona opera season is world-renowned but more importantly it was a chance to feel like Julia in her red gown in *Pretty Woman* – all heaving breasts and misty eyes. In a way, I was going one better than them. They had to make do with sitting in an enclosed theatre, I was going to an open-air former gladiator arena with 16,999 other people. Is there anything better than live music under the stars on a summer's night? Well, yeah, live music under the stars on a summer's night *with the one you love*, but this would do as a practice run.

The anticipation from the crowd was tangible as we took our seats. Row upon circular row of opera lovers from every walk of life, all in their best clothes, all rapt with wonder and appreciation from the first note. I found it incredible that with so many thousands of people present there was not a cough or a fidget in the place, everyone was concentrating so hard you could hear a pin drop. Or a programme. (I know because I dropped mine.)

I feel such a philistine admitting this but after forty minutes my mind started to drift. I briefly amused myself thinking how the English translation of *La Traviata* is 'The Woman Gone Astray' and that having joked with PM about being a prostitute our first night in the Piazzetta, I was now sitting with his son watching an opera about a courtesan, but that feeling passed. In a way, I was glad not to have to make conversation with Tyler so I could have some private time to think of Luca. But two hours in I was to-the-bone uncomfortable. We'd rented a cushion for our folding metal chairs but it just wasn't enough and I couldn't understand how everyone else managed to keep so still, especially the lesser-padded buttocks among us. And what with Violetta (the courtesan) dying of consumption and giving up her true love to avoid shaming him by association, things were looking pretty bleak. Then, during a lavish society ball scene, the most amazing bare-torsoed male dancer took centre stage and utterly wowed the audience.

'Strange that a dancer should get the most rapturous applause at an opera,' I mused during the third or fourth interval (I lost count).

'Which one's the hunchback?' I heard a woman with a Mancunian accent ask her husband.

'That's *Rigoletto*, you daft woman, you're on the wrong page,' he said, snatching her programme out of her hand.

I had to admit, if only to myself, that I was disappointed. Not in the production, but in myself, or at least in my reaction. I so wanted to be torn apart by emotion but it just didn't happen. Next time I think I'll wait for an 'Opera's Greatest Hits' night – bits of *Madam Butterfly*, *Carmen*, *La Bohème* . . .

Of course when Tyler asked me if I was enjoying

myself I said yes. In truth, by the final act, all I wanted was to crawl into bed with my imaginary Luca.

Back at the hotel, I take my last sip of nightcap brandy and announce that I'm going to bed.

'I think I can stand one more,' Tyler tells me, beckoning the barman. 'Are you sure you won't join me?'

'No but really, thank you for a wonderful evening!' I say, sliding off the velvety banquette and reviving the cushions I've compressed.

'Thank *you*!' Tyler smiles graciously. 'Sleep well.'

I'm at the door when he says, 'Oh, tomorrow . . .' as if having an afterthought.

'Yes?'

'I thought we might take the train to Rome, you know – make the most of the scenery.'

'Okay – great.' I nod.

'So we'll need to be at Porta Nuova station for 3p.m.'

'Right . . .' I pause. 'Well, goodnight.'

I have barely turned my toes towards the stairs when he enquires, 'Have you ever been on the Orient Express?'

I stop in my tracks.

Turning slowly around I inspect his face – a picture of nonchalance. 'You're kidding?' I test.

'I thought you might like it. But if you'd prefer to fly—'

'No!' I gasp. 'Oh my God – are we really going on the *Orient Express*?'

He smiles. 'Yes, Agatha, we are!'

39

'Did you know that Gracie Fields' second husband had a heart attack and died on the Orient Express on his way to Capri?' I enquire as we stand on the steam-swirled platform, admiring the regal splendour of the glossy navy and gold Wagons-Lits carriages.

Tyler gives me a look as if to say, 'A simple "wow" would suffice.'

I smile and revel in the envious glances of passers-by as a white-gloved hand extends and pulls us aboard the 1920s time machine.

The hand belongs to a sprightly young steward sporting a peaked cap and bright blue uniform with gold braid trim. He looks like a cross between a cavalry officer and a *Thunderbirds* puppet.

'My name is Steven and I would like to welcome you aboard the infamous Venice-Simplon Orient Express!'

Somebody pinch me!

'Shortly after we depart I will be serving tea in your private compartment,' he informs us.

It's all too fabulously civilized! I give Tyler a joyful grin then squeeze down the narrow corridor after

Steven, glad this isn't the 1980s or I would have to remove my shoulder pads.

'Don't suppose you get too many American footballers on this train!' I jest.

He smiles tolerantly. 'Here we are – compartments 7 and 8. Your rooms are adjoining so you can have the connecting door open if you want a bit more space.'

'Maybe when we have tea,' suggests Tyler. 'Shall we settle in first?'

I nod approval.

'Ms Rees – this is you,' Steven ushers me into my cubicle and gives me an enthusiastic rundown of the facilities, which include his full butler services – I just have to press the call button and he'll bring me a G&T, post my complimentary postcards (no stamp required) or share gems from yesteryear: 'Did you know that Agatha Christie's *Murder on the Orient Express* was originally published under the title *Murder in the Calais Coach*?' he asks as he sets the mini-fan whirring for me.

'Really?' I love a good bit of trivia. 'Were there any real murders?' I ask ghoulishly.

'Well,' he glances at his watch. 'Let me check on the other passengers and then when I bring the tea I shall tell you a tale of love, royalty and murder!'

I gurgle in delight. This is fun.

I'm just clambering up on the seat to get my suitcase down from the brass luggage rack when the train lurches into motion. Steven claims the train never travels faster than 75k.p.h. but it's certainly a rattling ride. When I decide to visit the loo at the end of the carriage I find myself stumbling and slamming into doors and window ledges. So much for the epitome of elegance, I'm going to look like I've been in a WWF fight by dinner. I'm relieved when I can safely slide the bathroom door closed behind me but my troubles have only just begun – trying to connect one's bottom with the moving target loo seat is like some kind of fairground game.

As I stagger like a drunkard back down the corridor to my room I notice all the other passengers are happy to leave their compartment doors open. It's like an open invitation to peer into their front rooms. A few of them have already hung out their finery for the evening; most are reading or gazing contentedly out of the window. One or two look up and bid me good afternoon.

I take a peak in at Tyler, surrounded by papers, mobile phone to his ear. 'Ah, here she is now!' he smiles, handing me his nifty Nokia. 'It's your mum – you can take it in your cabin, if you like.'

'Oh! Great, thanks,' I say, skipping next door and closing the door behind me. 'I take it you've heard!' I grin into the phone.

'Tony told me – I want every detail!' she whoops. 'Do you feel like a 1930s starlet?'

'Not yet,' I admit. 'I actually feel more like a wind-up ballerina in one of those lacquered music boxes.'

'Any particular reason?' She sounds confused.

'Well, the compartment is tiny and I'm surrounded by all this glossy wood panelling.'

'How tiny?'

'Well if I lie out on the banquette sofa thing I can

stretch my legs out straight but I can't point my toes. It would be a nightmare for Luca – he'd have to sleep folded in half!'

'Just as well he's not there, then,' Mum teases.

'Hey! I wouldn't say that,' I protest. 'How is he?'

'Fine, I explained everything. Tony could you pass me the water?'

That's her way of telling me PM's there and she can't go into any more detail.

'So you sleep on the sofa, do you?' Mum asks, getting back on track.

'Apparently the steward transforms it into a bed while you're at dinner,' I tell her. 'And if there's two of you sharing a cabin you get bunks – one above the other.'

'Oh.'

I can tell my mum's thinking what I thought when I discovered this: What if you're on your honeymoon? Now that would be tricky. Mind you, it's so jiggly-jolty that if you did want to have sex you could just lie on top of each other and let the train do the rest!

'But it's worth it for the ambience?' Mum enquires.

'Totally! And the view – you just sit back and watch this incredible ever-changing panorama sliding past the window,' I sigh. 'It's a bit like being in the world's smallest cinema: "*Coming soon to a window near you – Venice the movie!*"'

'Does the window open?'

'Yes – you use this handle that looks like you'd derail the train if you pulled it.'

'Are you sure it's for the window?' Mum frets.

'Almost sure – shall I try it now?'

'Kim! Don't!' Mum squeals.

'It's fine!' I laugh as I lower the window, inviting a hair-ruffling breeze into the compartment.

'Carry on,' Mum urges.

'Um, what else? Well, there's a ridiculous amount of hooks,' I say, looking around my cabin. 'I've counted fifteen so far. I would have brought some extra sets of keys and a dozen or so jackets if I'd known. There's even a special one with a circle of carpet underneath – apparently gentlemen would hang their fob watches overnight and the carpet bit protected it from bashing against the woodwork.'

'Gosh – they think of everything. Is there a full-length mirror?'

Ever the professional dresser.

'No but the wall facing me is nearly all mirrors. I suppose it's necessary to give the illusion of a bigger room but I'm convinced they're going to start playing *You're So Vain* any moment . . .'

'En-suite bathroom?'

'No bathroom anywhere! They've kept the detail authentic to how it was in the Twenties so there's just a little sink in the corner of the room with a hinged wooden lid so that when it's closed it becomes a table.'

'Oh my God!' Mum is aghast. 'So you can't shower or wash your hair?'

'No. Well, I suppose you could wash your hair if you used a cup but you couldn't use a hair-drier cos there's no socket.'

I half expect my mum to say, 'Tony could you pass

400

me that brown paper bag!' she's hyperventilating so badly.

'I'm not exactly sure how I'm supposed to transform myself into something fragrant and glamorous for dinner!' I say, trying to share her concern but it just makes things worse. It's as if I've pressed a Code Red emergency button – I can practically hear my mum's brain whirring as she reels off her emergency beauty regime strategy. Just as she's confessing that she sneaked her gas-powered hair tongs into my luggage, Steven the steward taps on the door bearing a tray of dainty china and outsize macaroons.

'Mum, I've got to go.'

'Why didn't I put a flannel in for you!' she laments.

'There appears to be a complimentary one here, don't worry,' I say, smiling apologetically at Steven. It seems terribly gauche to be talking on a mobile phone in a vintage carriage.

'Good luck, darling! Just put a bit of shimmer on your collarbones and cleavage. Hopefully he won't notice the rest.'

For once I smile rather than take offence. 'I might just paint myself gold and have done with it,' I tease. 'Byeee!'

'May I?' says Steven, offering to open the connecting doors.

As our two worlds become one, Tyler sets aside his papers and pats the seat beside him. I feel a little invasive – enter someone's cabin and you automatically enter their personal space. The train jolts as I step forward and Tyler has to stabilize me.

Quickly I take a seat so he can release me.

'Um, Steven was going to tell a story,' I say, wanting to keep a third party present for as long as possible.

'Are you sitting comfortably?' Steven obliges with a Disney smile.

'Wait!' Tyler passes me my cup of Earl Grey before nodding for him to begin.

'Once upon a time there was a Greek arms dealer . . .'

'Wha?!' I splutter.

Tyler nudges me quiet. 'I've heard this one, you'll like it.'

'He had many aliases but we shall call him Zaharoff. Though he grew up in the slums of Constantinople he became fantastically wealthy selling arms to rival governments and spent literally weeks on the Orient Express – always in Compartment 7 – becoming the train's most regular and distinguished patron. One day he boarded the train at Gare de L'Est in Paris along with a honeymoon couple connected with the Spanish royal house – an ethereal beauty named Maria, just seventeen years old and a strange weak-faced man, the Duke of Marchena. What Zaharoff didn't know was that the Duke was a childhood simpleton and beginning to show signs of dangerous insanity. Later that night, when everyone else had retired after dinner and the train was rattling towards Salzburg, an agonizing scream was heard. Zaharoff was confident his bodyguard would deal with the annoying disturbance and continued with his work. Suddenly there was frantic knocking at the door and when he opened it the young

402

bride fell into his arms, blood dripping from her throat where her crazed husband had tried to kill her.'

I let out a cry of mortification.

'The Duke was found with a jewel-encrusted dagger, frothing at the mouth!'

'Oh my God!'

'Zaharoff took charge of protecting young Maria and by the time the train reached Vienna, he was madly in love with her.'

I smile, delightedly.

'But as there was no divorce in Catholic Spain the lovers had to wait thirty-eight years until the Duke died before they were finally married in 1924.'

My heart sinks. I hope I won't have to wait thirty-eight years before Luca and I can be together legitimately.

'They even went on the Orient Express on their honeymoon!' Steven continues.

'So they had a happy ending, after all?' I brighten.

'Well . . . tragically she became ill and died eighteen months later.'

'Oh no!'

'He lived on, wretched, for another ten years and then died in November 1936 in Monte Carlo. The next day, his loyal bodyguard boarded the Orient Express at the Gare de L'Est and, following his last order from his master, tore up a photograph of the couple and scattered the pieces out of the window of Compartment 7 at precisely the same time that they first heard Maria's scream fifty years ago.'

I shudder.

'All true!' says Steven, leaving us open-mouthed.

'Have you got any more?'

'I'm sure he's got work to be getting along with,' Tyler decides before Steven can speak.

Once again I'm not sure whether he's being considerate or dismissive. Cleo would probably say he just wants to be alone with me but I feel a bit slapped down. Steven merely nods and bows out with the words, 'We'll be crossing the lagoon into Venice in about half an hour. Enjoy.'

For a second we're silent.

'The Orient Express has such great history,' Tyler understates.

'Yes, I would have liked to hear more,' I mutter under my breath.

'Amazing to think that it's been bombed, shot at, marooned in the snow . . .'

'Oh, you know all the stories too – perhaps you should be working as a steward!'

He doesn't like that. I give him my most innocent smile. He looks confused for a moment and then leans closer. 'The next carriage along – number 3544 – was actually a brothel!'

My eyes widen. 'Gosh – you wouldn't think they'd allow that kind of thing!'

'It wasn't running at the time,' Tyler tuts. 'It was during the war when the carriage was stored at Limoges.'

'Oh.' I feel somewhat foolish. 'So, how many times have you travelled on the Orient Express?'

'Just once – Lucerne to Paris. I wanted to see some of this legendary marquetry up close.'

'It is beautiful,' I say, studying the intricate design of poppies, grass reeds and what look like pimento olives inlaid in the wood panelling.

'Renét Prou was a true master of the floral art deco period.'

'Mmmm,' I agree, wishing I could plug an art history degree into my brain like in *The Matrix*. 'I love how the panels look like they've been varnished in honey!'

Tyler smiles and runs his finger along the syrupy sheen. 'You see these diagonal stripes of wood? Watch when we pass these buildings coming up – the sun gets blocked intermittently and you get a kind of strobe effect . . .'

'Oh wow – it looks like the stripes are flashing!' I gasp.

'Isn't that something?' Tyler smiles at my glee.

'I love it!'

'I love that you're here with me,' Tyler breathes.

I take a sip from my empty cup.

'More tea?' he offers.

'Er, no, I'm fine. I suppose I should be thinking about getting ready for dinner – you said we're at the 7p.m. sitting?'

He nods. 'I'm just going to have a shave then I'll wait for you in the Bar car.'

'Um, Tyler . . .'

'Um, Kim . . .'

405

'It says in the brochure, "You can never overdress on the Orient Express." Are you . . .?'

'Black tie,' he nods.

Looks like I'm going to get some use out of the bugle-beaded number my mum packed after all.

40

It's strange to think that Tyler is only a metre away from me. Especially as I am about to undress. I ensure that our connecting door is locked, check the wood panelling for peepholes and then contemplate the tiny sink. Strip wash it is, then.

Outside the countryside streaks by. It makes a change from staring at bathroom tiles, I suppose. I'm concentrating on scooping water into my armpits and not all over the faded turquoise and ginger carpet when I'm suddenly plunged into pitch blackness. It takes me a second to realize that we're going through a tunnel. I don't want to risk pressing the call button instead of the light switch so I just stand there sudsy and dripping until we emerge the other side. Finally – light.

As I rinse myself off I notice that we've slowed to a halt. On a train platform. It's like the Blue Grotto all over again, only this time my audience is a bemused old man, not a yachtful of yobs. I grab the blind and yank it down. I'm like some travelling soft porn show. I have got to stop exposing myself to Italians.

'What about Americans?' I hear Cleo goad me.

'No – no one except Luca!' I assert.

I peer at my reflection and wonder what I can do to look as if I've made some kind of effort. Not so much for Tyler, as the other passengers and the staff. I don't want to look like a runner who's accidentally wandered into shot on a Merchant Ivory film set. Then I remember my mum's gas-powered tongs and begin taming my curls – one eye on the mirror, one on the ever-changing scenery. Unfortunately the gas runs out when I'm only halfway done. Ah well, could be worse: imagine if I had poker straight hair like Cleo and had only curled one side – then I'd be stuffed. Now. Make-up – a new kit courtesy of Sophia. I go about the unfamiliar business of applying foundation. This can't be right – my skin looks like a freshly painted wall where you can make out the brushstrokes. 'Blend! Blend!' I beg. 'Give me Sophie Ellis Bextor skin, please.'

Oh no. *Oh no.* I peer closer. Please tell me I wasn't just having tea with Tyler with that spike sticking out of my chin? Where do these rogue hairs sprout from? It wasn't there yesterday and now it's at least a centimetre long. I pray he just thought it was an escapee from a blusher brush, not one of my own. Tweezers. Tweezers . . .

No tweezers.

As I flump back on the seat, I emit a bleep. Reaching beneath me I discover Tyler's phone. I should really give it back but . . .

I tap on Tyler's door. No reply. He must have

already gone to the bar. I mean, I would normally ask permission to phone abroad but I can't wait another minute to find out what happened with Cleo and Gareth yesterday. She finishes work early on a Wednesday, so she'll be able to give me the unedited version. I just pray that he's succumbed to her charms. Come on . . . Ring-ring. Click. Answermachine. Darn.

'Cleo! It's me! Are you there? Pick up the phone! You'll never guess where I'm ca—'

'Hello?' a feeble voice answers.

I feel instantly uneasy. Cleo never gets down. 'What's the matter?'

A heavy sigh and then: 'I developed his pictures.'

'And?'

'He wasn't in Cornwall. He was in the Caribbean.'

'Well, that's not exactly—'

'He was on his honeymoon,' she shuts me down.

I clunk my head back on the door.

'Those pictures of the lads' night out were his stag night.'

She sounds utterly despondent.

'Are you all right?' I ask, frustrated that I can't reach out and give her a hug.

'It's not even that – I didn't even know him, he was just another of my stupid crushes – it's just . . .' She sighs. 'I was looking at the pictures I was developing today: there was this dad at the hospital with his newborn baby and I mean, this thing was puce and bawling but he just looked so smitten! And then there was this smoochy couple in a four-poster bed at some chintzy hotel, and these women with a washing line pegged out with giant knickers . . .'

'What's to envy about that?'

'They were at a Tom Jones concert at Cardiff Castle! You should have seen their faces – they were singing along, having a right laugh. I was even jealous of this gang of mates at some tacky Costa del Hangover resort lunging all over each other pulling faces. It's not that I want to be sunburnt and sweating tequila, it's just that I feel like everybody else is out there, really living, except me.'

My heart goes out to her and I open my mouth to speak but she beats me to it.

'I'm not saying this to make you feel bad, but I only really noticed it since you've been gone. I don't do anything, I don't go anywhere . . . I tried to call one of my friends from back home but turns out she moved six months ago and I don't have her new number. So then I rang my dad and it was all, "Marlon this and Marlon that . . ." and when he asked what I'd been up to I had no news of my own.' She takes a breath. 'None of that mattered while you were here because staying in doing nothing is fun with you. But by myself, I don't know – I feel like I'm going crazy! A couple of nights there's been nothing on TV so I've been going to bed really early because I can't think of what to do with my time. I want the morning to come so I can get to work and then when I get there I don't enjoy it, I just go through the motions. Every day I feel a little less interested in the next. I think that's why I was fixating on Gareth. I just wanted something to be excited about. Look where that got me.'

I've never known her so introspective and low. Then again I've never been away for more than a night. 'I'm really sorry,' I mutter.

'You remember that woman who comes in asking to have people removed from her photos?'

'Yes,' I say, quietly.

'I feel like I've been erased from my own life.'

I slump down on the seat. I feel so helpless. 'Do you want me to come home?' I ask, prepared to walk back if I have to.

'No, no, no! That's not what I'm saying! Please don't think that! Oh God! I'm sorry to be such a moaner,' says Cleo, suddenly pulling herself together. 'Where did you say you're calling from?'

I look around my beautiful bijou cabin. I can't possibly tell her now. 'I'm on a train,' I say, still shaken by her words. There must be something I can do to cheer her up . . .

'To Rome?'

'Yes, but listen – I'll be back in Capri on Friday, what if you came out?'

She's obviously desperate for some fun. I could introduce her to the lovely Massimo at the Faraglioni restaurant. The smell from the kitchens alone would revive her.

'No, I'd only be in the way,' she demurs.

'Don't be ridiculous – you could never be in the way!'

Cleo sighs. 'Kim, you're all loved up with Luca and

that's great but I don't think I could be around a couple at the—' her voice breaks up. I hear her swallow hard, obviously fighting back the tears, and my own eyes fill up.

'It wouldn't be like that,' I say softly.

'Yes, it would. And I don't want you feeling you can't be happy just because I'm not. Really, I'm not being a killjoy, I just . . . couldn't . . .' She sniffs noisily and then takes a breath. 'I'll be fine tomorrow, I'm just having a lonesome cowboy moment.'

'Can't you get Marlon down for the weekend?' I hate to think of her alone. 'He always makes you laugh.'

'Yeah, good idea,' she says briskly. 'I'll give him a call in a minute. Maybe I could go and visit him for a change . . .'

She's bouncing back too quickly, just putting on a brave face for me, I know it. 'Was that the doorbell?' I ask.

'Yeah, it's Bongs.'

Solo take-away again. This is worse than I thought. She's given up the will to cook.

I hear her pay the delivery man and close the door.

'What are you doing for dinner tonight?' she asks, clattering plates and cutlery in the background.

'Actually we're eating on the train . . .'

'Oh, poor you! Sarnies with weirdly dense bread and microwave tikka masala – oh no, that's British Rail, you're in Italy. Maybe it won't be so bad. Do you know what you're getting?'

412

'Not sure,' I say, keeping shtum about my suspicions that there will be caviar involved.

'I'd better go or my prawn balls will go soggy.'

'Cleo—'

'Please don't worry about me. I feel fine now. I got out *Roseanna's Grave* on video the other day when you said Mario looked like Jean Réno and he's playing an Italian in it and I haven't watched it yet so . . .'

'Did you get any of those deep fried bananas?' I ask, wanting to keep her chatting so I can be sure she's okay.

'Yeah. I asked for extra sesame seeds this time.'

All is not lost.

'Hang in there. I'll call you tomorrow.'

'Okay.'

I can't bear to put the phone down.

'I'm going now,' she says.

Clunk.

I feel so bad. But what can I do? And when? Tonight is a write-off. Tomorrow I'm all tied up with the meeting with the artist's agent but after that . . . What if I flew back from Rome and went and got her – just filled a case with her things and marched her out the door? I wince, thinking of how panicked I felt when my mum yanked me out of my cocoon. I can see it was for the best now but I wasn't feeling anywhere near as raw as Cleo is right now. I've got a feeling she'd just refuse. I should know – I'm the one that taught her you should cut yourself off from the world when you're hurting.

The train jolts me back to the present moment.

Another jolt and I'm catapulted back to another era. It's still July 11th but the year has spun back to 1922.

I look at my watch – nearly 7p.m. I have to dress and get to the Bar car. I'll just get through dinner and then start working on a plan to put a smile back on Cleo's face.

'You are an art deco Aphrodite!' I tell myself as I wriggle into my rustling-swishing dress and apply an extra gleam of lipgloss. Heels. For the first time in years, heels. What else did Mum pack? A diamanté bracelet with a silver buckle fastening. A perfume miniature of Opium. Okay. This is the new me: Feminine. Alluring. Mysterious. Or Anita Dobson on her way to a soap awards ceremony – you decide.

As I ricochet along the carriages trying not to become impregnated by the men I pass, I wonder about the etiquette of corridor passing. Is it up to the men to face the wall and let you slide by their backs? Steven said the stewards must never turn their backs on their guests. Mind you, most of these stewards are such handsome devils and it's not exactly a hardship to brush past them full frontal.

In five carriages, there's only one guest I feel was perhaps taking advantage of the unpredictability of the train's motion. I wouldn't have minded but I lost three bugle beads on his belt buckle.

The glamorous heritage of the train creeps over me as I step into the Bar car – the setting sun has cast a golden glow across the dusty pink seats and low mahogany tables and if I scrunch up my eyes the man leaning on the baby grand piano, sipping his aperitif becomes Gregory Peck.

Of course there's one man that doesn't need distorting: Tyler. A good-looking fella by any account but in his sleek tuxedo . . . if they ever decide on a blond James Bond he's the template. An idea springs to mind – what about him and Cleo? She already likes the sound of him and there's nothing like the attentions of a stunning millionaire to un-break your heart. Ha! I feel better already. I don't even squirm when Tyler takes my hand and kisses it because I am looking at him through Cleo's eyes now.

'Shall we?' says Tyler, offering me his arm.

I take it and smile as the pianist begins to croon, *Almost Like Being In Love* . . .

41

The clickety-clackety motion of the train seems to be accentuated as I lie out in the darkness – I feel like my joints are dislocating then slotting back into place. I sneak another peek at my watch – 6.30a.m. Thanks to the invasive snoring from the man in the carriage to my right I've been awake since 5a.m. but somehow I haven't minded. There's something so snug about the compartment as a bedroom. Last night I returned to find the lights dimmed, the bed made up, my pyjamas on the pillow and a pair of VSOE slippers on the little bedside cloth. The only thing missing was a dead body and Hercule Poirot.

As I fluff up my pillow I wonder what conclusions Monsieur Moustache would come to about Tyler. We must have spent at least six intensive hours in each other's company last night and yet I still can't figure him out. Not even the free-flowing wine and liqueurs loosened him up. As for me, I was away on the first sip of champagne . . .

As we moved from the Bar car to the dining car, I felt a tingle of anticipation – even the tables were

416

dressed to impress in luxuriant linen accessorized with diamond cut crystal. We were seated by Venetian waiters who served us French cuisine: baked lobster tail in brandy sauce with stir-fried spring vegetables, roast duck supreme with white truffle foie gras (ick), a cheese course (which I skipped) and crispy bitter chocolate and bergamot ice-cream which was to sigh for. (I've kept a copy of the menu for Cleo.)

There are three dining cars: Etoile du Nord, Chinoise and ours, Lalique. As I sipped the velvety red wine, Tyler pointed to the frieze of opaque glass glowing with smooth classical figures entwined with bunches of plump grapes and told me that René Lalique actually trained as a jeweller and only got into glass at the age of forty-five when he was asked to design a perfume bottle by his good friend François Coty.

To which I replied, 'Do you know Coty now have a man's cologne called Stetson? And the woman's version is called Lady Stetson! Isn't that funny?'

Which pretty much sums up the difference in our conversation. He's just so sophisticated, I couldn't help thinking that he'd be better off with more ladylike company. I saw other female diners looking enviously in my direction then disappointedly back at their dining companion and actually felt a little guilty that I was hogging him. Then again I also felt: Hands off, I'm keeping him warm for a friend of mine!

Over dinner Tyler asked me a lot of questions about my life and my love life in particular, but revealed very little about himself. I couldn't even get a straight answer out of him when I asked him if he liked redheads. I was, of course, thinking of Cleo but he simply said, 'Why, are you thinking of dyeing yours?' At one point he did confess that he didn't think he'd ever truly been in love and lamented the fact that his lifestyle could be mistaken for that of an international playboy, but that was just a brief aberration. The only topic he spoke on effusively was art. It seems to be a family trait – his brother Morgan uses other people's words to make himself sound witty, Tyler uses other people's designs to make him sound creative, when really I think he is a businessman at heart.

Though I had attempted to put a ban on thoughts of Capri so I could enjoy the evening for what it was, my mind summoned Luca. I pictured him sitting next to Tyler sipping Colombian coffee – so raw and open and real in comparison. Everyone seems to be rooting for Tyler but I wonder how much of his appeal is his looks and status and his lifestyle. He's polished and charming when he wants to be, but I can't get a handle on his true character.

After dinner we returned to the atmospheric Bar car for a series of Amaretto nightcaps. One would have been enough for me but Tyler insisted on another and another. Though the room became rather blurry I remember noticing two things – one that the bar manager had one of the best comedy cross-breed accents I'd ever encountered (half Italian and half Australian) and secondly that the pianist played note-perfect as we jiggled along but whenever we came to a standstill he hit bum notes.

Tyler, however, continued to be flawless. Perfect teeth, perfect manicure, perfect gentleman. Not a hair out of place. Well, not until he tapped on my door half an hour after we'd said goodnight . . .

'I'm sorry to disturb you,' he apologized, leaning his arm on the door and peering through his newly tousled fringe like he was in a Seventies aftershave ad. 'You weren't in bed?'

'Not quite,' I pipped nervously. Surely he must have been aware that his dress shirt was unbuttoned to his navel. Was he trying to be provocative?

'I just wanted to ask . . .'

'Yes?' I croaked.

'If you still had my phone?'

I blushed at what was going through my mind.

'Only I might need to make some calls first thing,' he explained.

'Oh yes!' I blustered. 'I'm so sorry— I forgot.'

I fumbled on the table and handed him his Nokia.

'Thanks, I—' I was on the verge of confessing about the call to Cardiff, honest guv, but he distracted me by saying, 'That's a pretty bracelet' and taking my hand.

'It's my mother's' was all I could manage in response.

'Ah,' he nodded, adjusting the diamanté so it sent sparkling semaphore into the night. Then, seeming to sense my tension as his finger slipped to the underside of the bracelet, he added, 'Would you like me to undo the clasp for you?'

I wriggled my hand free from his. 'No, no, I'm fine, thank you!'

419

I didn't like him touching me. Even just his fingertips on my wrist felt disloyal to Luca. I know I'm over-reacting but every time he comes too close it's as though he's tripped the security system at a bank – sirens wail, lights flash and metal gates come clanking down around the vault.

When he nuzzled my ear with a goodnight kiss and whispered, 'Sweet dreams' I just went cold.

It's typical, isn't it – I find myself in the most romantic of settings and I'm with the *wrong guy*! Part of me feels like I'm being wasteful. I know my mother wouldn't have passed up the opportunity to be caressed on the Orient Express. And I can just hear Cleo's incredulous groans of, 'He was there, unbuttoned and ready to go and you said no?!'

Ah, what's a girl to do? It's got to feel right, hasn't it?

I sit forward and tentatively raise the blind to let the sunlight in. Just one more night to get through and I'll be going back to Capri, back to Luca ... In the meantime, it's time to embrace the day.

Learning from yesterday's mistake I turn on the light before I have my wash just in case we go through any tunnels. Miraculously I am decent when Steven comes to my compartment with a breakfast of croissants, fruit salad, orange juice and Earl Grey. I sit having my private tea party feeling like I'm in some kind of *Alice in Wonderland* dollhouse-cum-deluxe prison cell.

At about 8a.m. I hear Tyler on the phone, confirming his appointment with agent Aurora in Rome, then he taps on my door. I'm relieved to see that his hair has regained its Nicky Clarke precision flick and his shirt is buttoned to the collar once more.

'We're all set for this afternoon – how did you sleep?'

'Fine!' I lie.

'Rocks you like a baby, doesn't it?' Tyler smiles. 'We should be arriving in Florence in around half an hour so if you wanted to take those pictures you mentioned now would be a good time.'

'Oh yes! I definitely want to get a few of the bar.' It's my new favourite place.

'Okay, well, I've got a couple more calls to make so just give me a tap when you get back.'

I grab my camera and brace myself for the five-carriage bone-shaker. I'm halfway there when it occurs to me to check how many shots I have left. One. Curses – I have to go back. That's at least another three bruises added to my journey.

As I open my compartment door and reach in for my bag I hear Tyler groan, 'It's in the bag, I'm telling you!'

I look up, startled – can he see me? As he continues speaking I realize he's on the phone, presumably reassuring someone that he's secured Alessandro's work.

'No, of course not! He'd kill me if he knew – he's on the verge of proposing to her Goddamn mother!'

I freeze mid bag-rummage.

There's a silence while the person on the other end of the phone is speaking then Tyler insists, 'No, it'll never happen.'

Other voice.

'Because I won't allow it, that's why.'

Other voice.

'Listen – there's no way my father's marrying that slut!'

My mouth falls open. I'm stunned. How dare he? I suddenly feel incredibly protective and then I go cold. I called her that. And she heard me. Bad enough someone else speaking about your mother like that, imagine how hurtful it must have been for her to have heard that from her own daughter's mouth . . .

'No, she's not like that – bit more of a challenge.'

Other voice.

Tyler laughs. 'Five-star hotels, champagne, opera, Orient Express – I don't think so.'

Other voice.

'Tonight's the night, I'm telling you. They expect it before and then, when I don't make a move, they wonder why. By the third night they're coming on to *me*. Trust me, she's like all the rest: she'll give it up and then that's when the fun really starts . . .'

Other voice.

'No way. I promised Morgan I'd get her back.'

I feel sick.

Morgan and Tyler are in cahoots. I'm caught up in some rich boy's revenge game.

I'd run away but I'm on a speeding train. If I had the guts I'd burst in and punch him. But what good would that do? Maybe I should just disappear when we get off in Florence – leave him stranded and mess up his meeting in Rome. Then I think of Tomas. I disappeared without even making a ripple in his life. This is my chance to do things differently. My eyes dart around the carriage for inspiration. Think. Think! What if . . . ? I need more time.

Before Tyler ends his conversation I grab my bag, close my door oh-so-quietly and hurtle towards the bar. I've got the advantage. I know his intention. I'm not going to run. To think I nearly wished him on Cleo! On behalf of all the women who didn't see the humiliation coming I am going to make him pay.

42

Disembarking at Santa Maria Novella station, I fake-smile my way through our walking tour of Florence – I wasn't really looking at the Ponte Vecchio or Michelangelo's David, I was plotting. What would really get to him? What about the possible repercussions on Mum's relationship with PM? There has to be a way to get back at him without the finger pointing to me – but what?

We're back on the train in time for a highly photogenic lunch and then pull into Ostiense station in Rome at 4p.m. I feel a sentimental pang as we disembark for the last time. The staff are lined up to bid us farewell. This is the closest I'm ever going to get to royalty. The mystique of the Orient Express is real even if Tyler's charm is an illusion.

Once we've checked into the devastatingly sumptuous St Regis Grand Hotel (all Murano glass chandeliers and hand-painted frescos) we take the short stroll to the Spanish Steps, turn down a back street that would be called a crevice anywhere else in the world and find ourselves being welcomed into Alessandro's agent's tiny office.

I love Aurora on sight – an Italian Judi Dench with dominatrix overtones. Formalities are brief, negotiations fierce.

My first revenge tactic was to bugger up the deal but then the artist would lose out and the agent forgo her cut. Can't have that. As Aurora insists that her client is worth more than Tyler is offering, I start thinking that way myself. Something in the realm of an extra nought . . .

After a further ten minutes' haggling Aurora reluctantly agrees to 200,000,000 lire – just under $100,000.

'This lire shit is crazy!' Tyler's brow furrows as he studies the figures on his sleek pocket calculator. 'How many noughts is that again?' he asks me as he takes out his chequebook.

'One, two, three, four, five, six, seven, eight (and one for luck) *Nine*!' I tell him. What's an extra $900,000 between enemies?

'So that's Two Billion lire?' he says, writing out the words in full, still not twigging. 'It's like joke money, isn't it?'

'Just what I was thinking,' I smile.

I watch him sign the cheque then swiftly take it in my hand before he gives it to Aurora.

'This is Mr Hamilton's final offer,' I say, addressing her in Italian. 'May I recommend you neither look too surprised or delighted when you see the figure as it may cause him to reconsider.'

The agent gives me a curious look.

As does Tyler.

'I'm just emphasizing that this is a fair amount and you are delighted to have done business with her.'

425

Tyler nods graciously.

I push the cheque across the table to the agent.

She looks at the cheque. At me. At the cheque again.

Then she shrugs and sighs, 'Vale di più!'

'He's worth more!' I translate to Tyler, biting back a smile.

'Final offer,' Tyler confirms.

The agent gives Tyler's hand a firm shake but it's me she's looking at when she says, 'Grazie!'

Finally! It's happened – I've been acknowledged on a translating job! What I've said has made a difference!

'Now please, I am very busy.' Aurora ushers us out of the door, locking it behind us. 'I have to go to the bank!'

'I think we should celebrate!' says Tyler as we step back into the busy street.

'So do I!' I grin. I think I've just become a patron of the arts.

After a bottle of champagne (these rich folk drink it like Perrier), Tyler orders a pep-up 'expresso'.

'Out of curiosity – how are you spelling that?' I ask him as the waiter scurries away.

'E-x-p-'

'Can I just stop you there?' I interrupt. 'It's actually e-S-p-r-e-s-s-o – S, not X!'

'Oh. Oh. Actually you're right,' he concedes. 'Thank you.'

'Well, I'd hate for you to embarrass yourself in front of anyone important.'

I watch as Tyler mentally runs through the number of times he's made this particular *faux pas* then I make a

426

suggestion: 'Perhaps I could teach you a few Italian phrases for your next visit?'

'Sure – why not?' Tyler agrees.

He's a good student. In just a few minutes I get him inflection-perfect on, 'Ho un pene piccolissimo!' (I have a tiny penis.)

'And that's, '"You have a stunning city?"'

'Yes. Piccolissimo is like one step up from bellissimo.'

'Ahhh,' he nods.

'I think you'll be surprised at the reaction you get – especially from women,' I smile.

'They love it, don't they – an American speaking Italian.'

'Love it!' I agree.

'We'll have to try it out!' he enthuses.

'Well, no need until I've gone. I'm here to look after you until tomorrow morning,' I say, sliding a seductive hand on top of his.

He smiles in a 'Gotcha!' way. 'You're going to adore dinner tonight. I thought we'd eat at the hotel restaurant, Vivendo. The food should be incredible, it was founded by Escoffier . . .'

I look impressed on Cleo's behalf, whereas I'm simply wondering whether Escoffier is the origin of the word 'scoff'.

'It's been an amazing few days, Tyler. I'll never forget them,' I sigh. 'If you don't mind me saying, you're extremely generous with your money . . .'

'Money means nothing to me – it's just there to make life more fun.'

Hmmm. I wonder if he means that.

427

'What if you dropped a million dollars in an afternoon?' I ask, casually.

'I've done it before in Vegas,' he brazens. 'I always make it back.'

If that's true then the art deal isn't enough. It's not even going to make a dent. There must be something else. Something more personal.

As Tyler excuses himself to go to the Gents I watch him steal a glance at his reflection in the mirror above my head and flick his shimmering hair. *His halo is his trademark.* Morgan's words come back to me.

And then I think of Cleo with the hotel pillow chocolate in her hair . . .

I look around the café bar. I catch sight of a pair of gum-chewing teenage girls moaning in Italian about how all men are bastards. An international complaint if ever there was one. Every good criminal needs a sidekick or two so I duck over to their table and hurriedly enlist them in my plan.

'Have you noticed those girls keep looking over at you?' I ask Tyler when he returns.

'Where? Oh those two.' He acknowledges them with a nod.

They giggle and whisper between themselves.

'They think you look like a blond David Ginola. You know, the footballer with the long hair?'

He frowns. 'Is that a good thing?'

'Oh my God!' I simper. 'He's so handsome! A real sex symbol.'

He gives them a more confident smile.

'While you were in the bathroom they asked if I had a

camera so I could take a picture of you with them but I wasn't sure if . . .' I falter.

'Of course!' he smiles, good-naturedly.

'Really?' I gasp, giving the girls the thumbs-up. 'You're going to make their day! Ragazze venite qui!'

'I tuoi capelli sono morbitissimi, posso toccarli?'

'She wants to know if she can touch your hair,' I say, looking bashful.

'Sure,' he shrugs, lapping up the attention.

'Smile, everyone!' I cheer as the girls nuzzle in and ruffle his silken locks for the photograph. The second the shutter clicks the girls are off and running.

'Oh!' I gasp.

'Did you get their address to send the picture?' Tyler asks.

'No!' I laugh. 'I think maybe they just wanted to cop a feel, as you say in America!'

Tyler laughs and runs his hand through his hair. 'What the . . .'

'Something wrong?'

'Shit!'

'What is it?'

'The little bitches have put gum in my hair!'

'Not chewing gum? You're kidding!'

'Damn!' Tyler curses, thumping the table.

'Let me see . . .' I inspect his head. Nice job – right near the scalp. 'You know, I hate to say this but I think you're going to have to get it cut out.'

His hand shoots to the gum in a panic.

'No – don't touch it, it'll spread.'

'There must be—'

429

'You can't wash it out. Really – cutting is the only way.'

Tyler looks despairing. 'W-will you come with me to the hairdresser – make sure they understand I just want the minimum cut?'

'Oh yes,' I reassure him. 'I'll tell them exactly what you need.'

Turns out Tyler had reason to be protective about his hair. It did a beautiful job covering up his sticky-out ears.

Suddenly he doesn't seem so mannequin-perfect.

'I didn't know you dyed your hair,' I say, as we make our way back to the hotel.

'It's not dyed, it's highlights, I . . .' The poor guy is nearly in tears.

Now that the humiliation is complete, I doubt he would try it on with me tonight even if I did stay.

'You know, I think I might hop on a flight to Naples. Our work is complete and I'm missing my mum.'

Oddly this is kind of true.

Tyler doesn't raise any objections.

'You'll be fine without me,' I reassure him as I climb in the taxi for the airport. 'You've got all the Italian you need to get you by!'

43

As the Isle of Capri swims into view I feel my eyes gloss over with yearning and relief. It feels so good to be back. Who would have thought that I could feel such affinity with this intense beauty? Ten days ago this place meant nothing to me, if anything I was repelled by its elite reputation, but now it has me utterly beguiled.

The ferry churns into Marina Grande and I wonder, would I do things differently if I was arriving for the first time today but knew exactly what lay ahead? Obviously I would stay away from Tyler but could I have held back from Luca, even if I knew that being with him would be the emotional equivalent of extreme sports?

I bump my suitcase along the path to the Hotel Luna. Up on our bedroom balcony my mother sits engrossed in a book, twiddling a strand of her hair. From here she looks so young she could be reading *Anne of Green Gables* or *Little House on the Prairie*. It makes me stop and ponder, what if our roles were reversed and I were her mother? How would I feel? How would

I talk to her? I've always despaired of my mother's fussing but I realize that the first question I would ask myself would be, 'What can I do to make her more comfortable? Happier?' I'd watch her so closely to try and second-guess what her next need might be. I'd want to protect her and nurture her. I would probably feel that I had the right to try and mould her just a little or, at the very least, have the right to my say. And of course I would stroke her hair, because I would feel like she belonged to me.

I don't wait for the lift, I take the stairs two at a time.

'Kim!' Mum is startled by my premature appearance and, no doubt, the force of my hug. Suddenly she's all that matters.

'I wasn't expecting you back until tomorrow!'

'So Tyler hasn't called?' I say, loosening my grip.

'No,' she frowns, pushing a random curl from my eyes. 'Why? Did something happen?'

'No, nothing,' I breeze, deciding to leave his character assassination for now. 'Everything all right with PM?'

'Oh yes,' she brightens. 'He'll be here any minute, we're going to Lido del Faro for dinner – you have to come and tell us all about your wonderful trip.'

'Lido del Faro?' I repeat, hoping to distract her from further questions.

'It's over at Punta Carena – it's beautiful there on a clear night.'

I feel a pang. The lighthouse. That's where Luca was going to take me. 'Special occasion?' I test the water, wondering if Tyler's prediction was right.

'How did you guess?'

I shrug. 'Well?'

'Oh darling, he asked me to marry him!'

I love that my mother can work some surprise into her voice. By now she must be able to see a proposal coming a mile off.

'That's wonderful!' I tell her. 'When's the wedding?' (She normally likes a swift turnaround.)

'I don't know if there's going to be one.'

'What?'

'I haven't said yes yet!'

My jaw drops.

'I know you think I'm addicted to confetti—'

'It's not . . . I just . . .' I'm stunned. Finally some quality merchandise and she hesitates. 'Why?'

'I don't know – I want to think it through: if we marry he'd want me to move to Atlanta and I don't want to give up the shop yet.'

What's this? Pacing? Rationale? I'm impressed.

Mum leads me back into the room, saying she just needs to give her nails a second coat. 'I gave Luca your letter,' she informs me as she strokes on the oyster pearl.

'Right,' I say, looking at the tiled floor. Please don't let there be any bad news to follow.

'Obviously I didn't let on that I knew anything. I said I thought it was something to pass on to Ringo.'

'Thanks,' I say, still nervous of asking outright about him. 'Um, so is everything okay at the shop?'

'Well, let's just say most of the shoeboxes have got dents in them.'

433

I look up.

'I think Luca's feeling a little troubled right now,' she smiles, adding softly, 'You must have put him in quite a spin.'

'Is Tanya's sister here yet?' I ask, covering my blushes.

'She arrived today.'

'Did you meet her?'

Mum studies me. 'So you still feel the same way about him?'

I nod.

'Poor Tyler. He must be cut to the quick.'

I can't help but smile. 'Don't worry, it'll grow back.'

'What? What will grow back?' she yelps.

'Phone!' I trill.

'Kim!' my mother beseeches me, ignoring the rings.

'Hello?' I say, answering for her. 'Yes, I'm back early. I'd love to! Okay, here she is . . .'

My mother cradles the receiver in the nook of her neck so as not to smudge her nails and I dart into the bathroom to get ready for dinner.

Tonight I am happy to embrace my inner goose-berry.

The road to Punta Carena is leafy and peaceful. There is very little traffic other than the odd matchbox-size three-wheel truck chuntering by.

'Can you see us in one of those, Gina?' chuckles PM as one passes us with a work-scuffed man and a dolled-up woman compressed into the tiny driving compart-ment.

'They must have to put their arms and legs in the back of the truck – how *do* they fit in?' my mum ponders.

I decide they'd make marvellous magicians' assistants, ideally suited to contorting inside sword-sliced boxes. 'Perhaps we've just stumbled upon the secret training ground for Italian Debbie McGees,' I suggest.

'Ooh, Kim, look at her!' Mum points to a girl overtaking us on a sugar pink moped.

'I could see you on one of those!' PM nudges me. I smile. So could I. I'd ride it barefoot.

PM seems to be taking the semi-spurn in his stride. If anything, he's doting on my mother more than ever. Shame his sons didn't inherit his respect for women.

'Come on then, darling – tell us about your trip with Tyler!' Mum encourages as we pass through Capri's answer to suburbia.

'Yes, we're all ears,' adds PM.

As indeed is your son, I think to myself.

I give them the abridged version, keeping my references to Tyler entirely neutral.

'So no romance?' concludes PM.

'No.'

'I never really saw you two together,' PM admits. 'I know your mother was keen but frankly I wouldn't wish either of my sons on any woman. Ah. Here we are . . .'

We pull into a gravel carpark. The lighthouse stands at the furthest tip of the rocky coastline, striped peach and cream with a line of washing hanging from one of the windows. Down near the water's edge, lights sparkle and there's a welcoming clink of plates and hubbub of voices.

'The restaurant is down here,' says Mum, leading us to the steps. 'This was my father's favourite – this is such a treat!'

As we trot down the path, taking care not to catch our clothing on the spiky shrubbery, we round a corner and come face to face with Luca hand in hand with Ringo, followed by Tanya and Posh Blonde #2.

There's a flurry of 'Ciao!'s then my mother takes the initiative: 'You must be Tanya's sister . . .'

'Emma,' she says, a vision of peroxide perfection.

'This is Tony Hamilton and my daughter Kim.'

'Ow! Papa! You're hurting my hand.' Ringo squirms away from Luca, nursing his crushed fingers. Luca looks intently at the step as Tanya glares suspiciously.

I give Emma my most innocent 'I'm not remotely in love with your sister's husband!' look and wave at Ringo. Not being able to touch Luca is hard but within seconds his son fills my arms with his love. It's almost as though Ringo can sense the double helping of affection he's getting because he leans close to my ear and whispers, 'You give the best hugs, Kim. Mamma does not like to be squeezed too hard.'

'You go for dinner at the Lido?' Luca addresses PM.

'Yes,' he replies. 'Is that where you've been?'

'Sì!' Luca nods. 'It was wonderful.'

'It's a tough life sharing yourself between two beautiful women, isn't it, Luca?' PM winks.

Luca's eyes widen, my mouth goes dry.

'He means at dinner, you know: you with Tanya

and Emma. Him with Kim and myself,' my mother overcompensates, laughing shrilly.

'Ah, sì!' he nods.

If any of the neigbouring rock pools were deep enough I'd drown myself now.

'Well . . .' says Tanya, making a 'we should be off' motion.

'Won't you join us for a drink?' says PM, oblivious to the delicate politics of the situation.

Mum and Tanya wince and make reluctant 'umm-errr' noises.

'We really should be getting Nino home,' Tanya decides.

'I'm not tired!' he whoops. 'Can't we stay?'

'I'm sure Emma must be exhausted after her journey,' Mum attempts.

'Actually, I feel fine,' she chirrups, eyeing PM's Rolex.

'Really, we don't want to interrupt your evening,' Tanya insists.

'You wouldn't be,' PM begins, then – in response to a rib-dig from my mother – 'Of course, there's always another night. Maybe tomorrow?' Rib-dig. 'Or later in the week?'

A relieved chorus of 'Sì, grazie!' and 'Yes that would be lovely' puts us out of our misery. Ringo avails himself of one more hug and then both parties proceed as intended.

I stare at the menu but the words are a blur. When the waiter comes I order on autopilot and down a glass of wine in one. My heart continues to pound in my ears. It was the sweetest torture seeing Luca. Not that I could risk more than a glance – I wouldn't have been able to keep the love out of my eyes if I was looking directly at him. Just like I couldn't keep the unconditional affection out of my hug with Ringo. I think about his compliment 'You give the best hugs, Kim – Mamma does not like to be squeezed too hard.' And I can't help but delight in the knowledge that he prefers my hugs to those from his own mother. Of course, not wanting to be squeezed like a tube of toothpaste doesn't make you a bad mum but all the same ... I know what he means. Some people hug like they really mean it – they give something of themselves while they are in your arms. Others merely go through the motions – I call it hug-lite – and their unresponsive bodies leave you unsatisfied, as if you're embracing an empty sack.

After dinner Mum elects to stay at the Hotel Palace with PM. When the taxi pulls up at the Piazza Vittoria I too get out so I can give my mother a proper hug goodnight. She gives me a look that seems to say, Twice in one day? What's going on?

It makes me wonder what my mother has been getting from our hugs before today. Since my father left I'd say I've alternated between resistance and indifference. On a good day there may have been a veiled hint that I was *trying* to love her. Funny how easily it's coming now. I hope it doesn't change back.

I take the taxi as far as Capri town then hop out by the bus station and continue on foot. As I cross the

Piazzetta I spy the Luna hotel manager enjoying a latte with a few friends.

He looks up and smiles, 'Buona notte, Kim!'

'Buona notte, Alfredo!' I beam, chuffed that he remembered my name after-hours, delighted to be able to use his.

As the Quisisana comes into view I pass the waiter with the precision goatee who serves me at breakfast, stepping out with his girlfriend.

'Ciao!' he smiles.

'Ciao Francesco!' I reply, getting an absurd kick – I feel like part of the community!

I stroll back to the Luna feeling protected and known, totally reassured that my mother will be watched over when I leave.

When I leave? If I leave . . .

I take a deep breath. Whatever happens I'm going to be okay. I won't be sorry. I might even get a tattoo to remind me of that fact!

Andrea, the night concierge, turns his back on me the minute I enter the lobby. Ah well, you can't win them all. Then he turns back with a slip of paper.

'There is a message for you, Signorina Rees.'

'Grazie!' I say taking the folded note.

I don't open it until I get to the room.

It's from Luca.

My heart rips skyward.

Meet me tomorrow – 1p.m. at the Faraglioni rocks.

Here we go . . .

44

Last night I had that whole 'Que sera, sera' attitude off pat. Today my mantra is a less snappy 'Please, please, *please*, let me get the guy this time! Please can I have this one for keeps? I won't ask for anything else. Ever. Just let him choose me!'

The brick steps leading to the Faraglioni rocks are bordered by purple thistles and grasses that look like chives. In the shadier nooks heaps of pine needles hide wizened roots, out to ensnare unsuspecting ankles. The deeper down I go the more speed I gather; even the branches of the trees reach like outstretched arms towards the rocks.

I know I'm nearly there when I hear pre-recorded commentaries blown ashore from passing tour boats and the sound of children making a playmate out of the sea. I jump down from the final step on to what passes for a beach in these parts and weave around the splayed bodies contentedly filling themselves with solar energy. No Luca. Then I spy a spot shielded from both the sun and public view. There he sits. My heart bounces off the springboard and then belly-flops. He looks like he's got the weight of Pavarotti on his shoulders. There's an unfamiliar sunkenness to his frame. A look of confusion and despair – it must be love.

I hurry towards him, eager to ease back his shoulders and smooth his brow. But as I get closer a strange detachment creeps over me. It's not going to happen. We're not even going to have another night together. I can see it in his stoop. This is a man psyching himself up to do the right thing. I feel as though a wave is tumbling me in the surf and I can't tell whether I'm about to gasp air or seawater.

Part of me is tempted to keep walking right past him, but then he looks up – there's a moment's hesitation as though he intended to be guarded and remorseful and strong but then a genuine fondness fills his eyes and a smile spreads across his face. I stand before him and I know, *know 100 per cent* that he is The One for me. I have never felt so sure.

But it's not enough. The wariness creeps back into his face. He's torn. And I'm tearing him.

My instinct is to wrap myself around him so he can feel my love, to tell him how much I've missed him and how he rides tandem with every thought I have, but instead I lower myself on to the rock facing him and fold my hands neatly in my lap as if I'm composing myself for a work assessment interview.

'Okay!' I smile, exuding bravado. 'I'm guessing this is going to hurt.'

His eyes meet mine. Sad eyes. Silence. Pain.

I can't bear to see him like this. Just get it over with. 'I'm guessing this is goodbye.'

Damn, my voice wavered on the word 'goodbye'. I push out a breath and rein back the tears that are threatening to spill.

'It's Nino,' he says, bowing his head. 'Tanya said she would take him back to England if—'

'You didn't tell her?' I gasp.

'No. It was a warning. But she has suspicion. Even her sister ask me if something is going on.'

'I didn't realize other people could see those cartoon lovehearts above our heads!' I joke. I just want to see him smile again. It doesn't work.

'I have to be with my son.'

'I know,' I croak. Somewhere a small voice inside of me asks, Why didn't my father fight for me like this?

'I don't want to have to lie.'

'I understand,' I tell him.

He lets out an agonizing sigh and crumbles: 'This is the worst pain I have ever had! I can't look at you without wanting you. You are everything I ever wished for.'

He gets to his feet, angrily dislodging the pebbles around us with his heels. 'I want you to know, Kim, I want you to *really* know that being with you is the highest feeling I have ever experienced.'

I reach out and take his hand, remembering how his fingertips felt when they first touched my skin, arranging the necklace beads on my collarbone the day we met.

'Me too,' I tell him. 'The highest, the purest, the

442

happiest – look how happy I am!' I laugh, tears streaming down my face. 'Even standing here with you like this, I'm still happier than I have been with any other man.'

He steps forward and I tumble into him. His wet lashes stroke my damp cheeks. I can feel the love he is trying to hold back seep out through his skin.

'I felt so bad when you were gone but now I am alone with you again . . .' he wavers. 'I feel that I must do whatever it takes to be with you.'

Suddenly we're in this together.

When I first saw him I was shut out: he'd already made up his mind and it was just a matter of him informing me of his decision. It felt like every other relationship where I would passively go along with whatever the boyfriend decided. Now I get a say. The question is, how do I use my vote?

'Luca?'

'Yes?' He looks almost hopeful, as if I might have just come up with a miraculous solution that doesn't break any hearts or homes. If only.

'In case I don't get the chance again . . .'

'Don't say that!' he protests.

'I want to tell you what being with you has done for me. I want you to know.'

'I do know,' he says, eyes full of understanding.

'I want to say it out loud.'

He nods for me to go ahead.

'I'd given up on love. Whoever I've been with, however great they seemed on paper, I'd always feel unsure. So many boyfriends gave up on me saying,

"You'll never be happy. I'm offering you everything but you always convince yourself that something is missing." They seemed so certain that I started to think they were right – I was holding out for something that didn't exist. Years later I would reflect on the relationship and wonder why I had let them go. Was I so afraid of being hurt? Did I have unrealistic expectations? Was I simply incapable of love? Over and again I asked myself, "What's wrong with me?" There were always too many questions. All I knew was that it just didn't feel right to me – on some instinctive level my heart was saying *no*. But with you, there was none of that. I look at you and all I hear is a resounding, heartfelt *yes*!'

He sighs, looking almost proud.

'You have shown me that I can love. And that love can be uplifting and make you feel better about yourself. I actually like myself when I'm with you!' I laugh, amazed at the revelation. 'So, everything in me is saying, "Don't let this one go!"'

He kisses my hand.

'But I'm going to.'

He looks crushed.

'Neither of us want an affair – we want love. And I think sneaking around feeling sick with guilt at what this might do to Nino would be the quickest way to destroy what we have. I don't want an unhappy ending. I want to be able to smile when I think of you.'

It's amazing what you find yourself saying when you know someone is really listening to you.

'The hardest thing is that this still feels like the

beginning to me. I feel like I have all this love to give you and I have only said hello.'

Luca sighs. 'Maybe that is because there is more to come – we just don't know *when* yet.'

I don't know if I dare believe him but the alternative – making this the grand finale – is too bleak.

So I say, 'Yes, maybe one day.'

'Like Rosa and Vincenzo,' he smiles, then looks sad. 'But I don't ask you to wait for me. It would not be fair.'

'We'll see, but I think the memories will keep me going for a while.'

'Such good memories,' he sighs.

'I expect I'll have days when it will all seem like some fantasy but then I'll always have these . . .'

I reach in my bag and pull out an envelope of photos.

'I had them developed in Verona,' I explain as I place them one by one on the rocks: Our perfect kiss on the Terrace of Infinity. Me holding Rosa's wedding dress. Luca dressed in lurid polyester in Amalfi. A lopsided, arm's-length snap on board his boat at sunset, me snuggled in Luca's cashmere V-neck.

'You look good in my sweater,' he smiles.

'I think it's the only piece of designer clothing I actually approve of!'

'You'd look even better in that dress . . .' he says, wistfully eyeing the sheeny cream satin.

I feel a stab of regret. I only want to wear it for him.

'I got a double set,' I say, composing myself. 'I

445

thought maybe, if you wanted, you could keep them in Vincenzo's desk at the shop.'

Luca picks up the picture of our kiss and loses himself in the image.

I look on and smile – finally some pictures that have the power to block out Tomas and Britta. I can't even see them any more.

'When do you leave?'

'Tomorrow,' I say, as if it was already decided. I don't want him to know that I had prepared my mother for the possibility that I might stay on for several more weeks.

'How will I find you?'

'I'll write to you.'

His face brightens. 'From far off lands?'

'I'll tell you all my adventures,' I smile, hooking a finger in his belt-loop. 'But none will compare to this.'

He takes my head in his hands and kisses me firmly on the lips. When I open my eyes he looks so much lighter than when I first arrived – just a small Placido on his shoulders now.

'You should be getting back to the shop,' I suggest, looking at my watch. My resolve isn't going to hold for much longer.

He kisses me again. Softer this time. 'Kim, you are the kindest person I have ever met. Thank you.'

I keep smiling and waving until he rounds the corner. Then my heart splits apart and I fall to my knees.

When the sobbing finally subsides, I sit and stare out to

446

sea watching the sparkles get stretched and distorted through the blur of my left-over tears.

Finally I get to my feet, hitch up my trousers and wade into the sea to splash my face. The water trickles down my neck. The chill feels good. I plunge my arms deeper and take another step so the water creeps above my knees. Before I have time to change my mind, I whip off my shirt and trousers and throw the sopping bundle back on to the shore. My knickers and vest can pass as a tankini – I'm going for my first swim in the Med!

They say salt water is good for healing wounds.

45

'You can't go,' Mario sulks as I take my seat at the bar for the last time.

'Why not?' I ask, snaffling a glacé cherry. Even though my undies are still damp from my swim at the Faraglioni, I've come straight to the hotel bar – I don't want to fall back into the habit of hiding away like I did after Tomas. This time I am daring myself to keep going. Besides, Mario always makes me smile.

'I have not kept my promise,' he says gravely.

'What promise?'

'I promise myself I would make shaggy with you!'

'Oh Mario!' I laugh.

He raises an eyebrow.

'Oh go on then . . .' I say, pretending to unbutton my shirt.

'Really Kim, do you have to go?'

'Yes, I do,' I sigh.

'But what will you do?'

'No idea but I've still got £5,000 from Vincenzo's will to play with.'

'Five thousand pounds? Wow! That's 15 million lire!'

I look at Mario. '*Oh my God!*'

'What?'

'Mario you are a genius!' I lean across the bar and plant a smacker on his lips.

'What did I say?' he frowns.

I dash back to the room and feverishly dial Cleo, bungling the number three times in the excitement.

I've been thinking in pounds, not lire! Who says I have to go back to Wales to spend the money!

'Cleo!' I exclaim before she even completes the word Hello.

'Kim! Perfect timing! The New You Clinic just rang to confirm our liposuction appointment. They say they need a deposit of £200.'

'That's the price of a flight to Naples,' I tell her.

'Right.'

'Which would you prefer?' I pipe.

'What are you saying?'

'I'm saying that instead of spending £5,000 on trying to get skinny we could enjoy ourselves in a country where eating less than three courses at lunchtime is considered bad manners!'

'I told you before, I can't be around a couple right now. I know it's path—'

'No couple. No Capri,' I blurt, trying to find the quickest way of getting the information across.

'What's happened with Luca?'

'We've decided to wait a while before we have another date – something in the realm of ten years.'

'No!' Cleo gasps.

'It's okay but I certainly couldn't stay on the island with him, that would destroy me. I'm talking about exploring the rest of Italy.'

'You want to go on holiday?'

'No, I want to go on an adventure! And I want you to come with me.'

'Oh Kim, I don't know . . .'

'Five thousand pounds is 15 million lire, Cleo. We could buy a couple of sugar pink mopeds and go on tour!'

'*What?*' Cleo hoots.

'Or if you don't fancy driving we could go on six cookery courses in Tuscany. Or take 100 gondola rides in Venice. Or buy 72 pairs of Gucci sunglasses in Milan.'

'I have always wanted to go to Florence,' Cleo admits.

'We might be able to afford a fleck of sand on the shell Botticelli painted for *Birth of Venus*,' I suggest.

'What about work?'

'Ninety tarantella tambourines . . .' I rattle on.

'I suppose I could do with a change . . .'

'A lifetime's supply of grappa!'

'I can't!' Cleo suddenly snaps.

Silence. My heart sinks, remembering how hard it was for me to leave our bunker.

'I'm sorry. I can't do it,' she repeats.

I don't want to bully her. 'Okay,' I say, gently.

'I know I'm being pathetic.'

'You're not,' I reassure her. This is what I get for

450

pedalling all that Home Sweet Home propaganda over the past two years.

'It was just a thought,' I sigh.

'What will you do?' Cleo asks.

I waver. I don't know if I can take off on my own. I imagine myself sipping a solo mio cappuccino and spasm with self-pity. Maybe Italy would be too full of reminders of Luca. I can't believe that by this time tomorrow I'll be gone from his life. Suddenly the idea of being anaesthetized sounds appealing – it would take away this heartache. But it would also take away these newfound aspirations.

'Kim?'

'I'm coming home,' I hear myself say.

The word 'home' doesn't feel as comforting as it should.

'Brilliant!' Cleo whoops. 'Give me a ring when you get here – I'll come and meet you at the station.'

I feel gloom descend as I picture the familiar scene.

'You should be back in time for *An Audience with Victoria Beckham*.'

'Great,' I say. 'See you tomorrow.'

I wander back to the bar defeated, wondering where my mum has got to.

'Well?' asks Mario.

'Oh, nothing. I thought I'd come up with an answer.'

'From your face it looked like a good one.'

'I thought so too,' I say sadly.

Having Cleo come out would have been wonderful. There is so much I want to show her, so much I want

451

us to discover together. When she first came to Cardiff she was inspired to take pictures of her new surroundings and talked about the possibility of assisting a professional photographer on the weekends, but that somehow fell by the wayside. I just know she'd feel inspired again if she came out here. Every bit of scenery is calling, 'I'm ready for my close-up!'

But the fact is, she's afraid to come out and I'm afraid to go back. So we're in an impasse. Something – or rather someone – has to give. And it's my turn.

'Look who I found!' My mum waltzes into the bar with Ringo on her arm.

I can't help but beam.

'You are leaving?' he says sadly.

'Tomorrow morning,' I confirm.

'I have to say goodbye.'

I kneel beside him. 'Thank you.'

'Also my father ask me to give you this,' he says, handing me a carrier bag. Inside is Luca's dark grey cashmere sweater from the boat. 'He say you have problem finding a sweater that makes no itches and you like this one.'

'I do,' I say, wrapping the softness around me. I am overjoyed that I have something of his that I can snuggle up to.

'Cashmere is for ever,' Ringo informs me.

Suddenly the jumper becomes an eternity ring.

'Please tell your papa that I love it.'

'I also have something for you,' he says, handing me a little paper bag.

I open it and pull out a tiny plaque of the Blue Grotto.

'So you remember the magic!'

My stomach flips.

'I will never forget!' I gulp, clutching Ringo to my heart. I can't believe I'm leaving two men that I love.

'Please come back soon!' He gazes up at me with enormous dark brown eyes.

'I will!' I promise. 'You'll look after my mum for me, won't you? Make sure she orders the right combination of ice-cream!'

Ringo chuckles shyly. 'Yes, of course.'

Mum ruffles his hair. 'I'd better get you back to the shop.'

He nods. I watch them walk to the door and then he turns back and hurtles into me for one last hug.

'Ti amo, Kim!'

'I love you too,' I sigh, pressing my cheek against his silky hair.

When my mum returns half an hour later, I'm still stroking the cashmere sleeves in a trance.

'I'm so sorry about Luca,' she says, sitting beside me.

She looks like she really means it and is somewhat taken aback when I say, 'I'm not. Well, I'm sorry that it's over but I'm not going to regret that it happened, no matter how much it hurts.'

'Are you sure you're not giving up too soon?'

I sigh. 'I love Luca but I couldn't live with myself if Ringo lost his father because of me. In a way, I'd be doing to him what—' I halt myself.

453

Mum looks stung.

'I'm sorry,' I whisper.

'You'd be doing to Ringo what I did to you.' Mum looks downcast.

I can't keep making her feel guilty like this. 'Hold on,' I say. 'You know you said that it only happened once with Derek – that Dad found out and that was it.'

'Yes,' she nods, regretfully.

'The only difference between you and Derek and me and Luca is that you got caught. I can't go on blaming you for Dad leaving. I understand now that you can't always choose who you love, but you can choose what you do about it. I'm glad that I had what I had with Luca because now I understand you. And I'm glad that I broke the momentum by taking the trip with Tyler because it gave me the space to step back and think about what I really want, and I have to choose the option that lets me keep some self-respect. I'm not judging you, Mum. We all have to do what's right for us.'

'I admire you, Kim. You are so strong. All these men in my life . . .' she trails off. 'We've never really spoken about this.'

I'm about to tell her that it's not necessary but then I realize that she needs to have her say. And she needs me to listen.

'When your father left I felt so disgusted with myself – what I'd done to him, what I'd done to you – I just wanted someone to tell me that I was a good person. So when I met Mike and he thought I was this perfect creature I just lapped it up – I couldn't get enough of

454

him telling me how wonderful I was. His words filled my head and for a while everything was okay, but then it started to wear off. I'd see how you looked at me and I'd despise myself again and so I went looking for someone new to make it all right again.'

She looks into my eyes. 'It never lasted. I went from man to man, trying to find someone I could really believe but I was looking in the wrong place. All I ever wanted was for you to tell me that you'd forgiven me.'

I clutch her hand. 'Mum, I've forgiven you! I know it's been a long time coming but I mean it. If Dad had wanted to carry on seeing me he could've. He chose not to. It wasn't your fault.'

'I would have done anything to have made him stay,' she confesses. 'It breaks my heart that he vanished from your life like that.'

'I guess he didn't really care.'

'No, Kim. He loved you, he really did.'

'Would you have left me like that?'

'*Never!*' she sounds scandalized. 'I think he just saw the whole thing as . . . *messy*. I can't think of a better word. He liked order. He wanted to be in control, to be a success. When he looked at me he saw a failed marriage and with you, I think he didn't know how to handle not being in your life on a daily basis. It ruined this image he had of being this great father. I think he wanted to wipe the slate clean and start again.'

Wipe out a human life! I'd always seen my dad as a wounded animal who'd crept into the long grass to recuperate but never got his strength back. I pitied him. I raged at my mother on his behalf. Now I see him as someone who discards people who don't suit his self-image.

'That's such a cop-out! Why didn't you tell me this before?'

'You were already angry with me. What was the point in you losing faith in both your parents? I thought that one day he would come back into your life and we could clear things up. But he didn't.'

I glare at the floor.

'Please don't hold it against him, love. I bet there's been a million times when he wished he could get in contact. He probably just felt it was too late or that it would be disruptive if he came back.'

I sigh.

'I don't want to see you bitter like Granny Carmela. It's no way to live. You have to forgive him.'

'I will on one condition,' I say.

'What's that?'

'That you forgive me – all those years of resentment. I wouldn't have wanted me for a daughter.'

'Oh Kim!' Mum falls into my arms. 'I've always loved being your mother.'

46

I sit on the balcony with my back to the sun listening to the sound of the sea breathing in and out and watch my mother busily pottering around wrapping my shoes in plastic bags. This is a woman who loves to pack. As I lean forward to take a sip of apricot juice a breeze blows one of the french windows closed and I catch sight of my reflection in the glass. I recall how on the first day I stepped out on to this balcony and felt like I was superimposed on a foreign backdrop. Now I realize I am part of the view – the villas and Certosa arches are clustered around my shoulders, a seagull swoops and glides in the sky above my head and my bare feet are toasting themselves on the warm terracotta tiles. All this beauty. And it's real. And in two hours it will be gone.

I try to comfort myself with the knowledge that even Juliet had to squeeze a lifetime of love into one night with Romeo but I still feel crippled by the thought of leaving Luca.

'Do you want to take this with you or shall I keep it for you?' Mum asks, holding up Rosa's wedding dress.

'You keep it,' I tell her. If ever I need it, I'll come back for it. I could never marry someone else without first finding out for sure that Luca and I could not be reunited.

'I think I might call Rosa, to say goodbye,' I decide.

'I'll leave you to it,' says Mum, making a discreet exit.

The tears start to stream as I tell Rosa about what has happened with Luca, desperate for her to tell me that there is still some hope to cling to.

'Don't fight the love, Kim,' she says, softly. 'There is room in your heart for him, wherever you go, whoever else you love. It is a mistake to try and force yourself to get over someone before you are ready.'

I gulp back my tears so my hiccups don't delete any of her wise words.

'People try to find fault, to sour the sweetness they feel but every emotion has its own time. Enjoy experiencing the love and let yourself be sad when you need to be. It is your choice whether to curse the universe for not allowing you to be together or to feel blessed for the time you shared.'

My juddery breathing smooths out as she speaks.

'And remember: in the end everything is okay. And if it's not okay, it's not the end.'

Her words leave me feeling calm and accepting and even a little optimistic about the future. I thank her and promise to visit next time I come over from Cardiff to see my mum at the shop. Oh God. There it is again.

nagging, unsettling feeling I get when I think

about going back to my old life. On the bright side, it will be easier to think of Luca as a distant dream if I'm back watching *Linda Green* beneath a duvet. But I don't want to forget him. I'd rather keep moving forward and feel the pain than feel numb again. Luca has raised my game and it occurs to me that I would like to say thank you to the man who brought him into my life – my grandfather, Vincenzo.

My mother is nowhere to be found so I tell Mario to pass on the message that I'll be back in half an hour.

En route to the cemetery I stop at the flower shop. Then, kneeling at my grandfather's graveside, I place two magnolias beside the headstone – one from me, and one from Carmela. I decide it's about time she forgave him.

As I head back to the Luna I am filled with a new kind of assurance and daring. It's almost as if I can hear Carmela saying, 'Don't run away from life like I did, Kim!' And Vincenzo whispering, 'True love will always find you if you stay true to love.' I know now what I have to do.

Following a quick phone call to the airline, I drop into the perfumery to buy a bottle of Carthusia Man to tuck under Mum's pillow and then return to the hotel.

'Do you want to take my Paul Mitchell shampoo with you?' Mum asks. 'It seems to suit your hair . . .'

I decide to accept her gift though I'd really be better off with some Johnson's 'No more tears'.

The telephone rings. I answer. It's Mario. He wants a word with my mother.

'Hello? Yes? Great. Thanks for letting me know.'

'What did he want?'

'Um, he's just saying that he has a special farewell drink ready for us downstairs.'

'Is PM coming over before I leave?'

'Yes, he should be here any minute.'

'Have you decided what to do about him yet?'

Mum sighs. 'I'm not going to marry him. I don't need a man to make me feel good about myself any more.'

'But he's a good man, Mum. Don't let him go to prove something to me.'

'I'm not. I honestly don't think I'm ready for another big relationship yet. I want a chance to see how I get on here with the shop. Luca and I have decided to go 50/50 so that keeps my options open.'

I practise smiling at the mention of Luca. It comes easier than I expected. God, I love loving that man. I get the feeling that one day . . .

'Anyway, what's the rush?' Mum continues. 'Maybe in the winter when it's quiet I can go and visit Tony in Atlanta.'

'Sounds like a plan!' I approve. Then I feel wobbly. As much as I've despised so many of my mother's husbands at least I have never had to worry about her being lonely. 'Do you think you'll be all right here on your own?' I ask.

'I won't be on my own – I've got Sophia!'

'But, no man . . .'

'I don't think I'll be starved of attention on this island, do you?'

'No,' I concede with a smile.

460

'Anyway, I'm going to do my thing and I'm going to let you do yours. No more interfering! If you want to get liposuction—'

'What?'

'I won't stand in your way.'

'Are you crazy?' I screech.

'What do you mean?'

'I'm not letting some guy shove a tube in me and suck my stomach into a bucket!'

Mum looks stunned.

'This is quality fat! I've earned this belly!' I tell her. 'And now I've found a place where you can look like this and still get treated like a supermodel, I'm not leaving.'

'But . . .' she looks around at the suitcases.

'I'm leaving Capri but I'm not leaving Italy. I've already spoken to the airline.'

'When?'

'About half an hour ago, on the way back from grandad's grave,' I grin, knowing that Mum will be delighted to hear I've made my peace with him. 'I'm going to start in Venice and work my way through all the places I've never been: Pisa, Tuscany, Liguria – I've got a whole country to explore!'

'Alone?'

'Well, you know I would have loved it if Cleo could have come . . .' I say, fighting to avoid thinking about the one loophole in my plan. 'But I'm not ready to go back just yet.' I'm also not ready to give up on persuading her to join me – my plan is to call and read

461

her the menu in every restaurant I visit until she caves.

'How much?' Mum asks.

'How much what?' I frown.

'How much would you have loved it if Cleo could go travelling around Italy with you?'

I tilt my head and give my mother a quizzical look. She places her hands on my shoulders and marches me out to the balcony. Down below, sitting on the terrace with a giant Bellini, is my best friend Cleo.

Scream!

'What are you doing here?' I hoot, delirious with joy.

'Do you have any idea how much balsamic vinegar you can buy for 15 million lire?!'

I laugh out loud, feeling teary with euphoria.

'What about the TV?'

She holds up a shiny silver video camera. 'Thought we might make our own programme!'

'Where'd you get that?'

'Borrowed it from Ape Man at work!'

Suddenly the future seems full of luscious possibilities. I guess £5,000 can change your life if you pick the right thing to spend it on!

Co-conspirator Mario comes out to see what all the shouting is about. He looks up at me on the balcony and then back down at Cleo and sighs, 'In the old days it was Romeo and Juliet – now it's you two crazy women!'

'We're not women,' I yell back. 'We are *PARADISE*!'

Divas Las Vegas

Belinda Jones

A tale of love, friendship and sequinned underpants . . .

Jamie and Izzy, friends for ever, have a dream: a spangly double wedding in Las Vegas. And at twenty-seven, they decide they've had enough crap boyfriends and they're ready for crap husbands – all they have to do is find them. And where better than Las Vegas itself, where the air is 70% oxygen and 30% confetti?

But as they abandon their increasingly complicated lives in sleepy Devon for the eye-popping brilliance of Las Vegas, their groom-grabbing plan starts to look less than foolproof. And those niggling problems they thought they'd left behind – like Izzy's fiancé and the alarming reappearance of Jamie's first love – just won't go away . . .

'A wise and witty read about the secret desires deep with us'
Marie Claire

'A hilarious riot'
Company

'Great characters . . . hilariously written . . . buy it!'
New Woman

arrow books

The California Club

Belinda Jones

When Lara Richards jets off to glamorous California, the last thing she's expecting to find is her old friend Helen transformed from a clipboard-clasping frump into a shimmering surf goddess. The secret of her blissful new life? The mysterious California Club.

So the offer of guest membership – one wish guaranteed to come true by the end of their stay – is one Lara and her friends can't resist. Could this be Lara's chance to win her best friend Elliott's heart after ten years of longing? Or does the fact that he's travelling with his brand new fiancée mean that Lara will have to come up with a new dream?

arrow books

On the Road to Mr Right

Belinda Jones

'If adventures do not befall a young lady in her own village, she must seek them abroad' Jane Austen

Belinda loves America. Her best friend Emily loves men. So when they decide it's time to shake up their lives, they combine their two greatest passions in a fantastic road trip taking them from Eden to Valentine – via Climax – in pursuit of the American dream guy.

There's no shortage of men – a Casanova from Cazenovia, a male cheerleader from Darling, and a tattooed trucker from Kissimmee. But is romance really the answer to their problems? And is two women in search of the perfect man such a great idea anyway?

Theirs is a journey of revelations and surprises, of cactus kisses and errant snowploughs, but above all it's a journey in search of love. And you thought Thelma and Louise had an eventful trip . . .

arrow books

The Paradise Room

Belinda Jones

When Amber Pepper's jeweller boyfriend Hugh asks her to join him on a business trip to the paradise islands of Tahiti she's not keen – Amber loves big jumpers and rain. She'd rather be pedalling through puddles at home in Oxford than lolling in the gel-blue waters of the South Pacific. However, the prospect of sipping Mai Tais with her long-lost friend Felicity is incentive enough to coax her on the twenty-hour flight.

Within hours of touching down on coral sands the girls venture into a seductive new world of mesmerising music, exotic black pearls and sexy strangers. And for the first time Amber falls head over flip-flops in lust, only to receive an unexpected proposal of marriage.

Will she opt for a barefoot beach wedding or cast caution – and her coconut bra – to the wind? No easy decision for a drizzle-loving gal when it's ninety degrees in the shade . . .

'As essential as your SPF 15'
New Woman

'This is definitely worth cramming in your suitcase'
Cosmopolitan

arrow books

Let the best woman win . . .

Fair Game

Elizabeth Young

Up to her eyes with her friends' dramas, Harriet Grey has no time for her own. Let alone getting involved with John Mackenzie. He might be the most gorgeous man she's met in ages. But he's entangled with someone else, Nina.

Glamorous Nina wasn't exactly Harriet's best friend at school, but Harriet has principles. Still, surely one innocent little drink to repay a favour wouldn't hurt? Her friends aren't so sure.

Harriet tries to be strict, but John Mackenzie won't stay out of her life. When she finds herself alone at Christmas, she'd have to be a saint to walk away. And haloes never did suit Harriet . . .

Praise for Elizabeth Young:

'A warm sunny read that is as astute as it is humorous'
Good Housekeeping

'Feel-good romance'
Marie Claire

'Perfect comic timing and wickedly funny moments'
Cosmopolitan

'A lively Lisa Jewell-esque debut novel with a bit more bite than you would imagine'
Mirror

arrow books

The Love Academy

Belinda Jones

Do you have enough romance in your life?

Journalist Kirsty Bailey would have to answer no. She has the essential starter kit – a boyfriend – but somehow Joe seems to have skipped the vows of for better/for worse and gone straight to for granted.

But then just as she's on the verge of settling for a swoon-free existence, Kirsty's magazine sends her to a majestic Venetian palazzo to attend the much gossiped-about Love Academy . . . Her undercover mission? To prove her editor's theory that this 'school for singles' is nothing more than an escort agency with a sexy accent and fancy glass chandeliers.

But what if her editor is wrong and their promise of true amore is for real? Will Kirsty be able to resist the kind of moonlit temptations she's been dreaming of for years, or is her relationship with Joe going, going, *gondola*?

If you think Casanova was a bad boy, just wait until you see what Cupid has in store for Kirsty . . .

arrow books

It'll take more than a spoonful of sugar to sort this lot out . . .

The Nanny

Melissa Nathan

When Jo Green takes a nannying job in London to escape her annoying family, small-town routine and ineffectual boyfriend Shaun, culture shock doesn't even begin to describe it. Because walking into the Fitzgerald family's designer lifestyle is like entering a parallel universe . . .

Dick and Vanessa are the most incompatible pair since Tom and Jerry, and their children – glittery warrior pixie Cassandra, blood-thirsty Zak and shy little Tallulah – are downright mystifying. Suddenly village life seems terribly appealing.

Then, just as Jo's starting to get the hang of Tumble Tots, karate practice and cleaning out the guinea pigs, the Fitzgeralds acquire a new lodger – Dick's older son – and suddenly Jo's sharing her nanny flat with the distractingly good-looking but insufferably grumpy Josh. So when Shaun arrives on the scene, things can only get trickier . . .

Praise for Melissa Nathan:

'Tremendous fun'
Jilly Cooper

'A modern-day Lizzy and Darcy tale you won't be able to put down'
Company

arrow books

The Waitress

Melissa Nathan

Katie Simmonds wants to be an educational psychologist. Last week she wanted to be a teacher, and the week before that a film director. Katie isn't short of ambitions, but none of her ambitions are to be a waitress. Unfortunately, Katie Simmonds is a waitress.

Hassled by customers, badly paid and stuck with the boss from hell, Katie's life isn't turning out as she'd planned. And a career choice isn't the only commitment she has problems with. But just when she thinks things can't get any worse, the café where she works is taken over by the last man in the world she wants to see again.

Maybe Katie's been waiting at tables – and waiting for Mr Right – for far too long ...

'Highly entertaining'
heat

'You'll find this very moreish'
Daily Mirror

arrow books

The Learning Curve

Melissa Nathan

Nicky Hobbs loves teaching at the local primary school. She's idolised by her class – in particular ten-year-old Oscar Samuels – but she's starting to find she'd quite like some adult adoration for a change.

Mark Samuels is a frazzled single father working all the hours God gives to provide for his beloved son, Oscar. But he's unable to see that Oscar would prefer his presence to his presents once in a while.

Ms Hobbs knows Mr Samuels is a heartless workaholic. Mr Samuels is certain Ms Hobbs is an interfering busybody. But when they finally meet they start to discover that first impressions can be deceptive. And perhaps they've both got a bit of learning to do . . .

'Tremendous fun' Jilly Cooper

arrow books

THE POWER OF READING

Visit the Random House website and get connected with information on all our books and authors

EXTRACTS from our recently published books and selected backlist titles

COMPETITIONS AND PRIZE DRAWS Win signed books, audiobooks and more

AUTHOR EVENTS Find out which of our authors are on tour and where you can meet them

LATEST NEWS on bestsellers, awards and new publications

MINISITES with exclusive special features dedicated to our authors and their titles

READING GROUPS Reading guides, special features and all the information you need for your reading group

LISTEN to extracts from the latest audiobook publications

WATCH video clips of interviews and readings with our authors

RANDOM HOUSE INFORMATION including advice for writers, job vacancies and all your general queries answered

Come home to Random House
www.rbooks.co.uk